HAUNTINGS

Tales of the Supernatural

HAUNTINGS

Tales of the Supernatural

Edited by Henry Mazzeo
Illustrated by Edward Gorey

DOUBLEDAY & COMPANY, INC., GARDEN CITY, NEW YORK

Grateful acknowledgment is made for the use of the following:

"The Visiting Star" from *Powers of Darkness* by Robert Aickman. Copyright © 1966 by Robert Aickman. Reprinted by permission of William Collins & Sons, Ltd.

"The Face" from *Spook Stories* by E. F. Benson. Reprinted by permission of Reverend K. S. P. McDowall.

"The Man Who Collected Poe" by Robert Bloch. Copyright 1951 by Popular Publications, Inc. Reprinted by permission of the author's agent, Harry Altshuler.

"Levitation" from *Nine Horrors and a Dream* by Joseph Payne Brennan. Copyright 1958 by Joseph Payne Brennan. Reprinted by permission of Arkham House.

"Thus I Refute Beelzy" from *Fancies and Goodnights* by John Collier. Copyright 1940 by John Collier. Reprinted by permission of the Harold Matson Company, Inc.

"The Lonesome Place" by August Derleth. Copyright 1947 by All-Fiction Field, Inc.; copyright 1962 by August Derleth. Reprinted by permission of Arkham House.

"Lot No. 249" from *The Conan Doyle Stories* by Sir Arthur Conan Doyle. Reprinted by permission of the Trustees of the Estate of Sir Arthur Conan Doyle and John Murray, Ltd.

"The Whistling Room" by William Hope Hodgson. Copyright 1947 by August Derleth. Reprinted by permission of Arkham House.

"The Haunted Dolls' House" from *The Collected Ghost Stories of M. R. James* by Montangue Rhodes James. Reprinted by permission of Edward Arnold (Publishers) Ltd.

"In the Vault" by H. P. Lovecraft. Copyright 1932 by the Popular Fiction Publishing Company; copyright 1939, 1945 by August Derleth and Donald Wandrei; copyright 1963 by August Derleth. Reprinted by permission of Arkham House.

"Midnight Express" by Alfred Noyes. Reprinted by permission of Hugh Noyes.

"The Grey Ones" by J. B. Priestley. Reprinted by permission of A. D. Peters & Co.

This book is dedicated with thanks to Seon Manley

I am also indebted to John Ernst for his constant assistance, to Dr. Thomas G. Aylesworth for suggesting "Thus I Refute Beelzy" and "Midnight Express," and to Chris Steinbrunner, Lin Carter, Noël Vreeland Carter, Martin J. Swanson, and the staff of the Yonkers Public Library for all their help.

Contents

The Castle of Terror

The Gothic castle is the silent sovereign of literature casting its long shadow across time. It is the fortress of our fears and the summit of our hopes. Lofty, lonely, unattainable, it remains a challenge and a mystery to every age.

Storytellers, painters, poets, and dramatists have always employed the supernatural to give life and character to abstract ideas and put them in action. Human aspirations, states of mind, and hidden fears were portrayed as supernatural beings centuries before Freud penetrated our subconscious life of dreams and fantasies.

In the eighteenth century, Horace Walpole, mindful of Shakespeare's ghosts, shook the novel out of its routine realism with *The Castle of Otranto*. This book and its Gothic successors quickened the pace of fiction with action, atmosphere, and suspense. Even more important, it gave novelists a new license to range freely in time and space, to experiment with realities, and to call up images from the subconscious. Old myths took on new meanings, or deeper meanings were found in them again, and the novel acquired the breadth of poetry, the gusto of drama, the color of painting. Poets and painters took notice and the Gothic excitement spread to all the arts in the Romantic Movement.

In the year 1816, Byron, the Shelleys, and Dr. John William Polidori, Byron's physician and traveling companion, were stay-

ing on the southern shore of Lake Geneva. Heavy rains between
the tenth and twenty-second of June kept the company indoors.
For entertainment, they gathered around a blazing wood fire reading ghost stories and trying to devise new tales of terror and
wonder.

As a result of these sessions, Mary Shelley wrote *Frankenstein*
and Byron began a vampire novel, which he never completed.
Borrowing pretty much of Byron's idea, and also, perhaps, something of Matthew Gregory Lewis's melodrama *The Wood Dæ-
mon,* Polidori wrote a story called *The Vampyre,* which caricatured
Lord Byron himself as Lord Ruthven—the vampire, and created a
vogue for fictional vampires that has lasted down through *Dracula*
to the present.

The Frankenstein Monster and the Byronic Vampyre became
the rage of London and Paris in what we now would call a "horror
cycle" of dramas, musicals, and spoofs. T. P. Cooke, the Karloff
of his day, played Lord Ruthven in both capitals and was the first
of many Frankenstein Monsters on the stage. Mary Shelley
describes an 1823 performance:

> The playbill amused me extremely, for, in the list of *dramatis per-
> sonae,* came "_____, by Mr. T. Cooke;" this nameless mode
> of naming the unnameable is rather good. On Friday, August 29th,
> Jane, my Father, William, and I went to the theatre to see it. Wal-
> lack looked very well as Frankenstein. He is at the beginning full
> of hope and expectation. At the end of the first act the stage repre-
> sents a room with a staircase leading to Frankenstein's workshop;
> he goes to it, and you see his light at a small window, through which
> a frightened servant peeps, who runs off in terror when Franken-
> stein exclaims, "It lives." Presently Frankenstein himself rushes in
> horror and trepidation from the room, and, while still expressing his
> agony and terror, ("_____") throws down the door of the
> laboratory, leaps the staircase, and presents his unearthly and mon-
> strous person on the stage. The story is not well managed, but Cooke
> played _____'s part extremely well; his seeking, as it were,
> for support; his trying to grasp at the sounds he heard; all, indeed,
> he does was well imagined and executed. I was much amused, and
> it appeared to excite a breathless eagerness in the audience. . . .
> On the strength of the drama, my Father had published, for *my
> benefit,* a new edition of "Frankenstein."

Mary was amused, and Alexandre Dumas *Père* was so impressed by an 1823 revival of Charles Nodier's *Le Vampire*, a play about Lord Ruthven, that he devoted five chapters of his memoirs to the vampire, raised him again in *The Count of Monte Cristo*, and, in collaboration with Maquet, wrote a new play about him, also called *Le Vampire* (1851).

Plainly, it is no miracle of modern mass media that keeps the Frankensteins and Draculas going in our time; more likely, it is the daemonic power of the fabulous originals that supports the media. No matter how they are treated, they survive.

The Gothic experiment produced other lasting effects. Out of the ferment of techniques and ideas came stories of mystery, detection, horror, historical romance, and science fiction. Two great scholars of the Gothic novel, Montague Summers (*The Gothic Quest*, 1938; *A Gothic Bibliography*, 1941) and Dr. Devendra P. Varma (*The Gothic Flame*, 1957) discuss the Gothic influence on stream-of-consciousness narrative, expressionism, surrealism, and the psychological novel.

Supernatural tales and novels written in our time continue the tradition and extend the experiment, with Isaac Bashevis Singer, Claude Seignolle, and Robert Aickman proving how rich and relevant such things can be.

From here on in this book you are in the age-old yet ever unpredictable world of ghosts and demons. And what you think of them matters less than what they think of you. The stories that follow have various settings, some of them quite up-to-date. But they also have the timelessness of the Gothic castle—the castle of Elsinore, Otranto, Udolpho, Dracula, the Wicked Witch of the West, and Franz Kafka. There are subterranean passages connecting all of them.

Whether you are exploring these passages for the first time or rediscovering them, there will be many strange things. So, in the very words Count Dracula addressed to his guest, Jonathan Harker: "Let me advise you, my dear young friend—nay, let me warn you with all seriousness, that should you leave these rooms you will not by any chance go to sleep in any other part of the castle. It is old, and has many memories, and there are bad dreams for those who sleep unwisely. Be warned!"

H.M.

HAUNTINGS

Tales of the Supernatural

CHAPTER 1

The Lonesome Place

by August Derleth

America's foremost author, editor, and publisher of fantasy fiction, August Derleth writes half a million words a year—his own estimate— and has more than 120 books to his credit. About *The Lonesome Place,* he says: "There was such a place, though the streetlights are brighter today, and some of the trees have come down. When the story came out, in 1948, I suspect those local people who read it were pretty sure of the place I had in mind when I wrote the story—so to that extent it's grounded in experience. Something more, though—I think that more than most of my peers I was early in life aware of the essential loneliness of the individual, not just of the writer who is necessarily isolated from his fellow men at least on his creative plane; and this awareness certainly played a part in the writing of the story."

You who sit in your houses of nights, you who sit in the theaters, you who are gay at dances and parties—all you who are enclosed by four walls—you have no conception of what goes on outside in the dark. In the lonesome places. And there are so many of them, all over—in the country, in the small towns, in the cities. If you were out in the evenings, in the night, you would know about them, you would pass them and wonder, perhaps, and if you were a small boy you might be frightened . . . frightened the way Johnny Newell and I were frightened, the way thousands of small boys from one end of the country to the other are being frightened when they have to go out alone at night, past lonesome places, dark and lightless, somber and haunted. . . .

I want you to understand that if it had not been for the lonesome place at the grain elevator, the place with the big old trees and the sheds up close to the sidewalk, and the piles of lumber—if it had not been for that place Johnny Newell and I would never have been guilty of murder. I say it even if there is nothing the law can do about it. They cannot touch us, but it is true, and I know, and Johnny knows, but we never talk about it, we never say anything; it is just something we keep here, behind our eyes, deep in our thoughts where it is a fact which is lost among thousands of others, but no less there, something we know beyond cavil.

It goes back a long way. But as time goes, perhaps it is not long. We were young, we were little boys in a small town. Johnny lived three houses away and across the street from me, and both of us lived in the block west of the grain elevator. We were never afraid to go past the lonesome place together. But we were not often together. Sometimes one of us had to go that way alone, sometimes the other. I went that way most of time—there was no other, except to go far around, because that was the straight way down town, and I had to walk there, when my father was too tired to go.

In the evenings it would happen like this. My mother would discover that she had no sugar or salt or bologna, and she would say, "Steve, you go down town and get it. Your father's too tired."

I would say, "I don't wanna."

She would say, "You go."

I would say, "I can go in the morning before school."

She would say, "You go now. I don't want to hear another word out of you. Here's the money."

And I would have to go.

Going down was never quite so bad, because most of the time there was still some afterglow in the west, and a kind of pale light lay there, a luminousness, like part of the day lingering there, and all around town you could hear the kids hollering in the last hour they had to play, and you felt somehow not alone, you could go down into that dark place under the trees and you would never think of being lonesome. But when you came back—that was different. When you came back the afterglow was gone; if the stars were out, you could never see them for the trees; and though the streetlights were on—the old-fashioned lights arched over the crossroads—not a ray of them penetrated the lonesome place near the elevator. There it was, half a block long, black as black could be, dark as the deepest night, with the shadows of the trees making it a solid place of darkness, with the faint glow of light where a street-light pooled at the end of the street, far away it seemed, and that other glow behind, where the other corner light lay.

And when you came that way you walked slower and slower. Behind you lay the brightly lit stores; all along the way there had been houses, with lights in the windows and music playing and voices of people sitting to talk on their porches—but up there, ahead of you, there was the lonesome place, with no house nearby, and up beyond it the tall, dark grain elevator, gaunt and forbidding, the lonesome place of trees and sheds and lumber, in which any-thing might be lurking, anything at all, the lonesome place where you were sure that something haunted the darkness waiting for the moment and the hour and the night when you came through to burst forth from its secret place and leap upon you, tearing you and rending you and doing unmentionable things before it had done with you.

That was the lonesome place. By day it was oak and maple trees over a hundred years old, low enough so that you could al-most touch the big spreading limbs; it was sheds and lumber piles that were seldom disturbed; it was a sidewalk and long grass, never mowed or kept down until late fall, when somebody burned it off; it was a shady place in the hot summer days where some cool air always lingered. You were never afraid of it by day, but by night it was a different place; for then it was lonesome, away from sight or sound, a place of darkness and strangeness, a place of terror for little boys haunted by a thousand fears.

And every night, coming home from town, it happened like this. I would walk slower and slower, the closer I got to the lonesome place. I would think of every way around it. I would keep hoping somebody would come along, so that I could walk with him, Mr. Newell, maybe, or old Mrs. Potter, who lived farther up the street, or Reverend Bislor, who lived at the end of the block beyond the grain elevator. But nobody ever came. At this hour it was too soon after supper for them to go out, or, already out, too soon for them to return. So I walked slower and slower, until I got to the edge of the lonesome place—and then I ran as fast as I could, sometimes with my eyes closed.

Oh, I knew what was there, all right. I knew there was something in that dark, lonesome place. Perhaps it was the bogey-man. Sometimes my grandmother spoke of him, of how he waited in dark places for bad boys and girls. Perhaps it was an ogre. I knew about ogres in the books of fairy tales. Perhaps it was something else, something worse. I ran. I ran hard. Every blade of grass, every leaf, every twig that touched me was Its hand reaching for me. The sound of my footsteps slapping the sidewalk were Its steps pursuing. The hard breathing which was my own became Its breathing in Its frenetic struggle to reach me, to rend and tear me, to imbue my soul with terror.

I would burst out of that place like a flurry of wind, fly past the gaunt elevator, and not pause until I was safe in the yellow glow of the familiar streetlight. And then, in a few steps, I was home.

And mother would say, "For the Lord's sake, have you been running on a hot night like this?"

I would say, "I hurried."

"You didn't have to hurry that much. I don't need it till breakfast time."

And I would say, "I could-a got it in the morning. I could-a run down before breakfast. Next time, that's what I'm gonna do."

Nobody would pay any attention.

Some nights Johnny had to go down town, too. Things then weren't the way they are today, when every woman makes a ritual of afternoon shopping and seldom forgets anything; in those days, they didn't go down town so often, and when they did, they had such lists they usually forgot something. And after Johnny and I had been through the lonesome place on the same night, we compared notes next day.

"Did you see anything?" he would ask.

"No, but I heard it," I would say.

"I felt it," he would whisper tensely. "It's got big, flat clawed feet. You know what's the ugliest feet around?"

"Sure, one of those stinking yellow soft-shelled turtles."

"It's got feet like that. Oh, ugly, and soft, and sharp claws! I saw one out of the corner of my eye," he would say.

"Did you see its face?" I would ask.

"It ain't got no face. Cross my heart an' hope to die, there ain't no face. That's worse'n if there was one."

Oh, it was a horrible beast—not an animal, not a man—that

lurked in the lonesome place and came forth predatorily at night, waiting for us to pass. It grew like this, out of our mutual experiences. We discovered that it had scales, and a great long tail, like a dragon. It breathed from somewhere, hot as fire, but it had no face and no mouth in it, just a horrible opening in its throat. It was as big as an elephant, but it did not look like anything so friendly. It belonged there in the lonesome place; it would never go away; that was its home, and it had to wait for its food to come to it—the unwary boys and girls who had to pass through the lonesome place at night.

How I tried to keep from going near the lonesome place after dark!

"Why can't Mady go?" I would ask.

"Mady's too little," mother would answer.

"I'm not so big."

"Oh, shush! You're a big boy now. You're going to be seven years old. Just think of it."

"I don't think seven is old," I would say. I didn't, either. Seven wasn't nearly old enough to stand up against what was in the lonesome place.

"Your Sears Roebuck pants are long ones," she would say.

"I don't care about any old Sears Roebuck pants. I don't wanna go."

"I want you to go. You never get up early enough in the morning."

"But I will. I promise I will. I promise, Ma!" I would cry out.

"Tomorrow morning it will be a different story. No, you go."

That was the way it went every time. I had to go. And Mady was the only one who guessed. " 'Fraidy cat," she would whisper. Even she never really knew. She never had to go through the lonesome place after dark. They kept her at home. She never knew how something could lie up in those old trees, lie right along those old limbs across the sidewalk and drop down without a sound, clawing and tearing, something without a face, with ugly clawed feet like a soft-shelled turtle's, with scales and a tail like a dragon, something as big as a house, all black, like the darkness in that place.

But Johnny and I knew.

"It almost got me last night," he would say, his voice low, looking anxiously out of the woodshed where we sat as if It might hear us.

"Gee, I'm glad it didn't," I would say. "What was it like?"

"Big and black. Awful black. I looked around when I was running, and all of a sudden there wasn't any light way back at the other end. Then I knew it was coming. I ran like everything to get out of there. It was almost on me when I got away. Look there!"

And he would show me a rip in his shirt where a claw had come down.

"And you?" he would ask excitedly, big-eyed. "What about you?"

"It was back behind the lumber piles when I came through," I said. "I could just feel it waiting. I was running, but it got right up—you look, there's a pile of lumber tipped over there."

And we would walk down into the lonesome place in midday and look. Sure enough, there would be a pile of lumber tipped over, and we would look to where something had been lying down, the grass all pressed down. Sometimes we would find a handkerchief and wonder whether It had caught somebody; then we would go home and wait to hear if anyone was missing, speculating apprehensively all the way home whether It had got Mady or Christine or Helen, or any one of the girls in our class or Sunday School, or whether maybe It had got Miss Doyle, the young primary-grades teacher who had to walk that way sometimes after supper. But no one was ever reported missing, and the mystery grew. Maybe It had got some stranger who happened to be passing by and didn't know about the Thing that lived there in the lonesome place. We were sure It had got somebody. It scared us, bad, and after something like this I hated all the more to go down town after supper, even for candy or ice cream.

"Some night I won't come back, you'll see," I would say.

"Oh, don't be silly," my mother would say.

"You'll see. You'll see. It'll get me next, you'll see."

"What'll get you?" she would ask offhandedly.

"Whatever it is out there in the dark," I would say.

"There's nothing out there but the dark," she would say.

"What about the bogey-man?" I would protest.

"They caught him," she would say. "A long time ago. He's locked up for good."

But Johnny and I knew better. His parents didn't know, either. The minute he started to complain, his dad reached for a hickory switch they kept behind the door. He had to go out fast and never mind what was in the lonesome place.

What do grown-up people know about the things boys are afraid of? Oh, hickory switches and such like, they know that. But what about what goes on in their minds when they have to come home alone at night through the lonesome places? What do they know about lonesome places where no light from the street corner ever comes? What do they know about a place and time when a boy is very small and very alone, and the night is as big as the town, and the darkness is the whole world? When grownups are big, old people who cannot understand anything, no matter how plain? A boy looks up and out, but he can't look very far when the trees bend down over and press close, when the sheds rear up along one side and the trees on the other, when the darkness lies like a cloud along the sidewalk and the arc lights are far, far away. No wonder then that Things grow in the darkness of lonesome places that way It grew in that dark place near the grain elevator. No wonder a boy runs like the wind until his heartbeats sound like a drum and push up to suffocate him.

"You're white as a sheet," mother would say sometimes. "You've been running again."

"Yes," I would say. "I've been running." But I never said why; I knew they wouldn't believe me; I knew nothing I could say would convince them about the Thing that lived back there, down the block, down past the grain elevator in that dark, lonesome place.

"You don't have to run," my father would say. "Take it easy."

"I ran," I would say. But I wanted in the worst way to say I had to run and to tell them why I had to; but I knew they wouldn't believe me any more than Johnny's parents believed him when he told them, as he did once.

He got a licking with a strap and had to go to bed.

I never got licked. I never told them.

But now it must be told, now it must be set down.

For a long time we forgot about the lonesome place. We grew older and we grew bigger. We went on through school into high school, and somehow we forgot about the Thing in the lonesome place. That place never changed. The trees grew older. Sometimes the lumber piles were bigger or smaller. Once the sheds were painted—red, like blood. Seeing them that way the first time, I remembered. Then I forgot again. We took to playing baseball and basketball and football. We began to swim in the river and to date the girls. We never talked about the Thing in the lonesome place any more, and when we went through there at night it was like something forgotten that lurked back in a corner of the mind. We thought of something we ought to remember, but never could quite remember; that was the way it seemed—like a memory locked away, far away in childhood. We never ran through that place, and sometimes it was even a good place to walk through with a girl, because she always snuggled up close and said how spooky it was there under the overhanging trees. But even then we never lingered there, not exactly lingered; we didn't run through there, but we walked without faltering or loitering, no matter how pretty a girl she was.

The years went past, and we never thought about the lonesome place again.

We never thought how there would be other little boys going through it at night, running with fast-beating hearts, breathless with terror, anxious for the safety of the arc light beyond the margin of the shadow which confined the dweller in that place, the light-fearing creature that haunted the dark, like so many terrors dwelling in similar lonesome places in the cities and small towns and countrysides all over the world, waiting to frighten little boys and girls, waiting to invade them with horror and unshakable fear —waiting for something more. . . .

Three nights ago little Bobby Jeffers was killed in the lonesome place. He was all mauled and torn and partly crushed, as if something big had fallen on him. Johnny, who was on the Village Board, went to look at the place, and after he had been there, he telephoned me to go, too, before other people walked there.

I went down and saw the marks, too. It was just as the coroner said, only not an "animal of some kind," as he put it. Something with a dragging tail, with scales, with great clawed feet—and I knew it had no face.

I knew, too, that Johnny and I were guilty. We had murdered Bobby Jeffers because the thing that killed him was the thing Johnny and I had created out of our childhood fears and left in that lonesome place to wait for some scared little boy at some minute in some hour during some dark night, a little boy who, like fat Bobby Jeffers, couldn't run as fast as Johnny and I could run.

And the worst is not that there is nothing to do, but that the lonesome place is being changed. The village is cutting down some of the trees now, removing the sheds, and putting up a streetlight in the middle of that place; it will not be dark and lonesome any longer, and the Thing that lives there will have to go somewhere else, where people are unsuspecting, to some other lonesome place in some other small town or city or countryside, where It will wait as It did here, for some frightened little boy or girl to come along, waiting in the dark and the lonesomeness . . .

This story is from *Lonesome Places,* the fifth collection of macabre tales by August Derleth. Other current books by him include: *Walden West,* an autobiographical memoir; *The Moon Tenders,* a humorous novel; *The Casebook of Solar Pons,* Sherlockian detective stories; *Colonel Markeson and Less Pleasant People,* weird tales written in collaboration with Mark Schorer; and two anthologies of supernatural stories: *Travellers By Night* and *Over the Edge.* Mr. Derleth, who was born in 1909, owns and operates the publishing firm of Arkham House and he is literary editor of *The Capital Times* of Madison, Wisconsin.

CHAPTER 2

In the Vault

by H. P. Lovecraft

Until he died in 1937 (at the age of 47), Howard Phillips Lovecraft was known chiefly to readers of *Weird Tales, Astonishing Stories* and *Amazing Stories* magazines, and to fellow fantasy writers who were steadfast to him. Two of these colleagues, August Derleth and Donald Wandrei, founded the firm of Arkham House (*Arkham* after the mythicized, witch-ridden New England town of many Lovecraft tales) to publish Lovecraft to a wider audience. They have succeeded admirably. Today, Arkham House is the Mecca of the macabre, with a long list of British and American authors, and Lovecraft's fame is flourishing.

There is nothing more absurd, as I view it, than that conventional association of the homely and the wholesome which seems to pervade the psychology of the multitude. Mention a bucolic Yankee setting, a bungling and thick-fibered village undertaker, and a careless mishap in a tomb, and no average reader can be brought to expect more than a hearty albeit grotesque phase of comedy. God knows, though, that the prosy tale which George Birch's death permits me to tell has in it aspects beside which some of our darkest tragedies are light.

Birch acquired a limitation and changed his business in 1881, yet never discussed the case when he could avoid it. Neither did his old physician, Dr. Davis, who died years ago. It was generally stated that the affliction and shock were results of an unlucky slip whereby Birch had locked himself for nine hours in the receiving tomb of Peck Valley Cemetery, escaping only by crude and disastrous mechanical means; but while this much was undoubtedly true, there were other and blacker things which the man used to whisper to me in his drunken delirium toward the last. He confided in me because I was his doctor, and because he probably felt the need of confiding in someone else after Davis died. He was a bachelor, wholly without relatives.

Birch, before 1881, had been the village undertaker of Peck Valley, and was a very calloused and primitive specimen even as such specimens go. The practices I heard attributed to him would be unbelievable today, at least in a city; and even Peck Valley would have shuddered a bit had it known the easy ethics of its mortuary artist in such matters as the ownership of costly "laying-out" apparel invisible beneath the casket's lid, and the degrees of dignity to be maintained in posing and adapting the unseen members of lifeless tenants to containers not always calculated with sublimest accuracy. Most distinctly Birch was lax, insensitive, and professionally undesirable; yet I still think he was not an evil man. He was merely crass of fiber and function—thoughtless, careless, and liquorish, as his easily avoidable accident proves, and without that modicum of imagination that holds the average citizen within certain limits fixed by taste.

Just where to begin Birch's story I can hardly decide, since I am no practiced teller of tales. I suppose one should start in the cold December of 1880, when the ground froze and the cemetery delvers found they could dig no more graves till spring. Fortunately the village was small and the death rate low, so that it was possible to give all of Birch's inanimate charges a temporary haven in the single antiquated receiving tomb. The undertaker grew doubly lethargic in the bitter weather, and seemed to outdo even himself in carelessness. Never did he knock together flimsier and ungainlier caskets, nor disregard more flagrantly the needs of the rusty lock on the tomb door which he slammed open and shut with such nonchalant abandon.

At last the spring thaw came, and graves were laboriously prepared for the nine silent harvests of the grim reaper that waited in the tomb. Birch, though dreading the bother of removal and

interment, began his task of transference one disagreeable April
morning, but ceased before noon because of a heavy rain that
seemed to irritate his horse, after having laid but one body to its
permanent rest. That was Darius Peck, the nonagenarian, whose
grave was not far from the tomb. Birch decided that he would
begin the next day with little old Matthew Fenner, whose grave
was also near by; but actually postponed the matter for three days,
not getting to work until Good Friday, the fifteenth. Being without
superstition, he did not heed the day at all; though ever afterward
he refused to do anything of importance on that fateful sixth day of
the week. Certainly, the events of that evening greatly changed
George Birch.

On the afternoon of Friday, April fifteenth, then, Birch set out
for the tomb with horse and wagon to transfer the body of Matthew
Fenner. That he was not perfectly sober, he subsequently admitted; though he had not then taken to the wholesale drinking by
which he later tried to forget certain things. He was just dizzy
and careless enough to annoy his sensitive horse, which as he drew
it viciously up at the tomb neighed and pawed and tossed its
head, much as on that former occasion when the rain had seem-
ingly vexed it. The day was clear, but a high wind had sprung up;
and Birch was glad to get to shelter, as he unlocked the iron door
and entered the sidehill vault. Another might not have relished
the damp, odorous chamber with the eight carelessly placed coffins; but Birch in those days was insensitive, and was concerned
only in getting the right coffin for the right grave. He had not forgotten the criticism aroused when Hannah Bixby's relatives, wishing to transport her body to the cemetery in the city whither they
had moved, found the casket of Judge Capwell beneath her head-
stone.

The light was dim, but Birch's sight was good, and he did not
get Asaph Sawyer's coffin by mistake, although it was very similar.
He had, indeed, made the coffin for Matthew Fenner; but had cast
it aside at last as too awkward and flimsy, in a fit of curious
sentimentality aroused by recalling how kindly and generous the
little old man had been to him during his bankruptcy five years
before. He gave old Matt the very best his skill could produce,
but was thrifty enough to save the rejected specimen, and to use
it when Asaph Sawyer died of a malignant fever. Sawyer was not a
lovable man, and many stories were told of his almost inhuman

vindictiveness and tenacious memory for wrongs real or fancied. To him Birch had felt no compunction in assigning the carelessly made coffin which he now pushed out of the way in his quest for the Fenner casket.

It was just as he had recognized old Matt's coffin that the door slammed to in the wind, leaving him in a dusk even deeper than before. The narrow transom admitted only the feeblest rays, and the overhead ventilation funnel virtually none at all; so that he was reduced to a profane fumbling as he made his halting way among the long boxes toward the latch. In this funereal twilight he rattled the rusty handles, pushed at the iron panels, and wondered why the massive portal had grown so suddenly recalcitrant. In this twilight, too, he began to realize the truth and to shout loudly as if his horse outside could do more than neigh an unsympathetic reply. For the long-neglected latch was obviously broken, leaving the careless undertaker trapped in the vault, a victim of his own oversight.

The thing must have happened at about three-thirty in the afternoon. Birch, being by temperament phlegmatic and practical, did not shout long; but proceeded to grope about for some tools which he recalled seeing in a corner of the tomb. It is doubtful whether he was touched at all by the horror and exquisite weirdness of his position, but the bald fact of imprisonment so far from the daily paths of men was enough to exasperate him thoroughly. His day's work was sadly interrupted, and unless chance presently brought some rambler hither, he might have to remain all night or longer. The pile of tools soon reached, and a hammer and chisel selected, Birch returned over the coffins to the door. The air had begun to be exceedingly unwholesome, but to this detail he paid no attention as he toiled, half by feeling, at the heavy and corroded metal of the latch. He would have given much for a lantern or bit of candle; but, lacking these, bungled semi-sightlessly as best he might.

When he perceived that the latch was hopelessly unyielding, at least to such meager tools and under such tenebrous conditions as these, Birch glanced about for other possible points of escape. The vault had been dug from a sidehill, so that the narrow ventilation funnel in the top ran through several feet of earth, making this direction utterly useless to consider. Over the door, however, the high, slitlike transom in the brick façade gave promise of possible enlargement to a diligent worker; hence upon this his eyes long rested as he racked his brains for means to reach it. There was nothing like a ladder in the tomb, and the coffin niches on the sides and rear, which Birch seldom took the trouble to use, afforded no ascent to the space above the door. Only the coffins themselves remained as potential steppingstones, and as he considered these he speculated on the best mode of arranging them. Three coffin heights, he reckoned, would permit him to reach the transom; but he could do better with four. The boxes were fairly even, and could be piled up like blocks; so he began to compute how he might most stably use the eight to rear a scalable platform four deep. As he planned, he could not but wish that the units of his comtemplated staircase had been more securely made. Whether he had imagination enough to wish they were empty, is strongly to be doubted.

Finally he decided to lay a base of three parallel with the wall, to place upon this two layers of two each, and upon these a single box to serve as the platform. This arrangement could be ascended with a minimum of awkwardness, and would furnish the desired height. Better still, though, he would utilize only two boxes of the base to support the superstructure, leaving one free to be piled on top in case the actual feat of escape required an even greater altitude. And so the prisoner toiled in the twilight, heaving the unresponsive remnants of mortality with little ceremony as his miniature Tower of Babel rose course by course. Several of the coffins began to split under the stress of handling, and he planned to save the stoutly built casket of little Matthew Fenner for the top, in order that his feet might have as certain a surface as possible. In the semigloom he trusted mostly to touch to select the right one, and indeed came upon it almost by accident, since it tumbled into his hands as if through some odd volition after he had unwittingly placed it beside another on the third layer.

The tower at length finished, and his aching arms rested by a pause during which he sat on the bottom step of his grim device, Birch cautiously ascended with his tools and stood abreast of the narrow transom. The borders of the space were entirely of brick, and there seemed little doubt but that he could shortly chisel away enough to allow his body to pass. As his hammer blows began to fall, the horse outside whinnied in a tone which may have been encouraging and may have been mocking. In either case, it would have been appropriate, for the unexpected tenacity of the easy-looking brickwork was surely a sardonic commentary of the vanity of mortal hopes, and the source of a task whose performance deserved every possible stimulus.

Dusk fell and found Birch still toiling. He worked largely by feeling now, since newly gathered clouds hid the moon; and though progress was still slow, he felt heartened at the extent of his encroachments on the top and bottom of the aperture. He could, he was sure, get out by midnight; though it is characteristic of him that this thought was untinged with eery implications. Undisturbed by oppressive reflections on the time, the place, and the company beneath his feet, he philosophically chipped away the stony brickwork, cursing when a fragment hit him in the face, and laughing when one struck the increasingly excited horse that pawed near the cypress tree. In time the hole grew so large that he ventured to try his body in it now and then, shifting about so that the coffins beneath him rocked and creaked. He would not, he found, have to pile another on his platform to make the proper height, for the hole was on exactly the right level to use as soon as its size would permit.

It must have been midnight at least when Birch decided he could get through the transom. Tired and perspiring despite many rests, he descended to the floor and sat a while on the bottom box to gather strength for the final wriggle and leap to the ground outside. The hungry horse was neighing repeatedly and almost uncannily, and he vaguely wished it would stop. He was curiously unelated over his impending escape, and almost dreaded the exertion, for his form had the indolent stoutness of early middle age. As he remounted the splitting coffins he felt his weight very poignantly; especially when, upon reaching the topmost one, he heard that aggravated crackle which bespeaks the wholesale rending of wood. He had, it seems, planned in vain when choosing the stoutest coffin for the platform; for no sooner was his full bulk again upon it than the rotting lid gave way, jouncing him two feet down on a surface which even he did not care to imagine. Maddened by the sound, or by the stench which billowed forth even to the open air, the waiting horse gave a scream that was too frantic for a neigh, and plunged madly off through the night, the wagon rattling crazily behind it.

Birch, in his ghastly situation, was now too low for an easy scramble out of the enlarged transom, but gathered his energies for a determined try. Clutching the edges of the aperture, he sought to pull himself up, when he noticed a queer retardation in the form of an apparent drag on both his ankles. In another moment he knew fear for the first time that night; for struggle as he would, he could not shake clear of the unknown grasp which held his feet in relentless captivity. Horrible pains, as of savage wounds, shot through his calves; and in his mind was a vortex of fright mixed with an unquenchable materialism that suggested splinters, loose nails, or some other attribute of a breaking wooden box. Perhaps he screamed. At any rate, he kicked and squirmed frantically and automatically while his consciousness was almost eclipsed in a half swoon.

Instinct guided him in his wriggle through the transom, and in the crawl that followed his jarring thud on the damp ground. He could not walk, it appeared, and the emerging moon must have witnessed a horrible sight as he dragged his bleeding ankles toward the cemetery lodge, his fingers clawing the black mold in brainless haste, and his body responding with that maddening slowness from which one suffers when chased by the phantoms of nightmare. There was evidently, however, no pursuer; for he was alone and alive when Armington, the lodge keeper, responded to his feeble clawing at the door.

Armington helped Birch to the outside of a spare bed and sent his little son Edwin for Dr. Davis. The afflicted man was fully conscious, but would say nothing of any consequence, merely muttering such things as "Oh, my ankles!" "Let go!" or ". . . shut in the tomb." Then the doctor came in with his medicine case and asked crisp questions, and removed the patient's outer clothing, shoes, and socks. The wounds—for both ankles were frightfully lacerated about the Achilles' tendons—seemed to puzzle the old physician greatly, and finally almost to frighten him. His questioning grew more than medically tense, and his hands shook as he dressed the mangled members, binding them as if he wished to get the wounds out of sight as quickly as possible.

For an impersonal doctor, Davis's ominous and awestruck cross-examination became very strange indeed as he sought to drain from the weakened undertaker every last detail of his horrible experience. He was oddly anxious to know if Birch were sure—absolutely sure—of the identity of that top coffin of the pile, how he had chosen it, how he had been certain of it as the Fenner coffin in the dark, and how he had distinguished it from the inferior duplicate coffin of vicious Asaph Sawyer. Would the firm Fenner casket have caved in so readily? Davis, an old-time village practitioner, had of course seen both at the respective funerals, as indeed he had attended both Fenner and Sawyer in their last illnesses. He had even wondered, at Sawyer's funeral, how the vindictive farmer had managed to lie straight in a box so closely akin to that of the diminutive Fenner.

After a full two hours Dr. Davis left, urging Birch to insist at all times that his wounds were due entirely to loose nails and splintering wood. What else, he added, could ever in any case be proved or believed? But it would be well to say as little as could be said, and to let no other doctor treat the wounds. Birch heeded this advice all the rest of his life until he told me his story, and when I saw the scars—ancient and whitened as they then were—I agreed that he was wise in so doing. He always remained lame, for the great tendons had been severed; but I think the greatest lameness was in his soul. His thinking processes, once so phlegmatic and logical, had become ineffaceably scarred, and it was pitiful to note his reaction to certain chance allusions such as "Friday," "tomb," "coffin," and words of less obvious concatenation. His frightened horse had gone home, but his frightened wits never quite did that. He changed his business, but something always preyed upon him. It may have been just fear, and it may have been fear mixed with a queer belated sort of remorse for bygone crudities. His drinking, of course, only aggravated what he sought to alleviate.

When Dr. Davis left Birch that night, he had taken a lantern and gone to the old receiving tomb. The moon was shining on the scattered brick fragments and marred façade, and the latch of the great door yielded readily to a touch from the outside. Steeled by old ordeals in dissecting rooms, the doctor entered and looked about, stifling the nausea of mind and body that everything in sight and smell induced. He cried aloud once, and a little later gave a gasp that was more terrible than a cry. Then he fled back to the lodge and broke all the rules of his calling by rousing and shaking his patient, and hurling at him a succession of shuddering whispers that seared into the bewildered ears like the hissing of vitriol.

"It was Asaph's coffin, Birch, just as I thought! I knew his teeth, with the front ones missing on the upper jaw—never, for God's sake, show those wounds! The body was pretty badly gone, but if ever I saw vindictiveness on any face—or former face! . . . You know what a fiend he was for revenge—how he ruined old Raymond thirty years after their boundary suit, and how he stepped on the puppy that snapped at him a year ago last August. . . . He was the devil incarnate, Birch, and I believe his eye-for-an-eye fury could beat time and death! God, his rage—I'd hate to have it aimed at me!

"Why did you do it, Birch? He was a scoundrel, and I don't blame you for giving him a cast-aside coffin, but you always did go too damned far! Well enough to skimp on the thing in some way, but you knew what a little man old Fenner was.

"I'll never get the picture out of my head as long as I live. You kicked hard, for Asaph's coffin was on the floor. His head was broken in, and everything was tumbled about. I've seen sights before, but there was one thing too much here. An eye for an eye! Great heavens, Birch, but you got what you deserved! The skull turned my stomach, but the other was worse—*those ankles cut neatly off to fit Matt Fenner's cast-aside coffin!*"

A few years ago, much of Lovecraft's fiction was out-of-print and readers paid high prices for the original collections, *The Outsider and Others* and *Beyond the Wall of Sleep,* when they could be found. All of his fiction has since been reissued in three volumes: *The Dunwich Horror and Others; At the Mountains of Madness and Other Novels; Dagon and Other Macabre Tales*—with the *Collected Poems* in another volume. The first volume of *Selected Letters* came out in 1965 and these will run to five volumes. Some of the letters contain preliminary drafts for stories that are as entertaining as the published fiction. In addition, there are several books of Lovecraftiana. Among them, *The Dark Brotherhood and Others* has a detailed Lovecraft bibliography by Jack Laurence Chalker and Fritz Leiber's fine essay on Lovecraft's contribution to speculative fiction. Lovecraft's own survey of *Supernatural Horror in Literature* is included in the *Dagon* collection.

CHAPTER 3

The Man Who Collected Poe

by Robert Bloch

The author of *Psycho* needs little introduction. For the record, Robert Bloch was born in 1917 and, since 1935, he has written hundreds of stories of fantasy and suspense. Along with August Derleth, he is one of the most active writers of the famous Lovecraft circle. One of Mr. Bloch's earlier tales, "The Man Who Collected Poe" (1951) recalls H. P. Lovecraft's *The Case of Charles Dexter Ward* more than anything by Poe, but the grisly merriment of it is pure Bloch.

———————

During the whole of a dull, dark, and soundless day in the autumn of the year, when the clouds hung oppressively low in the heavens, I had been passing alone, by automobile, through a singularly dreary tract of country, and at length found myself, as the shades of the evening drew on, within view of my destination.

I looked upon the scene before me—upon the mere house, and the simple landscape features of the domain—upon the bleak walls —upon the vacant eyelike windows—upon a few rank sedges—and upon a few white trunks of decayed trees—with a feeling of utter confusion commingled with dismay. For it seemed to me as though I had visited this scene once before, or read of it, perhaps, in some frequently rescanned tale. And yet assuredly it could not be, for only three days had passed since I had made the acquaintance of Launcelot Canning and received an invitation to visit him at his Maryland residence.

The circumstances under which I met Canning were simple; I happened to attend a bibliophilic meeting in Washington and was introduced to him by a mutual friend. Casual conversation gave place to absorbed and interested discussion when he discovered my preoccupation with works of fantasy. Upon learning that I was traveling upon a vacation with no set itinerary, Canning urged me to become his guest for a day and to examine, at my leisure, his unusual display of memorabilia.

"I feel, from our conversation, that we have much in common," he told me. "For you see, sir, in my love of fantasy I bow to no man. It is a taste I have perhaps inherited from my father and from his father before him, together with their considerable acquisitions in the genre. No doubt you would be gratified with what I am prepared to show you, for in all due modesty, I beg to style myself the world's leading collector of the works of Edgar Allan Poe."

I confess that his invitation as such did not enthrall me, for I hold no brief for the literary hero-worshipper or the scholarly collector as a type. I own to a more than passing interest in the tales of Poe, but my interest does not extend to the point of ferreting out the exact date upon which Mr. Poe first decided to raise a mustache, nor would I be unduly intrigued by the opportunity to examine several hairs preserved from that hirsute appendage.

So it was rather the person and personality of Launcelot Canning himself which caused me to accept his proffered hospitality. For the man who proposed to become my host might have himself stepped from the pages of a Poe tale. His speech, as I have endeavored to indicate, was characterized by a courtly rodomontade so often exemplified in Poe's heroes—and beyond certainty, his appearance bore out the resemblance.

Launcelot Canning had the cadaverousness of complexion, the large, liquid, luminous eye, the thin, curved lips, the delicately modeled nose, finely molded chin, and dark, weblike hair of a typical Poe protagonist.

It was this phenomenon that prompted my acceptance and led me to journey to his Maryland estate which, as I now perceived, in itself manifested a Poe-esque quality of its own, intrinsic in the images of the gray sedge, the ghastly tree stems, and the vacant and eyelike windows of the mansion of gloom. All that was lacking was a tarn and a moat—and as I prepared to enter the dwelling I half expected to encounter therein the carved ceiling, the somber tapestries, the ebon floors, and the phantasmagoric armorial trophies so vividly described by the author of *Tales of the Grotesque and Arabesque.*

Nor, upon entering Launcelot Canning's home was I too greatly disappointed in my expectations. True to both the atmospheric quality of the decrepit mansion and to my own fanciful presentiments, the door was opened in response to my knock by a valet who conducted me, in silence, through dark and intricate passages to the study of his master.

The room in which I found myself was very large and lofty. The windows were long, narrow, and pointed, and at so vast a distance from the black oaken floor as to be altogether inaccessible from within. Feeble gleams of encrimsoned light made their way through the trellised panes, and served to render sufficiently distinct the more prominent objects around; the eye, however, struggled in vain to reach the remoter angles of the chamber or the recesses of the vaulted and fretted ceiling. Dark draperies hung upon the walls. The general furniture was profuse, comfortless, antique, and tattered. Many books and musical instruments lay scattered about, but failed to give any vitality to the scene.

Instead they rendered more distinct that peculiar quality of quasi recollection; it was as though I found myself once again, after a protracted absence, in a familiar setting. I had read, I had imagined, I had dreamed, or I had actually beheld this setting before.

Upon my entrance, Launcelot Canning arose from a sofa on which he had been lying at full length, and greeted me with a vivacious warmth which had much in it, I at first thought, of an overdone cordiality.

Yet his tone, as he spoke of the object of my visit, of his earnest desire to see me, and of the solace he expected me to afford him in a mutual discussion of our interests, soon alleviated my initial misapprehension.

Launcelot Canning welcomed me with the rapt enthusiasm of the born collector—and I came to realize that he was indeed just that. For the Poe collection he shortly proposed to unveil before me was actually his birthright.

Initially, he disclosed, the nucleus of the present accumulation had begun with his grandfather, Christopher Canning, a respected merchant of Baltimore. Almost eighty years ago he had been one of the leading patrons of the arts in his community and as such was partially instrumental in arranging for the removal of Poe's body to the southeastern corner of the Presbyterian Cemetery at Fayette and Green Streets, where a suitable monument might be erected. This event occurred in the year 1875, and it was a few years prior to that time that Canning laid the foundation of the Poe collection.

"Thanks to his zeal," his grandson informed me, "I am today the fortunate possessor of a copy of virtually every existing specimen of Poe's published works. If you will step over here"—and he led me to a remote corner of the vaulted study, past the dark draperies, to a bookshelf which rose remotely to the shadowy ceiling—"I shall be pleased to corroborate that claim. Here is a copy of *Al Araaf, Tamerlane and other Poems* in the 1829 edition, and here is the still earlier *Tamerlane and other Poems* of 1827. The Boston edition, which, as you doubtless know, is valued today at $15,000. I can assure you that Grandfather Canning parted with no such sum in order to gain possession of this rarity."

He displayed the volumes with an air of commingled pride and cupidity which is ofttimes characteristic of the collector and is by no means to be confused with either literary snobbery or ordinary greed. Realizing this, I remained patient as he exhibited further treasures—copies of the *Philadelphia Saturday Courier* containing early tales, bound volumes of *The Messenger* during the period of Poe's editorship, *Graham's Magazine,* editions of the *New York Sun* and the *New York Mirror* boasting, respectively, of *The Balloon Hoax* and *The Raven,* and files of *The Gentleman's Magazine.* Ascending a short library ladder, he handed down to me the Lea and Blanchard edition of *Tales of the Grotesque and Arabesque,* the *Conchologist's First Book,* the Putnam *Eureka,* and, finally the little paper booklet, published in 1843 and sold for 12½¢, entitled *The Prose Romances of Edgar A. Poe;* an insignificant trifle containing two tales which is valued by present-day collectors at $50,000.

Canning informed me of this last fact, and, indeed, kept up a running commentary upon each item he presented. There was no doubt but that he was a Poe scholar as well as a Poe collector, and his words informed tattered specimens of the *Broadway Journal* and *Godey's Lady's Book* with a singular fascination not necessarily inherent in the flimsy sheets or their contents.

"I owe a great debt to Grandfather Canning's obsession," he observed, descending the ladder and joining me before the bookshelves. "It is not altogether a breach of confidence to admit that his interest in Poe did reach the point of an obsession, and perhaps eventually of an absolute mania. The knowledge, alas, is public property, I fear.

"In the early seventies he built his house, and I am quite sure that you have been observant enough to note that it in itself is almost a replica of a typical Poe-esque mansion. This was his study, and it was here that he was wont to pore over the books, the letters, and the numerous mementos of Poe's life.

"What prompted a retired merchant to devote himself so fanatically to the pursuit of a hobby, I cannot say. Let it suffice that he virtually withdrew from the world and from all other normal interests. He conducted a voluminous and lengthy correspondence with aging men and women who had known Poe in their lifetime—made pilgrimages to Fordham, sent his agents to West Point, to England and Scotland, to virtually every locale in which Poe had set foot during his lifetime. He acquired letters and souvenirs as gifts, he bought them, and—I fear—stole them, if no other means of acquisition proved feasible."

Launcelot Canning smiled and nodded. "Does all this sound strange to you? I confess that once I, too, found it almost incredible, a fragment of romance. Now, after years spent here, I have lost my own objectivity."

"Yes, it is strange," I replied. "But are you quite sure that there was not some obscure personal reason for your grandfather's interest? Had he met Poe as a boy, or been closely associated with one of his friends? Was there, perhaps, a distant, undisclosed relationship?"

At the mention of the last word, Canning started visibly, and a tremor of agitation overspread his countenance.

"Ah!" he exclaimed. "There you voice my own inmost conviction. A relationship—assuredly there must have been one—I am morally, instinctively certain that Grandfather Canning felt or knew himself to be linked to Edgar Poe by ties of blood. Nothing else could account for his strong initial interest, his continuing

defense of Poe in the literary controversies of the day, and his
final melancholy lapse into a world of delusion and illusion.

"Yet he never voiced a statement or put an allegation upon
paper—and I have searched the collection of letters in vain for the
slightest clue.

"It is curious that you so promptly divine a suspicion held not
only by myself but by my father. He was only a child at the time
of my Grandfather Canning's death, but the attendant circumstances left a profound impression upon his sensitive nature. Although he was immediately removed from this house to the home
of his mother's people in Baltimore, he lost no time in returning
upon assuming his inheritance in early manhood.

"Fortunately being in possession of a considerable income, he
was able to devote his entire lifetime to further research. The
name of Arthur Canning is still well known in the world of literary
criticism, but for some reason he preferred to pursue his scholarly
examination of Poe's career in privacy. I believe this preference
was dictated by an inner sensibility; that he was endeavoring to
unearth some information which would prove his father's, his,
and for that matter, my own, kinship to Edgar Poe."

"You say your father was also a collector?" I prompted.

"A statement I am prepared to substantiate," replied my host, as
he led me to yet another corner of the shadow-shrouded study.
"But first, if you would accept a glass of wine?"

He filled, not glasses, but veritable beakers from a large carafe,
and we toasted one another in silent appreciation. It is perhaps
unnecessary for me to observe that the wine was a fine old Amon-
tillado.

"Now, then," said Launcelot Canning. "My father's special
province in Poe research consisted of the accumulation and study
of letters."

Opening a series of large trays or drawers beneath the bookshelves, he drew out file after file of glassined folios, and for the
space of the next half hour I examined Edgar Poe's correspondence—letters to Henry Herring, to Dr. Snodgrass, Sarah Shelton,
James P. Moss, Elizabeth Poe—missives to Mrs. Rockwood,
Helen Whitman, Anne Lynch, John Pendleton Kennedy—notes
to Mrs. Richmond, to John Allan, to Annie, to his brother, Henry
—a profusion of documents, a veritable epistolary cornucopia.

During the course of my perusal my host took occasion to refill our beakers with wine, and the heady draught began to take effect—for we had not eaten, and I own I gave no thought to food, so absorbed was I in the yellowed pages illumining Poe's past.

Here was wit, erudition, literary criticism; here were the muddled, maudlin outpourings of a mind gone in drink and despair; here was the draft of a projected story, the fragments of a poem; here were a pitiful cry for deliverance and a paean to living beauty; here were a dignified response to a dunning letter and an editorial pronunciamento to an admirer; here were love, hate, pride, anger, celestial serenity, abject penitence, authority, wonder, resolution, indecision, joy, and soul-sickening melancholia.

Here were the gifted elocutionist, the stammering drunkard, the adoring husband, the frantic lover, the proud editor, the indigent pauper, the grandiose dreamer, the shabby realist, the scientific inquirer, the gullible metaphysician, the dependent stepson, the free and untrammeled spirit, the hack, the poet, the enigma that was Edgar Allan Poe.

Again the beakers were filled and emptied.

I drank deeply with my lips, and with my eyes more deeply still.

For the first time the true enthusiasm of Launcelot Canning was communicated to my own sensibilities—I divined the eternal fascination found in a consideration of Poe the writer and Poe the man; he who wrote Tragedy, lived Tragedy, was Tragedy; he who penned Mystery, lived and died in Mystery, and who today looms on the literary scene as Mystery incarnate.

And Mystery Poe remained, despite Arthur Canning's careful study of the letters. "My father learned nothing," my host confided, "even though he assembled, as you see here, a collection to delight the heart of a Mabbott or a Quinn. So his search ranged further. By this time I was old enough to share both his interest and his inquiries. Come," and he led me to an ornate chest which rested beneath the windows against the west wall of the study.

Kneeling, he unlocked the repository, and then drew forth, in rapid and marvelous succession, a series of objects each of which boasted of intimate connection with Poe's life.

There were souvenirs of his youth and his schooling abroad—a book he had used during his sojourn at West Point—mementos of his days as a theatrical critic in the form of playbills, a pen used during his editorial period, a fan once owned by his girl-wife, Virginia, a brooch of Mrs. Clemm's; a profusion of objects including such diverse articles as a cravat stock and—curiously enough—Poe's battered and tarnished flute.

Again we drank, and I own the wine was potent. Canning's countenance remained cadaverously wan—but, moreover, there was a species of mad hilarity in his eye—an evident restrained hysteria in his whole demeanor. At length, from the scattered heap of curiosa, I happened to draw forth and examine a little box of no remarkable character, whereupon I was constrained to inquire its history and what part it had played in the life of Poe.

"In the *life* of Poe?" A visible tremor convulsed the features of my host, then rapidly passed in transformation to a grimace, a rictus of amusement. "This little box—and you will note how, by some fateful design or contrived coincidence it bears a resemblance to the box he himself conceived and described in his tale, *Berenice*—this little box is concerned with his death, rather than his life. It is, in fact, the self-same box my grandfather Christopher Canning clutched to his bosom when they found him down there."

Again the tremor, again the grimace. "But stay, I have not yet told you of the details. Perhaps you would be interested in seeing the spot where Christopher Canning was stricken; I have already told you of his madness, but I did not more than hint at the character of his delusions. You have been patient with me, and more than patient. Your understanding shall be rewarded, for I perceive you can be fully entrusted with the facts."

What further revelations Canning was prepared to make I could not say, but his manner was such as to inspire a vague disquiet and trepidation in my breast.

Upon perceiving my unease he laughed shortly and laid a hand upon my shoulder. "Come, this should interest you as an *aficionado* of fantasy," he said. "But first, another drink to speed our journey."

He poured, we drank, and then he led the way from that vaulted chamber, down the silent halls, down the staircase, and into the lowest recesses of the building until we reached what resembled a dungeon, its floor and the interior of a long archway carefully sheathed in copper. We paused before a door of massive iron. Again I felt in the aspect of this scene an element evocative of recognition or recollection.

Canning's intoxication was such that he misinterpreted, or chose to misinterpret, my reaction.

"You need not be afraid," he assured me. "Nothing has happened down here since that day, almost seventy years ago, when his servants discovered him stretched out before this door, the little box clutched to his bosom; collapsed, and in a state of delirium from which he never emerged. For six months he lingered, a hopeless maniac—raving as wildly from the very moment of his discovery as at the moment he died—babbling his visions of the giant horse, the fissured house collapsing into the tarn, the black cat, the pit, the pendulum, the raven on the pallid bust, the beating heart, the pearly teeth, and the nearly liquid mass of loathsome— of detestable putridity from which a voice emanated.

"Nor was that all he babbled," Canning confided, and here his voice sank to a whisper that reverberated through the copper-sheathed hall and against the iron door. "He hinted other things far worse than fantasy; of a ghastly reality surpassing all of the phantasms of Poe.

"For the first time my father and the servants learned the purpose of the room he had built beyond this iron door, and learned what Christopher Canning had done to establish his title as the world's foremost collector of Poe.

"For he babbled again of Poe's death, thirty years earlier, in 1849—of the burial in the Presbyterian Cemetery—and of the removal of the coffin in 1874 to the corner where the monument was raised. As I told you, and as was known then, my grandfather had played a public part in instigating that removal. But now we learned of the private part—learned that there was a monument and a grave, but no coffin in the earth beneath Poe's alleged resting place. The coffin now rested in the secret room at the end of this passage. That is why the room, the house itself, had been built.

"I tell you, he had stolen the body of Edgar Allan Poe—and as he shrieked aloud in his final madness, did not this indeed make him the greatest collector of Poe?

"His ultimate intent was never divined, but my father made one significant discovery—the little box clutched to Christopher Canning's bosom contained a portion of the crumbled bones, the veritable dust that was all that remained of Poe's corpse."

My host shuddered and turned away. He led me back along that hall of horror, up the stairs, into the study. Silently, he filled

our beakers and I drank as hastily, as deeply, as desperately as
he.

"What could my father do? To own the truth was to create
a public scandal. He chose instead to keep silence; to devote his
own life to study in retirement.

"Naturally the shock affected him profoundly; to my knowledge
he never entered the room beyond the iron door and, indeed, I
did not know of the room or its contents until the hour of his
death—and it was not until some years later that I myself found
the key among his effects.

"But find the key I did, and the story was immediately and
completely corroborated. Today I am the greatest collector of
Poe—for he lies in the keep below, my eternal trophy!"

This time I poured the wine. As I did so, I noted for the first
time the imminence of a storm; the impetuous fury of its gusts
shaking the casements, and the echoes of its thunder rolling and
rumbling down the time-corroded corridors of the old house.

The wild, overstrained vivacity with which my host harkened,
or apparently harkened, to these sounds did nothing to reassure
me—for his recent revelation led me to suspect his sanity.

That the body of Edgar Allan Poe had been stolen—that this
mansion had been built to house it—that it was indeed enshrined
in a crypt below—that grandsire, son, and grandson had dwelt here
alone, apart, enslaved to a sepulchral secret—was beyond sane
belief.

And yet, surrounded now by the night and the storm, in a setting torn from Poe's own frenzied fancies, I could not be sure.
Here the past was still alive, the very spirit of Poe's tales breathed
forth its corruption upon the scene.

As thunder boomed, Launcelot Canning took up Poe's flute,
and, whether in defiance of the storm without or as a mocking accompaniment, he played; blowing upon it with drunken persist-
ence, with eery atonality, with nerve-shattering shrillness. To the
shrieking of that infernal instrument the thunder added a braying
counterpoint.

Uneasy, uncertain, and unnerved, I retreated into the shadows
of the bookshelves at the farther end of the room, and idly
scanned the titles of a row of ancient tomes. Here was the
Chiromancy of Robert Flud, the *Directorium Inquisitorum,* a
rare and curious book in quarto Gothic that was the manual of a

forgotten church; and betwixt and between the volumes of pseudoscientific inquiry, theological speculation, and sundry incunabula I found titles that arrested and appalled me. *De Vermis Mysteriis* and the *Liber Eibon,* treatises on demonology, on witchcraft, on sorcery moldered in crumbling binding. The books were old, but the books were not dusty. They had been read—

"Read them?" It was as though Canning divined my inmost thoughts. He had put aside his flute and now approached me, tittering as though in continued drunken defiance of the storm. Odd echoes and boomings now sounded through the long halls of the house, and curious grating sounds threatened to drown out his words and his laughter.

"Read them?" said Canning. "I study them. Yes, I have gone beyond grandfather and father, too. It was I who procured the books that held the key, and it was I who found the key. A key more difficult to discover, and more important, than the key to the vaults below. I often wonder if Poe himself had access to these selfsame tomes, knew the selfsame secrets. The secrets of the grave and what lies beyond, and what can be summoned forth if one but holds the key."

He stumbled away and returned with wine. "Drink," he said. "Drink to the night and the storm."

I brushed the proffered glass aside. "Enough," I said. "I must be on my way."

Was it fancy or did I find fear frozen on his features? Canning clutched my arm and cried, "No, stay with me! This is no night on which to be alone; I swear I cannot abide the thought of being alone, I can bear to be alone no more!"

His incoherent babble mingled with the thunder and the echoes; I drew back and confronted him. "Control yourself," I counseled. "Confess that this is a hoax, an elaborate imposture arranged to please your fancy."

"Hoax? Imposture? Stay, and I shall prove to you beyond all doubt"—and so saying, Launcelot Canning stooped and opened a small drawer set in the wall beneath and beside the bookshelves. "This should repay you for your interest in my story, and in Poe," he murmured. "Know that you are the first, other person than myself, to glimpse these treasures."

He handed me a sheaf of manuscripts on plain white paper; documents written in ink curiously similar to that I had noted while perusing Poe's letters. Pages were clipped together in groups, and for a moment I scanned titles alone.

"*The Worm of Midnight, by Edgar Poe*," I read, aloud. "*The Crypt*," I breathed. And here, "*The Further Adventures of Arthur Gordon Pym*"—and in my agitation I came close to dropping the precious pages. "Are these what they appear to be—the unpublished tales of Poe?"

My host bowed.

"Unpublished, undiscovered, unknown, save to me—and to you."

"But this cannot be," I protested. "Surely there would have been a mention of them somewhere, in Poe's own letters or those of his contemporaries. There would have been a clue, an indication, somewhere, some place, somehow."

Thunder mingled with my words, and thunder echoed in Canning's shouted reply.

"You dare to presume an imposture? Then compare!" He stooped again and brought out a glassined folio of letters. "Here —is this not the veritable script of Edgar Poe? Look at the calligraphy of the letter, then at the manuscripts. Can you say they are not penned by the selfsame hand?"

I looked at the handwriting, wondered at the possibilities of a monomaniac's forgery. Could Launcelot Canning, a victim of mental disorder, thus painstakingly simulate Poe's hand?

"Read, then!" Canning screamed through the thunder. "Read, and dare to say that these tales were written by any other than Edgar Poe, whose genius defies the corruption of Time and the Conqueror Worm!"

I read but a line or two, holding the topmost manuscript close to eyes that strained beneath wavering candlelight; but even in the flickering illumination I noted that which told me the only, the incontestable truth. For the paper, the curiously *unyellowed* paper, bore a visible watermark; the name of a firm of well-known modeern stationers, and the date—1949.

Putting the sheaf aside, I endeavored to compose myself as I moved away from Launcelot Canning. For now I knew the truth; knew that, one hundred years after Poe's death a semblance of his spirit still lived in the distorted and disordered soul of Canning. Incarnation, reincarnation, call it what you will; Canning was, in his own irrational mind, Edgar Allan Poe.

Stifled and dull echoes of thunder from a remote portion of the mansion now commingled with the soundless seething of my own inner turmoil, as I turned and rashly addressed my host.

"Confess!" I cried. "Is it not true that you have written these tales, fancying yourself the embodiment of Poe? Is it not true that you suffer from a singular delusion born of solitude and everlasting brooding upon the past; that you have reached a stage character-ized by the conviction that Poe still lives on in your own person?"

A strong shudder came over him and a sickly smile quivered about his lips as he replied, "Fool! I say to you that I have spoken the truth. Can you doubt the evidence of your senses? This house is real, the Poe collection exists, and the stories exist—they exist, I swear, as truly as the body lying in the crypt below!"

I took up the little box from the table and removed the lid. "Not so," I answered. "You said your grandfather was found with this box clutched to his breast, before the door of the vault, and that it contained Poe's dust. Yet you cannot escape the fact that the box is empty." I faced him furiously. "Admit it, the story is a fabrica-tion, a romance. Poe's body does not lie beneath this house, nor are these his unpublished works, written during his lifetime and concealed."

"True enough." Canning's smile was ghastly beyond belief. "The dust is gone because I took it and used it—because in the works of wizardry I found the formulae, the arcana whereby I could raise the flesh, recreate the body from the essential salts of the grave. Poe does not *lie* beneath this house—he *lives!* And the tales are *his posthumous works!*"

Accented by thunder, his words crashed against my conscious-ness.

"That was the end-all and the be-all of my planning, of my stud-ies, of my work, of my life! To raise, by sorcery, the veritable spirit of Edgar Poe from the grave—reclothed and animate in flesh—set him to dwell and dream and do his work again in the private cham-bers I built in the vaults below—and this I have done! To steal a corpse is but a ghoulish prank; mine is the achievement of true genius!"

The distinct, hollow, metallic, and clangorous, yet apparently muffled reverberation accompanying his words caused him to turn in his seat and face the door of the study, so that I could not see the workings of his countenance—nor could he read my own reaction to his ravings.

His words came but faintly to my ears through the thunder that now shook the house in a relentless grip; the wind rattling the casements and flickering the candle flame from the great silver candelabra sent a soaring sighing in an anguished accompaniment to his speech.

"I would show him to you, but I dare not; for he hates me as he hates life. I have locked him in the vault, alone, for the resurrected have no need of food nor drink. And he sits there, pen moving over paper, endlessly moving, endlessly pouring out the evil essence of all he guessed and hinted at in life and which he learned in death.

"Do you not see the tragic pity of my plight? I sought to raise his spirit from the dead, to give the world anew of his genius—and yet these tales, these works, are filled and fraught with a terror not to be endured. They cannot be shown to the world, he cannot be shown to the world; in bringing back the dead I have brought back the fruits of death!"

Echoes sounded anew as I moved toward the door—moved, I confess, to flee this accursed house and its accursed owner.

Canning clutched my hand, my arm, my shoulder. "You cannot go!" he shouted above the storm. "I spoke of his escaping, but did you not guess? Did you not hear it through the thunder—the grating of the door?"

I pushed him aside and he blundered backward upsetting the candelabra, so that flames licked now across the carpeting.

"Wait!" he cried. "Have you not heard his footstep on the stair? *Madman, I tell you that he now stands without the door!*"

A rush of wind, a roar of flame, a shroud of smoke rose all about us. Throwing open the huge, antique panels to which Canning pointed, I staggered into the hall.

I speak of wind, of flame, of smoke—enough to obscure all vision. I speak of Canning's screams, and of thunder loud enough to drown all sound. I speak of terror born of loathing and of desperation enough to shatter all my sanity.

Despite these things, I can never erase from my consciousness that which I beheld as I fled past the doorway and down the hall.

There without the doors there *did* stand a lofty and enshrouded figure; a figure all too familiar, with pallid features, high, domed forehead, mustache set above a mouth. My glimpse lasted but an instant, an instant during which the man—the corpse—the apparition—the hallucination, call it what you will—moved forward into the chamber and clasped Canning to his breast in an unbreakable embrace. Together, the two figures tottered toward the flames, which now rose to blot out vision forevermore.

From that chamber, and from that mansion, I fled aghast. The storm was still abroad in all its wrath, and now fire came to claim the house of Canning for its own.

Suddenly there shot along the path before me a wild light, and I turned to see whence a gleam so unusual could have issued—but it was only the flames, rising in supernatural splendor to consume the mansion, and the secrets, of the man who collected Poe.

Dr. Thomas Ollive Mabbott, the distinguished Poe scholar, liked "The Man Who Collected Poe" so much that he asked Robert Bloch to complete Poe's unfinished tale "The Light-House." Mr. Bloch complied and the finished product appears in the collection called *Pleasant Dreams—Nightmares* by Robert Bloch. Poe's part in the collaboration was, of course, posthumous. But there is no reason to suspect that Mr. Bloch practices the black arts he describes so vividly—unless he goes on turning out such uncanny tales.

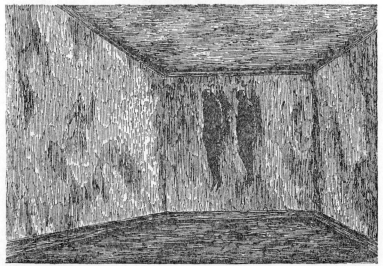

CHAPTER 4

Where Angels Fear

by Manly Wade Wellman

African tales of magic and spirits awakened Manly Wade Wellman's interest in folklore when he was a boy. Though his family goes back to colonial Virginia, he was born, in 1903, in Portuguese West Africa where his father founded a mission hospital. Mr. Wellman's first tales of mystery and fantasy were published while he was a student at Columbia. Since then, he has written some 500 short stories and more than forty books dealing with America's past and legends. A collection of his tales, *Who Fears the Devil?*, deals with the Southern mountains and "supernatural matters not to be found anywhere else in America." But the locale of "Where Angels Fear" might be any place that has an old dark house to challenge the curious.

Half a mile from McCormack's cabin a paved highway crossed the rutted woodland road, and here a post held aloft in the misty darkness an electric light. Muriel Fisher paused in its brightest glow, and turned up her spectacled, good-humored young face. "Let's interview that whisky, Scotty," she said.

McCormack smiled, and drew the silver flask from under the tail of his old shooting coat. He was a tall, gaunt young man, made sturdy just now by rough, heavy clothes. Between his plaid scarf and the brim of his felt hat showed a fine, bony face, Gaelicly wide in jaw and brow, with a narrowness through the cheeks. "Drink," he invited, and drew the stopper for her.

She drank, with honest heartiness. Her bandanna-framed face, tilting back under the white light, seemed to have lost a touch of its healthy pink, but she looked ready enough in her tweed suit, turtleneck brown sweater, woollen stockings, and oxfords. "That braces me to the adventure," she said, handing back the flask. "This is like the beginning of a Sherlock Holmes story—old clothes, thick walking sticks, a bottle of liquor, and a dark road to travel." Her spectacles turned to scan the extension of the road on the other side of the pavement. It seemed suddenly to dwindle, to become no more than a trail in the deepening fog. "Only," she added, "Sherlock Holmes was too rational to believe in haunted houses."

"His creator wasn't," said McCormack, and drank in turn. The potent whisky cut from his mouth the savor of those sardines they had eaten together, just before starting into the night. "Conan Doyle believed in ghosts, fairies, and God. What time is it, Muriel?"

She peeled down a knitted glove and looked at her wrist watch. "Twenty minutes after eleven. We'd better hurry if we're going to reach this boogey bin of yours before midnight."

They crossed the highway, and plunged into the half gloom beyond. Only a narrow strip of the sky hung between the two blocky masses of trees, and from it there filtered a slaty blue light. The moon would be full, or almost, but the wholly mist clouds obscured it. Underfoot the going was uneven and turfy, and the tip of McCormack's walking stick sent a pebble scuttling. Muriel started violently, laughed to deprecate her own nervousness, and fumbled for a cigarette. McCormack found himself grateful for the brief flare of her match.

"Tell me all about the house, Scotty," she begged.

"It's a treasure-trove of goblins, if it's authentic," he complied. "I've seen it only twice, and by daylight both times. It has the traditional look, all right—a big, square-roofed ruin, two stories high, on a rock above a stream. The local gossips tell me that it was built maybe sixty years ago, by a young couple who were found one morning in an upstairs room, hanging by the necks."

"Suicide," asked Muriel, "or murder?"

"Nobody's sure. After a while, some relatives moved in, a man with his wife and young son. During the first week, so I understand, the mother died suddenly and mysteriously. And the little boy was so scared by something that he had to be taken to a hospital. Next morning, the father was dangling and dead—in the same upstairs room. That was the last of regular residence at the place."

Muriel drew up her shoulders. "I don't wonder. What about the poor little boy?"

"He didn't entirely recover—the groceryman down at the village says he's at the State Hospital. Mental case—can't rightly remember who he is or how he got there. Quiet, harmless—but they don't dare leave as much as three feet of rope where he can get to it."

"And nobody's lived in the house since?" prompted the girl.

"Well—not lived in it," McCormack told her. "Once a convict escaped from the prison camp and ran away through the woods. That was year before last. I was spending the summer at my cabin. The state police tracked him to the house, and cut him down from the hook where he was hanging."

"Wooh!" gasped Muriel with shivery relish. "In the upstairs room?"

"In the upstairs room."

McCormack lighted his pipe. Its bowl sent forth a soft rose colored glimmer, that relieved his strong, bony features with an impression of whimsical gentleness. The night was strangely still, except for the footfalls and respirations of man and woman. No insect chirped or creaked, the autumn leaves did not rustle on the branches. McCormack thought that cold perspiration was starting on his forehead, but perhaps it was the condensation of the mist.

"I dare hope that nobody knows we're out ghost hunting," he remarked. "Some heavy-handed jokester might dress up in a sheet and come to call."

"Have you brought any charms along?" his companion asked. "Wolfbane, a crucifix, holy water—anything of that description?"

McCormack shook his head. "I'm out to see ghosts, not drive them away," he replied, and smiled. He had an agreeable smile, but with his pipe fire half screened in ashes, his face looked like a clay mask in the blue dimness. Muriel Fisher felt less cheerful than she had at the beginning of the walk, and far less sceptical of ghosts than when she and McCormack had shared sandwiches and coffee in his snug cabin. That cabin seemed far away just now, but she refused to wish herself back. She had come out here tonight expressly to see a haunted house.

"Where's the scene of all these Gothic horrors?" she asked after a time.

"Almost directly ahead," her companion informed her. "Yes, here's the creek, and the road ends. There was a bridge once, I daresay, but not now."

The trees shrank away from this spot, and the fog-strained moonlight was almost strong around the two adventurers. Before them, set deep between rocky banks, ran black, swift water. Mc-Cormack stepped cautiously to the very edge, peered down, and then across.

"It looked narrower by day, I must confess," he remarked. "However, I think I can jump it." He flung his walking stick to the far bank, gathered his body suddenly, and straddled his long legs into a skipping leap. He seemed to swing across the stream, gained the rough-looking rocks beyond, and turned back. His thin face was like a genial skull in the moonlight.

"If you go only a little way down, it's narrower," he called to Muriel.

But she, too, flung her stick across. "Don't coddle me," she cried gaily. "I can jump as far as you can."

She suited the action to the word, and bravely, but her stride could not match McCormack's, and her skirt hampered the scissory thrash of her legs. One blunt oxford touched the edge of the far bank, rock crunched and crumbled beneath it. She felt herself falling backward. McCormack, moving quickly for so big a man, shot out a hand and clutched her by the wrist. With a mighty heave, he fairly whipped her to safety.

"Thanks, Scotty," she gasped, and straightened her spectacles, then the bandanna that was bound over her head and beneath her chin, peasant style. "You spared me a cold bath." They both smiled, and breathed deeply in mutual relief. "I take that escape as a good omen," she went on. "Now, is this the haunted house? It looks to be."

They had come into a larger clearing, but here the mist had thickened to a pearly cloud. In its heart rose a great clifflike structure, with towering walls and a flat roof. The walls had weathered to a gloomy night-gray, in which shuttered windows formed indistinct deviations. A porch had once run the entire width of the front, but the roof was collapsed, the pillars fallen, and the floor all but in ruins.

"Isn't that a lightning-blasted oak in the front yard?" asked Muriel, pointing with her recovered stick. "I suppose owls hoot in its branches to foretell the death of the heir."

"There aren't any heirs," McCormack reminded her. "All of them died, or were hanged. Come around to the side. There's supposed to be an open window there."

He led the way, up a rise in the overgrown yard and through thickset brambles that may once have been a bank of roses. Three windows were ranged in line on the right side of the house, and the rearmost showed blacker than its fellows. McCormack pushed close to it, knee-deep in rank shrubs that showed one or two wax-petalled flowers.

"No shutters," he reported, "and the glass is all broken out of the sash. Where are you, Muriel?"

"Right with you," came her reply from just behind his arm. He turned, set his hands to her waist, and lifted her lightly through the opening.

"Whee, it's dark," she cried in protest as her feet came to light on the dully echoing floor. At once she struck a match. It gave blotchy glimpses of a big, crumbling room, apparently running all the way from front to back of this part of the house. McCormack struggled in through the gap where the window had been. His bracing fingers found the wood spongily dry, as if the house had been decaying for six centuries instead of sixty years.

"I brought no flashlight," he informed Muriel. "Only a candle."

"You did exactly right. Why chase away spirits with electricity?" She watched as he ignited the fat tallow cylinder, which yielded a clear, courageous tag of flame. "Now where?" she asked him.

"There should be stairs leading upward," he said, and moved across the room. Its boards creaked and buckled under his shoes, and crumbs of plaster fallen from the shattered ceiling made harsh, crunching noises. The candle showed them a doorway, through which they walked together.

Beyond, they found themselves in a central hall. Here was the flight of stairs they sought, its railings fallen away in a heap, and clotted blackness above. The plaster of the walls had broken away in sheets. Again they were aware of the presence in the house of decay's very soul.

"Do we go up?" inquired Muriel, her voice automatically hushed, and McCormack nodded and again led the way. His left hand held the candle high, his right clutched his stick tightly, as though to be ready to strike a blow. He could not have told what he feared to meet.

The upper landing was encircled with moldy-looking doors, two of them fallen from their hinges. McCormack went to each, Muriel close at his heels, and held in his candle for quick examination. He stopped at the right rear chamber, just above the window by which they had entered.

"Here's our haunted room," he announced. "See the hooks there, on the wall at the back?"

The hooks he mentioned were set well into the plaster, within inches of the ceiling. Strangely enough for that house of ruin and rot, they appeared to shine in the candlelight as if new and rustless. Elsewhere clung a strange pall of gloom, though the flaked and ragged wallpaper must have been reasonably light in color.

"I wonder if a hundred-watt lamp would help this room any," grunted the tall man. "It looks to be in mourning for the four who were hanged. But we'll douse the candle anyway, in a minute. Hold it, Muriel, while I spread something for us to sit down."

From a big pocket of his shooting coat he fished a folded newspaper, and, spreading it out, covered a space against the wall directly beneath the hooks. "Now," he said, "light another cigarette if you like. I'll put a fresh fill in this pipe. Ready?"

He took back the candle and blew it out, and they sat down in the dark. After a blinded moment, they saw that a dim radiance stole into the room. There must have been chinks in the window shutter somewhere, and the moon, now close to zenith, was fighting its way through the mist so as to peer in. The two ghost challengers sat shoulder to shoulder, each silently grateful for touch of the other. Muriel again peered at the illuminated dial of her watch.

"It lacks only seven or eight minutes of midnight," she announced in half a whisper. "Scotty, you're quite willing to stay?"

"Strange as it may seem," returned McCormack, "I'm suddenly quite willing to depart. But I won't. I came here to see ghosts, if there are any, and I don't intend to leave so close to the proverbial witching hour."

It was not much of a success as careless chatter. Silence fell again, and awkwardly. Muriel broke in, in a voice no louder than a sigh:

"Look——"

They both saw, or thought they saw, a stir in the soft shimmer of gauzy light. It might have been streaks of silent rain falling, had the roof been open. Again, it might have been the rhythmic creeping of long, spider legs without a tangible body. McCormack felt something fasten tightly upon his biceps, and started violently; but it was Muriel's fingers, closing for comfort on his flesh. Her hand slid down into his own grasp. He, too, regained something of serenity and strength in being able to reassure her.

"Scotty," she was breathing at his ear, "I wonder if there's something the matter with the doorway. Is it closing?"

He stared. His eyes had grown more used to the almost darkness.

"Not closing," he made easy-sounding reply. "The door's off the hinges, there it leans against the wall. But the opening does look smaller, somehow. Growing narrower."

"And lower," she added. "It's only an optical illusion, of course," and she chuckled nervously, "but I'd bet good money that you'd have to stoop to get through it."

Again the illusion of bandy leg lines stirring in the room, this time very near. McCormack, at least, fancied that he heard something like a stealthy scramble, and once again he lifted the stick that had never quitted his strong right hand. His left squeezed Muriel's wrist, trying to win back some of the calmness he had transmitted to her. But when he tried to fix his eyes on the spidery movement, it seemed to fade, to retreat. He echoed in his heart the words of his companion: optical illusion, of course——

"I'd have to stoop, too," Muriel was telling him. "It looks like the door to . . . to a dollhouse." Again her chuckle, more hysterical than before.

"Chin up," McCormack exhorted her. "When we get up from here and walk toward it, there'll be width and height enough."

"Are you . . . so anxious to see ghosts . . . now?" she fairly quavered.

McCormack did not wish to heighten her terror by denying; he did not wish to tempt any strange and sudden visitation by agreeing. He therefore kept his peace, and quartered the floor and walls with his straining eyes. Once again, something rustled nearby, menacingly stealthy. He leaned hard against the wall, and drew up his legs so that his feet would come under him and bring him, if necessary, swiftly erect.

Too much imagination, he accused himself. This was undoubtedly the way that psychical investigators conditioned themselves to experience phenomena that never really happened. No wonder people had been frightened into hanging themselves on those hooks overhead. But he was too rational a being to be thus stampeded.

Optical illusion, he insisted once again to his thundering heart. At most, none of the things he almost saw or heard would be too terrible to face. A blow of his stick—but what if it lashed out and met no substance?

"I keep thinking I hear voices," Muriel said once again. "Not human voices—not exactly. They're too soft and——"

"Like whispers?" McCormack suggested, as casually as he could manage.

"No. Less audible than that. They're like an echo, a memory—they can be felt not heard."

"Imagination," said McCormack, rather rudely. His eyes sought the door again.

There was no door. Only blank wall, solidly pale in the dimness. He felt a tightness on his heart and throat, and with real savagery tried to persuade himself that this was no more than curious—notable—absorbing.

"We're shut in," Muriel said aloud, and the ring of apprehension in her voice made him jump. Next moment a bell rang, clear and far away—rang again, again, again——

"It's midnight," he said briskly, and with the greatest relief he had known in years. "Hear that clock striking? Let's clear out, and head back to the cabin."

He rose to his feet, feeling unaccountably light, as though he had floated up. Once more he led the way, trying to make out the vanished door through which they had come short minutes ago.

Muriel's cry of agonized terror brought him up short.

"Scotty! *Look back there where we were sitting!*"

"What do you mean?" He spun around, still with that strange, airy lightness.

Against the wall dangled two silent figures. Bands, or nooses of rope, held them by the necks to the gleaming hooks that jutted close to the ceiling. The figures hung limp, lank, unmistakably dead.

One was long and thin, in rough coat and trousers. The other, smaller and unmistakably feminine, wore a tweed suit and scuffed walking shoes.

To McCormack, those two corpses looked vaguely familiar.

Again Muriel's fear-loud cry beside him: "Scotty, I can't see you! Where have you gone?"

"I'm right here," he said hoarsely, and turned in the direction of her wail.

He could not see her, either. He put out a hand to touch her.

He could not see the hand.

Immediately he knew what man and woman were hanged on the wall of the haunted room.

Clearly, the author of this story has more respect for Sir Arthur Conan Doyle than the late Scotty McCormack expressed. Sherlock Holmes was "too rational to believe in haunted houses," but Doyle was no skeptic. After the death of his son, Kingsley Doyle, Sir Arthur spent some time investigating, writing, and lecturing about spirit communication.

CHAPTER 5

Lot No. 249

by Sir Arthur Conan Doyle

I hate to disappoint you: this is not a story about Sherlock Holmes. In his entire career, Holmes never encountered a genuine spook, and that's the only kind allowed in this book. In fact, he went so far as to express complete skepticism in "The Adventure of the Sussex Vampire": "Rubbish, Watson, rubbish! What have we to do with walking corpses who can only be held in their graves by stakes driven through their hearts? It's pure lunacy. . . . This agency stands flat-footed upon the ground, and there it must remain. No ghosts need apply." But, if you've read "The Sussex Vampire," *The Hound of the Baskervilles,* "The Adventure of the Devil's Foot," "The Adventure of the Lion's Mane," and many more, you know very well that the adventures of Sherlock Holmes are macabre enough to satisfy the most Halloweenish appetites. Holmes himself possesses the brooding intensity and dramatic flair of a Gothic villain, as befits a descendant of Edgar Allan Poe's detective, C. Auguste Dupin.

Sir Arthur Conan Doyle (1859–1930) received his Bachelor of Medicine degree in 1881 and wrote *The Adventures of Sherlock Holmes* while waiting for his medical practice to pick up. The practice never thrived, the stories did.

Of the dealings of Edward Bellingham with William Monkhouse Lee, and of the cause of the great terror of Abercrombie Smith, it

may be that no absolute and final judgment will ever be delivered.
It is true that we have the full and clear narrative of Smith himself, and such corroboration as he could look for from Thomas
Styles the servant, from the Reverend Plumptree Peterson, Fellow
of Old's, and from such other people as chanced to gain some passing glance at this or that incident in a singular chain of events.
Yet, in the main, the story must rest upon Smith alone, and the
most will think that it is more likely that one brain, however out-
wardly sane, has some subtle warp in its texture, some strange
flaw in its workings, than that the path of Nature has been over-
stepped in open day in so famed a center of learning and light as
the University of Oxford. Yet when we think how narrow and
how devious this path of Nature is, how dimly we can trace it, for
all our lamps of science, and how from the darkness that girds
it round great and terrible possibilities loom ever shadowly upward, it is a bold and confident man who will put a limit to the
strange bypaths into which the human spirit may wander.

In a certain wing of what we will call Old College in Oxford
there is a corner turret of an exceeding great age. The heavy arch
that spans the open door has bent downward in the center under
the weight of its years, and the gray, lichen-blotched blocks of
stone are bound and knitted together with withes and strands of
ivy, as though the old mother had set herself to brace them up
against wind and weather. From the door a stone stair curves upward spirally, passing two landings, and terminating in a third one,
its steps all shapeless and hollowed by the tread of so many gen-
erations of the seekers after knowledge. Life has flowed like water
down this winding stair, and, waterlike, has left these smooth-
worn grooves behind it. From the long-gowned, pedantic scholars
of Plantagenet days down to the young bloods of a later age, how
full and strong had been that tide of young, English life. And what
was left now of all those hopes, those strivings, those fiery energies, save here and there in some old-world churchyard a few
scratches upon a stone, and perchance a handful of dust in a mold-
ering coffin? Yet here were the silent stair and the gray, old wall,
with bend and saltire and many another heraldic device still to be
read upon its surface, like grotesque shadows thrown back from
the days that had passed.

In the month of May, in the year 1884, three young men occupied the sets of rooms which opened on to the separate landings

of the old stair. Each set consisted simply of a sitting room and of a bedroom, while the two corresponding rooms upon the ground floor were used, the one as a coal cellar, and the other as the living room of the servant, or scout, Thomas Styles, whose duty it was to wait upon the three men above him. To right and to left was a line of lecture rooms and of offices, so that the dwellers in the old turret enjoyed a certain seclusion, which made the chambers popular among the more studious undergraduates. Such were the three who occupied them now—Abercrombie Smith above, Edward Bellingham beneath him, and William Monkhouse Lee upon the lowest story.

It was ten o'clock on a bright, spring night, and Abercrombie Smith lay back in his armchair, his feet upon the fender, and his brierroot pipe between his lips. In a similar chair, and equally at his ease, there lounged on the other side of the fireplace his old school friend Jephro Hastie. Both men were in flannels, for they had spent their evening upon the river, but apart from their dress no one could look at their hard-cut, alert faces without seeing that they were open-air men—men whose minds and tastes turned naturally to all that was manly and robust. Hastie, indeed, was stroke of his college boat, and Smith was an even better oar, but a coming examination had already cast its shadow over him and held him to his work, save for the few hours a week which health demanded. A litter of medical books upon the table, with scattered bones, models, and anatomical plates, pointed to the extent as well as the nature of his studies, while a couple of singlesticks and a set of boxing gloves above the mantelpiece hinted at the means by which, with Hastie's help, he might take his exercise in its most compressed and least distant form. They knew each other very well —so well that they could sit now in that soothing silence which is the very highest development of companionship.

"Have some whisky," said Abercrombie Smith at last between two cloudbursts. "Scotch in the jug and Irish in the bottle."

"No, thanks. I'm in for the sculls. I don't liquor when I'm training. How about you?"

"I'm reading hard. I think it best to leave it alone."

Hastie nodded, and they relapsed into a contented silence.

"By the way, Smith," asked Hastie, presently, "have you made the acquaintance of either of the fellows on your stair yet?"

"Just a nod when we pass. Nothing more."

"Hum! I should be inclined to let it stand at that. I know something of them both. Not much, but as much as I want. I don't think I should take them to my bosom if I were you. Not that there's much amiss with Monkhouse Lee."

"Meaning the thin one?"

"Precisely. He is a gentlemanly little fellow. I don't think there is any vice in him. But then you can't know him without knowing Bellingham."

"Meaning the fat one?"

"Yes, the fat one. And he's a man whom I, for one, would rather not know."

Abercrombie Smith raised his eyebrows and glanced across at his companion.

"What's up, then?" he asked. "Drink? Cards? Cad? You used not to be censorious."

"Ah! you evidently don't know the man, or you wouldn't ask. There's something damnable about him—something reptilian. My gorge always rises at him. I should put him down as a man with secret vices—an evil liver. He's no fool, though. They say that he is one of the best men in his line that they have ever had in the college."

"Medicine or classics?"

"Eastern languages. He's a demon at them. Chillingworth met him somewhere above the second cataract last summer vacation, and he told me that he just prattled to the Arabs as if he had been born and nursed and weaned among them. He talked Coptic to the Copts, and Hebrew to the Jews, and Arabic to the Bedouins, and they were all ready to kiss the hem of his frock coat. There are some old hermit Johnnies up in those parts who sit on rocks and scowl and spit at the casual stranger. Well, when they saw this chap Bellingham, before he had said five words they just lay down on their bellies and wriggled. Chillingworth said that he never saw anything like it. Bellingham seemed to take it as his right, too, and strutted about among them and talked down to them like a Dutch uncle. Pretty good for an undergrad of Old's, wasn't it?"

"Why do you say you can't know Lee without knowing Bellingham?"

"Because Bellingham is engaged to his sister Eveline. Such a bright little girl, Smith! I know the whole family well. It's disgusting to see that brute with her. A toad and a dove, that's what they always remind me of."

Abercrombie Smith grinned and knocked his ashes out against the side of the grate.

"You show every card in your hand, old chap," said he. "What a prejudiced, green-eyed, evil-thinking old man it is! You have really nothing against the fellow except that."

"Well, I've known her ever since she was as long as that cherry-wood pipe, and I don't like to see her taking risks. And it is a risk. He looks beastly. And he has a beastly temper, a venomous temper. You remember his row with Long Norton?"

"No; you always forget that I am a freshman."

"Ah, it was last winter. Of course. Well, you know the tow-path along by the river. There were several fellows going along it, Bellingham in front, when they came on an old market woman coming the other way. It had been raining—you know what those fields are like when it has rained—and the path ran between the river and a great puddle that was nearly as broad. Well, what does this swine do but keep the path, and push the old girl into the mud, where she and her marketings came to terrible grief. It was a blackguard thing to do, and Long Norton, who is as gentle a fellow as ever stepped, told him what he thought of it. One word led to another, and it ended in Norton laying his stick across the fellow's shoulders. There was the deuce of a fuss about it, and it's a treat to see the way in which Bellingham looks at Norton when they meet now. By Jove, Smith, it's nearly eleven o'clock!"

"No hurry. Light your pipe again."

"Not I. I'm supposed to be in training. Here I've been sitting gossiping when I ought to have been safely tucked up. I'll borrow your skull, if you can share it. Williams has had mine for a month. I'll take the little bones of your ear, too, if you are sure you won't need them. Thanks very much. Never mind a bag, I can carry them very well under my arm. Good night, my son, and take my tip as to your neighbor."

When Hastie, bearing his anatomical plunder, had clattered off down the winding stair, Abercrombie Smith hurled his pipe into the wastepaper basket, and drawing his chair nearer to the lamp, plunged into a formidable, green-covered volume, adorned with great, colored maps of that strange, internal kingdom of which we are the hapless and helpless monarchs. Though a freshman at

Oxford, the student was not so in medicine, for he had worked for four years at Glasgow and at Berlin, and this coming examination would place him finally as a member of his profession. With his firm mouth, broad forehead, and clear-cut, somewhat hard-featured face, he was a man who, if he had no brilliant talent, was yet so dogged, so patient, and so strong that he might in the end overtop a more showy genius. A man who can hold his own among Scotchmen and North Germans is not a man to be easily set back. Smith had left a name at Glasgow and at Berlin, and he was bent upon doing as much at Oxford, if hard work and devotion could accomplish it.

He had sat reading for about an hour, and the hands of the noisy carriage clock upon the side table were rapidly closing together upon the twelve, when a sudden sound fell upon his student's ear—a sharp, rather shrill sound, like the hissing intake of a man's breath who gasps under some strong emotion. Smith laid down his book and slanted his ear to listen. There was no one on either side or above him, so that the interruption came certainly from the neighbor beneath—the same neighbor of whom Hastie had given so unsavory an account. Smith knew him only as a flabby, pale-faced man of silent and studious habits, a man whose lamp threw a golden bar from the old turret even after he had extinguished his own. This community in lateness had formed a certain silent bond between them. It was soothing to Smith when the hours stole on toward dawn to feel that there was another so close who set as small a value upon his sleep as he did. Even now, as his thoughts turned toward him, Smith's feelings were kindly. Hastie was a good fellow, but he was rough, strong-fibered, with no imagination or sympathy. He could not tolerate departures from what he looked upon as the model type of manliness. If a man could not be measured by a public-school standard, then he was beyond the pale with Hastie. Like so many who are themselves robust, he was apt to confuse the constitution with the character, to ascribe to want of principle what was really a want of circulation. Smith, with his stronger mind, knew his friend's habit, and made allowance for it now as his thoughts turned toward the man beneath him.

There was no return of the singular sound, and Smith was about to turn to his work once more, when suddenly there broke out in the silence of the night a hoarse cry, a positive scream—the call of a man who is moved and shaken beyond all control. Smith sprang out of his chair and dropped his book. He was a man of fairly firm fiber, but there was something in this sudden, uncontrollable shriek of horror that chilled his blood and pringled in his skin. Coming in such a place and at such an hour, it brought a thousand fantastic possibilities into his head. Should he rush down, or was it better to wait? He had all the national hatred of making a scene, and he knew so little of his neighbor that he would not lightly intrude upon his affairs. For a moment he stood in doubt and even as he balanced the matter there was a quick rattle of footsteps upon the stairs, and young Monkhouse Lee, half-dressed and as white as ashes, burst into his room.

"Come down!" he gasped. "Bellingham's ill."

Abercrombie Smith followed him closely downstairs into the sitting room which was beneath his own, and intent as he was upon the matter in hand, he could not but take an amazed glance around him as he crossed the threshold. It was such a chamber as he had never seen before—a museum rather than a study. Walls and ceiling were thickly covered with a thousand strange relics from Egypt and the East. Tall, angular figures bearing burdens or weapons stalked in an uncouth frieze round the apartment. Above were bull-headed, stork-headed, cat-headed, owl-headed statues, with viper-crowned, almond-eyed monarchs, and strange, beetlelike deities cut out of the blue Egyptian lapis lazuli. Horus and Isis and Osiris peeped down from every niche and shelf, while across the ceiling a true son of Old Nile, a great, hanging-jawed crocodile, was slung in a double noose.

In the center of this singular chamber was a large, square table, littered with papers, bottles, and the dried leaves of some graceful, palmlike plant. These varied objects had all been heaped together in order to make room for a mummy case, which had been conveyed from the wall, as was evident from the gap there, and laid across the front of the table. The mummy itself, a horrid, black, withered thing, like a charred head on a gnarled bush, was lying half out of the case, with its clawlike hand and bony forearm resting upon the table. Propped up against the sarcophagus was an old, yellow scroll of papyrus, and in front of it, in a wooden armchair, sat the owner of the room, his head thrown back, his widely opened eyes directed in a horrified stare to the crocodile above him, and his blue, thick lips puffing loudly with every expiration.

"My God! He's dying!" cried Monkhouse Lee, distractedly.

He was a slim, handsome young fellow, olive-skinned and dark-eyed, of a Spanish rather than of an English type, with a Celtic intensity of manner which contrasted with the Saxon phlegm of Abercrombie Smith.

"Only a faint, I think," said the medical student. "Just give me a hand with him. You take his feet. Now on to the sofa. Can you kick all those little wooden devils off? What a litter it is! Now he will be all right if we undo his collar and give him some water. What has he been up to at all?"

"I don't know. I heard him cry out. I ran up. I know him pretty well, you know. It is very good of you to come down."

"His heart is going like a pair of castanets," said Smith, laying his hand on the breast of the unconscious man. "He seems to me to be frightened all to pieces. Chuck the water over him! What a face he has got on him!"

It was indeed a strange and most repellent face, for color and outline were equally unnatural. It was white, not with the ordinary pallor of fear, but with an absolutely bloodless white, like the underside of a sole. He was very fat, but gave the impression of having at some time been considerably fatter, for his skin hung loosely in creases and folds, and was shot with a meshwork of wrinkles. Short, stubby brown hair bristled up from his scalp, with a pair of thick, wrinkled ears protruding at the sides. His light gray eyes were still open, the pupils dilated and the balls projecting in a fixed and horrid stare. It seemed to Smith as he looked down upon him that he had never seen Nature's danger signals flying so plainly upon a man's countenance, and his thoughts turned more seriously to the warning which Hastie had given him an hour before.

"What the deuce can have frightened him so?" he asked.

"It's the mummy."

"The mummy? How, then?"

"I don't know. It's beastly and morbid. I wish he would drop it. It's the second fright he has given me. It was the same last winter. I found him just like this, with that horrid thing in front of him."

"What does he want with the mummy, then?"

"Oh, he's a crank, you know. It's his hobby. He knows more

about these things than any man in England. But I wish he wouldn't! Ah, he's beginning to come to."

A faint tinge of color had begun to steal back into Bellingham's ghastly cheeks, and his eyelids shivered like a sail after a calm. He clasped and unclasped his hands, drew a long, thin breath between his teeth, and suddenly jerking up his head, threw a glance of recognition around him. As his eyes fell upon the mummy, he sprang off the sofa, seized the roll of papyrus, thrust it into a drawer, turned the key, and then staggered back on to the sofa.

"What's up?" he asked. "What do you chaps want?"

"You've been shrieking out and making no end of a fuss," said Monkhouse Lee. "If our neighbor here from above hadn't come down, I'm sure I don't know what I should have done with you."

"Ah, it's Abercrombie Smith," said Bellingham, glancing up at him. "How very good of you to come in! What a fool I am! Oh, my God, what a fool I am!"

He sank his head on to his hands, and burst into peal after peal of hysterical laughter.

"Look here! Drop it!" cried Smith, shaking him roughly by the shoulder.

"Your nerves are all in a jangle. You must drop these little midnight games with mummies, or you'll be going off your chump. You're all on wires now."

"I wonder," said Bellingham, "whether you would be as cool as I am if you had seen——"

"What then?"

"Oh, nothing. I meant that I wonder if you could sit up at night with a mummy without trying your nerves. I have no doubt that you are quite right. I dare say that I have been taking it out of myself too much lately. But I am all right now. Please don't go, though. Just wait for a few minutes until I am quite myself."

"The room is very close," remarked Lee, throwing open the window and letting in the cool night air.

"It's balsamic resin," said Bellingham. He lifted up one of the dried palmate leaves from the table and frizzled it over the chimney of the lamp. It broke away into heavy smoke wreaths, and a pungent, biting odor filled the chamber. "It's the sacred plant— the plant of the priests," he remarked. "Do you know anything of Eastern languages, Smith?"

"Nothing at all. Not a word."

The answer seemed to lift a weight from the Egyptologist's mind.

"By the way," he continued, "how long was it from the time that you ran down, until I came to my senses?"

"Not long. Some four or five minutes."

"I thought it could not be very long," said he, drawing a long breath. "But what a strange thing unconsciousness is! There is no measurement to it. I could not tell from my own sensations if it were seconds or weeks. Now that gentleman on the table was packed up in the days of the eleventh dynasty, some forty centuries ago, and yet if he could find his tongue, he would tell us that this lapse of time has been but a closing of the eyes and a reopening of them. He is a singularly fine mummy, Smith."

Smith stepped over to the table and looked down with a professional eye at the black and twisted form in front of him. The features, though horribly discolored, were perfect, and two little nutlike eyes still lurked in the depths of the black, hollow sockets. The blotched skin was drawn tightly from bone to bone, and a tangled wrap of black, coarse hair fell over the ears. Two thin teeth, like those of a rat, overlay the shriveled lower lip. In its crouching position, with bent joints and craned head, there was a suggestion of energy about the horrid thing which made Smith's gorge rise. The gaunt ribs, with their parchmentlike covering, were exposed, and the sunken, leaden-hued abdomen, with the long slit where the embalmer had left his mark; but the lower limbs were wrapped round with coarse, yellow bandages. A number of little clovelike pieces of myrrh and of cassia were sprinkled over the body, and lay scattered on the inside of the case.

"I don't know his name," said Bellingham, passing his hand over the shriveled head. "You see the outer sarcophagus with the inscriptions is missing. Lot 249 is all the title he has now. You see it printed on his case. That was his number in the auction at which I picked him up."

"He has been a very pretty sort of fellow in his day," remarked Abercrombie Smith.

"He has been a giant. His mummy is six feet seven in length, and that would be a giant over there, for they were never a very robust race. Feel these great, knotted bones, too. He would be a nasty fellow to tackle."

"Perhaps these very hands helped to build the stones into the pyramids," suggested Monkhouse Lee, looking down with disgust in his eyes at the crooked, unclean talons.

"No fear. This fellow has been pickled in natron, and looked after in the most approved style. They did not serve hodsmen in that fashion. Salt or bitumen was enough for them. It has been calculated that this sort of thing cost about seven hundred and thirty pounds in our money. Our friend was a noble at the least. What do you make of that small inscription near his feet, Smith?"

"I told you that I know no Eastern tongue."

"Ah, so you did. It is the name of the embalmer, I take it. A very conscientious worker he must have been. I wonder how many modern works will survive four thousand years?"

He kept on speaking lightly and rapidly, but it was evident to Abercrombie Smith that he was still palpitating with fear. His hands shook, his lower lip trembled, and look where he would, his eye always came sliding round to his gruesome companion. Through all his fear, however, there was a suspicion of triumph in his tone and manner. His eyes shone, and his footstep, as he paced the room, was brisk and jaunty. He gave the impression of a man who has gone through an ordeal, the marks of which he still bears upon him, but which has helped him to his end.

"You're not going yet?" he cried, as Smith rose from the sofa.

At the prospect of solitude, his fears seemed to crowd back upon him, and he stretched out a hand to detain him.

"Yes, I must go. I have my work to do. You are all right now. I think that with your nervous system you should take up some less morbid study."

"Oh, I am not nervous as a rule; and I have unwrapped mummies before."

"You fainted last time," observed Monkhouse Lee.

"Ah, yes, so I did. Well, I must have a nerve tonic or a course of electricity. You are not going, Lee?"

"I'll do whatever you wish, Ned."

"Then I'll come down with you and have a shakedown on your sofa. Good night, Smith. I am so sorry to have disturbed you with my foolishness."

They shook hands, and as the medical student stumbled up the spiral and irregular stair he heard a key turn in a door, and the steps of his two new acquaintances as they descended to the lower floor.

In this strange way began the acquaintance between Edward Bellingham and Abercrombie Smith, an acquaintance which the latter, at least, had no desire to push further. Bellingham, however, appeared to have taken a fancy to his rough-spoken neighbor, and made his advances in such a way that he could hardly be repulsed without absolute brutality. Twice he called to thank Smith for his assistance, and many times afterward he looked in with books, papers, and such other civilities as two bachelor neighbors can offer each other. He was, as Smith soon found, a man of wide reading, with catholic tastes and an extraordinary memory. His manner, too, was so pleasing and suave that one came, after a time, to overlook his repellent appearance. For a jaded and wearied man he was no unpleasant companion, and Smith found himself, after a time, looking forward to his visits, and even returning them.

Clever as he undoubtedly was, however, the medical student seemed to detect a dash of insanity in the man. He broke out at times into a high, inflated style of talk which was in contrast with the simplicity of his life.

"It is a wonderful thing," he cried, "to feel that one can command powers of good and of evil—a ministering angel or a demon of vengeance." And again, of Monkhouse Lee, he said—"Lee is a good fellow, an honest fellow, but he is without strength or ambition. He would not make a fit partner for a man with a great enterprise. He would not make a fit partner for me."

At such hints and innuendoes stolid Smith, puffing solemnly at his pipe, would simply raise his eyebrows and shake his head, with little interjections of medical wisdom as to earlier hours and fresher air.

One habit Bellingham had developed of late which Smith knew to be a frequent herald of a weakening mind. He appeared to be forever talking to himself. At late hours of the night, when there could be no visitor with him, Smith could still hear his voice beneath him in a low, muffled monologue, sunk almost to a whisper, and yet very audible in the silence. This solitary babbling annoyed and distracted the student, so that he spoke more than once to his neighbor about it. Bellingham, however, flushed up at the charge, and denied curtly that he had uttered a sound; indeed, he showed more annoyance over the matter than the occasion seemed to demand.

Had Abercrombie Smith had any doubt as to his own ears he had not to go far to find corroboration. Tom Styles, the little wrinkled man-servant who had attended to the wants of the lodgers in the turret for a longer time than any man's memory could carry him, was sorely put to it over the same matter.

"If you please, sir," said he, as he tidied down the top chamber one morning, "do you think Mr. Bellingham is all right, sir?"

"All right, Styles?"

"Yes, sir. Right in his head, sir."

"Why should he not be, then?"

"Well, I don't know, sir. His habits has changed of late. He's not the same man he used to be, though I make free to say that he was never quite one of my gentlemen, like Mr. Hastie or yourself, sir. He's took to talkin' to himself something awful. I wonder it don't disturb you. I don't know what to make of him, sir."

"I don't know what business it is of yours, Styles."

"Well, I takes an interest, Mr. Smith. It may be forward of me, but I can't help it. I feel sometimes as if I was mother and father to my young gentlemen. It all falls on me when things go wrong and the relations come. But Mr. Bellingham, sir. I want to know what it is that walks about his room sometimes when he's out and when the door's locked on the outside."

"Eh? You're talking nonsense, Styles."

"Maybe so, sir; but I heard it more'n once with my own ears."

"Rubbish, Styles."

"Very good, sir. You'll ring the bell if you want me."

Abercrombie Smith gave little heed to the gossip of the old man-servant, but a small incident occurred a few days later which left an unpleasant effect upon his mind, and brought the words of Styles forcibly to his memory.

Bellingham had come up to see him late one night, and was entertaining him with an interesting account of the rock tombs of Beni Hassan in Upper Egypt, when Smith, whose hearing was remarkably acute, distinctly heard the sound of a door opening on the landing below.

"There's some fellow gone in or out of your room," he remarked.

Bellingham sprang up and stood helpless for a moment, with the expression of a man who is half incredulous and half afraid.

"I surely locked it. I am almost positive that I locked it," he stammered. "No one could have opened it."

"Why, I hear someone coming up the steps now," said Smith.

Bellingham rushed out through the door, slammed it loudly behind him, and hurried down the stairs. About halfway down Smith heard him stop, and thought he caught the sound of whispering. A moment later the door beneath him shut, a key creaked in a lock, and Bellingham, with beads of moisture upon his pale face, ascended the stairs once more, and re-entered the room.

"It's all right," he said, throwing himself down in a chair. "It was that fool of a dog. He had pushed the door open. I don't know how I came to forget to lock it."

"I didn't know you kept a dog," said Smith, looking very thoughtfully at the disturbed face of his companion.

"Yes, I haven't had him long. I must get rid of him. He's a great nuisance."

"He must be, if you find it so hard to shut him up. I should have thought that shutting the door would have been enough, without locking it."

"I want to prevent old Styles from letting him out. He's of some value, you know, and it would be awkward to lose him."

"I am a bit of a dog fancier myself," said Smith, still gazing hard at his companion from the corner of his eyes. "Perhaps you'll let me have a look at it."

"Certainly. But I am afraid it cannot be tonight; I have an appointment. Is that clock right? Then I am a quarter of an hour late already. You'll excuse me, I am sure."

He picked up his cap and hurried from the room. In spite of his appointment, Smith heard him re-enter his own chamber and lock his door upon the inside.

This interview left a disagreeable impression upon the medical student's mind. Bellingham had lied to him, and lied so clumsily that it looked as if he had desperate reasons for concealing the truth. Smith knew that his neighbor had no dog. He knew, also, that the step which he had heard upon the stairs was not the step of an animal. But if it were not, then what could it be? There was old Styles's statement about the something that used to pace the room at times when the owner was absent. Could it be a woman? Smith rather inclined to the view. If so, it would mean disgrace and expulsion to Bellingham if it were discovered by the authorities, so that his anxiety and falsehoods might be accounted for. And yet it was inconceivable that an undergraduate could keep a woman in his rooms without being instantly detected. Be the explanation what it might, there was something ugly about it, and Smith determined, as he turned to his books, to discourage all further attempts at intimacy on the part of his soft-spoken and ill-favored neighbor.

But his work was destined to interruption that night. He had hardly caught up the broken threads when a firm, heavy footfall came three steps at a time from below, and Hastie, in blazer and flannels, burst into the room.

"Still at it!" said he, plumping down into his wonted armchair. "What a chap you are to stew! I believe an earthquake might come and knock Oxford into a cocked hat, and you would sit perfectly placid with your books among the ruins. However, I won't bore you long. Three whiffs of baccy, and I am off."

"What's the news, then?" asked Smith, cramming a plug of bird's-eye into his brier with his forefinger.

"Nothing very much. Wilson made seventy for the freshmen against the eleven. They say that they will play him instead of Buddicomb, for Buddicomb is clean off color. He used to be able to bowl a little, but it's nothing but half volleys and long hops now."

"Medium right," suggested Smith, with the intense gravity that comes upon a 'varsity man when he speaks of athletics.

"Inclining to fast, with a work from leg. Comes with the arm about three inches or so. He used to be nasty on a wet wicket. Oh, by the way, have you heard about Long Norton?"

"What's that?"

"He's been attacked."

"Attacked?"

"Yes, just as he was turning out of the High Street, and within a hundred yards of the gate of Old's."

"But who——"

"Ah, that's the rub! If you said 'what', you would be more grammatical. Norton swears that it was not human, and, indeed, from the scratches on his throat, I should be inclined to agree with him."

"What, then? Have we come down to spooks?"

Abercrombie Smith puffed his scientific contempt.

"Well, no; I don't think that is quite the idea, either. I am inclined to think that if any showman has lost a great ape lately, and

the brute is in these parts, a jury would find a true bill against it.
Norton passes that way every night, you know, about the same
hour. There's a tree that hangs low over the path—the big elm from
Rainy's garden. Norton thinks the thing dropped on him out of the
tree. Anyhow, he was nearly strangled by two arms, which, he
says, were as strong and as thin as steel bands. He saw nothing;
only those beastly arms that tightened and tightened on him. He
yelled his head off, and a couple of chaps came running, and the
thing went over the wall like a cat. He never got a fair sight of it
the whole time. It gave Norton a shake up, I can tell you. I tell
him it has been as good as a change at the seaside for him."

"A garroter, most likely," said Smith.

"Very possibly. Norton says not; but we don't mind what he
says. The garroter has long nails, and was pretty smart at swinging
himself over walls. By the way, your beautiful neighbor would be
pleased if he heard about it. He had a grudge against Norton, and
he's not a man, from what I know of him, to forget his little debts.
But hallo, old chap, what have you got in your noddle?"

"Nothing," Smith answered curtly.

He had started in his chair, and the look had flashed over his
face which comes upon a man who is struck suddenly by some
unpleasant idea.

"You looked as if something I had said had taken you on the
raw. By the way, you have made the acquaintance of Master B.
since I looked in last, have you not? Young Monkhouse Lee told
me something to that effect."

"Yes; I know him slightly. He has been up here once or twice."

"Well, you're big enough and ugly enough to take care of yourself. He's not what I should call exactly a healthy sort of Johnny,
though, no doubt, he's very clever, and all that. But you'll soon
find out for yourself. Lee is all right; he's a very decent little fellow.
Well, so long, old chap! I row Mullins for the Vice-Chancellor's
pot on Wednesday week, so mind you come down, in case I don't
see you before."

Bovine Smith laid down his pipe and turned stolidly to his books
once more. But with all the will in the world, he found it very hard
to keep his mind upon his work. It would slip away to brood upon
the man beneath him, and upon the little mystery which hung
round his chambers. Then his thoughts turned to this singular attack of which Hastie had spoken, and to the grudge which Belling-

ham was said to owe the object of it. The two ideas would persist in rising together in his mind, as though there were some close and intimate connection between them. And yet the suspicion was so dim and vague that it could not be put down in words.

"Confound the chap!" cried Smith, as he shied his book on pathology across the room. "He has spoiled my night's reading, and that's reason enough, if there were no other, why I should steer clear of him in the future."

For ten days the medical student confined himself so closely to his studies that he neither saw nor heard anything of either of the men beneath him. At the hours when Bellingham had been accustomed to visit him, he took care to sport his oak, and though he more than once heard a knocking at his outer door, he resolutely refused to answer it. One afternoon, however, he was descending the stairs when, just as he was passing it, Bellingham's door flew open, and young Monkhouse Lee came out with his eyes sparkling and a dark flush of anger upon his olive cheeks. Close at his heels followed Bellingham, his fat, unhealthy face all quivering with malignant passion.

"You fool!" he hissed. "You'll be sorry."

"Very likely," cried the other. "Mind what I say. It's off! I won't hear of it!"

"You've promised, anyhow."

"Oh, I'll keep that! I won't speak. But I'd rather little Eva was in her grave. Once for all, it's off. She'll do what I say. We don't want to see you again."

So much Smith could not avoid hearing, but he hurried on, for he had no wish to be involved in their dispute. There had been a serious breach between them, that was clear enough, and Lee was going to cause the engagement with his sister to be broken off. Smith thought of Hastie's comparison of the toad and the dove, and was glad to think that the matter was at an end. Bellingham's face when he was in a passion was not pleasant to look upon. He was not a man to whom an innocent girl could be trusted for life. As he walked, Smith wondered languidly what could have caused the quarrel, and what the promise might be which Bellingham had been so anxious that Monkhouse Lee should keep.

It was the day of the sculling match between Hastie and Mullins, and a stream of men were making their way down to the banks of the Isis. A May sun was shining brightly, and the yellow path was barred with the black shadows of the tall elm trees. On either side the gray colleges lay back from the road, the hoary old mothers of minds looking out from their high, mullioned windows at the tide of young life which swept so merrily past them. Black-clad tutors, prim officials, pale, reading men, brown-faced, straw-hatted young athletes in white sweaters or many-colored blazers, all were hurrying toward the blue, winding river which curves through the Oxford meadows.

Abercrombie Smith, with the intuition of an old oarsman, chose his position at the point where he knew that the struggle, if there were a struggle, would come. Far off he heard the hum that announced the start, the gathering roar of the approach, the thunder of running feet, and the shouts of the men in the boats beneath him. A spray of half-clad, deep-breathing runners shot past him, and craning over their shoulders, he saw Hastie pulling a steady thirty-six, while his opponent, with a jerky forty, was a good boat's length behind him. Smith gave a cheer for his friend, and pulling out his watch, was starting off again for his chambers, when he felt a touch upon his shoulder, and found that young Monkhouse Lee was beside him.

"I saw you there," he said, in a timid, deprecating way. "I wanted to speak to you, if you could spare me a half hour. This cottage is mine. I share it with Harrington of King's. Come in and have a cup of tea."

"I must be back presently," said Smith. "I am hard on the grind at present. But I'll come in for a few minutes with pleasure. I wouldn't have come out only Hastie is a friend of mine."

"So he is of mine. Hasn't he a beautiful style? Mullins wasn't in it. But come into the cottage. It's a little den of a place, but it is pleasant to work in during the summer months."

It was a small, square, white building, with green doors and shutters, and a rustic trelliswork porch, standing back some fifty yards from the river's bank. Inside, the main room was roughly fitted up as a study—deal table, unpainted shelves with books, and a few cheap oleographs upon the wall. A kettle sang upon a spirit-stove, and there were tea things upon a tray on the table.

"Try that chair and have a cigarette," said Lee. "Let me pour you out a cup of tea. It's so good of you to come in, for I know that your time is a good deal taken up. I wanted to say to you that, if I were you, I should change my rooms at once."

"Eh?"

Smith sat staring with a lighted match in one hand and his unlit cigarette in the other.

"Yes; it must seem very extraordinary, and the worst of it is that I cannot give my reasons, for I am under a solemn promise— a very solemn promise. But I may go so far as to say that I don't think Bellingham is a very safe man to live near. I intend to camp out here as much as I can for a time."

"Not safe! What do you mean?"

"Ah, that's what I mustn't say. But do take my advice and move your rooms. We had a grand row today. You must have heard us, for you came down the stairs."

"I saw that you had fallen out."

"He's a horrible chap, Smith. That is the only word for him. I have had doubts about him ever since that night when he fainted— you remember, when you came down. I taxed him today, and he told me things that made my hair rise, and wanted me to stand in with him. I'm not straight-laced, but I am a clergyman's son, you know, and I think there are some things which are quite beyond the pale. I only thank God that I found him out before it was too late, for he was to have married into my family."

"This is all very fine, Lee," said Abercrombie Smith curtly. "But either you are saying a great deal too much or a great deal too little."

"I give you a warning."

"If there is real reason for warning, no promise can bind you. If I see a rascal about to blow a place up with dynamite no pledge will stand in my way of preventing him."

"Ah, but I cannot prevent him, and I can do nothing but warn you."

"Without saying what you warn me against."

"Against Bellingham."

"But that is childish. Why should I fear him, or any man?"

"I can't tell you. I can only entreat you to change your rooms. You are in danger where you are. I don't even say that Bellingham would wish to injure you. But it might happen, for he is a dangerous neighbor just now."

"Perhaps I know more than you think," said Smith, looking keenly at the young man's boyish, earnest face. "Suppose I tell you that someone else shares Bellingham's rooms."

Monkhouse Lee sprang from his chair in uncontrollable excitement.

"You know, then?" he gasped.

"A woman."

Lee dropped back again with a groan.

"My lips are sealed," he said. "I must not speak."

"Well, anyhow," said Smith, rising, "it is not likely that I should allow myself to be frightened out of rooms which suit me very nicely. It would be a little too feeble for me to move out all my goods and chattels because you say that Bellingham might in some unexplained way do me an injury. I think that I'll just take my chance, and stay where I am, and as I see that it's nearly five o'clock, I must ask you to excuse me."

He bade the young student adieu in a few curt words, and made his way homeward through the sweet spring evening, feeling half ruffled, half amused, as any other strong, unimaginative man might who has been menaced by a vague and shadowy danger.

There was one little indulgence which Abercrombie Smith always allowed himself, however closely his work might press upon him. Twice a week, on the Tuesday and the Friday, it was his invariable custom to walk over to Farlingford, the residence of Dr. Plumptree Peterson, situated about a mile and a half out of Oxford. Peterson had been a close friend of Smith's elder brother, Francis, and as he was a bachelor, fairly well-to-do, with a good cellar and a better library, his house was a pleasant goal for a man who was in need of a brisk walk. Twice a week, then, the medical student would swing out there along the dark country roads and spend a pleasant hour in Peterson's comfortable study, discussing, over a glass of old port, the gossip of the 'varsity or the latest developments of medicine or of surgery.

On the day that followed his interview with Monkhouse Lee, Smith shut up his books at a quarter past eight, the hour when he usually started for his friend's house. As he was leaving his room, however, his eyes chanced to fall upon one of the books which Bellingham had lent him, and his conscience pricked him for not having returned it. However repellent the man might be, he should not be treated with discourtesy. Taking the book, he walked downstairs and knocked at his neighbor's door. There was no answer; but on turning the handle he found that it was unlocked. Pleased at the thought of avoiding an interview, he stepped inside, and placed the book with his card upon the table.

The lamp was turned half down, but Smith could see the details of the room plainly enough. It was all much as he had seen it before—the frieze, the animal-headed gods, the hanging crocodile, and the table littered over with papers and dried leaves. The mummy case stood upright against the wall, but the mummy itself was missing. There was no sign of any second occupant of the room, and he felt as he withdrew that he had probably done Bellingham an injustice. Had he a guilty secret to preserve, he would hardly leave his door open so that all the world might enter.

The spiral stair was as black as pitch, and Smith was slowly making his way down its irregular steps, when he was suddenly conscious that something had passed him in the darkness. There was a faint sound, a whiff of air, a light brushing past his elbow, but so slight that he could scarcely be certain of it. He stopped and listened, but the wind was rustling among the ivy outside, and he could hear nothing else.

"Is that you, Styles?" he shouted.

There was no answer, and all was still behind him. It must have been a sudden gust of air, for there were crannies and cracks in the old turret. And yet he could almost have sworn that he heard a footfall by his very side. He had emerged into the quadrangle, still turning the matter over in his head, when a man came running swiftly across the smooth-cropped lawn.

"Is that you, Smith?"

"Hullo, Hastie!"

"For God's sake come at once! Young Lee is drowned! Here's Harrington of King's with the news. The doctor is out. You'll do, but come along at once. There may be life in him."

"Have you brandy?"

"No."

"I'll bring some. There's a flask on my table."

Smith bounded up the stairs, taking three at a time, seized the flask, and was rushing down with it, when, as he passed Bellingham's room, his eyes fell upon something which left him gasping and staring upon the landing.

The door, which he had closed behind him, was now open, and right in front of him, with the lamplight shining upon it, was the mummy case. Three minutes ago it had been empty. He could swear to that. Now it framed the lank body of its horrible occupant, who stood, grim and stark, with his black, shriveled face toward the door. The form was lifeless and inert, but it seemed to Smith as he gazed that there still lingered a lurid spark of vitality, some faint sign of consciousness in the little eyes which lurked in the depths of the hollow sockets. So astounded and shaken was he that he had forgotten his errand, and was still staring at the lean, sunken figure when the voice of his friend below recalled him to himself.

"Come on, Smith!" he shouted. "It's life and death, you know. Hurry up! Now, then," he added, as the medical student reappeared, "let us do a sprint. It is well under a mile, and we should do it in five minutes. A human life is better worth running for than a pot."

Neck and neck they dashed through the darkness, and did not pull up until, panting and spent, they had reached the little cottage by the river. Young Lee, limp and dripping like a broken water plant, was stretched upon the sofa, the green scum of the river upon his black hair, and a fringe of white foam upon his leaden-hued lips. Beside him knelt his fellow student, Harrington, endeavoring to chafe some warmth back into his rigid limbs.

"I think there's life in him," said Smith, with his hand to the lad's side. "Put your watch glass to his lips. Yes, there's dimming on it. You take one arm, Hastie. Now work it as I do, and we'll soon pull him round."

For ten minutes they worked in silence, inflating and depressing the chest of the unconscious man. At the end of that time a shiver ran through his body, his lips trembled, and he opened his eyes. The three students burst out into an irrepressible cheer.

"Wake up, old chap. You've frightened us quite enough."

"Have some brandy. Take a sip from the flask."

"He's all right now," said his companion Harrington. "Heavens, what a fright I got! I was reading here, and he had gone out for a stroll as far as the river, when I heard a scream and a splash. Out I ran, and by the time I could find him and fish him out, all life seemed to have gone. Then Simpson couldn't get a doctor, for he has a game leg, and I had to run, and I don't know what I'd have done without you fellows. That's right, old chap. Sit up."

Monkhouse Lee had raised himself on his hands, and looked wildly about him.

"What's up?" he asked. "I've been in the water. Ah, yes; I remember."

A look of fear came into his eyes, and he sank his face into his hands.

"How did you fall in?"

"I didn't fall in."

"How then?"

"I was thrown in. I was standing by the bank, and something from behind picked me up like a feather and hurled me in. I heard nothing, and I saw nothing. But I know what it was, for all that."

"And so do I," whispered Smith.

Lee looked up with a quick glance of surprise.

"You've learned, then?" he said. "You remember the advice I gave you?"

"Yes, and I begin to think that I shall take it."

"I don't know what the deuce you fellows are talking about," said Hastie, "but I think, if I were you, Harrington, I should get Lee to bed at once. It will be time enough to discuss the why and the wherefore when he is a little stronger. I think, Smith, you and I can leave him alone now. I am walking back to college; if you are coming in that direction, we can have a chat."

But it was little chat that they had upon their homeward path. Smith's mind was too full of the incidents of the evening, the absence of the mummy from his neighbor's rooms, the step that passed him on the stair, the reappearance—the extraordinary, inexplicable reappearance—of the grisly thing, and then this attack upon Lee, corresponding so closely to the previous outrage upon another man against whom Bellingham bore a grudge. All this settled in his thoughts, together with the many little incidents which had previously turned him against his neighbor, and the singular circumstances under which he was first called in to him. What had been a dim suspicion, a vague, fantastic conjecture, had suddenly taken form, and stood out in his mind as a grim fact, a thing not to be denied. And yet, how monstrous it was! how unheard of! how entirely beyond all bounds of human experience. An impartial judge, or even the friend who walked by his side, would simply tell him that his eyes had deceived him, that the mummy had been there all the time, that young Lee had tumbled into the river as any other man tumbles into a river, and the blue pill was the best thing for a disordered liver. He felt that he would

have said as much if the positions had been reversed. And yet he
could swear that Bellingham was a murderer at heart, and that he
wielded a weapon such as no man had ever used in all the grim
history of crime.

Hastie had branched off to his rooms with a few crisp and em-
phatic comments upon his friend's unsociability, and Abercrombie
Smith crossed the quadrangle to his corner turret with a strong
feeling of repulsion for his chambers and their associations. He
would take Lee's advice, and move his quarters as soon as possible, for how could a man study when his ear was ever straining
for every murmur or footstep in the room below? He observed,
as he crossed over the lawn, that the light was still shining in Bellingham's window, and as he passed up the staircase the door
opened, and the man himself looked out at him. With his fat, evil
face he was like some bloated spider fresh from the weaving of his
poisonous web.

"Good evening," said he. "Won't you come in?"

"No," cried Smith fiercely.

"No? You are as busy as ever? I wanted to ask you about Lee.
I was sorry to hear that there was a rumor that something was
amiss with him."

His features were grave, but there was the gleam of a hidden
laugh in his eyes as he spoke. Smith saw it, and he could have
knocked him down for it.

"You'll be sorrier still to hear that Monkhouse Lee is doing
very well, and is out of all danger," he answered. "Your hellish
tricks have not come off this time. Oh, you needn't try to brazen it
out. I know all about it."

Bellingham took a step back from the angry student, and half
closed the door as if to protect himself.

"You are mad," he said. "What do you mean? Do you assert
that I had anything to do with Lee's accident?"

"Yes," thundered Smith. "You and that bag of bones behind
you; you worked it between you. I tell you what it is, Master B.,
they have given up burning folk like you, but we still keep a hang-
man, and, by George! if any man in this college meets his death
while you are here, I'll have you up, and if you don't swing for it,
it won't be my fault. You'll find that your filthy Egyptian tricks
won't answer in England."

"You're a raving lunatic," said Bellingham.

"All right. You just remember what I say, for you'll find that I'll be better than my word."

The door slammed, and Smith went fuming up to his chamber, where he locked the door upon the inside, and spent half the night in smoking his old brier, and brooding over the strange events of the evening.

Next morning Abercrombie Smith heard nothing of his neighbor, but Harrington called upon him in the afternoon to say that Lee was almost himself again. All day Smith stuck fast to his work, but in the evening he determined to pay the visit to his friend Dr. Peterson upon which he had started the night before. A good walk and a friendly chat would be welcome to his jangled nerves.

Bellingham's door was shut as he passed, but glancing back when he was some distance from the turret, he saw his neighbor's head at the window outlined against the lamplight, his face pressed apparently against the glass as he gazed out into the darkness. It was a blessing to be away from all contact with him, if but for a few hours, and Smith stepped out briskly, and breathed the soft spring air into his lungs. The half moon lay in the west between two Gothic pinnacles, and threw upon the silvered street a dark tracery from the stonework above. There was a brisk breeze, and light, fleecy clouds drifted swiftly across the sky. Old's was on the very border of the town, and in five minutes Smith found himself beyond the houses and between the hedges of a May-scented, Oxfordshire lane.

It was a lonely and little-frequented road which led to his friend's house. Early as it was, Smith did not meet a single soul upon his way. He walked briskly along until he came to the avenue gate, which opened into the long, gravel drive leading up to Farlingford. In front of him he could see the cozy, red light of the windows glimmering through the foliage. He stood with his hand upon the iron latch of the swinging gate, and he glanced back at the road along which he had come. Something was coming swiftly down it.

It moved in the shadow of the hedge, silently and furtively, a dark, crouching figure, dimly visible against the black background. Even as he gazed back at it, it had lessened its distance by twenty paces, and was fast closing upon him. Out of the darkness he had a glimpse of a scraggy neck, and of two eyes that will ever haunt him in his dreams. He turned, and with a cry of terror he ran for his life up the avenue. There were the red lights, the signals of safety, almost within a stone's throw of him. He was a famous runner, but never had he run as he ran that night.

The heavy gate had swung into place behind him but he heard it dash open again before his pursuer. As he rushed madly and wildly through the night, he could hear a swift, dry patter behind him, and could see, as he threw back a glance, that this horror was bounding like a tiger at his heels, with blazing eyes and one stringy arm outthrown. Thank God, the door was ajar. He could see the thin bar of light which shot from the lamp in the hall. Nearer yet sounded the clatter from behind. He heard a hoarse gurgling at his very shoulder. With a shriek he flung himself against the door, slammed and bolted it behind him, and sank half fainting on the hall chair.

"My goodness, Smith, what's the matter?" asked Peterson, appearing at the door of his study.

"Give me some brandy."

Peterson disappeared, and came rushing out again with a glass and a decanter.

"You need it," he said, as his visitor drank off what he poured out for him. "Why, man, you are as white as a cheese."

Smith laid down his glass, rose up, and took a deep breath.

"I am my own man again now," said he. "I was never so unmanned before. But, with your leave, Peterson, I will sleep here tonight, for I don't think I could face that road again except by daylight. It's weak, I know, but I can't help it."

Peterson looked at his visitor with a very questioning eye.

"Of course you shall sleep here if you wish. I'll tell Mrs. Burney to make up the spare bed. Where are you off to now?"

"Come up with me to the window that overlooks the door. I want you to see what I have seen."

They went up to the window of the upper hall whence they could look down upon the approach to the house. The drive and the fields on either side lay quiet and still, bathed in the peaceful moonlight.

"Well, really, Smith," remarked Peterson, "it is well that I know you to be an abstemious man. What in the world can have frightened you?"

"I'll tell you presently. But where can it have gone? Ah, now, look, look! See the curve of the road just beyond your gate."

"Yes, I see; you needn't pinch my arm off. I saw someone pass. I should say a man, rather thin, apparently, and tall, very tall. But what of him? And what of yourself? You are still shaking like an aspen leaf."

"I have been within handgrip of the devil, that's all. But come down to your study, and I shall tell you the whole story."

He did so. Under the cheery lamplight with a glass of wine on the table beside him, and the portly form and florid face of his friend in front, he narrated, in their order, all the events, great and small, which had formed so singular a chain, from the night on which he had found Bellingham fainting in front of the mummy case until this horrid experience of an hour ago.

"There now," he said as he concluded, "that's the whole, black business. It is monstrous and incredible, but it is true."

Doctor Plumptree Peterson sat for some time in silence with a very puzzled expression upon his face.

"I never heard of such a thing in my life, never!" he said at last. "You have told me the facts. Now tell me your inferences."

"You can draw your own."

"But I should like to hear yours. You have thought over the matter, and I have not."

"Well, it must be a little vague in detail, but the main points seem to me to be clear enough. This fellow Bellingham, in his Eastern studies, has got hold of some infernal secret by which a mummy—or possibly only this particular mummy—can be temporarily brought to life. He was trying this disgusting business on the night when he fainted. No doubt the sight of the creature moving had shaken his nerve, even though he had expected it. You remember that almost the first words he said were to call out upon himself as a fool. Well, he got more hardened afterward, and carried the matter through without fainting. The vitality which he could put into it was evidently only a passing thing, for I have seen it continually in its case as dead as this table. He has some elaborate process, I fancy, by which he brings the thing to pass. Having done it, he naturally bethought him that he might use the creature as an agent. It has intelligence and it has strength. For some purpose he took Lee into his confidence; but Lee, like a decent Christian, would have nothing to do with such a business. Then they had a row, and Lee vowed that he would tell his sister of Bellingham's true character. Bellingham's game was to prevent him, and he nearly managed it, by setting this creature of his on his track. He had already tried its powers upon another man—Norton—toward whom he had a grudge. It is the merest chance that he has not two murders upon his soul. Then, when I taxed him with the matter, he had the strongest reasons for wishing to get me out of the way before I could convey my knowledge to anyone else. He got his chance when I went out, for he knew my habits and where I was bound for. I have had a narrow shave, Peterson, and it is mere luck you didn't find me on your doorstep in the morning. I'm not a nervous man as a rule, and I never thought to have the fear of death put upon me as it was tonight."

"My dear boy, you take the matter too seriously," said his companion. "Your nerves are out of order with your work, and you make too much of it. How could such a thing as this stride about the streets of Oxford, even at night, without being seen?"

"It has been seen. There is quite a scare in the town about an escaped ape, as they imagine the creature to be. It is the talk of the place."

"Well, it's a striking chain of events. And yet, my dear fellow, you must allow that each incident in itself is capable of a more natural explanation."

"What! even my adventure of tonight?"

"Certainly. You come out with your nerves all unstrung, and your head full of this theory of yours. Some gaunt, half-famished tramp steals after you, and seeing you run, is emboldened to pursue you. Your fears and imagination do the rest."

"It won't do, Peterson; it won't do."

"And again, in the instance of your finding the mummy case empty, and then a few moments later with an occupant, you know that it was lamplight, that the lamp was half-turned down, and that you had no special reason to look hard at the case. It is quite possible that you may have overlooked the creature in the first instance."

"No, no; it is out of the question."

"And then Lee may have fallen into the river, and Norton been garroted. It is certainly a formidable indictment that you have against Bellingham; but if you were to place it before a police magistrate, he would simply laugh in your face."

"I know he would. That is why I mean to take the matter into my own hands."

"Eh?"

"Yes; I feel that a public duty rests upon me, and, besides, I must do it for my own safety, unless I choose to allow myself to be hunted by this beast out of the college, and that would be a little too feeble. I have quite made up my mind what I shall do. And first of all, may I use your paper and pens for an hour?"

"Most certainly. You will find all that you want upon that side table."

Abercrombie Smith sat down before a sheet of foolscap, and for an hour, and then for a second hour, his pen traveled swiftly over it. Page after page was finished and tossed aside while his friend leaned back in his armchair, looking across at him with patient curiosity. At last, with an exclamation of satisfaction, Smith sprang to his feet, gathered his papers up into order, and laid the last one upon Peterson's desk.

"Kindly sign this as a witness," he said.

"A witness? Of what?"

"Of my signature, and of the date. The date is the most important. Why, Peterson, my life might hang upon it."

"My dear Smith, you are talking wildly. Let me beg you to go to bed."

"On the contrary, I never spoke so deliberately in my life. And I will promise to go to bed the moment you have signed it."

"But what is it?"

"It is a statement of all that I have been telling you tonight. I wish you to witness it."

"Certainly," said Peterson, signing his name under that of his companion. "There you are! But what is the idea?"

"You will kindly retain it, and produce it in case I am arrested."

"Arrested? For what?"

"For murder. It is quite on the cards. I wish to be ready for every event. There is only one course open to me, and I am determined to take it."

"For heaven's sake, don't do anything rash!"

"Believe me, it would be far more rash to adopt any other course. I hope that we won't need to bother you, but it will ease my mind to know that you have this statement of my motives. And

now I am ready to take your advice and to go to roost, for I want
to be at my best in the morning."

Abercrombie Smith was not an entirely pleasant man to have as
an enemy. Slow and easy tempered, he was formidable when driven
to action. He brought to every purpose in life the same deliberate
resoluteness that had distinguished him as a scientific student. He
had laid his studies aside for a day, but he intended that the day
should not be wasted. Not a word did he say to his host as to his
plans, but by nine o'clock he was well on his way to Oxford.

In the High Street he stopped at Clifford's, the gunmaker's, and
bought a heavy revolver, with a box of center-fire cartridges. Six of
them he slipped into the chambers, and half cocking the weapon,
placed it in the pocket of his coat. He then made his way to Hastie's
rooms, where the big oarsman was lounging over his breakfast, with
the *Sporting Times* propped up against the coffeepot.

"Hullo! What's up?" he asked. "Have some coffee?"

"No, thank you. I want you to come with me, Hastie, and do
what I ask you."

"Certainly, my boy."

"And bring a heavy stick with you."

"Hullo!" Hastie stared. "Here's a hunting crop that would fell an
ox."

"One other thing. You have a box of amputating knives. Give me
the longest of them."

"There you are. You seem to be fairly on the war trail. Anything else?"

"No; that will do." Smith placed the knife inside his coat, and
led the way to the quadrangle. "We are neither of us chickens,
Hastie," said he. "I think I can do this job alone, but I take you
as a precaution. I am going to have a little talk with Bellingham.
If I have only him to deal with, I won't, of course, need you. If I
shout, however, up you come, and lam out with your whip as hard
as you can lick. Do you understand?"

"All right. I'll come if I hear you bellow."

"Stay here, then. I may be a little time, but don't budge until I
come down."

"I'm a fixture."

Smith ascended the stairs, opened Bellingham's door and stepped in. Bellingham was seated behind his table, writing. Beside him, among his litter of strange possessions, towered the mummy case, with its sale number 249 still stuck upon its front, and its hideous occupant stiff and stark within it. Smith looked very deliberately round him, closed the door, and then, stepping across to the fireplace, struck a match and set the fire alight. Bellingham sat staring, with amazement and rage upon his bloated face.

"Well, really now, you make yourself at home," he gasped.

Smith sat himself deliberately down, placing his watch upon the table, drew out his pistol, cocked it, and laid it in his lap. Then he took the long amputating knife from his bosom, and threw it down in front of Bellingham.

"Now, then," said he, "just get to work and cut up that mummy."

"Oh, is that it?" said Bellingham with a sneer.

"Yes, that is it. They tell me that the law can't touch you. But I have a law that will set matters straight. If in five minutes you have not set to work, I swear by the God who made me that I will put a bullet through your brain!"

"You would murder me?"

Bellingham had half risen, and his face was the color of putty.

"Yes."

"And for what?"

"To stop your mischief. One minute has gone."

"But what have I done?"

"I know and you know."

"This is mere bullying."

"Two minutes are gone."

"But you must give reasons. You are a madman—a dangerous madman. Why should I destroy my own property? It is a valuable mummy."

"You must cut it up, and you must burn it."

"I will do no such thing."

"Four minutes are gone."

Smith took up the pistol and he looked toward Bellingham with an inexorable face. As the second-hand stole round, he raised his hand, and the finger twitched upon the trigger.

"There! there! I'll do it!" screamed Bellingham.

In frantic haste he caught up the knife and hacked at the figure of the mummy, ever glancing round to see the eye and the weapon

of his terrible visitor bent upon him. The creature crackled and
snapped under every stab of the keen blade. A thick, yellow dust
rose up from it. Spices and dried essences rained down upon the
floor. Suddenly, with a rending crack, its backbone snapped
asunder, and it fell, a brown heap of sprawling limbs, upon the
floor.

"Now into the fire!" said Smith.

The flames leaped and roared as the dried and tinderlike debris
was piled upon it. The little room was like the stokehole of a
steamer and the sweat ran down the faces of the two men; but
still the one stooped and worked, while the other sat watching him
with a set face. A thick, fat smoke oozed out from the fire, and a
heavy smell of burned resin and singed hair filled the air. In a
quarter of an hour a few charred and brittle sticks were all that was
left of Lot No. 249.

"Perhaps that will satisfy you," snarled Bellingham, with hate
and fear in his little gray eyes as he glanced back at his tormentor.

"No; I must make a clean sweep of all your materials. We must
have no more devil's tricks. In with all these leaves! They may have
something to do with it."

"And what now?" asked Bellingham, when the leaves also had
been added to the blaze.

"Now the roll of papyrus which you had on the table that night.
It is in that drawer, I think."

"No, no," shouted Bellingham. "Don't burn that! Why, man,
you don't know what you do. It is unique; it contains wisdom
which is nowhere else to be found."

"Out with it!"

"But look here, Smith, you can't really mean it. I'll share the
knowledge with you. I'll teach you all that is in it. Or, stay, let me
only copy it before you burn it!"

Smith stepped forward and turned the key in the drawer. Taking
out the yellow, curled roll of paper, he threw it into the fire, and
pressed it down with his heel. Bellingham screamed, and grabbed
at it; but Smith pushed him back and stood over it until it was
reduced to a formless, gray ash.

"Now, Master B.," said he, "I think I have pretty well drawn
your teeth. You'll hear from me again, if you return to your old
tricks. And now good morning, for I must go back to my studies."

And such is the narrative of Abercrombie Smith as to the

singular events that occurred in Old College, Oxford, in the spring of '84. As Bellingham left the university immediately afterward, and was last heard of in the Soudan, there is no one who can contradict his statement. But the wisdom of men is small, and the ways of Nature are strange, and who shall put a bound to the dark things that may be found by those who seek for them?

Reanimated mummies are less frequent in literature than ghosts, vampires, and werewolves, but they are catching up in the movies. Two novels, Bran Stoker's *The Jewel of Seven Stars* and Lin Carter's *The Curse of the Black Pharaoh* involve resuscitation of mummies. But I wonder if the movie mummies owe a little to "Lot No. 249"; it's the earliest story I've seen about a mummy used to commit murder and that is the pattern of all mummy films but one: Karl Freund's stylish and unusual 1932 film *The Mummy*. This one was credited to an original (it was) story by Nina Wilcox Putnam and Richard Schayer. In this film, Karloff did *not* stalk around in mummy wrappings; he appeared in socially acceptable guise and was less violent and far more chilling than his bandaged-up successors.

CHAPTER 6

The Haunted Dolls' House

by M. R. James

Dolls and dollhouses were buried in the tombs of ancient Egypt to serve the needs of Pharaohs in the afterworld. The most famous dolls' house in this world is the one that was presented to Her Majesty Queen Mary in 1924. Its garage holds a fleet of limousines, among them a Rolls-Royce; the wine cellar (a scandal to prohibitionists) is stocked with small bottles of 1820 Madeira; and the library boasts two hundred doll-size books written by eminent British authors, in their own hand, expressly for this collection. The volume that concerns us is titled *The Haunted Dolls' House* by Dr. Montague Rhodes James, Provost of Eton. But you should be warned before you read it, that title is disarming.

"I suppose you get stuff of that kind through your hands pretty often?" said Mr. Dillet, as he pointed with his stick to an object that shall be described when the time comes: and when he said it, he lied in his throat, and knew that he lied. Not once in twenty years—perhaps not once in a lifetime—could Mr. Chittenden, skilled as he was in ferreting out the forgotten treasures of half a dozen counties, expect to handle such a specimen. It was collectors' palaver, and Mr. Chittenden recognized it as such.

"Stuff of that kind, Mr. Dillet! It's a museum piece, that is."

"Well, I suppose there are museums that'll take anything."

"I've seen one, not as good as that, years back," said Mr. Chittenden thoughtfully. "But that's not likely to come into the market: and I'm told they 'ave some fine ones of the period over the water. No: I'm only telling you the truth, Mr. Dillet, when I say that if you was to place an unlimited order with me for the very best that could be got—and you know I 'ave facilities for getting to know of such things, and a reputation to maintain—well, all I can say is, I should lead you straight up to that one and say, 'I can't do no better for you than that, sir.' "

"Hear, hear!" said Mr. Dillet, applauding ironically with the end of his stick on the floor of the shop. "How much are you sticking the innocent American buyer for it, eh?"

"Oh, I shan't be overhard on the buyer, American or otherwise. You see, it stands this way, Mr. Dillet—if I knew just a bit more about the pedigree——"

"Or just a bit less," Mr. Dillet put in.

"Ha, ha! you will have your joke, sir. No, but as I was saying, if I knew just a little more than what I do about the piece—though anyone can see for themselves it's a genuine thing, every last corner of it, and there's not been one of my men allowed to so much as touch it since it came into the shop—there'd be another figure in the price I'm asking."

"And what's that: five and twenty?"

"Multiply that by three and you've got it, sir. Seventy-five's my price."

"And fifty's mine," said Mr. Dillet.

The point of agreement was, of course, somewhere between the two, it does not matter exactly where—I think sixty guineas. But half an hour later the object was being packed, and within an hour Mr. Dillet had called for it in his car and driven away. Mr. Chittenden, holding the check in his hand, saw him off from the door with smiles, and returned, still smiling, to the parlor where his wife was making the tea. He stopped at the door.

"It's gone," he said.

"Thank God for that!" said Mrs. Chittenden, putting down the teapot. "Mr. Dillet, was it?"

"Yes, it was."

"Well, I'd sooner it was him than another."

"Oh, I don't know; he ain't a bad feller, my dear."

"Maybe not, but in my opinion he'd be none the worse for a bit of a shake-up."

"Well, if that's your opinion, it's my opinion he's put himself into the way of getting one. Anyhow, *we* shan't have no more of it, and that's something to be thankful for."

And so Mr. and Mrs. Chittenden sat down to tea.

And what of Mr. Dillet and of his new acquisition? What it was, the title of this story will have told you. What it was like, I shall have to indicate as well as I can.

There was only just room enough for it in the car, and Mr. Dillet had to sit with the driver: he had also to go slow, for though the rooms of the Dolls' House had all been stuffed carefully with soft cotton, jolting was to be avoided, in view of the immense number of small objects which thronged them; and the ten-mile drive was an anxious time for him, in spite of all the precautions he insisted upon. At last his front door was reached, and Collins, the butler, came out.

"Look here, Collins, you must help me with this thing—it's a delicate job. We must get it out upright, see? It's full of little things that mustn't be displaced more than we can help. Let's see, where shall we have it? (After a pause for consideration.) Really, I think I shall have to put it in my own room, to begin with at any rate. On the big table—that's it."

It was conveyed—with much talking—to Mr. Dillet's spacious room on the first floor, looking out on the drive. The sheeting was unwound from it, and the front thrown open, and for the next hour or two Mr. Dillet was fully occupied in extracting the padding and setting in order the contents of the rooms.

When this thoroughly congenial task was finished, I must say that it would have been difficult to find a more perfect and attractive specimen of a Dolls' House in Strawberry Hill Gothic than that which now stood on Mr. Dillet's large kneehole table, lighted up by the evening sun which came slanting through three tall sash windows.

It was quite six-feet long, including the chapel or oratory, which flanked the front on the left as you faced it, and the stable on the right. The main block of the house was, as I have said, in the Gothic manner: that is to say, the windows had pointed arches and were surmounted by what are called ogival hoods, with crockets and finials such as we see on the canopies of tombs built into church walls. At the angles were absurd turrets covered with arched panels. The chapel had pinnacles and buttresses, and a bell in the turret, and colored glass in the windows. When the front of the house was open you saw four large rooms, bedroom, dining room, drawing room, and kitchen, each with its appropriate furniture in a very complete state.

The stable on the right was in two stories, with its proper complement of horses, coaches, and grooms, and with its clock and Gothic cupola for the clock bell.

Pages, of course, might be written on the outfit of the mansion—how many frying pans, how many gilt chairs, what pictures, carpets, chandeliers, four-posters, table linen, glass, crockery, and plate it possessed; but all this must be left to the imagination. I will only say that the base or plinth on which the house stood (for it was fitted with one of some depth which allowed of a flight of steps to the front door and a terrace, partly balustraded) contained a shallow drawer or drawers in which were neatly stored sets of embroidered curtains, changes of raiment for the inmates, and, in short, all the materials for an infinite series of variations and re-fittings of the most absorbing and delightful kind.

"Quintessence of Horace Walpole, that's what it is: he must have had something to do with the making of it." Such was Mr. Dillet's murmured reflection as he knelt before it in a reverent ecstasy. "Simply wonderful! this is my day and no mistake. Five hundred pounds coming in this morning for that cabinet which I never cared about, and now this tumbling into my hands for a tenth, at the very most, of what it would fetch in town. Well, well! It almost makes one afraid something'll happen to counter it. Let's have a look at the population, anyhow."

Accordingly, he set them before him in a row. Again, here is an opportunity, which some would snatch at, of making an inventory of costume: I am incapable of it.

There were a gentleman and lady, in blue satin and brocade respectively. There were two children, a boy and a girl. There was a cook, a nurse, a footman, and there were the stable servants, two postilions, a coachman, two grooms.

"Anyone else? Yes, possibly."

The curtains of the four-poster in the bedroom were closely drawn round all four sides of it, and he put his finger in between them and felt in the bed. He drew the finger back hastily, for it almost seemed to him as if something had—not stirred, perhaps, but yielded—in an odd live way as he pressed it. Then he put back the curtains, which ran on rods in the proper manner, and extracted from the bed a white-haired old gentleman in a long linen nightdress and cap, and laid him down by the rest. The tale was complete.

Dinnertime was now near, so Mr. Dillet spent but five minutes in putting the lady and children into the drawing room, the gentleman into the dining room, the servants into the kitchen and stables, and the old man back into his bed. He retired into his dressing room next door, and we see and hear no more of him until something like eleven o'clock at night.

His whim was to sleep surrounded by some of the gems of his collection. The big room in which we have seen him contained his bed: bath, wardrobe, and all the appliances of dressing were in a commodious room adjoining: but his four-poster, which itself was a valued treasure, stood in the large room where he sometimes wrote, and often sat, and even received visitors. Tonight he repaired to it in a highly complacent frame of mind.

There was no striking clock within earshot—none on the staircase, none in the stable, none in the distant church tower. Yet it is indubitable that Mr. Dillet was startled out of a very pleasant slumber by a bell tolling One.

He was so much startled that he did not merely lie breathless with wide-open eyes, but actually sat up in his bed.

He never asked himself, till the morning hours, how it was that, though there was no light at all in the room, the Dolls' House on the kneehole table stood out with complete clearness. But it was so. The effect was that of a bright harvest moon shining full on the front of a big white stone mansion—a quarter of a mile away it might be, and yet every detail was photographically sharp. There were trees about it, too—trees rising behind the chapel and the house. He seemed to be conscious of the scent of a cool, still September night. He thought he could hear an occasional stamp and clink from the stables, as of horses stirring. And with another shock he realized that, above the house, he was looking, not at the wall of his room with its pictures, but into the profound blue of a night sky.

There were lights, more than one, in the windows, and he quickly saw that this was no four-roomed house with a movable front, but one of many rooms, and staircases—a real house, but seen as if through the wrong end of a telescope. "You mean to show me something," he muttered to himself, and he gazed earnestly on the lighted windows. They would in real life have been shuttered or curtained, no doubt, he thought; but, as it was, there was nothing to intercept his view of what was being transacted inside the rooms.

Two rooms were lighted—one on the ground floor to the right of the door, one upstairs, on the left—the first brightly enough, the other rather dimly. The lower room was the dining room: a table was laid, but the meal was over, and only wine and glasses were left on the table. The man of the blue satin and the woman of the brocade were alone in the room, and they were talking very earnestly, seated close together at the table, their elbows on it: every now and again stopping to listen, as it seemed. Once *he* rose, came to the window and opened it and put his head out and his hand to his ear. There was a lighted taper in a silver candlestick on a sideboard. When the man left the window he seemed to leave the room also; and the lady, taper in hand, remained standing and listening. The expression on her face was that of one striving her utmost to keep down a fear that threatened to master her—and succeeding. It was a hateful face, too; broad, flat, and sly. Now the man came back and she took some small thing from him and hurried out of the room. He, too, disappeared, but only for a moment or two. The front door slowly opened and he stepped out and stood on the top of the perron, looking this way and that; then turned toward the upper window that was lighted, and shook his fist.

It was time to look at that upper window. Through it was seen a four-post bed: a nurse or other servant in an armchair, evidently sound asleep; in the bed an old man lying: awake, and, one would say, anxious, from the way in which he shifted about and moved his fingers, beating tunes on the coverlet. Beyond the bed a door opened. Light was seen on the ceiling, and the lady came in: she set down her candle on a table, came to the fireside and roused the nurse. In her hand she had an old-fashioned wine bottle, ready uncorked. The nurse took it, poured some of the contents into a little silver saucepan, added some spice and sugar from casters on the table, and set it to warm on the fire. Meanwhile the old man in the bed beckoned feebly to the lady, who came to him, smiling, took his wrist as if to feel his pulse, and bit her lip as if in consternation. He looked at her anxiously, and then pointed to the window, and spoke. She nodded, and did as the man below had done; opened the casement and listened—perhaps rather ostentatiously: then drew in her head and shook it, looking at the old man, who seemed to sigh.

By this time the posset on the fire was steaming, and the nurse poured it into a small two-handled silver bowl and brought it to the bedside. The old man seemed disinclined for it and was waving it away, but the lady and the nurse together bent over him and evidently pressed it upon him. He must have yielded, for they supported him into a sitting position, and put it to his lips. He drank most of it, in several draughts, and they laid him down. The lady left the room, smiling good night to him, and took the bowl, the bottle, and the silver saucepan with her. The nurse returned to the chair, and there was an interval of complete quiet.

Suddenly the old man started up in his bed—and he must have uttered some cry, for the nurse started out of her chair and made but one step of it to the bedside. He was a sad and terrible sight—flushed in the face, almost to blackness, the eyes glaring whitely, both hands clutching at his heart, foam at his lips.

For a moment the nurse left him, ran to the door, flung it wide open, and, one supposes, screamed aloud for help, then darted back to the bed and seemed to try feverishly to soothe him—to lay him down—anything. But as the lady, her husband, and several servants, rushed into the room with horrified faces, the old man collapsed under the nurse's hands and lay back, and the features, contorted with agony and rage, relaxed slowly into calm.

A few moments later, lights showed out to the left of the house, and a coach with flambeaux drove up to the door. A white-wigged man in black got nimbly out and ran up the steps, carrying a small leather trunk-shaped box. He was met in the doorway by the man and his wife, she with her handkerchief clutched between her hands, he with a tragic face, but retaining his self-control. They led the newcomer into the dining room, where he set his box of papers on the table, and, turning to them, listened with a face of consternation at what they had to tell. He nodded his head again and again, threw out his hands slightly, declined, it seemed, offers of refreshment and lodging for the night, and within a few minutes came slowly down the steps, entering the coach and driving off the way he had come. As the man in blue watched him from the top of the steps, a smile not pleasant to see stole slowly over his fat white face. Darkness fell over the whole scene as the lights of the coach disappeared.

But Mr. Dillet remained sitting up in the bed: he had rightly guessed that there would be a sequel. The house front glimmered out again before long. But now there was a difference. The lights were in other windows, one at the top of the house, the other illuminating the range of colored windows of the chapel. How he saw through these is not quite obvious, but he did. The interior was as carefully furnished as the rest of the establishment, with its minute red cushions on the desks, its Gothic stall canopies, and its western gallery and pinnacled organ with gold pipes. On the center of the black and white pavement was a bier: four tall candles burned at the corners. On the bier was a coffin with a pall of black velvet.

As he looked the folds of the pall stirred. It seemed to rise at one end: it slid downward: it fell away, exposing the black coffin with its silver handles and nameplate. One of the tall candlesticks swayed and toppled over. Ask no more, but turn, as Mr. Dillet hastily did, and look in at the lighted window at the top of the house, where a boy and girl lay in two truckle beds, and a four-poster for the nurse rose above them. The nurse was not visible for the moment; but the father and mother were there, dressed now in mourning, but with very little sign of mourning in their demeanor. Indeed, they were laughing and talking with a good deal of animation, sometimes to each other, and sometimes throwing a remark to one or other of the children, and again laughing at the answers. Then the father was seen to go on tiptoe out of the room, taking with him as he went a white garment that hung on a peg near the door. He shut the door after him. A minute or two later it was slowly opened again, and a muffled head poked round it. A bent form of sinister shape stepped across to the truckle beds, and suddenly stopped, threw up its arms and revealed, of course, the father, laughing. The children were in agonies of terror, the boy with the bedclothes over his head, the girl throwing herself out of bed into her mother's arms. Attempts at consolation followed—the parents took the children on their laps, patted them, picked up the white gown and showed there was no harm in it, and so forth; and at last, putting the children back into bed, left the room with encouraging waves of the hand. As they left it, the nurse came in, and soon the light died down.

Still Mr. Dillet watched immovable.

A new sort of light—not of lamp or candle—a pale ugly light, began to dawn around the doorcase at the back of the room. The door was opening again. The seer does not like to dwell upon what he saw entering the room: he says it might be described as a frog— the size of a man—but it had scanty white hair about its head. It was busy about the truckle beds, but not for long. The sound of cries—faint, as if coming out of a vast distance—but, even so, infinitely appalling, reached the ear.

There were signs of a hideous commotion all over the house: lights moved along and up, and doors opened and shut, and running figures passed within the windows. The clock in the stable turret tolled one, and darkness fell again.

It was only dispelled once more, to show the house front. At the bottom of the steps dark figures were drawn up in two lines, holding flaming torches. More dark figures came down the steps, bearing, first one, then another small coffin. And the lines of torch-bearers with the coffins between them moved silently onward to the left.

The hours of night passed on—never so slowly, Mr. Dillet thought. Gradually he sank down from sitting to lying in his bed— but he did not close an eye: and early next morning he sent for the doctor.

The doctor found him in a disquieting state of nerves, and recommended sea air. To a quiet place on the East Coast he accordingly repaired by easy stages in his car.

One of the first people he met on the sea front was Mr. Chitten-den, who, it appeared, had likewise been advised to take his wife away for a bit of a change.

Mr. Chittenden looked somewhat askance upon him when they met: and not without cause.

"Well, I don't wonder at you being a bit upset, Mr. Dillet. What? yes, well, I might say 'orrible upset, to be sure, seeing what me and my poor wife went through ourselves. But I put it to you, Mr. Dillet, one of two things: was I going to scrap a lovely piece like that on the one 'and, or was I going to tell customers: 'I'm selling you a regular picture-palace-dramar in reel life of the olden time, billed to perform regular at one o'clock A.M.'? Why, what would you 'ave said yourself? And next thing you know, two jus-tices of the peace in the back parlor, and pore Mr. and Mrs. Chittenden off in a spring cart to the county asylum and everyone in the street saying, 'Ah, I thought it 'ud come to that. Look at the way the man drank!'—and me next door, or next door but one, to a total abstainer, as you know. Well, there was my position. What? Me 'ave it back in the shop? Well, what do *you* think? No, but I'll tell you what I will do. You shall have your money back, bar the ten pounds I paid for it, and you make what you can."

Later in the day, in what is offensively called the "smoke room" of the hotel, a murmured conversation between the two went on for some time.

"How much do you really know about that thing, and where it came from?"

"Honest, Mr. Dillet, I don't know the 'ouse. Of course, it came out of the lumber room of a country 'ouse—that anyone could guess. But I'll go as far as say this, that I believe it's not a hundred miles from this place. Which direction and how far I've no notion. I'm only judging by guesswork. The man as I actually paid the check to ain't one of my regular men, and I've lost sight of him; but I 'ave the idea that this part of the country was his beat, and that's every word I can tell you. But now, Mr. Dillet, there's one thing that rather physicks me. That old chap,—I suppose you saw him drive up to the door—I thought so: now, would he have been the medical man, do you take it? My wife would have it so, but I stuck to it that was the lawyer, because he had papers with him, and one he took out was folded up."

"I agree," said Mr. Dillet. "Thinking it over, I came to the conclusion that was the old man's will, ready to be signed."

"Just what I thought," said Mr. Chittenden, "and I took it that will would have cut out the young people, eh? Well, well! It's been a lesson to me, I know that. I shan't buy no more dolls' houses, nor waste no more money on the pictures—and as to this business of poisonin' grandpa, well, if I know myself, I never 'ad much of a turn for that. Live and let live: that's bin my motto throughout life, and I ain't found it a bad one."

Filled with these elevated sentiments, Mr. Chittenden retired to his lodgings. Mr. Dillet next day repaired to the local institute, where he hoped to find some clue to the riddle that absorbed him. He gazed in despair at a long file of the Canterbury and York society's publications of the parish registers of the district. No print resembling the house of his nightmare was among those that hung on the staircase and in the passages. Disconsolate, he found himself at last in a derelict room, staring at a dusty model of a church in a dusty glass case: *Model of St. Stephen's Church, Coxham. Presented by J. Merewether, Esq., of Ilbridge House, 1877. The work of his ancestor James Merewether, d. 1786.* There was something in the fashion of it that reminded him dimly of his horror. He retraced his steps to a wall map he had noticed, and made out that Ilbridge House was in Coxham Parish. Coxham was, as it happened, one of the parishes of which he had retained the name when he glanced over the file of printed registers, and it was not long before he found in them the record of the burial of Roger Milford, aged seventy-six on the eleventh of September, 1757, and of Roger and Elizabeth Merewether, aged nine and seven, on the nineteenth of the same month. It seemed worth while to follow up this clue, frail as it was; and in the afternoon he drove out to Coxham. The east end of the north aisle of the church is a Milford chapel, and on its north wall are tablets to the same persons; Roger, the elder, it seems, was distinguished by all the qualities that adorn "the Father, the Magistrate, and the Man": the memorial was erected by his attached daughter Elizabeth, "who did not long survive the loss of a parent ever solicitous for her welfare, and of two amiable children." The last sentence was plainly an addition to the original inscription.

A yet later slab told of James Merewether, husband of Elizabeth, "who in the dawn of life practised, not without success, those arts which, had he continued their exercise, might in the opinion of the most competent judges have earned for him the name of the British Vitruvius: but who, overwhelmed by the visitation which deprived him of an affectionate partner and a blooming offspring, passed his Prime and Age in a secluded yet elegant Retirement: his grateful Nephew and Heir indulges a pious sorrow by this too brief recital of his excellences."

The children were more simply commemorated. Both died on the night of the twelfth of September.

Mr. Dillet felt sure that in Ilbridge House he had found the scene of his drama. In some old sketchbook, possibly in some old print, he may yet find convincing evidence that he is right. But the Ilbridge House of today is not that which he sought; it is an Elizabethan erection of the forties, in red brick with stone quoins and dressings. A quarter of a mile from it, in a low part of the park, backed by ancient, stag-horned, ivy-strangled trees and thick under-growth are marks of a terraced platform overgrown with rough grass. A few stone balusters lie here and there, and a heap or two, covered with nettles and ivy, of wrought stones with badly carved crockets. This, someone told Mr. Dillet, was the site of an older house.

As he drove out of the village, the hall clock struck four, and Mr. Dillet started up and clapped his hands to his ears. It was not the first time he had heard that bell.

Awaiting an offer from the other side of the Atlantic, the dolls' house still reposes, carefully sheeted, in a loft over Mr. Dillet's stables, whither Collins conveyed it on the day when Mr. Dillet started for the sea coast.

M. R. James (1862–1936), a noted English scholar, wrote, as Basil Davenport often and truly remarked, "more first-rate ghost stories than any other man who has ever tried." They are gathered in one volume, *The Collected Ghost Stories of M. R. James,* frequently published in England though it has yet to appear in an American edition. "Count Magnus" and several other stories appear in many anthologies. Dr. James admired the ghost stories of Joseph Sheridan Le Fanu whose "Carmilla" inspired Bram Stoker's vampire novel *Dracula.*

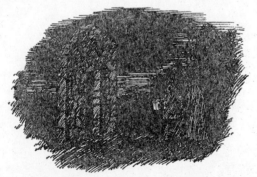

CHAPTER 7

The Open Door

by Mrs. Oliphant

Women are eminent in the annals of supernatural fiction. Anne Radcliffe, Emily Brontë, and Mary Shelley reign in terror to this day. Any man might dream up a Frankenstein Monster; only a woman would think of making him human, and lonely, as well as monstrous. There lies the power of these enchantresses. They evoke pity and terror simultaneously.

Margaret Oliphant (1828–1897), was a very popular novelist. Born in Scotland, she moved to London in 1850 where she contributed to *Blackwood's Magazine*. She wrote 123 books and numerous stories. Among them, one of the most beautiful ghost stories ever written—this one.

I took the house of Brentwood on my return from India in 18—, for the temporary accommodation of my family, until I could find a permanent home for them. It had many advantages which made it peculiarly appropriate. It was within reach of Edinburgh, and my boy Roland, whose education had been considerably neglected, could go in and out to school, which was thought to be better for him than either leaving home altogether or staying there always with a tutor. The first of these expedients would have seemed preferable to me, the second commended itself to his mother. The

doctor, like a judicious man, took the midway between. "Put
him on his pony, and let him ride into the high school every morning; it will do him all the good in the world," Dr. Simson said; "and
when it is bad weather there is the train." His mother accepted this
solution of the difficulty more easily than I could have hoped;
and our pale-faced boy, who had never known anything more
invigorating than Simla, began to encounter the brisk breezes of
the North in the subdued severity of the month of May. Before
the time of the vacation in July we had the satisfaction of seeing
him begin to acquire something of the brown and ruddy complexion of his schoolfellows. The English system did not com-
mend itself to Scotland in these days. There was no little Eton at
Fettes; nor do I think, if there had been, that a genteel exotic of that
class would have tempted either my wife or me. The lad was
doubly precious to us, being the only one left us of many; and he
was fragile in body, we believed, and deeply sensitive in mind.
To keep him at home, and yet to send him to school—to combine
the advantages of the two systems—seemed to be everything that
could be desired. The two girls also found at Brentwood everything
they wanted. They were near enough to Edinburgh to have masters
and lessons as many as they required for completing that never-
ending education which the young people seem to require nowadays. Their mother married me when she was younger than Agatha,
and I should like to see them improve upon their mother! I myself
was then no more than twenty-five—an age at which I see the young
fellows now groping about them, with no notion what they are
going to do with their lives. However, I suppose every generation
has a conceit of itself which elevates it, in its own opinion, above
that which comes after it.

Brentwood stands on that fine and wealthy slope of country, one
of the richest in Scotland, which lies between the Pentland Hills
and the Firth. In clear weather you could see the blue gleam—like a
bent bow, embracing the wealthy fields and scattered houses—of the
great estuary on one side of you; and on the other the blue heights,
not gigantic like those we had been used to, but just high enough
for all the glories of the atmosphere, the play of clouds, and sweet
reflections, which give to a hilly country an interest and a charm
that nothing else can emulate. Edinburgh, with its two lesser
heights—the Castle and the Calton Hill—its spires and towers piercing through the smoke, and Arthur's Seat lying crouched behind,

like a guardian no longer very needful, taking his repose beside the
well-beloved charge, which is now, so to speak, able to take care
of itself without him—lay at our right hand. From the lawn and
drawing-room windows we could see all these varieties of landscape. The color was sometimes a little chilly, but sometimes, also,
as animated and full of vicissitude as a drama. I was never tired of
it. Its color and freshness revived the eyes which had grown weary
of arid plains and blazing skies. It was always cheery, and fresh,
and full of repose.

The village of Brentwood lay almost under the house, on the
other side of the deep little ravine, down which a stream—which
ought to have been a lovely, wild, and frolicsome little river—
flowed between its rocks and trees. The river, like so many in
that district, had, however, in its earlier life been sacrificed to
trade, and was grimy with paper making. But this did not affect
our pleasure in it so much as I have known it to affect other
streams. Perhaps our water was more rapid—perhaps less clogged
with dirt and refuse. Our side of the dell was charmingly *accidenté,*
and clothed with fine trees, through which various paths wound
down to the riverside and to the village bridge that crossed the
stream. The village lay in the hollow, and climbed, with very
prosaic houses, the other side. Village architecture does not
flourish in Scotland. The blue slates and the gray stone are sworn
foes to the picturesque; and though I do not, for my own part,
dislike the interior of an old-fashioned pewed and galleried
church, with its little family settlements on all sides, the square
box outside, with its bit of a spire like a handle to lift it by, is not
an improvement to the landscape. Still, a cluster of houses on
differing elevations—with scraps of garden coming in between,
a hedgerow with clothes laid out to dry, the opening of a street
with its rural sociability, the women at their doors, the slow wagon
lumbering along—gives a center to the landscape. It was cheerful
to look at, and convenient in a hundred ways. Within ourselves
we had walks in plenty, the glen being always beautiful in all its
phases, whether the woods were green in the spring or ruddy in
the autumn. In the park that surrounded the house were the ruins
of the former mansion of Brentwood, a much smaller and less
important house than the solid Georgian edifice that we inhabited.
The ruins were picturesque, however, and gave importance to the
place. Even we, who were but temporary tenants, felt a vague pride

in them, as if they somehow reflected a certain consequence upon ourselves. The old building had the remains of a tower, an indistinguishable mass of masonwork, overgrown with ivy, and the shells of walls attached to this were half filled up with soil. I had never examined it closely, I am ashamed to say. There was a large room, or what had been a large room, with the lower part of the windows still existing, on the principal floor, and underneath other windows, which were perfect, though half filled up with fallen soil, and waving with a wild growth of brambles and chance growths of all kinds. This was the oldest part of all. At a little distance were some very commonplace and disjointed fragments of the building, one of them suggesting a certain pathos by its very commonness and the complete wreck which it showed. This was the end of a low gable, a bit of gray wall, all encrusted with lichens, in which was a common doorway. Probably it had been a servants' entrance, a backdoor, or opening into what are called "the offices" in Scotland. No offices remained to be entered—pantry and kitchen had all been swept out of being; but there stood the doorway open and vacant, free to all the winds, to the rabbits, and every wild creature. It struck my eye, the first time I went to Brentwood, like a melancholy comment upon a life that was over. A door that led to nothing—closed once perhaps with anxious care, bolted and guarded, now void of any meaning. It impressed me, I remember, from the first; so perhaps it may be said that my mind was prepared to attach to it an importance which nothing justified.

The summer was a very happy period of repose for us all. The warmth of Indian suns was still in our veins. It seemed to us that we could never have enough of the greenness, the dewiness, the freshness of the northern landscape. Even its mists were pleasant to us, taking all the fever out of us, and pouring in vigor and refreshment. In autumn we followed the fashion of the time, and went away for change which we did not in the least require. It was when the family had settled down for the winter, when the days were short and dark, and the rigorous reign of frost upon us, that the incidents occurred which alone could justify me in intruding upon the world my private affairs. These incidents were, however, of so curious a character, that I hope my inevitable references to my own family and pressing personal interests will meet with a general pardon.

I was absent in London when these events began. In London an old Indian plunges back into the interests with which all his previous life has been associated, and meets old friends at every step. I had been circulating among some half dozen of these— enjoying the return to my former life in shadow, though I had been so thankful in substance to throw it aside—and had missed some of my home letters, what with going down from Friday to Monday to old Benbow's place in the country, and stopping on the way back to dine and sleep at Sellar's and to take a look into Cross's stables, which occupied another day. It is never safe to miss one's letters. In this transitory life, as the prayer book says, how can one ever be certain what is going to happen? All was well at home. I knew exactly (I thought) what they would have to say to me: "The weather has been so fine, that Roland has not once gone by train, and he enjoys the ride beyond anything." "Dear Papa, be sure that you don't forget anything, but bring us so-and-so and so-and-so"—a list as long as my arm. Dear girls and dearer Mother! I would not for the world have forgotten their commissions, or lost their little letters, for all the Benbows and Crosses in the world.

But I was confident in my home comfort and peacefulness. When I got back to my club, however, three or four letters were lying for me, upon some of which I noticed the "immediate," "urgent," which old-fashioned people and anxious people still believe will influence the post office and quicken the speed of the mails. I was about to open one of these, when the club porter brought me two telegrams, one of which, he said, had arrived the night before. I opened, as was to be expected, the last first, and this was what I read: "Why don't you come or answer? For God's sake, come. He is much worse." This was a thunderbolt to fall upon a man's head who had one only son, and he the light of his eyes! The other telegram, which I opened with hands trembling so much that I lost time by my haste, was to much the same purport: "No better; doctor afraid of brain fever. Calls for you day and night. Let nothing detain you." The first thing I did was to look up the timetables to see if there were any way of getting off sooner than by the night train, though I knew well enough there was not; and then I read the letters, which furnished, alas! too clearly, all the details. They told me that the boy had been pale for some time, with a scared look. His mother had noticed it before I left home, but would not say anything to alarm me. This

look had increased day by day; and soon it was observed that
Roland came home at a wild gallop through the park, his pony
panting and in foam, himself "as white as a sheet," but with the
perspiration streaming from his forehead. For a long time he had
resisted all questioning, but at length had developed such strange
changes of mood, showing a reluctance to go to school, a desire
to be fetched in the carriage at night—which was a ridiculous piece
of luxury—an unwillingness to go out into the grounds, and nervous start at every sound, that his mother had insisted upon an
explanation. When the boy—our boy Roland, who had never
known what fear was—began to talk to her of the voices he had
heard in the park, and shadows that had appeared to him among
the ruins, my wife promptly put him to bed and sent for Dr.
Simson—which, of course, was the only thing to do.

I hurried off that evening, as may be supposed, with an anxious
heart. How I got through the hours before the starting of the
train, I cannot tell. We must all be thankful for the quickness of
the railway when in anxiety; but to have thrown myself into a post
chaise as soon as horses could be put to, would have been a relief.
I got to Edinburgh very early in the blackness of the winter
morning, and scarcely dared look the man in the face at whom I
gasped, "What news?" My wife had sent the brougham for me,
which I concluded, before the man spoke, was a bad sign. His
answer was that stereotyped answer which leaves the imagination
so wildly free—"Just the same." Just the same! What might that
mean? The horses seemed to me to creep along the long dark
country road. As we dashed through the park, I thought I heard
some one moaning among the trees, and clenched my fist at him
(whoever he might be) with fury. Why had the fool of a woman
at the gate allowed any one to come in to disturb the quiet of the
place? If I had not been in such hot haste to get home, I think I
should have stopped the carriage and got out to see what tramp
it was that had made an entrance, and chosen my grounds, of all
places in the world,—when my boy was ill!—to grumble and groan
in. But I had no reason to complain of our slow pace here. The
horses flew like lightning along the intervening path, and drew up
at the door all panting, as if they had run a race. My wife stood
waiting to receive me with a pale face, and a candle in her hand,
which made her look paler still as the wind blew the flame about.
"He is sleeping," she said in a whisper, as if her voice might wake

him. And I replied, when I could find my voice, also in a whisper, as though the jingling of the horses' furniture and the sound of their hoofs must not have been more dangerous. I stood on the steps with her a moment, almost afraid to go in, now that I was here; and it seemed to me that I saw without observing, if I may say so, that the horses were unwilling to turn round, though their stables lay that way, or that the men were unwilling. These things occurred to me afterward, though at the moment I was not capable of anything but to ask questions and to hear of the condition of the boy.

I looked at him from the door of his room, for we were afraid to go near, lest we should disturb that blessed sleep. It looked like actual sleep—not the lethargy into which my wife told me he would sometimes fall. She told me everything in the next room, which communicated with his, rising now and then and going to the door of communication; and in this there was much that was very startling and confusing to the mind. It appeared that ever since the winter began, since it was early dark and night had fallen before his return from school, he had been hearing voices among the ruins—at first only a groaning, he said, at which his pony was as much alarmed as he was, but by degrees a voice. The tears ran down my wife's cheeks as she described to me how he would start up in the night and cry out, "Oh, Mother, let me in! Oh, Mother, let me in!" with a pathos which rent her heart. And she sitting there all the time, only longing to do everything his heart could desire! But though she would try to soothe him, crying, "You are at home, my darling. I am here. Don't you know me? Your mother is here," he would only stare at her, and after a while spring up again with the same cry. At other times he would be quite reasonable, she said, asking eagerly when I was coming, but declaring that he must go with me as soon as I did so, "to let them in." "The doctor thinks his nervous system must have received a shock," my wife said. "Oh, Henry, can it be that we have pushed him on too much with his work—a delicate boy like Roland?—and what is his work in comparison with his health? Even you would think little of honors or prizes if it hurt the boy's health." Even I! as if I were an inhuman father sacrificing my child to my ambition. But I would not increase her trouble by taking any notice. After a while they persuaded me to lie down, to rest, and to eat—none of which things had been possible since I

received their letters. The mere fact of being on the spot, of
course, in itself was a great thing; and when I knew that I could
be called in a moment, as soon as he was awake and wanted me, I
felt capable, even in the dark, chill morning twilight, to snatch an
hour or two's sleep. As it happened, I was so worn out with the
strain of anxiety, and he so quieted and consoled by knowing I
had come, that I was not disturbed till the afternoon, when the
twilight had again settled down. There was just daylight enough to
see his face when I went to him; and what a change in a fortnight!
He was paler and more worn, I thought, than even in those dreadful days in the plains before we left India. His hair seemed to
me to have grown long and lank; his eyes were like blazing lights
projecting out of his white face. He got hold of my hand in a cold
and tremulous clutch, and waved to everybody to go away. "Go
away—even Mother," he said,—"go away." This went to her heart,
for she did not like that even I should have more of the boy's
confidence than herself; but my wife has never been a woman to
think of herself, and she left us alone. "Are they all gone?" he said,
eagerly. "They would not let me speak. The doctor treated me as
if I were a fool. You know I am not a fool, Papa."

"Yes, yes, my boy, I know; but you are ill, and quiet is so
necessary. You are not only not a fool, Roland, but you are reasonable and understand. When you are ill you must deny yourself;
you must not do everything that you might do being well."

He waved his thin hand with a sort of indignation. "Then,
Father, I am not ill," he cried. "Oh, I thought when you came
you would not stop me,—you would see the sense of it! What do
you think is the matter with me, all of you? Simson is well enough,
but he is only a doctor. What do you think is the matter with me?
I am no more ill than you are. A doctor, of course, he thinks you
are ill the moment he looks at you—that's what he's there for—and
claps you into bed."

"Which is the best place for you at present, my dear boy."

"I made up my mind," cried the little fellow, "that I would stand
it till you came home. I said to myself, I won't frighten Mother and
the girls. But now, Father," he cried, half jumping out of bed,
"it's not illness, it's a secret."

His eyes shone so wildly, his face was so swept with strong
feeling, that my heart sank within me. It could be nothing but
fever that did it, and fever had been so fatal. I got him into my

arms to put him back into bed. "Roland," I said, humoring the poor child, which I knew was the only way, "if you are going to tell me this secret to do any good, you know you must be quite quiet, and not excite yourself. If you excite yourself, I must not let you speak."

"Yes, Father," said the boy. He was quiet directly, like a man, as if he quite understood. When I had laid him back on his pillow, he looked up at me with that grateful sweet look with which children, when they are ill, break one's heart, the water coming into his eyes in his weakness. "I was sure as soon as you were here you would know what to do," he said.

"To be sure, my boy. Now keep quiet, and tell it all out like a man." To think I was telling lies to my own child! for I did it only to humor him, thinking, poor little fellow, his brain was wrong.

"Yes, Father. Father, there is someone in the park,—someone that has been badly used."

"Hush, my dear; you remember, there is to be no excitement. Well, who is this somebody, and who has been ill-using him? We will soon put a stop to that."

"Ah," cried Roland, "but it is not so easy as you think. I don't know who it is. It is just a cry. Oh, if you could hear it! It gets into my head in my sleep. I heard it as clear—as clear;—and they think that I am dreaming—or raving perhaps," the boy said, with a sort of disdainful smile.

This look of his perplexed me; it was less like fever than I thought. "Are you quite sure you have not dreamed it, Roland?" I said.

"Dreamed?—that!" He was springing up again when he suddenly bethought himself, and lay down flat with the same sort of smile on his face. "The pony heard it too," he said. "She jumped as if she had been shot. If I had not grasped at the reins,—for I was frightened, Father——"

"No shame to you, my boy," said I, though I scarcely knew why.

"If I hadn't held to her like a leech, she'd have pitched me over her head, and she never drew breath till we were at the door. Did the pony dream it?" he said, with a soft disdain, yet indulgence for my foolishness. Then he added slowly: "It was only a cry the first time, and all the time before you went away. I wouldn't tell you, for it was so wretched to be frightened. I thought it might be a hare or a rabbit snared, and I went in the morning and looked, but there was nothing. It was after you went I heard it really first, and this is what he says." He raised himself on his elbow close to me, and looked me in the face. "'Oh, Mother, let me in! oh, Mother, let me in!'" As he said the words a mist came over his face, the mouth quivered, the soft features all melted and changed, and when he had ended these pitiful words, dissolved in a shower of heavy tears.

Was it a hallucination? Was it the fever of the brain? Was it the disordered fancy caused by great bodily weakness? How could I tell? I thought it wisest to accept it as if it were all true.

"This is very touching, Roland," I said.

"Oh, if you had just heard it, Father! I said to myself, if Father heard it he would do something; but Mamma, you know, she's given over to Simson, and that fellow's a doctor, and never thinks of anything but clapping you into bed."

"We must not blame Simson for being a doctor, Roland."

"No, no," said my boy, with delightful toleration and indulgence; "oh, no; that's the good of him—that's what he's for; I know that. But you—you are different; you are just Father: and you'll do something,—directly, Papa, directly,—this very night."

"Surely," I said. "No doubt it is some little lost child."

He gave me a sudden, swift look, investigating my face as though to see whether, after all, this was everything my eminence as "Father" came to,—no more than that? Then he got hold of my shoulder, clutching it with his thin hand: "Look here," he said, with a quiver in his voice; "suppose it wasn't—living at all!"

"My dear boy, how then could you have heard it?" I said.

He turned away from me with a pettish exclamation—"As if you didn't know better than that!"

"Do you want to tell me it is a ghost?" I said.

Roland withdrew his hand; his countenance assumed an aspect of great dignity and gravity; a slight quiver remained about his lips. "Whatever it was—you always said we were not to call names. It was something—in trouble. Oh, Father, in terrible trouble!"

"But, my boy," I said—I was at my wits' end—"if it was a child that was lost, or any poor human creature——but, Roland, what do you want me to do?"

"I should know if I was you," said the child, eagerly. "That is what I always said to myself—Father will know. Oh, Papa, Papa,

to have to face it night after night, in such terrible, terrible
trouble! and never to be able to do it any good. I don't want to
cry; it's like a baby, I know; but what can I do else?—out there
all by itself in the ruin, and nobody to help it. I can't bear it, I
can't bear it!" cried my generous boy. And in his weakness he
burst out, after many attempts to restrain it, into a great childish
fit of sobbing and tears.

I do not know that I ever was in a greater perplexity in my life;
and afterward, when I thought of it, there was something comic
in it too. It is bad enough to find your child's mind possessed
with the conviction that he has seen—or heard—a ghost. But that
he should require you to go instantly and help that ghost, was
the most bewildering experience that had ever come my way. I am
a sober man myself, and not superstitious—at least any more than
everybody is superstitious. Of course I do not believe in ghosts;
but I don't deny, any more than other people, that there are stories
which I cannot pretend to understand. My blood got a sort of
chill in my veins at the idea that Roland should be a ghost seer;
for that generally means a hysterical temperament and weak
health, and all that men most hate and fear for their children.
But that I should take up his ghost and right its wrongs, and save
it from its trouble, was such a mission as was enough to confuse
any man. I did my best to console my boy without giving any
promise of this astonishing kind; but he was too sharp for me. He
would have none of my caresses. With sobs breaking in at intervals upon his voice, and the raindrops hanging on his eyelids, he
yet returned to the charge.

"It will be there now—it will be there all the night. Oh think,
Papa, think, if it was me! I can't rest for thinking of it. Don't!"
he cried, putting away my hand—"don't! You go and help it, and
Mother can take care of me."

"But, Roland, what can I do?"

My boy opened his eyes, which were large with weakness and
fever, and gave me a smile such, I think, as sick children only
know the secret of. "I was sure you would know as soon as you
came. I always said—Father will know: and Mother," he cried,
with a softening of repose upon his face, his limbs relaxing, his
form sinking with a luxurious ease in his bed—"Mother can come
and take care of me."

I called her, and saw him turn to her with the complete dependence of a child, and then I went away and left them, as perplexed a man as any in Scotland. I must say, however, I had this consolation, that my mind was greatly eased about Roland. He might be under a hallucination, but his head was clear enough, and I did not think him so ill as everybody else did. The girls were astonished even at the ease with which I took it. "How do you think he is?" they said in a breath, coming round me, laying hold of me. "Not half so ill as I expected," I said; "not very bad at all."

"Oh, Papa, you are a darling," cried Agatha, kissing me, and crying upon my shoulder; while little Jeanie, who was as pale as Roland, clasped both her arms round mine, and could not speak at all. I knew nothing about it, not half so much as Simson: but they believed in me; they had a feeling that all would go right now. God is very good to you when your children look to you like that. It makes one humble, not proud. I was not worthy of it; and then I recollected that I had to act the part of a father to Roland's ghost, which made me almost laugh, though I might just as well have cried. It was the strangest mission that ever was entrusted to mortal man.

It was then I remembered suddenly the looks of the men when they turned to take the brougham to the stables in the dark that morning: they had not liked it, and the horses had not liked it. I remembered that even in my anxiety about Roland I had heard them tearing along the avenue back to the stables, and had made a memorandum mentally that I must speak of it. It seemed to me that the best thing I could do was to go to the stables now and make a few inquiries. It is impossible to fathom the minds of rustics; there might be some devilry of practical joking, for anything I knew; or they might have some interest in getting up a bad reputation for the Brentwood avenue. It was getting dark by the time I went out, and nobody who knows the country will need to be told how black is the darkness of a November night under high laurel bushes and yew trees. I walked into the heart of the shrubberies two or three times, not seeing a step before me, till I came out upon the broader carriage road, where the trees opened a little, and there was a faint gray glimmer of sky visible, under which the great limes and elms stood darkling like ghosts; but it grew black again as I approached the corner where the ruins lay. Both eyes and ears were on the alert, as may be supposed; but I

could see nothing in the absolute gloom, and, so far as I can recol-
lect, I heard nothing. Nevertheless there came a strong impression
upon me that somebody was there. It is a sensation that most
people have felt. I have seen when it has been strong enough to
awake me out of sleep, the sense of some one looking at me. I
suppose my imagination had been affected by Roland's story; and
the mystery of the darkness is always full of suggestions. I
stamped my feet violently on the gravel to rouse myself, and called
out sharply, "Who's there?" Nobody answered, nor did I expect
any one to answer, but the impression had been made. I was so
foolish that I did not like to look back, but went sideways, keeping an eye on the gloom behind. It was with great relief that I
spied the light in the stables, making a sort of oasis in the darkness. I walked very quickly into the midst of that lighted and
cheerful place, and thought the clank of the groom's pail one of
the pleasantest sounds I had ever heard. The coachman was the
head of this little colony, and it was to his house I went to pursue
my investigations. He was a native of the district, and had taken
care of the place in the absence of the family for years; it was
impossible but that he must know everything that was going on,
and all the traditions of the place. The men, I could see, eyed me
anxiously when I thus appeared at such an hour among them, and
followed me with their eyes to Jarvis's house, where he lived alone
with his old wife, their children being all married and out in the
world. Mrs. Jarvis met me with anxious questions. How was the
poor young gentleman? but the others knew, I could see by their
faces, that not even this was the foremost thing in my mind.

"Noises?—ou ay, there'll be noises—the wind in the trees, and
the water soughing down the glen. As for tramps, Cornel, no,
there's little o' that kind o' cattle about here; and Merran at the
gate's a careful body." Jarvis moved about with some embarrassment from one leg to another as he spoke. He kept in the shade,
and did not look at me more than he could help. Evidently his
mind was perturbed, and he had reasons for keeping his own
counsel. His wife sat by, giving him a quick look now and then,
but saying nothing. The kitchen was very snug, and warm, and
bright—as different as could be from the chill and mystery of the
night outside.

"I think you are trifling with me, Jarvis," I said.

"Triflin', Cornel? No me. What would I trifle for? If the deevil himsel was in the auld hoose, I have no interest in't one way or another——"

"Sandy, hold your peace!" cried his wife imperatively.

"And what am I to hold my peace for, wi' the Cornel standing there asking a' thae questions? I'm saying, if the deevil himsel——"

"And I'm telling ye hold your peace!" cried the woman, in great excitement. "Dark November weather and lang nichts, and us that ken a' we ken. How daur ye name—a name that shouldna be spoken?" She threw down her stocking and got up, also in great agitation. "I tell't ye you never could keep it. It's no a thing that will hide; and the haill toun kens as weel as you or me. Tell the Cornel straight out—or see, I'll do it. I dinna hold wi' your secrets: and a secret that the haill toun kens!" She snapped her fingers with an air of large disdain. As for Jarvis, ruddy and big as he was, he shrank to nothing before this decided woman. He repeated to her two or three times her own adjuration, "Hold your peace!" then, suddenly changing his tone, cried out, "Tell him then, confound ye! I'll wash my hands o't. If a' the ghosts in Scotland were in the auld hoose, is that ony concern o' mine?"

After this I elicited without much difficulty the whole story. In the opinion of the Jarvises, and of everybody about, the certainty that the place was haunted was beyond all doubt. As Sandy and his wife warmed to the tale, one tripping up another in their eagerness to tell everything, it gradually developed as distinct a superstition as I ever heard, and not without poetry and pathos. How long it was since the voice had been heard first, nobody could tell with certainty. Jarvis's opinion was that his father, who had been coachman at Brentwood before him, had never heard anything about it, and that the whole thing had arisen within the last ten years, since the complete dismantling of the old house: which was a wonderfully modern date for a tale so well authenticated. According to these witnesses, and to several whom I questioned afterward, and who were all in perfect agreement, it was only in the months of November and December that "the visitation" occurred. During these months, the darkest of the year, scarcely a night passed without the recurrence of these inexplicable cries. Nothing, it was said, had ever been seen—at least nothing that could be identified. Some people, bolder or more imaginative than the others, had seen the darkness moving, Mrs. Jarvis

said, with unconscious poetry. It began when night fell and continued, at intervals, till day broke. Very often it was only an inarticulate cry and moaning, but sometimes the words which had
taken possession of my poor boy's fancy had been distinctly
audible—"Oh, Mother, let me in!" The Jarvises were not aware
that there had ever been any investigation into it. The estate of
Brentwood had lapsed into the hands of a distant branch of the
family, who had lived but little there; and of the many people who
had taken it, as I had done, few had remained through two
Decembers. And nobody had taken the trouble to make a very
close examination into the facts. "No, no," Jarvis said, shaking
his head, "No, no, Cornel. Wha wad set themsels up for a laughingstock to a' the countryside, making a wark about a ghost?
Naebody believes in ghosts. It bid to be the wind in the trees, the
last gentleman said, or some effec' o' the water wrastlin' among
the rocks. He said it was a' quite easy explained: but he gave up
the hoose. And when you cam, Cornel, we were awfu' anxious
you should never hear. What for should I have spoiled the bargain
and hairmed the property for no-thing?"

"Do you call my child's life nothing?" I said in the trouble of
the moment, unable to restrain myself. "And instead of telling this
all to me, you have told it to him—to a delicate boy, a child unable
to sift evidence, or judge for himself, a tenderhearted young
creature—"

I was walking about the room with an anger all the hotter that I
felt it to be most likely quite unjust. My heart was full of bitterness
against the stolid retainers of a family who were content to risk
other people's children and comfort rather than let the house lie
empty. If I had been warned I might have taken precautions, or
left the place, or sent Roland away, a hundred things which now
I could not do; and here I was with my boy in a brain fever, and
his life the most precious life on earth, hanging in the balance,
dependent on whether or not I could get to the reason of a commonplace ghost story! I paced about in high wrath, not seeing
what I was to do; for, to take Roland away, even if he were able to
travel, would not settle his agitated mind; and I feared even that
a scientific explanation of refracted sound, or reverberation, or
any other of the easy certainties with which we elder men are
silenced, would have very little effect upon the boy.

"Cornel," said Jarvis, solemnly, "and *she'll* bear me witness—

the young gentleman never heard a word from me—no, nor from either groom or gardener; I'll gie ye my word for that. In the first place, he's no a lad that invites ye to talk. There are some that are, and some that arena. Some will draw ye on, till ye've tellt them a' the clatter of the toun, and a' ye ken, and whiles mair. But Maister Roland, his mind's fu' of his books. He's aye civil and kind, and a fine lad; but no that sort. And ye see it's for a' our interest, Cornel, that you should stay at Brentwood. I took it upon me mysel to pass the word—'No a syllable to Maister Roland, nor to the young leddies—no a syllable.' The women servants, that have little reason to be out at night, ken little or nothing about it. And some think it grand to have a ghost so long as they're no in the way of coming across it. If you had been tellt the story to begin with, maybe ye would have thought so yourself."

This was true enough, though it did not throw any light upon my perplexity. If we had heard of it to start with, it is possible that all the family would have considered the possession of a ghost a distinct advantage. It is the fashion of the times. We never think what a risk it is to play with young imaginations, but cry out, in the fashionable jargon, "A ghost!—nothing else was wanted to make it perfect." I should not have been above this myself. I should have smiled, of course, at the idea of the ghost at all, but then to feel that it was mine would have pleased my vanity. Oh, yes, I claim no exemption. The girls would have been delighted. I could fancy their eagerness, their interest, and excitement. No; if we had been told, it would have done no good—we should have made the bargain all the more eagerly, the fools that we are. "And there has been no attempt to investigate it," I said, "to see what it really is?"

"Eh, Cornel," said the coachman's wife, "wha would investigate, as ye call it, a thing that nobody believes in? Ye would be the laughingstock of a' the countryside, as my man says."

"But you believe in it," I said, turning upon her hastily. The woman was taken by surprise. She made a step backward out of my way.

"Lord, Cornel, how ye frichten a body! Me!—there's awful strange things in this world. An unlearned person doesna ken what to think. But the minister and the gentry they just laugh in your face. Inquire into the thing that is not! Na, na, we just let it be."

"Come with me, Jarvis," I said, hastily, "and we'll make an attempt at least. Say nothing to the men or to anybody. I'll come back after dinner, and we'll make a serious attempt to see what it is, if it is anything. If I hear it—which I doubt—you may be sure I shall never rest till I make it out. Be ready for me about ten o'clock."

"Me, Cornel!" Jarvis said, in a faint voice. I had not been looking at him in my own preoccupation, but when I did so, I found that the greatest change had come over the fat and ruddy coachman. "Me, Cornel!" he repeated, wiping the perspiration from his brow. His ruddy face hung in flabby folds, his knees knocked together, his voice seemed half extinguished in his throat. Then he began to rub his hands and smile upon me in a deprecating, imbecile way. "There's nothing I wouldna do to pleasure ye, Cornel," taking a step further back. "I'm sure *she* kens I've aye said I never had to do with a mair fair, weel-spoken gentleman—" Here Jarvis came to a pause, again looking at me, rubbing his hands.

"Well?" I said.

"But eh, sir!" he went on, with the same imbecile yet insinuating smile, "if ye'll reflect that I am no used to my feet. With a horse atween my legs, or the reins in my hand, I'm maybe nae worse than other men; but on fit, Cornel— It's no the—bogles; but I've been cavalry, ye see," with a little hoarse laugh, "a' my life. To face a thing ye didna understan'—on your feet, Cornel."

"Well, sir, if *I* do it," said I tartly, "why shouldn't you?"

"Eh, Cornel, there's an awfu' difference. In the first place, ye tramp about the haill countryside, and think naething of it; but a walk tires me mair than a hunard miles' drive: and then ye'e a gentleman, and do your ain pleasure; and you're no so auld as me; and it's for your ain bairn, ye see, Cornel; and then——"

"He believes in it, Cornel, and you dinna believe in it," the woman said.

"Will you come with me?" I said, turning to her.

She jumped back, upsetting her chair in her bewilderment. "Me!" with a scream, and then fell into a sort of hysterical laugh. "I wouldna say but what I would go; but what would the folk say to hear of Cornel Mortimer with an auld silly woman at his heels?"

The suggestion made me laugh too, though I had little inclination for it. "I'm sorry you have so little spirit, Jarvis," I said. "I must find some one else, I suppose."

Jarvis, touched by this, began to remonstrate, but I cut him short. My butler was a soldier who had been with me in India, and was not supposed to fear anything—man or devil,—certainly not the former; and I felt that I was losing time. The Jarvises were too thankful to get rid of me. They attended me to the door with the most anxious courtesies. Outside, the two grooms stood close by, a little confused by my sudden exit. I don't know if perhaps they had been listening—at least standing as near as possible, to catch any scrap of the conversation. I waved my hand to them as I went past, in answer to their salutations, and it was very apparent to me that they also were glad to see me go.

And it will be thought very strange, but it would be weak not to add, that I myself, though bent on the investigation I have spoken of, pledged to Roland to carry it out, and feeling that my boy's health, perhaps his life, depended on the result of my inquiry,—I felt the most unaccountable reluctance to pass these ruins on my way home. My curiosity was intense; and yet it was all my mind could do to pull my body along. I daresay the scientific people would describe it the other way, and attribute my cowardice to the state of my stomach. I went on; but if I had followed my impulse, I should have turned and bolted. Everything in me seemed to cry out against it; my heart thumped, my pulses all began, like sledge hammers, beating against my ears and every sensitive part. It was very dark, as I have said; the old house, with its shapeless tower, loomed a heavy mass through the darkness, which was only not entirely so solid as itself. On the other hand, the great dark cedars of which we were so proud seemed to fill up the night. My foot strayed out of the path in my confusion and the gloom together, and I brought myself up with a cry as I felt myself knock against something solid. What was it? The contact with hard stone and lime, and prickly bramblebushes restored me a little to myself. "Oh, it's only the old gable," I said aloud, with a little laugh to reassure myself. The rough feeling of the stones reconciled me. As I groped about thus, I shook off my visionary folly. What so easily explained as that I should have strayed from the path in the darkness? This brought me back to common existence, as if I had been shaken by a wise hand out of all the silliness of superstition. How silly it was, after all! What did it matter

which path I took? I laughed again, this time with better heart—
when suddenly, in a moment, the blood was chilled in my veins,
a shiver stole along my spine, my faculties seemed to forsake me.
Close by me at my side, at my feet, there was a sigh. No, not a
groan, not a moaning, not anything so tangible—a perfectly soft,
faint, inarticulate sigh. I sprang back, and my heart stopped beating. Mistaken! no, mistake was impossible. I heard it as clearly
as I hear myself speak; a long, soft, weary sigh, as if drawn to
the utmost, and emptying out a load of sadness that filled the
breast. To hear this in the solitude, in the dark, in the night
(though it was still early), had an effect which I cannot describe.
I feel it now—something cold creeping over me, up into my hair,
and down to my feet, which refused to move. I cried out, with a
trembling voice, "Who is there?" as I had done before—but there
was no reply.

I got home I don't quite know how; but in my mind there was
no longer any indifference as to the thing, whatever it was, that
haunted these ruins. My skepticism disappeared like a mist. I was
as firmly determined that there was something as Roland was.
I did not for a moment pretend to myself that it was possible I
could be deceived; there were movements and noises which I
understood all about, cracklings of small branches in the frost,
and little rolls of gravel on the path, such as have a very eerie
sound sometimes, and perplex you with wonder as to who has
done it, *when there is no real mystery;* but I assure you all these
little movements of nature don't affect you one bit *when there is
something.* I understood *them.* I did not understand the sigh. That
was not simple nature; there was meaning in it—feeling, the soul
of a creature invisible. This is the thing that human nature trembles
at—a creature invisible, yet with sensations, feelings, a power
somehow of expressing itself. I had not the same sense of unwillingness to turn my back upon the scene of the mystery which
I had experienced in going to the stables; but I almost ran home,
impelled by eagerness to get everything done that had to be done
in order to apply myself to finding it out. Bagley was in the hall
as usual when I went in. He was always there in the afternoon,
always with the appearance of perfect occupation, yet, so far as I
know, never doing anything. The door was open, so that I hurried
in without any pause, breathless; but the sight of his calm regard,
as he came to help me off with my overcoat, subdued me in a

moment. Anything out of the way, anything incomprehensible, faded to nothing in the presence of Bagley. You saw and wondered how *he* was made: the parting of his hair, the tie of his white neckcloth, the fit of his trousers, all perfect as works of art; but you could see how they were done, which makes all the difference. I flung myself upon him, so to speak, without waiting to note the extreme unlikeness of the man to anything of the kind I meant. "Bagley," I said, "I want you to come out with me tonight to watch for—"

"Poachers, Colonel," he said, a gleam of pleasure running all over him.

"No, Bagley; a great deal worse," I cried.

"Yes, Colonel; at what hour, sir?" the man said; but then I had not told him what it was.

It was ten o'clock when we set out. All was perfectly quiet indoors. My wife was with Roland, who had been quite calm, she said, and who (though, no doubt, the fever must run its course) had been better since I came. I told Bagley to put on a thick greatcoat over his evening coat, and did the same myself—with strong boots; for the soil was like a sponge, or worse. Talking to him, I almost forgot what we were going to do. It was darker even than it had been before, and Bagley kept very close to me as we went along. I had a small lantern in my hand, which gave us a partial guidance. We had come to the corner where the path turns. On one side was the bowling green, which the girls had taken possession of for their croquet ground—a wonderful enclosure surrounded by high hedges of holly, three hundred years old and more; on the other, the ruins. Both were black as night; but before we got so far, there was a little opening in which we could just discern the trees and the lighter line of the road. I thought it best to pause there and take breath. "Bagley," I said, "there is something about these ruins I don't understand. It is there I am going. Keep your eyes open and your wits about you. Be ready to pounce upon any stranger you see—anything, man or woman. Don't hurt, but seize—anything you see." "Colonel," said Bagley, with a little tremor in his breath, "they do say there's things there—as is neither man nor woman." There was no time for words. "Are you game to follow me, my man? that's the question," I said. Bagley fell in without a word, and saluted. I knew then I had nothing to fear.

We went, so far as I could guess, exactly as I had come, when I heard that sigh. The darkness, however, was so complete that all marks, as of trees or paths, disappeared. One moment we felt our feet on the gravel, another sinking noiselessly into the slippery grass, that was all. I had shut up my lantern, not wishing to scare any one, whoever it might be. Bagley followed, it seemed to me, exactly in my footsteps as I made my way, as I supposed, toward the mass of the ruined house. We seemed to take a long time groping along seeking this; the squash of the wet soil under our feet was the only thing that marked our progress. After a while I stood still to see, or rather feel, where we were. The darkness was very still, but no stiller than is usual in a winter's night. The sounds I mentioned—the crackling of twigs, the roll of a pebble, the sound of some rustle in the dead leaves, or creeping creature on the grass—were audible when you listened, all mysterious enough when your mind is disengaged, but to me cheering now as signs of the livingness of nature, even in the death of the frost. As we stood still, there came up from the trees in the glen the prolonged hoot of an owl. Bagley started with alarm, being in a state of general nervousness, and not knowing what he was afraid of. But to me the sound was encouraging and pleasant, being so comprehensible. "An owl," I said, under my breath. "Y—es, Colonel," said Bagley, his teeth chattering. We stood still about five minutes, while it broke into the still brooding of the air, the sound widening out in circles, dying upon the darkness. This sound, which is not a cheerful one, made me almost gay. It was natural, and relieved the tension of the mind. I moved on with new courage, my nervous excitement calming down.

When all at once, quite suddenly, close to us, at our feet, there broke out a cry. I made a spring backward in the first moment of surprise and horror, and in doing so came sharply against the same rough masonry and brambles that had struck me before. This new sound came upward from the ground—a low, moaning, wailing voice, full of suffering and pain. The contrast between it and the hoot of the owl was indescribable; the one with a wholesome wildness and naturalness that hurt nobody—the other, a sound that made one's blood curdle, full of human misery. With a great deal of fumbling—for in spite of everything I could do to keep up my courage my hands shook—I managed to remove the slide of my lantern. The light leaped out like something living,

and made the place visible in a moment. We were what would
have been inside the ruined building had anything remained but
the gable wall which I have described. It was close to us, the
vacant doorway in it going out straight into the blackness outside.
The light showed the bit of wall, the ivy glistening upon it in
clouds of dark green, the bramble branches waving, and below,
the open door—a door that led to nothing. It was from this the
voice came that died out just as the light flashed upon this strange
scene. There was a moment's silence, and then it broke forth
again. The sound was so near, so penetrating, so pitiful, that, on the
nervous start I gave, the light fell out of my hand. As I groped
for it in the dark my hand was clutched by Bagley, who I think
must have dropped upon his knees; but I was too much perturbed myself to think much of this. He clutched at me in the
confusion of his terror, forgetting all his usual decorum. "For
God's sake, what is it, sir?" he gasped. If I yielded, there was
evidently an end of both of us. "I can't tell," I said, "any more
than you; that's what we've got to find out: up, man, up!" I
pulled him to his feet. "Will you go round and examine the other
side, or will you stay here with the lantern?" Bagley gasped at
me with a face of horror. "Can't we stay together, Colonel?" he
said—his knees were trembling under him. I pushed him against
the corner of the wall, and put the light into his hands. "Stand
fast till I come back; shake yourself together, man; let nothing
pass you," I said. The voice was within two or three feet of us, of
that there could be no doubt.

I went myself to the other side of the wall, keeping close to it.
The light shook in Bagley's hand, but, tremulous though it was,
shone out through the vacant door, one oblong block of light
marking all the crumbling corners and hanging masses of foliage.
Was that something dark huddled in a heap by the side of it? I
pushed forward across the light in the doorway, and fell upon it
with my hands; but it was only a juniper bush growing close
against the wall. Meanwhile, the sight of my figure crossing the
doorway had brought Bagley's nervous excitement to a height:
he flew at me, gripping my shoulder. "I've got him, Colonel! I've
got him!" he cried, with a voice of sudden exultation. He thought
it was a man, and was at once relieved. But at that moment the
voice burst forth again between us, at our feet—more close to us
than any separate being could be. He dropped off from me, and fell

against the wall, his jaw dropping as if he were dying. I suppose, at the same moment, he saw that it was me whom he had clutched. I, for my part, had scarcely more command of myself. I snatched the light out of his hand, and flashed it all about me wildly. Nothing,—the juniper bush which I thought I had never seen before, the heavy growth of the glistening ivy, the brambles waving. It was close to my ears now, crying, crying, pleading as if for life. Either I heard the same words Roland had heard, or else, in my excitement, his imagination got possession of mine. The voice went on, growing into distinct articulation, but wavering about, now from one point, now from another, as if the owner of it were moving slowly back and forward.—"Mother! Mother!" and then an outburst of wailing. As my mind steadied, getting accustomed (as one's mind gets accustomed to anything), it seemed to me as if some uneasy, miserable creature was pacing up and down before a closed door. Sometimes—but that must have been excitement—I thought I heard a sound like knocking, and then another burst, "Oh, Mother! Mother!" All this close, close to the space where I was standing with my lantern—now before me, now behind me: a creature restless, unhappy, moaning, crying, before the vacant doorway, which no one could either shut or open more.

"Do you hear it, Bagley? do you hear what it is saying?" I cried, stepping in through the doorway. He was lying against the wall— his eyes glazed, half dead with terror. He made a motion of his lips as if to answer me, but no sounds came; then lifted his hand with a curious imperative movement as if ordering me to be silent and listen. And how long I did so I cannot tell. It began to have an interest, an exciting hold upon me, which I could not describe. It seemed to call up visibly a scene any one could understand—a something shut out, restlessly wandering to and fro; sometimes the voice dropped, as if throwing itself down—sometimes wandered off a few paces, growing sharp and clear. "Oh, Mother, let me in! Oh, Mother, Mother, let me in! Oh, let me in!" Every word was clear to me. No wonder the boy had gone wild with pity. I tried to steady my mind upon Roland, upon his conviction that I could do something, but my head swam with the excitement, even when I partially overcame the terror. At last the words died away, and there was a sound of sobs and moaning. I cried out, "In the name of God who are you?" with a kind of feeling in my mind that to use the name of God was profane, seeing that I did not believe in

ghosts or anything supernatural; but I did it all the same, and
waited, my heart giving a leap of terror lest there should be a reply.
Why this should have been I cannot tell, but I had a feeling that if
there was an answer it would be more than I could bear. But there
was no answer; the moaning went on, and then, as if it had been
real, the voice rose, a little higher again, the words recommenced,
"Oh, Mother, let me in! Oh, Mother, let me in!" with an expression
that was heartbreaking to hear.

As if it had been real! What do I mean by that? I suppose I got
less alarmed as the thing went on. I began to recover the use of my
senses—I seemed to explain it all to myself by saying that this had
once happened, that it was a recollection of a real scene. Why
there should have seemed something quite satisfactory and compos-
ing in this explanation I cannot tell, but so it was. I began to listen
almost as if it had been a play, forgetting Bagley, who, I almost
think, had fainted, leaning against the wall. I was startled out of
this strange spectatorship that had fallen upon me by the sudden
rush of something which made my heart jump once more, a large
black figure in the doorway waving its arms. "Come in! come in!
come in!" it shouted out hoarsely at the top of a deep bass voice,
and then poor Bagley fell down senseless across the threshold. He
was less sophisticated than I,—he had not been able to bear it any
longer. I took him for something supernatural, as he took me, and
it was some time before I awoke to the necessities of the moment.
I remembered only after, that from the time I began to give my attention to the man, I heard the other voice no more. It was some
time before I brought him to. It must have been a strange scene;
the lantern making a luminous spot in the darkness, the man's
white face lying on the black earth, I over him, doing what I
could for him. Probably I should have been thought to be murder-
ing him had any one seen us. When at last I succeeded in pouring a
little brandy down his throat he sat up and looked about him wildly.
"What's up?" he said; then recognizing me, tried to struggle to his
feet with a faint "Beg your pardon, Colonel." I got him home as
best I could, making him lean upon my arm. The great fellow was
as weak as a child. Fortunately he did not for some time remember
what had happened. From the time Bagley fell the voice had
stopped, and all was still.

"You've got an epidemic in your house, Colonel," Simson said to me next morning. "What's the meaning of it all? Here's your butler raving about a voice. This will never do, you know; and so far as I can make out, you are in it too."

"Yes, I am in it, doctor. I thought I had better speak to you. Of course you are treating Roland all right—but the boy is not raving, he is as sane as you or me. It's all true."

"As sane as—I—or you. I never thought the boy insane. He's got cerebral excitement, fever. I don't know what you've got. There's something very queer about the look of your eyes."

"Come," said I, "you can't put us all to bed, you know. You had better listen and hear the symptoms in full."

The doctor shrugged his shoulders, but he listened to me patiently. He did not believe a word of the story, that was clear; but he heard it all from beginning to end. "My dear fellow," he said, "the boy told me just the same. It's an epidemic. When one person falls a victim to this sort of thing, it's as safe as can be—there's always two or three."

"Then how do you account for it?" I said.

"Oh, account for it!—that's a different matter; there's no accounting for the freaks our brains are subject to. If it's delusion; if it's some trick of the echoes or the winds—some phonetic disturbance or other——"

"Come with me tonight, and judge for yourself," I said.

Upon this he laughed aloud, then said, "That's not such a bad idea; but it would ruin me for ever if it were known that John Simson was ghost hunting."

"There it is," said I; "you dart down on us who are unlearned with your phonetic disturbances, but you daren't examine what the thing really is for fear of being laughed at. That's science!"

"It's not science—it's common sense," said the doctor. "The thing has delusion on the front of it. It is encouraging an unwholesome tendency even to examine. What good could come of it? Even if I am convinced, I shouldn't believe."

"I should have said so yesterday; and I don't want you to be convinced or to believe," said I. "If you prove it to be a delusion, I shall be very much obliged to you for one. Come; somebody must go with me."

"You are cool," said the doctor. "You've disabled this poor fellow of yours, and made him—on that point—a lunatic for life; and now you want to disable me. But for once, I'll do it. To save appearance, if you'll give me a bed, I'll come over after my last rounds."

It was agreed that I should meet him at the gate, and that we should visit the scene of last night's occurrences before we came to the house, so that nobody might be the wiser. It was scarcely possible to hope that the cause of Bagley's sudden illness should not somehow steal into the knowledge of the servants at least, and it was better that all should be done as quietly as possible. The day seemed to me a very long one. I had to spend a certain part of it with Roland, which was a terrible ordeal for me—for what could I say to the boy? The improvement continued, but he was still in a very precarious state, and the trembling vehemence with which he turned to me when his mother left the room filled me with alarm. "Father!" he said, quietly. "Yes, my boy; I am giving my best attention to it—all is being done that I can do. I have not come to any conclusion—yet. I am neglecting nothing you said," I cried. What I could not do was to give his active mind any encouragement to dwell upon the mystery. It was a hard predicament, for some satisfaction had to be given him. He looked at me very wistfully, with the great blue eyes that shone so large and brilliant out of his white and worn face. "You must trust me," I said. "Yes, Father. Father understands," he said to himself, as if to soothe some inward doubt. I left him as soon as I could. He was about the most precious thing I had on earth, and his health my first thought; but yet somehow, in the excitement of this other subject, I put that aside, and preferred not to dwell upon Roland, which was the most curious part of it all.

That night at eleven I met Simson at the gate. He had come by train, and I let him in gently myself. I had been so much absorbed in the coming experiment that I passed the ruins in going to meet him, almost without thought, if you can understand that. I had my lantern; and he showed me a coil of taper which he had ready for use. "There is nothing like light," he said, in his scoffing tone. It was a very still night, scarcely a sound, but not so dark. We could keep the path without difficulty as we went along. As we approached the spot we could hear a low moaning, broken occasionally by a bitter cry. "Perhaps that is your voice," said the doctor; "I thought it must be something of the kind. That's a poor brute caught in some of these infernal traps of yours; you'll find it among the bushes somewhere." I said nothing. I felt no

particular fear, but a triumphant satisfaction in what was to follow.
I led him to the spot where Bagley and I had stood on the previous
night. All was silent as a winter night could be—so silent that we
heard far off the sound of the horses in the stables, the shutting of
a window at the house. Simson lighted his taper and went peering
about, poking into all the corners. We looked like two conspirators
lying in wait for some unfortunate traveler; but not a sound broke
the quiet. The moaning had stopped before we came up; a star or
two shone over us in the sky, looking down as if surprised at our
strange proceedings. Dr. Simson did nothing but utter subdued
laughs under his breath. "I thought as much," he said. "It is just
the same with tables and all other kinds of ghostly apparatus; a
skeptic's presence stops everything. When I am present nothing
ever comes off. How long do you think it will be necessary to stay
here? Oh, I don't complain; only, when *you* are satisfied, *I* am—
quite."

I will not deny that I was disappointed beyond measure by this
result. It made me look like a credulous fool. It gave the doctor
such a pull over me as nothing else could. I should point all his
morals for years to come, and his materialism, his skepticism, would
be increased beyond endurance. "It seems, indeed," I said, "that
there is to be no——" "Manifestation," he said, laughing; "that is
what all the mediums say. No manifestations, in consequence of
the presence of an unbeliever." His laugh sounded very uncomfortable to me in the silence; and it was now near midnight. But that
laugh seemed the signal; before it died away the moaning we had
heard before was resumed. It started from some distance off, and
came toward us, nearer and nearer, like some one walking along
and moaning to himself. There could be no idea now that it was a
hare caught in a trap. The approach was slow, like that of a weak
person with little halts and pauses. We heard it coming along the
grass straight toward the vacant doorway. Simson had been a little
startled by the first sound. He said hastily, "That child has no business to be out so late." But he felt, as well as I, that this was no
child's voice. As it came nearer, he grew silent, and, going to the
doorway with his taper, stood looking out toward the sound. The
taper being unprotected blew in the night air, though there was
scarcely any wind. I threw the light of my lantern steady and white
across the same space. It was a blaze of light in the midst of the
blackness. A little icy thrill had gone over me at the first sound, but

as it came close, I confess that the only feeling was satisfaction. The scoffer could scoff no more. The light touched his own face, and showed a very perplexed countenance. If he was afraid, he concealed it with great success, but he was perplexed. And then all that had happened on the previous night was enacted once more. It fell strangely upon me with a sense of repetition. Every cry, every sob seemed the same as before. I listened almost without any emotion at all in my own person, thinking of its effect upon Simson. He maintained a very bold front on the whole. All that coming and going of the voice was, if our ears could be trusted, exactly in front of the vacant, blank doorway, blazing full of light, which caught and shone in the glistening leaves of the great hollies at a little distance. Not a rabbit could have crossed the turf without being seen;—but there was nothing. After a time, Simson, with a certain caution and bodily reluctance, as it seemed to me, went out with his roll of taper into this space. His figure showed against the holly in full outline. Just at this moment the voice sank, as was its custom, and seemed to fling itself down at the door. Simson recoiled violently, as if some one had come up against him, then turned, and held his taper low as if examining something. "Do you see anybody?" I cried in a whisper, feeling the chill of nervous panic steal over me at this action. "It's nothing but a——confounded juniper bush," he said. This I knew very well to be nonsense, for the juniper bush was on the other side. He went about after this, round and round, poking his taper everywhere, then returned to me on the inner side of the wall. He scoffed no longer; his face was contracted and pale. "How long does this go on?" he whispered to me, like a man who does not wish to interrupt some one who is speaking. I had become too much perturbed myself to remark whether the successions and changes of the voice were the same as last night. It suddenly went out in the air almost as he was speaking, with a soft reiterated sob dying away. If there had been anything to be seen, I should have said that the person was at that moment crouching on the ground close to the door.

We walked home very silent afterward. It was only when we were in sight of the house that I said, "What do you think of it?" "I can't tell what to think of it," he said, quickly. He took—though he was a very temperate man—not the claret I was going to offer him, but some brandy from the tray, and swallowed it almost undiluted. "Mind you, I don't believe a word of it," he said, when he had lighted his candle; "but I can't tell what to think," he turned round to add, when he was half way upstairs.

All of this, however, did me no good with the solution of my problem. I was to help this weeping, sobbing thing, which was already to me as distinct a personality as anything I knew—or what should I say to Roland? It was on my heart that my boy would die if I could not find some way of helping this creature. You may be surprised that I should speak of it in this way. I did not know if it was man or woman; but I no more doubted that it was a soul in pain than I doubted my own being; and it was my business to soothe this pain—to deliver it, if that was possible. Was ever such a task given to an anxious father trembling for his only boy? I felt in my heart, fantastic as it may appear, that I must fulfill this somehow, or part with my child; and you may conceive that rather than do that I was ready to die. But even my dying would not have advanced me—unless by bringing me into the same world with that seeker at the door.

Next morning Simson was out before breakfast, and came in with evident signs of the damp grass on his boots, and a look of worry and weariness, which did not say much for the night he had passed. He improved a little after breakfast, and visited his two patients, for Bagley was still an invalid. I went out with him on his way to the train, to hear what he had to say about the boy. "He is going on very well," he said; "there are no complications as yet. But mind you, that's not a boy to be trifled with, Mortimer. Not a word to him about last night." I had to tell him then of my last interview with Roland, and of the impossible demand he had made upon me —by which, though he tried to laugh, he was much discomposed, as I could see. "We must just perjure ourselves all round," he said, "and swear you exorcized it"; but the man was too kindhearted to be satisfied with that. "It's frightfully serious for you, Mortimer. I can't laugh as I should like to. I wish I saw a way out of it, for your sake. By the way," he added shortly, "didn't you notice that juniper bush on the left-hand side?" "There was one on the right hand of the door. I noticed you made that mistake last night." "Mistake!" he cried, with a curious low laugh, pulling up the collar of his coat as though he felt the cold,—"there's no juniper there this morning, left or right. Just go and see." As he stepped into the train a few minutes after, he looked back upon me and

beckoned me for a parting word. "I'm coming back tonight,"
he said.

I don't think I had any feeling about this as I turned away from
that common bustle of the railway which made my private pre-
occupations feel so strangely out of date. There had been a distinct
satisfaction in my mind before that his skepticism had been so
entirely defeated. But the more serious part of the matter pressed
upon me now. I went straight from the railway to the manse, which
stood on a little plateau on the side of the river opposite to the
woods of Brentwood. The minister was one of a class which is not
so common in Scotland as it used to be. He was a man of good
family, well educated in the Scotch way, strong in philosophy, not
so strong in Greek, strongest of all in experience,—a man who had
"come across," in the course of his life, most people of note that
had ever been in Scotland—and who was said to be very sound in
doctrine, without infringing the toleration with which old men, who
are good men, are generally endowed. He was old-fashioned; perhaps he did not think so much about the troublesome problems of
theology as many of the young men, nor ask himself any hard
questions about the Confession of Faith—but he understood human
nature, which is perhaps better. He received me with a cordial
welcome. "Come away, Colonel Mortimer," he said; "I'm all the
more glad to see you, that I feel it's a good sign for the boy. He's
doing well?—God be praised—and the Lord bless him and keep
him. He has many a poor body's prayers—and that can do nobody
harm."

"He will need them all, Dr. Moncrieff," I said, "and your counsel
too." And I told him the story—more than I had told Simson. The
old clergyman listened to me with many suppressed exclamations,
and at the end the water stood in his eyes.

"That's just beautiful," he said. "I do not mind to have heard
anything like it; it's as fine as Burns when he wished deliverance
to one—that is prayed for in no kirk. Ay, ay! so he would have you
console the poor lost spirit? God bless the boy! There's something
more than common in that, Colonel Mortimer. And also the faith
of him in his father!—I would like to put that into a sermon." Then
the old gentleman gave me an alarmed look, and said, "No, no; I
was not meaning a sermon; but I must write it down for the *Children's Record*." I saw the thought that passed through his mind.

Either he thought, or he feared I would think, of a funeral sermon.
You may believe this did not make me more cheerful.

I can scarcely say that Dr. Moncrieff gave me any advice. How
could any one advise on such a subject? But he said, "I think I'll
come too. I'm an old man; I'm less liable to be frightened than
those that are further off the world unseen. It behoves me to
think of my own journey there. I've no cut-and-dry beliefs on the
subject. I'll come too: and maybe at the moment the Lord will put
into our heads what to do."

This gave me a little comfort—more than Simson had given me.
To be clear about the cause of it was not my grand desire. It was
another thing that was in my mind—my boy. As for the poor soul
at the open door, I had no more doubt, as I have said, of its existence than I had of my own. It was no ghost to me. I knew the
creature, and it was in trouble. That was my feeling about it, as it
was Roland's. To hear it first was a great shock to my nerves, but
not now; a man will get accustomed to anything. But to do something for it was the great problem; how was I to be serviceable to a
being that was invisible, that was mortal no longer? "Maybe at
the moment the Lord will put it into our heads." This is very
old-fashioned phraseology, and a week before, most likely, I
should have smiled (though always with kindness) at Dr. Moncrieff's credulity; but there was a great comfort, whether rational
or otherwise I cannot say, in the mere sound of the words.

The road to the station and the village lay through the glen—
not by the ruins; but though the sunshine and the fresh air, and
the beauty of the trees, and the sound of the water were all very
soothing to the spirits, my mind was so full of my own subject
that I could not refrain from turning to the right hand as I got to the
top of the glen, and going straight to the place which I may call the
scene of all my thoughts. It was lying full in the sunshine, like all
the rest of the world. The ruined gable looked due east, and in
the present aspect of the sun the light streamed down through the
doorway as our lantern had done, throwing a flood of light upon
the damp grass beyond. There was a strange suggestion in the
open door—so futile, a kind of emblem of vanity—all free around,
so that you could go where you pleased, and yet that semblance
of an enclosure—that way of entrance, unnecessary, leading to
nothing. And why any creature should pray and weep to get in—to
nothing: or be kept out—by nothing! You could not dwell upon it,

or it made your brain go round. I remembered, however, what
Simson said about the juniper, with a little smile on my own mind
as to the inaccuracy of recollection, which even a scientific man
will be guilty of. I could see now the light of my lantern gleaming
upon the wet glistening surface of the spiky leaves at the right
hand—and he ready to go to the stake for it that it was the left! I
went round to make sure. And then I saw what he had said. Right
or left there was no juniper at all. I was confounded by this, though
it was entirely a matter of detail: nothing at all: a bush of brambles
waving, the grass growing up to the very walls. But after all, though
it gave me a shock for a moment, what did that matter? There were
marks as if a number of footsteps had been up and down in front
of the door; but these might have been our steps; and all was
bright, and peaceful, and still. I poked about the other ruin—the
larger ruins of the old house—for some time, as I had done before.
There were marks upon the grass here and there, I could not call
them footsteps, all about; but that told for nothing one way or
another. I had examined the ruined rooms closely the first day.
They were half filled up with soil and debris, withered brackens and
bramble—no refuge for any one there. It vexed me that Jarvis
should see me coming from that spot when he came up to me for
his orders. I don't know whether my nocturnal expeditions had got
wind among the servants. But there was a significant look in his
face. Something in it I felt was like my own sensation when Simson
in the midst of his skepticism was struck dumb. Jarvis felt satisfied
that his veracity had been put beyond question. I never spoke to a
servant of mine in such a peremptory tone before. I sent him away
"with a flea in his lug," as the man described it afterward. Interference of any kind was intolerable to me at such a moment.

But what was strangest of all was, that I could not face Roland.
I did not go up to his room as I would have naturally done at once.
This the girls could not understand. They saw there was some
mystery in it. "Mother has gone to lie down," Agatha said; "he has
had such a good night." "But he wants you so, Papa!" cried little
Jeanie, always with her two arms embracing mine in a pretty
way she had. I was obliged to go at last—but what could I say? I
could only kiss him, and tell him to keep still—that I was doing all
I could. There is something mystical about the patience of a child.
"It will come all right, won't it, Father?" he said. "God grant it
may! I hope so, Roland." "Oh yes, it will come all right." Perhaps

he understood that in the midst of my anxiety I could not stay with
him as I should have done otherwise. But the girls were more
surprised than it is possible to describe. They looked at me with
wondering eyes. "If I were ill, Papa, and you only stayed with me a
moment, I should break my heart," said Agatha. But the boy had
a sympathetic feeling. He knew that of my own will I would not
have done it. I shut myself up in the library, where I could not
rest, but kept pacing up and down like a caged beast. What could
I do? and if I could do nothing, what would become of my
boy? These were the questions that, without ceasing, pursued each
other through my mind.

Simson came out to dinner, and when the house was still, and
most of the servants in bed, we went out and met Dr. Moncrieff,
as we had appointed, at the head of the glen. Simson, for his part,
was disposed to scoff at the doctor. "If there are to be any spells,
you know, I'll cut the whole concern," he said. I did not make him
any reply. I had not invited him; he could go or come as he pleased.
He was very talkative, far more than suited my humor, as we went
on. "One thing is certain, you know, there must be some human
agency," he said. "It is all bosh about apparitions. I never have
investigated the laws of sound to any great extent, and there's a
great deal in ventriloquism that we don't know much about." "If
it's the same to you," I said, "I wish you'd keep all that to yourself, Simson. It doesn't suit my state of mind." "Oh, I hope I know
how to respect idiosyncrasy," he said. The very tone of his voice
irritated me beyond measure. These scientific fellows, I wonder
people put up with them as they do, when you have no mind for
their cold-blooded confidence. Dr. Moncrieff met us about
eleven o'clock, the same time as on the previous night. He was a
large man, with a venerable countenance and white hair—old,
but in full vigor, and thinking less of a cold night walk than many
a younger man. He had his lantern as I had. We were fully provided with means of lighting the place, and we were all of us
resolute men. We had a rapid consultation as we went up, and the
result was that we divided to different posts. Dr. Moncrieff remained inside the wall—if you can call that inside where there was
no wall but one. Simson placed himself on the side next the ruins,
so as to intercept any communication with the old house, which
was what his mind was fixed upon. I was posted on the other
side. To say that nothing could come near without being seen

was self-evident. It had been so also on the previous night. Now, with our three lights in the midst of the darkness, the whole place seemed illuminated. Dr. Moncrieff's lantern, which was a large one, without any means of shutting up—an old-fashioned lantern with a pierced and ornamental top—shone steadily, the rays shooting out of it upward into the gloom. He placed it on the grass, where the middle of the room, if this had been a room, would have been. The usual effect of the light streaming out of the doorway was prevented by the illumination which Simson and I on either side supplied. With these differences, everything seemed as on the previous night.

And what occurred was exactly the same, with the same air of repetition, point for point, as I had formerly remarked. I declare that it seemed to me as if I were pushed against, put aside, by the owner of the voice as he paced up and down in his trouble,— though these are perfectly futile words, seeing that the stream of light from my lantern, and that from Simson's taper, lay broad and clear, without a shadow, without the smallest break, across the entire breadth of the grass. I had ceased even to be alarmed, for my part. My heart was rent with pity and trouble—pity for the poor suffering human creature that moaned and pleaded so, and trouble for myself and my boy. God! if I could not find any help— and what help could I find?—Roland would die.

We were all perfectly still till the first outburst was exhausted, as I knew (by experience) it would be. Dr. Moncrieff, to whom it was new, was quite motionless on the other side of the wall, as we were in our places. My heart had remained almost at its usual beating during the voice. I was used to it; it did not rouse all my pulses as it did at first. But just as it threw itself sobbing at the door (I cannot use other words), there suddenly came something which sent the blood coursing through my veins and my heart into my mouth. It was a voice inside the wall—the minister's well-known voice. I would have been prepared for it in any kind of adjuration, but I was not prepared for what I heard. It came out with a sort of stammering, as if too much moved for utterance. "Willie, Willie! Oh, God preserve us! is it you?"

These simple words had an effect upon me that the voice of the invisible creature had ceased to have. I thought the old man, whom I had brought into this danger, had gone mad with terror. I made a dash round to the other side of the wall, half crazed myself with the thought. He was standing where I had left him, his shadow thrown vague and large upon the grass by the lantern which stood at his feet. I lifted my own light to see his face as I rushed forward. He was very pale, his eyes wet and glistening, his mouth quivering with parted lips. He neither saw nor heard me. We that had gone through this experience before, had crouched toward each other to get a little strength to bear it. But he was not even aware that I was there. His whole being seemed absorbed in anxiety and tenderness. He held out his hands, which trembled, but it seemed to me with eagerness, not fear. He went on speaking all the time. "Willie, if it is you—and it's you, if it is not a delusion of Satan,—Willie, lad! why come ye here fighting them that know you not? Why come ye not to me?"

He seemed to wait for an answer. When his voice ceased, his countenance, every line moving, continued to speak. Simson gave me another terrible shock, stealing into the open doorway with his light, as much awe-stricken, as wildly curious, as I. But the minister resumed, without seeing Simson, speaking to some one else. His voice took a tone of expostulation—

"Is this right to come here? Your mother's gone with your name on her lips. Do you think she would ever close her door on her own lad? Do ye think the Lord will close the door, ye fainthearted creature? No!—I forbid ye! I forbid ye!" cried the old man. The sobbing voice had begun to resume its cries. He made a step forward, calling out the last words in a voice of command. "I forbid ye! Cry out no more to man. Go home, ye wandering spirit! go home! Do you hear me?—me that christened ye, that have struggled with ye, that have wrestled for ye with the Lord!" Here the loud tones of his voice sank into tenderness. "And her too, poor woman! poor woman! her you are calling upon. She's not here. You'll find her with the Lord. Go there and seek her, not here. Do you hear me, lad? go after her there. He'll let you in, though it's late. Man, take heart! if you will lie and sob and greet, let it be at heaven's gate, and not your poor mother's ruined door."

He stopped to get his breath: and the voice had stopped, not as it had done before, when its time was exhausted and all its repetitions said, but with a sobbing catch in the breath as if overruled. Then the minister spoke again, "Are you hearing me, Will? Oh, laddie, you've liked the beggarly elements all your days. Be done with them now. Go home to the Father—the Father! Are you hear-

ing me?" Here the old man sank down upon his knees, his face
raised upward, his hands held up with a tremble in them, all white
in the light in the midst of the darkness. I resisted as long as I could,
though I cannot tell why,—then I, too, dropped upon my knees.
Simson all the time stood in the doorway, with an expression in his
face such as words could not tell, his underlip dropped, his eyes
wild, staring. It seemed to be to him, that image of blank ignorance
and wonder, that we were praying. All the time the voice, with a
low arrested sobbing, lay just where he was standing, as I thought.

"Lord," the minister said—"Lord, take him into Thy everlasting
habitations. The mother he cries to is with Thee. Who can open
to him but Thee? Lord, when is it too late for Thee, or what is too
hard for Thee? Lord, let the woman there draw him inower! Let
her draw him inower!"

I sprang forward to catch something in my arms that flung itself wildly within the door. The illusion was so strong, that I never
paused till I felt my forehead graze against the wall and my hands
clutch the ground—for there was nobody there to save from falling,
as in my foolishness I thought. Simson held out his hand to me to
help me up. He was trembling and cold, his lower lip hanging, his
speech almost inarticulate. "It's gone," he said, stammering—"it's
gone!" We leant upon each other for a moment, trembling so much
both of us that the whole scene trembled as if it were going to dis-
solve and disappear; and yet as long as I live I will never forget it
—the shining of the strange lights, the blackness all round, the
kneeling figure with all the whiteness of the light concentrated on
its white venerable head and uplifted hands. A strange solemn
stillness seemed to close all round us. By intervals a single syllable,
"Lord! Lord!" came from the old minister's lips. He saw none of
us, nor thought of us. I never knew how long we stood, like senti-
nels guarding him at his prayers, holding our lights in a confused
dazed way, not knowing what we did. But at last he rose from his
knees, and standing up at his full height, raised his arms, as the
Scotch manner is at the end of a religious service, and solemnly
gave the apostolical benediction—to what? to the silent earth, the
dark woods, the wide breathing atmosphere—for we were but spec-
tators gasping an Amen!

It seemed to me that it must be the middle of the night, as we
all walked back. It was in reality very late. Dr. Moncrieff put his
arm into mine. He walked slowly, with an air of exhaustion. It

was as if we were coming from a deathbed. Something hushed and solemnized the very air. There was that sense of relief in it which there always is at the end of a death struggle. And nature persistent, never daunted, came back in all of us, as we returned into the ways of life. We said nothing to each other, indeed, for a time; but when we got clear of the trees and reached the opening near the house, where we could see the sky, Dr. Moncrieff himself was the first to speak. "I must be going," he said; "it's very late, I'm afraid. I will go down the glen, as I came."

"But not alone. I am going with you, doctor."

"Well, I will not oppose it. I am an old man, and agitation wearies more than work. Yes; I'll be thankful of your arm. Tonight, Colonel, you've done me more good turns than one."

I pressed his hand on my arm, not feeling able to speak. But Simson, who turned with us, and who had gone along all this time with his taper flaring, in entire unconsciousness, came to himself, apparently at the sound of our voices, and put out that wild little torch with a quick movement, as if of shame. "Let me carry your lantern," he said; "it is heavy." He recovered with a spring, and in a moment, from the awe-stricken spectator he had been, became himself, skeptical and cynical. "I should like to ask you a question," he said. "Do you believe in purgatory, Doctor? It's not in the tenets of the Church, so far as I know."

"Sir," said Dr. Moncrieff, "an old man like me is sometimes not very sure what he believes. There is just one thing I am certain of —and that is the loving-kindness of God."

"But I thought that was in this life. I am no theologian——"

"Sir," said the old man again, with a tremor in him which I could feel going over all his frame, "if I saw a friend of mine within the gates of hell, I would not despair but his Father would take him by the hand still—if he cried like *yon.*"

"I allow it is very strange—very strange. I cannot see through it. That there must be human agency, I feel sure. Doctor, what made you decide upon the person and the name?"

The minister put out his hand with the impatience which a man might show if he were asked how he recognized his brother. "Tuts!" he said, in familiar speech—then more solemnly, "how should I not recognize a person that I know better—far better— than I know you?"

"Then you saw the man?"

Dr. Moncrieff made no reply. He moved his hand again with a little impatient movement, and walked on, leaning heavily on my arm. And we went on for a long time without another word, threading the dark paths, which were steep and slippery with the damp of the winter. The air was very still—not more than enough to make a faint sighing in the branches, which mingled with the sound of the water to which we were descending. When we spoke again, it was about indifferent matters—about the height of the river, and the recent rains. We parted with the minister at his own door, where his old housekeeper appeared in great perturbation, waiting for him. "Eh me, Minister! the young gentleman will be worse?" she cried.

"Far from that—better. God bless him!" Dr. Moncrieff said.

I think if Simson had begun again to me with his questions, I should have pitched him over the rocks as we returned up the glen; but he was silent, by a good inspiration. And the sky was clearer than it had been for many nights, shining high over the trees, with here and there a star faintly gleaming through the wilderness of dark and bare branches. The air, as I have said, was very soft in them, with a subdued and peaceful cadence. It was real, like every natural sound, and came to us like a hush of peace and relief. I thought there was a sound in it as of the breath of a sleeper, and it seemed clear to me that Roland must be sleeping, satisfied and calm. We went up to his room when we went in. There we found the complete hush of rest. My wife looked up out of a doze, and gave me a smile; "I think he is a great deal better: but you are very late," she said in a whisper, shading the light with her hand that the doctor might see his patient. The boy had got back something like his own color. He woke as we stood all round his bed. His eyes had the happy half-awakened look of childhood, glad to shut again, yet pleased with the interruption and glimmer of the light. I stooped over him and kissed his forehead, which was moist and cool. "All is well, Roland," I said. He looked up at me with a glance of pleasure, and took my hand and laid his cheek upon it, and so went to sleep.

For some nights after, I watched among the ruins, spending all the dark hours up to midnight patrolling about the bit of wall which was associated with so many emotions; but I heard nothing, and saw nothing beyond the quiet course of nature: nor, so far as I

am aware, has anything been heard again. Dr. Moncrieff gave me
the history of the youth, whom he never hesitated to name. I did
not ask, as Simson did, how he recognized him. He had been a
prodigal—weak, foolish, easily imposed upon, and "led away," as
people say. All that we had heard had passed actually in life, the
doctor said. The young man had come home thus a day or two
after his mother died—who was no more than the housekeeper in
the old house—and distracted with the news, had thrown himself
down at the door and called upon her to let him in. The old man
could scarcely speak of it for tears. To me it seemed as if—heaven
help us, how little do we know about anything!—a scene like that
might impress itself somehow upon the hidden heart of nature. I
do not pretend to know how, but the repetition had struck me at
the time as, in its terrible strangeness and incomprehensibility, almost mechanical—as if the unseen actor could not exceed or vary,
but was bound to re-enact the whole. One thing that struck me,
however, greatly, was the likeness between the old minister and
my boy in the manner of regarding these strange phenomena. Dr.
Moncrieff was not terrified, as I had been myself, and all the rest
of us. It was no "ghost," as I fear we all vulgarly considered it, to
him—but a poor creature whom he knew under these conditions,
just as he had known him in the flesh, having no doubt of his identity. And to Roland it was the same. This spirit in pain—if it was a
spirit—this voice out of the unseen—was a poor fellow creature in
misery, to be succored and helped out of his trouble, to my boy.
He spoke to me quite frankly about it when he got better. "I knew
Father would find out some way," he said. And this was when he
was strong and well, and all idea that he would turn hysterical or
become a seer of visions had happily passed away.

I must add one curious fact that does not seem to me to have
any relation to the above, but which Simson made great use of, as
the human agency which he was determined to find somehow.
We had examined the ruins very closely at the time of these occurrences; but afterward, when all was over, as we went casually
about them one Sunday afternoon in the idleness of that unem-
ployed day, Simson with his stick penetrated an old window which
had been entirely blocked up with fallen soil. He jumped down into
it in great excitement, and called me to follow. There we found a

little hole—for it was more a hole than a room—entirely hidden
under the ivy ruins, in which there was a quantity of straw laid in
a corner, as if someone had made a bed there, and some remains
of crusts about the floor. Someone had lodged there, and not very
long before, he made out; and that this unknown being was the
author of all the mysterious sounds we heard he is convinced. "I
told you it was human agency," he said, triumphantly. He forgets,
I suppose, how he and I stood with our lights seeing nothing, while
the space between us was audibly traversed by something that
could speak, and sob, and suffer. There is no argument with men
of this kind. He is ready to get up a laugh against me on this slen-
der ground. "I was puzzled myself—I could not make it out—but I
always felt convinced human agency was at the bottom of it. And
here it is—and a clever fellow he must have been," the doctor says.

Bagley left my service as soon as he got well. He assured me it
was no want of respect; but he could not stand "them kind of
things," and the man was so shaken and ghastly that I was glad to
give him a present and let him go. For my own part, I made a point
of staying out the time, two years, for which I had taken Brentwood; but I did not renew my tenancy. But that time we had settled, and found for ourselves a pleasant home of our own.

I must add that when the doctor defies me, I can always bring
back gravity to his countenance, and a pause in his railing, when I
remind him of the juniper bush. To me that was a matter of little
importance. I could believe I was mistaken. I did not care about it
one way or other; but on his mind the effect was different. The
miserable voice, the spirit in pain, he could think of as the result of
ventriloquism, or reverberation, or—anything you please: an elaborate prolonged hoax executed somehow by the tramp that had
found a lodging in the old tower. But the juniper bush staggered
him. Things have effects so different on the minds of different men.

M. R. James admired both "The Open Door" and Mrs. Oliphant's
"equally beautiful book" *A Beleagured City*. He suggests that a very old
story might have furnished the idea for "The Open Door"—"I mean
the history of Mr. Ruddle of Launceston. He tells it himself as a veritable experience he went through in the year 1665. Here, too, there was
a young boy who was troubled by the appearance of the ghost of a
woman, whom he knew to have been dead about eight years, which

met him in a field every day on his way to school. The story is
interestingly told: I do not know if it has ever been critically treated.
The only text I can now lay hands on is in *News from the Invisible
World,* by T. Charley. Mr. Ruddle keeps his counsel as to what the
ghost (whom he eventually interviewed and exorcized) said to him:
the end was that 'it quietly vanished, and neither doth appear since, or
ever will more to any man's disturbance.' "*

*Dr. Montague Rhodes James in his introduction to *Ghosts and Marvels, a
Selection of Uncanny Tales from Daniel Defoe to Algernon Blackwood* made
by V. H. Collins (Oxford University Press, 1924). Another outstanding
writer of ghost stories, Oliver Onions, has developed Mr. Ruddle's account
as a story called "The Woman in the Way."

CHAPTER 8

Thus I Refute Beelzy

by John Collier

The identity of Beelzy is just hinted in this story, but you might guess he is Beelzebub, "the prince of the devils" (Matt. 12:24). Milton makes him second only to Satan himself in rank and power. The boy in the story, Small Simon, is named after his father, but perhaps the author was also thinking of the biblical sorcerer Simon Magus. It is evident that Small Simon is engaged in some sort of sorcery and that, like Faust, he has made a pact with the devil.

"There goes the tea bell," said Mrs. Carter. "I hope Simon hears it."

They looked out from the window of the drawing room. The long garden, agreeably neglected, ended in a waste plot. Here a little summer house was passing close by beauty on its way to complete decay. This was Simon's retreat: it was almost completely screened by the tangled branches of the apple tree and the pear tree, planted too close together, as they always are in suburban gardens. They caught a glimpse of him now and then, as he strutted up and down, mouthing and gesticulating, performing all the solemn mumbo jumbo of small boys who spend long afternoons at the forgotten ends of long gardens.

"There he is, bless him," said Betty.

"Playing his game," said Mrs. Carter. "He won't play with the other children any more. And if I go down there—the temper! He comes in tired out."

"He doesn't have his sleep in the afternoons?" asked Betty.

"You know what Big Simon's ideas are," said Mrs. Carter. " 'Let him choose for himself,' he says. That's what he chooses, and he comes in as white as a sheet."

"Look. He's heard the bell," said Betty. The expression was justified, though the bell had ceased ringing a full minute ago. Small Simon stopped in his parade exactly as if its tinny dingle had at that moment reached his ear. They watched him perform certain ritual sweeps and scratchings with his little stick, and come lagging over the hot and flaggy grass toward the house.

Mrs. Carter led the way down to the playroom or garden room, which was also the tearoom for hot days. It had been the huge scullery of this tall Georgian house. Now the walls were cream-washed, there was coarse blue net in the windows, canvas-covered armchairs on the stone floor, and a reproduction of Van Gogh's "Sunflowers" over the mantelpiece.

Small Simon came drifting in, and accorded Betty a perfunctory greeting. His face was an almost perfect triangle, pointed at the chin, and he was paler than he should have been. "The little elf child!" cried Betty.

Simon looked at her. "No," said he.

At that moment the door opened, and Mr. Carter came in, rubbing his hands. He was a dentist, and washed them before and after everything he did. "You!" said his wife. "Home already!"

"Not unwelcome, I hope," said Mr. Carter, nodding to Betty. "Two people cancelled their appointments: I decided to come home. I said, I hope I am not unwelcome."

"Silly!" said his wife. "Of course not."

"Small Simon seems doubtful," continued Mr. Carter. "Small Simon, are you sorry to see me at tea with you?"

"No, Daddy."

"No what?"

"No, Big Simon."

"That's right. Big Simon and Small Simon. That sounds more like friends, doesn't it? At one time little boys had to call their father 'sir.' If they forgot—a good spanking. On the bottom, Small Simon! On the bottom!" said Mr. Carter, washing his hands once more with his invisible soap and water.

The little boy turned crimson with shame or rage.

"But now, you see," said Betty, to help, "you can call your father whatever you like."

"And what," asked Mr. Carter, "has Small Simon being doing this afternoon, while Big Simon has been at work?"

"Nothing," muttered his son.

"Then you have been bored," said Mr. Carter. "Learn from experience, Small Simon. Tomorrow, do something amusing, and you will not be bored. I want him to learn from experience, Betty. That is my way, the new way."

"I have learned," said the boy, speaking like an old tired man, as little boys so often do.

"It would hardly seem so," said Mr. Carter. "If you sit on your behind all the afternoon, doing nothing. Had *my* father caught me doing nothing, I should not have sat very comfortably."

"He played," said Mrs. Carter.

"A bit," said the boy, shifting on his chair.

"Too much," said Mrs. Carter. "He comes in all nervy and dazed. He ought to have his rest."

"He is six," said her husband. "He is a reasonable being. He must choose for himself. But what game is this, Small Simon, that is worth getting nervy and dazed over? There are very few games as good as all that."

"It's nothing," said the boy.

"Oh, come," said his father. "We are friends, are we not? You can tell me. I was a Small Simon once, just like you, and played the same games you play. Of course there were no airplanes in those days. With whom do you play this fine game? Come on, we must all answer civil questions, or the world would never go round. With whom do you play?"

"Mr. Beelzy," said the boy, unable to resist.

"Mr. Beelzy?" said his father, raising his eyebrows inquiringly at his wife.

"It's a game he makes up," said she.

"Not makes up," cried the boy. "Fool!"

"That is telling stories," said his mother. "And rude as well. We had better talk of something different."

"No wonder he is rude," said Mr. Carter. "If you say he tells lies, and then insist on changing the subject. He tells you his fantasy: you implant a guilt feeling. What can you expect? A defense mechanism. Then you get a real lie."

"Like in *These Three*," said Betty. "Only different, of course. *She* was an unblushing little liar."

"I would have made her blush," said Mr. Carter, "in the proper part of her anatomy. But Small Simon is in the fantasy stage. Are you not, Small Simon? You just make things up."

"No, I don't," said the boy.

"You do," said his father. "And because you do, it is not too late to reason with you. There is no harm in a fantasy, old chap. There is no harm in a bit of make-believe. Only you have to know the difference between daydreams and real things, or your brain will never grow. It will never be the brain of a Big Simon. So come on. Let us hear about this Mr. Beelzy of yours. Come on. What is he like?"

"He isn't like any thing," said the boy.

"Like nothing on earth," said his father. "That's a terrible fellow."

"I'm not frightened of him," said the child, smiling. "Not a bit."

"I should hope not," said his father. "If you were, you would be frightening yourself. I am always telling people, older people than you are, that they are just frightening themselves. Is he a funny man? Is he a giant?"

"Sometimes he is," said the little boy.

"Sometimes one thing, sometimes another," said his father. "Sounds pretty vague. Why can't you tell us just what he's like?"

"I love him," said the small boy. "He loves me."

"That's a big word," said Mr. Carter. "That might be better kept for real things, like Big Simon and Small Simon."

"He is real," said the boy, passionately. "He's not a fool. He's real."

"Listen," said his father. "When you go down the garden there's nobody there. Is there?"

"No," said the boy.

"Then you think of him, inside your head, and he comes."

"No," said Small Simon. "I have to do something with my stick."

"That doesn't matter."

"Yes, it does."

"Small Simon, you are being obstinate," said Mr. Carter. "I am

trying to explain something to you. I have been longer in the
world than you have, so naturally I am older and wiser. I am explaining that Mr. Beelzy is a fantasy of yours. Do you hear? Do
you understand?"

"Yes, Daddy."

"He is a game. He is a 'let's-pretend.' "

The little boy looked down at his plate, smiling resignedly.

"I hope you are listening to me," said his father. "All you have
to do is to say, 'I have been playing a game of let's-pretend. With
someone I make up, called Mr. Beelzy.' Then no one will say you
tell lies, and you will know the difference between dreams and
reality. Mr. Beelzy is a daydream."

The little boy still stared at his plate.

"He is sometimes there and sometimes not there," pursued Mr.
Carter. "Sometimes he's like one thing, sometimes another. You
can't really see him. Not as you see me. I am real. You can't touch
him. You can touch me. I can touch you." Mr. Carter stretched out
his big, white, dentist's hand, and took his little son by the
shoulder. He stopped speaking for a moment and tightened his
hand. The little boy sunk his head still lower.

"Now you know the difference," said Mr. Carter, "between
a pretend and a real thing. You and I are one thing; he is another.
Which is the pretend? Come on. Answer me. Which is the
pretend?"

"Big Simon and Small Simon," said the little boy.

"Don't!" cried Betty, and at once put her hand over her mouth,
for why should a visitor cry "don't" when a father is explaining
things in a scientific and modern way?

"Well, my boy," said Mr. Carter, "I have said you must be
allowed to learn from experience. Go upstairs. Right up to your
room. You shall learn whether it is better to reason, or to be
perverse and obstinate. Go up. I shall follow you."

"You are not going to beat the child?" cried Mrs. Carter.

"No," said the little boy. "Mr. Beelzy won't let him."

"Go on up with you," shouted his father.

Small Simon stopped at the door. "He said he wouldn't let
anyone hurt me," he whimpered. "He said he'd come like a lion,
with wings on, and eat them up."

"You'll learn how real he is," shouted his father after him. "If
you can't learn it at one end, you shall learn it at the other. I'll

have your breeches down. I shall finish my cup of tea first, how-ever," said he to the two women.

Neither of them spoke. Mr. Carter finished his tea, and un-hurriedly left the room, washing his hands with his invisible soap and water.

Mrs. Carter said nothing. Betty could think of nothing to say. She wanted to be talking: she was afraid of what they might hear.

Suddenly it came. It seemed to tear the air apart. "Good God!" she cried. "What was that? He's hurt him." She sprang out of her chair, her silly eyes flashing behind her glasses. "I'm going up there," she cried, trembling.

"Yes, let us go up," said Mrs. Carter. "Let us go up. That was not Small Simon."

It was on the second-floor landing that they found the shoe, with the man's foot still in it, like that morsel of a mouse which sometimes falls unnoticed from the side of the jaws of the cat.

John Collier (born 1901), English novelist, satirist and short-story writer, began his literary career as a poet. He is best known for his wryly humorous and fantastic fiction. Some of his most popular books are: *His Monkey Wife, or Married to a Chimp; Full Circle; Defy the Foul Fiend: or, the Misadventures of a Heart; The Devil and All; Presenting Moonshine; A Touch of Nutmeg and More Unlikely Stories; No Traveller Returns; Fancies and Goodnights.* Clifton Fadiman once commented that Collier "carries the small, neat mantle of 'Saki' " (the pen name of Hector Hugh Munro). "Thus I Refute Beelzy" affords an interesting comparison to Saki's tale, "Sredni Vashtar," about a boy named Conradin who invokes the powers of darkness.

CHAPTER 9

Levitation

by Joseph Payne Brennan

Carnivals and poetry, if we are susceptible to them, renew our sense of wonder. The author of this story is a poet, and the carnival Hypnotist he describes might be Bela Lugosi himself, commanding and chilling as he appeared in *Dracula, White Zombie,* and *Murders in the Rue Morgue.* This Hypnotist is no charlatan, and the strange power he wields is something more than hypnotism as modern science knows it.

Morgan's Wonder Carnival moved into Riverville for an overnight stand, setting up its tents in the big ball park on the edge of the village. It was a warm evening in early October and by seven o'clock a sizable crowd had made its way to the scene of raucous amusement.

The traveling show was neither large nor particularly impressive of its type, but its appearance was eagerly welcomed in Riverville, an isolated mountain community many miles from the motion picture houses, vaudeville theaters, and sports arenas situated in larger towns.

The natives of Riverville did not demand sophisticated entertainment; consequently the inevitable Fat Lady, the Tattooed Man, and the Monkey Boy kept them chattering animatedly for many minutes at a time. They crammed peanuts and buttered popcorn into their mouths, drank cup after cup of pink lemonade, and got

their fingers all but stuck together trying to scrape the paper
wrappers off colored taffy candies.

Everyone appeared to be in a relaxed and tolerant state of mind
when the barker for the Hypnotist began his spiel. The barker, a
short stocky man wearing a checkered suit, bellowed through an
improvised megaphone, while the Hypnotist himself remained
aloof at the rear of the plank platform erected in front of his tent.
He appeared disinterested, scornful, and he scarcely deigned to
glance at the gathering crowd.

At length, however, when some fifty souls had assembled in
front of the platform, he stepped forward into the light. A murmur
went up from the crowd.

In the harsh overhead electric glare, the Hypnotist made a striking appearance. His tall figure, thin to the point of emaciation, his
pale complexion, and most of all his dark, sunken eyes, enormous
and brilliant, compelled immediate attention. His dress, a severe
black suit and an archaic black string tie, added a final Mephis-
tophelean touch.

He surveyed the crowd coolly, with an expression betraying
resignation and a kind of quiet contempt.

His sonorous voice reached to the far edge of the throng. "I will
require one volunteer from among you," he said. "If someone will
kindly step up—"

Everyone glanced around, or nudged his neighbor, but nobody
advanced toward the platform.

The Hypnotist shrugged. "There can be no demonstration," he
said in a weary voice, "unless one of you is kind enough to come
up. I assure you, ladies and gentlemen, the demonstration is quite
harmless, quite without danger."

He looked around expectantly and presently a young man slowly
elbowed through the crowd toward the platform.

The Hypnotist helped him up the steps and seated him in a
chair.

"Relax," said the Hypnotist. "Presently you will be asleep and
you will do exactly what I tell you to do."

The young man squirmed on the chair, grinning self-consciously
toward the crowd.

The Hypnotist caught his attention, fixing his enormous eyes on
him, and the young man stopped squirming.

Suddenly someone in the crowd threw a large ball of colored

popcorn toward the platform. The popcorn arched over the lights, landing squarely atop the head of the young man sitting in the chair.

He jerked sideways, almost falling off the chair, and the crowd, quiet a moment before, guffawed boisterously.

The Hypnotist was furious. He turned scarlet and literally shook with rage as he glared at the crowd.

"Who threw that?" he demanded in a choking voice.

The crowd grew silent.

The Hypnotist continued to glare at them. At length the color left his face and he stopped trembling, but his brilliant eyes remained baleful.

Finally he nodded to the young man seated on the platform, dismissing him with brief thanks, and turned again toward the crowd.

"Due to the interruption," he announced in a low voice, "it will be necessary to recommence the demonstration—with a new subject. Perhaps the person who threw the popcorn would care to come up?"

At least a dozen people in the crowd turned to gaze at someone who stood half in shadow at the rear of the gathering.

The Hypnotist spotted him at once; his dark eyes seemed to smoulder. "Perhaps," he said in a purring, mocking voice, "the one who interrupted is afraid to come up. He prefers to hide in the shadows and throw popcorn!"

The culprit voiced a sudden exclamation and then pushed belligerently toward the platform. His appearance was not in any way remarkable; in fact, he somewhat resembled the first young man, and any casual observer would have placed the two of them in the farm-laborer class, neither more nor less capable than the average.

The second young man sat down in the platform chair with a distinct air of defiance and for some minutes visibly fought the Hypnotist's suggestion to relax. Presently, however, his aggressiveness disappeared and he dutifully stared into the smouldering eyes opposite his own.

In another minute or two he arose at the Hypnotist's command and lay flat on his back on the hard planks of the platform. The crowd gasped.

"You will fall asleep," the Hypnotist told him. "You will fall asleep. You are falling asleep. You are falling asleep. You are asleep. You are asleep and you will do anything which I command you to do. Anything which I command you to do. Anything. . . ."

His voice droned on, repeating repetitious phrases, and the crowd grew perfectly silent.

Suddenly a new note entered the Hypnotist's voice and the audience became tense.

"Do not stand up—but *rise from the platform!*" the Hypnotist commanded. *"Rise from the platform!"* His dark eyes became wild and luminous-looking and the crowd shivered.

"Rise!"

Then the crowd drew in its collective breath with an audible start.

The young man lying rigid on the platform, without moving a muscle, began to ascend horizontally. He arose slowly, almost imperceptively at first, but soon with a steady and unmistakable acceleration.

"Rise!" the Hypnotist's voice rang out.

The young man continued to ascend, until he was five feet off the platform, and still he did not stop.

The crowd was sure it was some kind of trick, but in spite of themselves they stared open-mouthed. The young man appeared to be suspended and moving in mid-air without any possible means of physical support.

Abruptly the focus of the crowd's attention was shifted; the Hypnotist clasped a hand to his chest, staggered, and crumpled to the platform.

There were calls for a doctor. The barker in the checkered suit appeared out of the tent and bent over the motionless form.

He felt for a pulse, shook his head and straightened up. Someone offered a bottle of whiskey, but he merely shrugged.

Suddenly a woman in the crowd screamed.

Everyone turned to look at her and a second later followed the direction of her gaze.

Immediately there were further cries—for the young man whom the Hypnotist had put to sleep was still ascending. While the crowd's attention had been distracted by the fatal collapse of the Hypnotist, he had continued to rise. He was now a good seven feet above the platform and moving inexorably upward. Even after the death of the Hypnotist, he continued to obey that final ringing command: *"Rise!"*

The barker, eyes all but popping out of his head, made a frantic upward leap, but he was too short. His fingers barely brushed the moving figure above and he fell heavily back to the platform.

The rigid form of the young man continued to float upward, as if he were being hoisted by some kind of invisible pulley.

Women began screaming hysterically; men shouted. But no one knew what to do. A look of terror crept over the face of the barker as he stared up. Once he glanced wildly toward the sprawled shape of the Hypnotist.

"Come down, Frank! Come down!" the crowd shrieked. "Frank! Wake up! Come down! Stop! Frank!"

But the rigid form of Frank moved ever upward. Up, up, until he was level with the top of the carnival tent, until he reached the height of the tallest trees—until he passed the trees and moved on into the soft moonlit sky of early October.

Many in the crowd threw hands over horror-stricken faces and turned away.

Those who continued to stare saw the floating form ascend into the sky. It was no more than a tiny speck, like a little cinder drifting far up near the moon.

Then it disappeared altogether.

———

A native of Connecticut, Joseph Payne Brennan was born in 1918. He is the author of four collections of verse—*Heart of Earth, The Humming Stair, The Wind of Time, Nightmare Need,* and three collections of weird fiction—*Nine Horrors and a Dream, The Dark Returners, Scream at Midnight.* He has contributed to *Weird Tales, The London Evening Standard, Esquire, The American Scholar, The Chicago Review, The New York Times, The Christian Science Monitor,* and many other periodicals.

CHAPTER 10

The Ghostly Rental

by Henry James

Skipping all palaver about the nature of ghosts and whether they exist, Henry James (1843–1916) leaves the topic wide open: they are what you think they are; fill in the details yourself. His characters are so convincing that you readily feel what they feel and see what they see. The most artful example of this technique is "The Turn of the Screw," written in 1897. But "The Ghostly Rental," written twenty-two years before that, gives a fine foretaste of things to come and has, besides, an engaging clarity. James's lifelong interest in ghosts is traced in full detail in Leon Edel's collection of *The Ghostly Tales of Henry James*.

I was in my twenty-second year, and I had just left college. I was at liberty to choose my career, and I chose it with much promptness. I afterward renounced it, in truth, with equal ardor, but I have never regretted those two youthful years of perplexed and excited, but also of agreeable and fruitful, experiment. I had a taste for theology, and during my college term I had been an admiring reader of Dr. Channing. This was the theology of a grateful and succulent savor; it seemed to offer one the rose of faith delightfully stripped of its thorns. And then (for I rather think this had something to do with it), I had taken a fancy to the old Divinity School. I have always had an eye to the back scene in the human drama, and it seemed to me that I might play my part with a fair chance of

applause (from myself at least), in that detached and tranquil
home of mild casuistry, with its respectable avenue on one side,
and its prospect of green fields and contact with acres of woodland on the other. Cambridge, for the lovers of woods and fields,
has changed for the worse since those days, and the precinct in
question has forfeited much of its mingled pastoral and scholastic
quietude. It was then a college hall in the woods—a charming
mixture. What it is now has nothing to do with my story; and I
have no doubt that there are still doctrine-haunted young seniors
who, as they stroll near it in the summer dusk, promise themselves,
later, to taste of its fine leisurely quality. For myself, I was not
disappointed. I established myself in a great square, low-browed
room, with deep window benches; I hung prints from Overbeck
and Ary Scheffer on the walls; I arranged my books, with great
refinement of classification, in the alcoves beside the high chimney
shelf, and I began to read Plotinus and St. Augustine. Among my
companions were two or three men of ability and of good fellowship, with whom I occasionally brewed a fireside bowl; and with
adventurous reading, deep discourse, potations conscientiously
shallow, and long country walks, my initiation into the clerical
mystery progressed agreeably enough.

With one of my comrades I formed a special friendship, and
we passed a great deal of time together. Unfortunately he had a
chronic weakness of one of his knees, which compelled him to
lead a very sedentary life, and as I was a methodical pedestrian,
this made some difference in our habits. I used often to stretch
away for my daily ramble, with no companion but the stick in my
hand or the book in my pocket. But in the use of my legs and the
sense of unstinted open air, I have always found company enough.
I should, perhaps, add that in the enjoyment of a very sharp pair
of eyes, I found something of a social pleasure. My eyes and I were
on excellent terms; they were indefatigable observers of all wayside incidents, and so long as they were amused I was contented.
It is, indeed, owing to their inquisitive habits that I came into
possession of this remarkable story. Much of the country about the
old college town is pretty now, but it was prettier thirty years ago.
That multitudinous eruption of domiciliary pasteboard which now
graces the landscape, in the direction of the low, blue Waltham
hills, had not yet taken place; there were no genteel cottages to put
the shabby meadows and scrubby orchards to shame—a juxtaposi-

tion by which, in later years, neither element of the contrast has gained. Certain crooked crossroads, then, as I remember them, were more deeply and naturally rural, and the solitary dwellings on the long grassy slopes beside them, under the tall, customary elm that curved its foliage in mid-air like the outward dropping ears of a girdled wheat sheaf, sat with their shingled hoods well pulled down on their ears, and no prescience whatever of the fashion of French roofs—weather-wrinkled old peasant women, as you might call them, quietly wearing the native coif, and never dreaming of mounting bonnets, and indecently exposing their venerable brows. That winter was what is called an "open" one; there was much cold, but little snow; the roads were firm and free, and I was rarely compelled by the weather to forego my exercise.

One gray December afternoon I had sought it in the direction of the adjacent town of Medford, and I was retracing my steps at an even pace, and watching the pale, cold tints—the transparent amber and faded rose color—which curtained, in wintry fashion, the western sky, and reminded me of a skeptical smile on the lips of a beautiful woman. I came, as dusk was falling, to a narrow road which I had never traversed and which I imagined offered me a short cut homeward. I was about three miles away; I was late, and would have been thankful to make them two. I diverged, walked some ten minutes, and then perceived that the road had a very unfrequented air. The wheel ruts looked old; the stillness seemed peculiarly sensible. And yet down the road stood a house, so that it must in some degree have been a thoroughfare. On one side was a high, natural embankment, on the top of which was perched an apple orchard, whose tangled boughs made a stretch of coarse black lacework, hung across the coldly rosy west. In a short time I came to the house, and I immediately found myself interested in it. I stopped in front of it gazing hard, I hardly knew why, but with a vague mixture of curiosity and timidity. It was a house like most of the houses thereabouts, except that it was decidedly a handsome specimen of its class. It stood on a grassy slope, it had its tall, impartially drooping elm beside it, and its old black well cover at its shoulder. But it was of very large proportions, and it had a striking look of solidity and stoutness of timber. It had lived to a good old age, too, for the woodwork on its doorway and under its eaves, carefully and abundantly carved, referred it to the middle, at the latest, of the last century. All this had once

been painted white, but the broad back of time, leaning against the
doorposts for a hundred years, had laid bare the grain of the wood.
Behind the house stretched an orchard of apple trees, more gnarled
and fantastic than usual, and wearing, in the deepening dusk, a
blighted and exhausted aspect. All the windows of the house had
rusty shutters, without slats, and these were closely drawn. There
was no sign of life about it; it looked blank, bare, and vacant, and
yet, as I lingered near it, it seemed to have a familiar meaning—an
audible eloquence. I have always thought of the impression made
upon me at first sight, by that gray colonial dwelling, as a proof
that induction may sometimes be near akin to divination; for after
all, there was nothing on the face of the matter to warrant the very
serious induction that I made. I fell back and crossed the road. The
last red light of the sunset disengaged itself, as it was about to
vanish, and rested faintly for a moment on the time-silvered front
of the old house. It touched, with perfect regularity, the series of
small panes in the fan-shaped window above the door, and twinkled
there fantastically. Then it died away, and left the place more intensely somber. At this moment, I said to myself with the accent
of profound conviction—"The house is simply haunted!"

Somehow, immediately, I believed it, and so long as I was not
shut up inside, the idea gave me pleasure. It was implied in the
aspect of the house, and it explained it. Half an hour before, if I
had been asked, I would have said, as befitted a young man who
was explicitly cultivating cheerful views of the supernatural, that
there were no such things as haunted houses. But the dwelling
before me gave a vivid meaning to the empty words; it had been
spiritually blighted.

The longer I looked at it, the intenser seemed the secret that
it held. I walked all round it, I tried to peep here and there,
through a crevice in the shutters, and I took a puerile satisfaction
in laying my hand on the doorknob and gently turning it. If the door
had yielded, would I have gone in?—would I have penetrated the
dusky stillness? My audacity, fortunately, was not put to the test.
The portal was admirably solid, and I was unable ever to shake
it. At last I turned away, casting many looks behind me. I pursued
my way, and, after a longer walk than I had bargained for, reached
the highroad. At a certain distance below the point at which the
long lane I have mentioned entered it, stood a comfortable, tidy
dwelling, which might have offered itself as the model of the house

which is in no sense haunted—which has no sinister secrets, and knows nothing but blooming prosperity. Its clean white paint stared placidly through the dusk, and its vine-covered porch had been dressed in straw for the winter. An old, one-horse chaise, freighted with two departing visitors, was leaving the door, and through the undraped windows, I saw the lamplit sitting room, and the table spread with the early "tea," which had been improvised for the comfort of the guests. The mistress of the house had come to the gate with her friends; she lingered there after the chaise had wheeled creakingly away, half to watch them down the road, and half to give me, as I passed in the twilight, a questioning look. She was a comely, quick young woman, with a sharp, dark eye, and I ventured to stop and speak to her.

"That house down that side road," I said, "about a mile from here—the only one—can you tell me whom it belongs to?"

She stared at me a moment, and, I thought, colored a little. "Our folks never go down that road," she said, briefly.

"But it's a short way to Medford," I answered.

She gave a little toss of her head. "Perhaps it would turn out a long way. At any rate, we don't use it."

This was interesting. A thrifty Yankee household must have good reasons for this scorn of timesaving processes. "But you know the house, at least?" I said.

"Well, I have seen it."

"And to whom does it belong?"

She gave a little laugh and looked away, as if she were aware that, to a stranger, her words might seem to savor of agricultural superstition. "I guess it belongs to them that are in it."

"But is there any one in it? It is completely closed."

"That makes no difference. They never come out, and no one ever goes in." And she turned away.

But I laid my hand on her arm, respectfully. "You mean," I said, "that the house is haunted?"

She drew herself away, colored, raised her finger to her lips, and hurried into the house, where, in a moment, the curtains were dropped over the windows.

For several days, I thought repeatedly of this little adventure, but I took some satisfaction in keeping it to myself. If the house was not haunted, it was useless to expose my imaginative whims, and if it was, it was agreeable to drain the cup of horror without assistance. I determined, of course, to pass that way again; and a week later—it was the last day of the year—I retraced my steps. I approached the house from the opposite direction, and found myself before it at about the same hour as before. The light was failing, the sky low and gray; the wind wailed along the hard, bare ground, and made slow eddies of the frost-blackened leaves. The melancholy mansion stood there, seeming to gather the winter twilight around it, and mask itself in it, inscrutably. I hardly knew on what errand I had come, but I had a vague feeling that if this time the doorknob were to turn and the door to open, I should take my heart in my hands, and let them close behind me. Who were the mysterious tenants to whom the good woman at the corner had alluded? What had been seen or heard—what was related? The door was as stubborn as before, and my impertinent fumblings with the latch caused no upper window to be thrown open, nor any strange, pale face to be thrust out. I ventured even to raise the rusty knocker and give it half a dozen raps, but they made a flat, dead sound, and aroused no echo. Familiarity breeds contempt; I don't know what I should have done next, if, in the distance, up the road (the same one I had followed), I had not seen a solitary figure advancing. I was unwilling to be observed hanging about this ill-famed dwelling, and I sought refuge among the dense shadows of a grove of pines nearby, where I might peep forth, and yet remain invisible. Presently, the newcomer drew near, and I perceived that he was making straight for the house. He was a little, old man, the most striking feature of whose appearance was a voluminous cloak, of a sort of military cut. He carried a walking stick, and advanced in a slow, painful, somewhat hobbling fashion, but with an air of extreme resolution. He turned off from the road, and followed the vague wheel track, and within a few yards of the house he paused. He looked up at it, fixedly and searchingly, as if he were counting the windows, or noting certain familiar marks. Then he took off his hat, and bent over slowly and solemnly, as if he were performing an obeisance. As he stood uncovered, I had a good look at him. He was, as I have said, a diminutive old man, but it would have been hard to decide whether he belonged to this world or to the other. His head reminded me, vaguely, of the portraits of Andrew Jackson. He had a crop of grizzled hair, as stiff as a brush, a lean, pale, smooth-shaven face, and an eye of intense brilliancy, surmounted with thick brows, which had remained perfectly black. His face, as well as his cloak, seemed to belong to an old soldier; he looked like a retired military man of a modest rank; but he struck me as exceeding the classic privilege of even such a personage to be eccentric and grotesque. When he had finished his salute, he advanced to the door, fumbled in the folds of his cloak, which hung down much farther in front than behind, and produced a key. This he slowly and carefully inserted into the lock, and then, apparently, he turned it. But the door did not immediately open; first he bent his head, turned his ear, and stood listening, and then he looked up and down the road. Satisfied or reassured, he applied his aged shoulder to one of the deep-set panels, and pressed a moment. The door yielded—opening into perfect darkness. He stopped again on the threshold, and again removed his hat and made his bow. Then he went in, and carefully closed the door behind him.

Who in the world was he, and what was his errand? He might have been a figure out of one of Hoffmann's tales. Was he vision or a reality—an inmate of the house, or a familiar, friendly visitor? What had been the meaning, in either case, of his mystic genuflections, and how did he propose to proceed, in that inner darkness? I emerged from my retirement, and observed narrowly, several of the windows. In each of them, at an interval, a ray of light became visible in the chink between the two leaves of the shutters. Evidently, he was lighting up; was he going to give a party—a ghostly revel? My curiosity grew intense, but I was quite at a loss how to satisfy it. For a moment I thought of rapping peremptorily at the door; but I dismissed this idea as unmannerly, and calculated to break the spell, if spell there was. I walked round the house and tried, without violence, to open one of the lower windows. It resisted, but I had better fortune, in a moment, with another. There was a risk, certainly, in the trick I was playing—a risk of being seen from within, or (worse) seeing, myself, something that I should repent of seeing. But curiosity, as I say, had become an inspiration, and the risk was highly agreeable. Through the parting of the shutters I looked into a lighted room—a room lighted by two candles in old brass flambeaux, placed upon the mantelshelf. It was apparently a sort of back parlor, and it had retained all its furniture. This was of a homely, old-fashioned pattern, and consisted of haircloth chairs and sofas, spare mahogany tables, and framed samplers hung upon the walls. But although the room was furnished, it had a strangely uninhabited look; the tables and chairs were in rigid positions, and no small, familiar objects were visible. I could not see everything, and I could only guess at the existence, on my right, of a large folding door. It was apparently open, and the light of the neighboring room passed through it. I waited for some time, but the room remained empty. At last I became conscious that a large shadow was projected upon the wall opposite the folding door—the shadow, evidently, of a figure in the adjoining room. It was tall and grotesque, and seemed to represent a person sitting perfectly motionless, in profile. I thought I recognized the perpendicular bristles and far-arching nose of my little old man. There was a strange fixedness in his posture; he appeared to be seated, and looking intently at something. I watched the shadow a long time, but it never stirred. At last, however, just as my patience began to ebb, it moved slowly, rose to the ceiling, and became indistinct. I don't know what I should have seen next, but by an irresistible impulse, I closed the shutter. Was it delicacy?—was it pusillanimity? I can hardly say. I lingered, nevertheless, near the house, hoping that my friend would reappear. I was not disappointed; for he at last emerged, looking just as when he had gone in, and taking his leave in the same ceremonious fashion. (The lights, I had already observed, had disappeared from the crevice of each of the windows.) He faced about before the door, took off his hat, and made an obsequious bow. As he turned away I had a hundred minds to speak to him, but I let him depart in peace. This, I may say, was pure delicacy;—you will answer, perhaps, that it came too late. It seemed to me that he had a right to resent my observation; though my own right to exercise it (if ghosts were in the question) struck me as equally positive. I continued to watch him as he hobbled softly down the bank, and along the lonely road. Then I musingly retreated in the opposite direction. I was tempted to follow him, at a distance, to see what became of him; but this, too, seemed indelicate; and I confess, moreover, that I felt the inclination to coquet a little, as it were, with my discovery—to pull apart the petals of the flower one by one.

I continued to smell the flower, from time to time, for its oddity of perfume had fascinated me. I passed by the house on the cross-road again, but never encountered the old man in the cloak, or any other wayfarer. It seemed to keep observers at a distance, and I was careful not to gossip about it: one inquirer, I said to myself, may edge his way into the secret, but there is no room for two. At the same time, of course, I would have been thankful for any chance side light that might fall across the matter—though I could not well see whence it was to come. I hoped to meet the old man in the cloak elsewhere, but as the days passed by without his reappearing, I ceased to expect it. And yet I reflected that he probably lived in that neighborhood, inasmuch as he had made his pilgrimage to the vacant house on foot. If he had come from a distance, he would have been sure to arrive in some old deep-hooded gig with yellow wheels—a vehicle as venerably grotesque as himself. One day I took a stroll in Mount Auburn cemetery—an institution at that period in its infancy, and full of a sylvan charm which it has now completely forfeited. It contained more maple and birch than willow and cypress, and the sleepers had ample elbow room. It was not a city of the dead, but at the most a village, and a meditative pedestrian might stroll there without too importunate reminder of the grotesque side of our claims to posthumous consideration. I had come out to enjoy the first foretaste of spring —one of those mild days of late winter, when the torpid earth seems to draw the first long breath that marks the rupture of the spell of sleep. The sun was veiled in haze, and yet warm, and the frost was oozing from its deepest lurking places. I had been treading for half an hour the winding ways of the cemetery, when suddenly I perceived a familiar figure seated on a bench against a southward-facing evergreen hedge. I call the figure familiar, because I had seen it often in memory and in fancy; in fact, I had beheld it but once. Its back was turned to me, but it wore a voluminous cloak, which there was no mistaking. Here, at last, was my fellow visitor at the haunted house, and here was my chance, if I wished to approach him! I made a circuit, and came toward him from in front. He saw me, at the end of the alley, and sat motionless, with his hands on the head of his stick, watching me from under his black eyebrows as I drew near. At a distance these black eyebrows looked formidable; they were the only thing I saw in his face. But on a closer view I was reassured, simply because I immediately felt that no man could really be as fantastically fierce as this poor old gentleman looked. His face was a kind of caricature of martial truculence. I stopped in front of him, and respectfully asked leave to sit and rest upon his bench. He granted it with a silent gesture, of much dignity, and I placed myself beside him. In this position I was able, covertly, to observe him. He was quite as much an oddity in the morning sunshine, as he had been in the dubious twilight. The lines in his face were as rigid as if they had been hacked out of a block by a clumsy woodcarver. His eyes were flamboyant, his nose terrific, his mouth implacable. And yet, after a while, when he slowly turned and looked at me, fixedly, I perceived that in spite of this portentous mask, he was a very mild old man. I was sure he even would have been glad to smile, but, evidently, his facial muscles were too stiff—they had taken a different fold, once for all. I wondered whether he was demented, but I dismissed the idea; the fixed glitter in his eye was not that of insanity. What his face really expressed was deep and simple sadness; his heart perhaps was broken, but his brain was intact. His dress was shabby but neat, and his old blue cloak had known half a century's brushing.

I hastened to make some observation upon the exceptional softness of the day, and he answered me in a gentle, mellow voice, which it was almost startling to hear proceed from such bellicose lips.

"This is a very comfortable place," he presently added.

"I am fond of walking in graveyards," I rejoined deliberately; flattering myself that I had struck a vein that might lead to something.

I was encouraged; he turned and fixed me with his duskily glowing eyes. Then very gravely—"Walking, yes. Take all your exercise now. Someday you will have to settle down in a graveyard in a fixed position."

"Very true," said I. "But you know there are some people who are said to take exercise even after that day."

He had been looking at me still; at this he looked away.

"You don't understand?" I said gently.

He continued to gaze straight before him.

"Some people, you know, walk about after death," I went on.

At last he turned and looked at me more portentously than ever. "You don't believe that," he said simply.

"How do you know I don't?"

"Because you are young and foolish." This was said without acerbity—even kindly; but in the tone of an old man whose consciousness of his own heavy experience made everything else seem light.

"I am certainly young," I answered; "but I don't think that, on the whole, I am foolish. But say I don't believe in ghosts—most people would be on my side."

"Most people are fools!" said the old man.

I let the question rest, and talked of other things. My companion seemed on his guard, he eyed me defiantly, and made brief answers to my remarks; but I nevertheless gathered an impression that our meeting was an agreeable thing to him, and even a social incident of some importance. He was evidently a lonely creature, and his opportunities for gossip were rare. He had had troubles, and they had detached him from the world, and driven him back upon himself; but the social chord in his antiquated soul was not entirely broken, and I was sure he was gratified to find that it could still feebly resound. At last, he began to ask questions himself; he inquired whether I was a student.

"I am a student of divinity," I answered.

"Of divinity?"

"Of theology. I am studying for the ministry."

At this he eyed me with peculiar intensity—after which his gaze wandered away again. "There are certain things you ought to know, then," he said at last.

"I have a great desire for knowledge," I answered. "What things do you mean?"

He looked at me again awhile, but without heeding my question.

"I like your appearance," he said. "You seem to me a sober lad."

"Oh, I am perfectly sober!" I exclaimed—yet departing for a moment from my soberness.

"I think you are fair-minded," he went on.

"I don't any longer strike you as foolish, then?" I asked.

"I stick to what I said about people who deny the power of departed spirits to return. They *are* fools!" And he rapped fiercely with his staff on the earth.

I hesitated a moment, and then, abruptly, "You have seen a ghost!" I said.

He appeared not at all startled.

"You are right, sir!" he answered with great dignity. "With me it's not a matter of cold theory—I have not had to pry into old books to learn what to believe. I *know!* With these eyes I have be-

held the departed spirit standing before me as near as you are!"
And his eyes, as he spoke, certainly looked as if they had rested
upon strange things.

I was irresistibly impressed—I was touched with credulity.

"And was it very terrible?" I asked.

"I am an old soldier—I am not afraid!"

"When was it?—where was it?" I asked.

He looked at me mistrustfully, and I saw that I was going too
fast.

"Excuse me from going into particulars," he said. "I am not at
liberty to speak more fully. I have told you so much, because I
cannot bear to hear this subject spoken of lightly. Remember in
future, that you have seen a very honest old man who told you—
on his honor—that he had seen a ghost!" And he got up, as if he
thought he had said enough. Reserve, shyness, pride, the fear of
being laughed at, the memory, possibly, of former strokes of sarcasm—all this, on one side, had its weight with him; but I suspected
that on the other, his tongue was loosened by the garrulity of old
age, the sense of solitude, and the need of sympathy—and perhaps, also, by the friendliness which he had been so good as to express toward myself. Evidently it would be unwise to press him,
but I hoped to see him again.

"To give greater weight to my words," he added, "let me mention my name—Captain Diamond, sir. I have seen service."

"I hope I may have the pleasure of meeting you again," I said.

"The same to you, sir!" And brandishing his stick portentously
—though with the friendliest intentions—he marched stiffly away.

I asked two or three persons—selected with discretion—whether
they knew anything about Captain Diamond, but they were quite
unable to enlighten me. At last, suddenly, I smote my forehead,
and, dubbing myself a dolt, remembered that I was neglecting a
source of information to which I had never applied in vain. The
excellent person at whose table I habitually dined, and who dis-
pensed hospitality to students at so much a week, had a sister as
good as herself, and of conversational powers more varied. This
sister, who was known as Miss Deborah, was an old maid in all
the force of the term. She was deformed, and she never went out
of the house; she sat all day at the window, between a bird cage
and a flowerpot, stitching small linen articles—mysterious bands
and frills. She wielded, I was assured, an exquisite needle, and her

work was highly prized. In spite of her deformity and her confinement, she had a little, fresh, round face, and an imperturbable serenity of spirit. She had also a very quick little wit of her own, she was extremely observant, and she had a high relish for a friendly chat. Nothing pleased her so much as to have you—especially, I think, if you were a young divinity student—move your chair near her sunny window, and settle yourself for twenty minutes' "talk." "Well, sir," she used always to say, "what is the latest monstrosity in biblical criticism?"—for she used to pretend to be horrified at the rationalistic tendency of the age. But she was an inexorable little philosopher, and I am convinced that she was a keener rationalist than any of us, and that, if she had chosen, she could have propounded questions that would have made the boldest of us wince. Her window commanded the whole town—or rather, the whole country. Knowledge came to her as she sat singing, with her little, cracked voice, in her low rocking chair. She was the first to learn everything, and the last to forget it. She had the town gossip at her fingers' ends, and she knew everything about people she had never seen. When I asked her how she had acquired her learning, she said simply—"Oh, I observe!" "Observe closely enough," she once said, "and it doesn't matter where you are. You may be in a pitch-dark closet. All you want is something to start with; one thing leads to another, and all things are mixed up. Shut me up in a dark closet and I will observe after a while, that some places in it are darker than others. After that (give me time), and I will tell you what the President of the United States is going to have for dinner." Once I paid her a compliment. "Your observation," I said, "is as fine as your needle, and your statements are as true as your stitches."

Of course Miss Deborah had heard of Captain Diamond. He had been much talked about many years before, but he had survived the scandal that attached to his name.

"What was the scandal?" I asked.

"He killed his daughter."

"Killed her?" I cried; "How so?"

"Oh, not with a pistol, or a dagger, or a dose of arsenic! With his tongue. Talk of women's tongues! He cursed her—with some horrible oath—and she died!"

"What had she done?"

"She had received a visit from a young man who loved her, and whom he had forbidden the house."

"The house," I said. "Ah yes! The house is out in the country, two or three miles from here, on a lonely crossroad."

Miss Deborah looked sharply at me, as she bit her thread.

"Ah, you know about the house?" she said.

"A little," I answered; "I have seen it. But I want you to tell me more."

But here Miss Deborah betrayed an incommunicativeness which was most unusual.

"You wouldn't call me superstitious, would you?" she asked.

"You?—you are the quintessence of pure reason."

"Well, every thread has its rotten place, and every needle its grain of rust. I would rather not talk about that house."

"You have no idea how you excite my curiosity!" I said.

"I can feel for you. But it would make me very nervous."

"What harm can come to you?" I asked.

"Some harm came to a friend of mine." And Miss Deborah gave a very positive nod.

"What had your friend done?"

"She had told me Captain Diamond's secret, which he had told her with a mighty mystery. She had been an old flame of his, and he took her into his confidence. He bade her tell no one, and assured her that if she did, something dreadful would happen to her."

"And what happened to her?"

"She died."

"Oh, we are all mortal!" I said. "Had she given him a promise?"

"She had not taken it seriously, she had not believed him. She repeated the story to me, and three days afterward, she was taken with inflammation of the lungs. A month afterward, here where I sit now, I was stitching her grave clothes. Since then, I have never mentioned what she told me."

"Was it very strange?"

"It was strange, but it was ridiculous too. It is a thing to make you shudder and to make you laugh, both. But you can't worry it out of me. I am sure that if I were to tell you, I should immediately break a needle in my finger and die the next week of lockjaw."

I retired, and urged Miss Deborah no further; but every two or three days, after dinner, I came and sat down by her rocking chair.

I made no further allusion to Captain Diamond; I sat silent, clip-
ping tape with her scissors. At last, one day, she told me I was
looking poorly. I was pale.

"I am dying of curiosity," I said. "I have lost my appetite. I have
eaten no dinner." "

"Remember Blue Beard's wife!" said Miss Deborah.

"One may as well perish by the sword as by famine!" I answered.

Still she said nothing, and at last I rose with a melodramatic
sigh and departed. As I reached the door she called me and
pointed to the chair I had vacated. "I never was hardhearted," she
said. "Sit down, and if we are to perish, may we at least perish together." And then, in very few words, she communicated what
she knew of Captain Diamond's secret. "He was a very high-
tempered old man, and though he was very fond of his daughter,
his will was law. He had picked out a husband for her, and given
her due notice. Her mother was dead, and they lived alone together. The house had been Mrs. Diamond's own marriage portion; the Captain, I believe, hadn't a penny. After his marriage
they had come to live there, and he had begun to work the farm.
The poor girl's lover was a young man with whiskers from Boston.
The Captain came in one evening and found them together; he
collared the young man, and hurled a terrible curse at the poor
girl. The young man cried that she was his wife, and he asked her
if it was true. She said, No! Thereupon Captain Diamond, his fury
growing fiercer, repeated his imprecation, ordered her out of the
house, and disowned her forever. She swooned away, but her father went raging off and left her. Several hours later, he came back
and found the house empty. On the table was a note from the
young man telling him that he had killed his daughter, repeating
the assurance that she was his own wife, and declaring that he
himself claimed the sole right to commit her remains to earth. He
had carried the body away in a gig! Captain Diamond wrote him
a dreadful note in answer, saying that he didn't believe his daughter was dead, but that, whether or no, she was dead to him. A
week later, in the middle of the night, he saw her ghost. Then, I
suppose, he was convinced. The ghost reappeared several times,
and finally began regularly to haunt the house. It made the old
man very uncomfortable, for little by little his passion had passed
away, and he was given up to grief. He determined at last to leave

the place, and tried to sell it or rent it; but meanwhile the story had gone abroad, the ghost had been seen by other persons, the house had a bad name, and it was impossible to dispose of it. With the farm, it was the old man's only property, and his only means of subsistence; if he could neither live in it nor rent it he was beggared. But the ghost had no mercy, as he had had none. He struggled for six months, and at last he broke down. He put on his old blue cloak and took up his staff, and prepared to wander away and beg his bread. Then the ghost relented, and proposed a compromise. 'Leave the house to me!' it said; 'I have marked it for my own. Go off and live elsewhere. But to enable you to live, I will be your tenant, since you can find no other. I will hire the house of you and pay you a certain rent.' And the ghost named a sum. The old man consented, and he goes every quarter to collect his rent!"

I laughed at this recital, but I confess I shuddered too, for my own observation had exactly confirmed it. Had I not been witness of one of the Captain's quarterly visits, had I not all but seen him sit watching his spectral tenant count out the rent money, and when he trudged away in the dark, had he not a little bag of strangely gotten coin hidden in the folds of his old blue cloak? I imparted none of these reflections to Miss Deborah, for I was determined that my observations should have a sequel, and I promised myself the pleasure of treating her to my story in its full maturity. "Captain Diamond," I asked, "has no other known means of subsistence?"

"None whatever. He toils not, neither does he spin—his ghost supports him. A haunted house is valuable property!"

"And in what coin does the ghost pay?"

"In good American gold and silver. It has only this peculiarity —that the pieces are all dated before the young girl's death. It's a strange mixture of matter and spirit!"

"And does the ghost do things handsomely; is the rent large?"

"The old man, I believe, lives decently, and has his pipe and his glass. He took a little house down by the river; the door is sidewise to the street, and there is a little garden before it. There he spends his days, and has an old colored woman to do for him. Some years ago, he used to wander about a good deal, he was a familiar figure in the town, and most people knew his legend. But of late he has drawn back into his shell; he sits over his fire, and curiosity has forgotten him. I suppose he is falling into his dotage. But I am sure, I trust," said Miss Deborah in conclusion, "that he won't outlive his faculties or his powers of locomotion, for, if I remember rightly, it was part of the bargain that he should come in person to collect his rent."

We neither of us seemed likely to suffer any special penalty for Miss Deborah's indiscretion; I found her, day after day, singing over her work, neither more nor less active than usual. For myself, I boldly pursued my observations. I went again, more than once, to the great graveyard, but I was disappointed in my hope of finding Captain Diamond there. I had a prospect, however, which afforded me compensation. I shrewdly inferred that the old man's quarterly pilgrimages were made upon the last day of the old quarter. My first sight of him had been on the thirty-first of December, and it was probable that he would return to his haunted house on the last day of March. This was near at hand; at last it arrived. I betook myself late in the afternoon to the old house on the crossroad, supposing that the hour of twilight was the appointed season. I was not wrong. I had been hovering about for a short time, feeling very much like a restless ghost myself, when he appeared in the same manner as before, and wearing the same costume. I again concealed myself, and saw him enter the house with the ceremonial which he had used on the former occasion. A light appeared successively in the crevice of each pair of shutters, and I opened the window which had yielded to my importunity before. Again I saw the great shadow on the wall, motionless and solemn. But I saw nothing else. The old man reappeared at last, made his fantastic salaam before the house, and crept away into the dusk.

One day, more than a month after this, I met him again at Mount Auburn. The air was full of the voice of spring; the birds had come back and were twittering over their winter's travels, and a mild west wind was making a thin murmur in the raw verdure. He was seated on a bench in the sun, still muffled in his enormous mantle, and he recognized me as soon as I approached him. He nodded at me as if he were an old Bashaw giving the signal for my decapitation, but it was apparent that he was pleased to see me.

"I have looked for you here more than once," I said. "You don't come often."

"What did you want of me?" he asked.

"I wanted to enjoy your conversation. I did so greatly when I met you here before."

"You found me amusing?"

"Interesting!" I said.

"You didn't think me cracked?"

"Cracked? My dear sir—!" I protested.

"I'm the sanest man in the country. I know that is what insane people always say; but generally they can't prove it. I can!"

"I believe it," I said. "But I am curious to know how such a thing can be proved."

He was silent awhile.

"I will tell you. I once committed, unintentionally, a great crime. Now I pay the penalty. I give up my life to it. I don't shirk it; I face it squarely, knowing perfectly what it is. I haven't tried to bluff it off; I haven't begged off from it; I haven't run away from it. The penalty is terrible, but I have accepted it. I have been a philosopher!

"If I were a Catholic, I might have turned monk, and spent the rest of my life in fasting and praying. That is no penalty; that is an evasion. I might have blown my brains out—I might have gone mad. I wouldn't do either. I would simply face the music, take the consequences. As I say, they are awful! I take them on certain days, four times a year. So it has been these twenty years; so it will be as long as I last. It's my business; it's my avocation. That's the way I feel about it. I call that reasonable!"

"Admirably so!" I said. "But you fill me with curiosity and with compassion."

"Especially with curiosity," he said, cunningly.

"Why," I answered, "if I know exactly what you suffer I can pity you more."

"I'm much obliged. I don't want your pity; it won't help me. I'll tell you something, but it's not for myself; it's for your own sake." He paused a long time and looked all round him, as if for chance eavesdroppers. I anxiously awaited his revelation, but he disappointed me. "Are you still studying theology?" he asked.

"Oh, yes," I answered, perhaps with a shade of irritation. "It's a thing one can't learn in six months."

"I should think not, so long as you have nothing but your books. Do you know the proverb, 'A grain of experience is worth a pound of precept'? I'm a great theologian."

"Ah, you have had experience," I murmured sympathetically.

"You have read about the immortality of the soul; you have

seen Jonathan Edwards and Dr. Hopkins chopping logic over it, and deciding, by chapter and verse, that it is true. But I have seen it with these eyes; I have touched it with these hands!" And the old man held up his rugged old fists and shook them portentously. "That's better!" he went on; "but I have bought it dearly. You had better take it from the books—evidently you always will. You are a very good young man; you will never have a crime on your conscience."

I answered with some juvenile fatuity, that I certainly hoped I had my share of human passions, good young man and prospective Doctor of Divinity as I was.

"Ah, but you have a nice, quiet little temper," he said. "So have I—now! But once I was very brutal—very brutal. You ought to know that such things are. I killed my own child."

"Your own child?"

"I struck her down to the earth and left her to die. They could not hang me, for it was not with my hand I struck her. It was with foul and damnable words. That makes a difference; it's a grand law we live under! Well, sir, I can answer for it that *her* soul is immortal. We have an appointment to meet four times a year, and then I catch it!"

"She has never forgiven you?"

"She has forgiven me as the angels forgive! That's what I can't stand—the soft, quiet way she looks at me. I'd rather she twisted a knife about in my heart—O Lord, Lord, Lord!" and Captain Diamond bowed his head over his stick and leaned his forehead on his crossed hands.

I was impressed and moved, and his attitude seemed for the moment a check to further questions. Before I ventured to ask him anything more, he slowly rose and pulled his old cloak around him. He was unused to talking about his troubles, and his memories overwhelmed him. "I must go my way," he said; "I must be creeping along."

"I shall perhaps meet you here again," I said.

"Oh, I'm a stiff-jointed old fellow," he answered, "and this is rather far for me to come. I have to reserve myself. I have sat sometimes a month at a time smoking my pipe in my chair. But I should like to see you again." And he stopped and looked at me, terribly and kindly. "Some day, perhaps, I shall be glad to be able to lay my hand on a young, unperverted soul. If a man can make a friend, it is always something gained. What is your name?"

I had in my pocket a small volume of Pascal's *Thoughts,* on the flyleaf of which were written my name and address. I took it out and offered it to my old friend. "Pray keep this little book," I said. "It is one I am very fond of, and it will tell you something about me."

He took it and turned it over slowly, then looking up at me with a scowl of gratitude, "I'm not much of a reader," he said; "but I won't refuse the first present I shall have received since—my troubles; and the last. Thank you, sir!" And with the little book in his hand he took his departure.

I was left to imagine him for some weeks after that sitting solitary in his armchair with his pipe. I had not another glimpse of him. But I was awaiting my chance, and on the last day of June, another quarter having elapsed, I deemed that it had come. The evening dusk in June falls late, and I was impatient for its coming. At last, toward the end of a lovely summer's day, I revisited Captain Diamond's property. Everything now was green around it save the blighted orchard in its rear, but its own immitigable grayness and sadness were as striking as when I had first beheld it beneath a December sky. As I drew near it, I saw that I was late for my purpose, for my purpose had simply been to step forward on Captain Diamond's arrival, and bravely ask him to let me go in with him. He had preceded me, and there were lights already in the windows. I was unwilling, of course, to disturb him during his ghostly interview, and I waited till he came forth. The lights disappeared in the course of time; then the door opened and Captain Diamond stole out. That evening he made no bow to the haunted house, for the first object he beheld was his fair-minded young friend planted, modestly but firmly, near the doorstep. He stopped short, looking at me, and this time his terrible scowl was in keeping with the situation.

"I knew you were here," I said. "I came on purpose."

He seemed dismayed, and looked round at the house uneasily.

"I beg your pardon if I have ventured too far," I added, "but you know you have encouraged me."

"How did you know I was here?"

"I reasoned it out. You told me half your story, and I guessed the other half. I am a great observer, and I had noticed this house in passing. It seemed to me to have a mystery. When you kindly confided to me that you saw spirits, I was sure that it could only be here that you saw them."

"You are mighty clever," cried the old man. "And what brought you here this evening?"

I was obliged to evade this question.

"Oh, I often come; I like to look at the house—it fascinates me."

He turned and looked up at it himself. "It's nothing to look at outside." He was evidently quite unaware of its peculiar outward appearance, and this odd fact, communicated to me thus in the twilight, and under the very brow of the sinister dwelling, seemed to make his vision of the strange things within more real.

"I have been hoping," I said, "for a chance to see the inside. I thought I might find you here, and that you would let me go in with you. I should like to see what you see."

He seemed confounded by my boldness, but not altogether displeased. He laid his hand on my arm. "Do you know what I see?" he asked.

"How can I know, except as you said the other day, by experience? I want to have the experience. Pray, open the door and take me in."

Captain Diamond's brilliant eyes expanded beneath their dusky brows, and after holding his breath a moment, he indulged in the first and last apology for a laugh by which I was to see his solemn visage contorted. It was profoundly grotesque, but it was perfectly noiseless. "Take you in?" he softly growled. "I wouldn't go in again before my time's up for a thousand times that sum." And he thrust out his hand from the folds of his cloak and exhibited a small agglomeration of coin, knotted into the corner of an old silk pocket handkerchief. "I stick to my bargain no less, but no more!"

"But you told me the first time I had the pleasure of talking with you that it was not so terrible."

"I don't say it's terrible—now. But it's damned disagreeable!"

This adjective was uttered with a force that made me hesitate and reflect. While I did so, I thought I heard a slight movement of one of the window shutters above us. I looked up, but everything seemed motionless. Captain Diamond, too, had been thinking; suddenly he turned toward the house. "If you will go in alone," he said, "you are welcome."

"Will you wait for me here?"

"Yes, you will not stop long."

"But the house is pitch dark. When you go you have lights."

He thrust his hand into the depths of his cloak and produced some matches. "Take these," he said. "You will find two candlesticks with candles on the table in the hall. Light them, take one in each hand and go ahead."

"Where shall I go?"

"Anywhere—everywhere. You can trust the ghost to find you."

I will not pretend to deny that by this time my heart was beating. And yet I imagine I motioned the old man with a sufficiently dignified gesture to open the door. I had made up my mind that there was in fact a ghost. I had conceded the premise. Only I had assured myself that once the mind was prepared, and the thing was not a surprise, it was possible to keep cool. Captain Diamond turned the lock, flung open the door, and bowed low to me as I passed in. I stood in the darkness, and heard the door close behind me. For some moments, I stirred neither finger nor toe; I stared bravely into the impenetrable dusk. But I saw nothing and heard nothing, and at last I struck a match. On the table were two old brass candlesticks rusty from disuse. I lighted the candles and began my tour of exploration.

A wide staircase rose in front of me, guarded by an antique balustrade of that rigidly delicate carving which is found so often in old New England houses. I postponed ascending it, and turned into the room on my right. This was an old-fashioned parlor, meagerly furnished, and musty with the absence of human life. I raised my two lights aloft and saw nothing but its empty chairs and its blank walls. Behind it was the room into which I had peeped from without, and which, in fact, communicated with it, as I had supposed, by folding doors. Here, too, I found myself confronted by no menacing specter. I crossed the hall again, and visited the rooms on the other side; a dining room in front, where I might have written my name with my finger in the deep dust of the great square table; a kitchen behind with its pots and pans eternally cold. All this was hard and grim, but it was not formidable. I came back into the hall, and walked to the foot of the staircase, holding up my candles; to ascend required a fresh effort, and I was scanning the gloom above. Suddenly, with an inexpressible sensation, I became aware that this gloom was animated; it seemed to move and gather itself together. Slowly—I say slowly, for to my tense expectancy the instants appeared ages—it took the shape of a large, definite figure, and this figure advanced and stood at the top of the stairs. I frankly confess that by this time I was conscious of a feeling to which I am in duty bound to apply the vulgar name of fear. I may poetize it and call it Dread, with a capital letter; it was at any rate the feeling that makes a man yield ground. I measured it as it grew, and it seemed perfectly irresistible; for it did not appear to come from within but from without, and to be embodied in the dark image at the head of the staircase. After a fashion I reasoned—I remember reasoning. I said to myself, "I had always thought ghosts were white and transparent; this is a thing of thick shadows, densely opaque." I reminded myself that the occasion was momentous, and that if fear were to overcome me I should gather all possible impressions while my wits remained. I stepped back, foot behind foot, with my eyes still on the figure and placed my candles on the table. I was perfectly conscious that the proper thing was to ascend the stairs resolutely, face to face with the image, but the soles of my shoes seemed suddenly to have been transformed into leaden weights. I had got what I wanted; I was seeing the ghost. I tried to look at the figure distinctly so that I could remember it, and fairly claim, afterward, not to have lost my self-possession. I even asked myself how long it was expected I should stand looking, and how soon I could honorably retire. All this, of course, passed through my mind with extreme rapidity, and it was checked by a further movement on the part of the figure. Two white hands appeared in the dark perpendicular mass, and were slowly raised to what seemed to be the level of the head. Here they were pressed together, over the region of the face, and then they were removed, and the face was disclosed. It was dim, white, strange, in every way ghostly. It looked down at me for an instant, after which one of the hands was raised again, slowly, and waved to and fro before it. There was something very singular in this gesture; it seemed to denote resentment and dismissal, and yet it had a sort of trivial, familiar motion. Familiarity on the part of the haunting Presence had not entered into my calculations, and did not strike me pleasantly. I agreed with Captain Diamond that it was "damned disagreeable." I was pervaded by an intense desire to make an orderly, and, if possible, a graceful retreat. I wished to do it gallantly, and it seemed to me that it would be gallant to blow out my candles. I turned and did so, punctiliously, and then I made my way to the door, groped a moment and opened it. The outer light, almost extinct as it was, entered for a moment, played over the dusty depths of the house and showed me the solid shadow.

Standing on the grass, bent over his stick, under the early glimmering stars, I found Captain Diamond. He looked up at me fixedly for a moment, but asked no questions, and then he went and locked the door. This duty performed, he discharged the other—made his obeisance like the priest before the altar—and then without heeding me further, took his departure.

A few days later, I suspended my studies and went off for the summer's vacation. I was absent for several weeks, during which I had plenty of leisure to analyze my impressions of the supernatural. I took some satisfaction in the reflection that I had not been ignobly terrified; I had not bolted nor swooned—I had proceeded with dignity. Nevertheless, I was certainly more comfortable when I had put thirty miles between me and the scene of my exploit, and I continued for many days to prefer the daylight to the dark. My nerves had been powerfully excited; of this I was particularly conscious when, under the influence of the drowsy air of the seaside, my excitement began slowly to ebb. As it disappeared, I attempted to take a sternly rational view of my experience. Certainly I had seen *something*—that was not fancy; but what had I seen? I regretted extremely now that I had not been bolder, that I had not gone nearer and inspected the apparition more minutely. But it was very well to talk; I had done as much as any man in the circumstances would have dared; it was indeed a physical impossibility that I should have advanced. Was not this paralyzation of my powers in itself a supernatural influence? Not necessarily, perhaps, for a sham ghost that one accepted might do as much execution as a real ghost. But why had I so easily accepted the sable phantom that waved its hand? Why had it so impressed itself? Unquestionably, true or false, it was a very clever phantom, I greatly preferred that it should have been true—in the first place because I did not care to have shivered and shaken for nothing, and in the second place because to have seen a well-authenticated goblin is, as things go, a feather in a quiet man's cap. I tried, therefore, to let my vision rest and to stop turning it over. But an impulse stronger than my will recurred at intervals and set a mocking question on my lips. Granted that the apparition was Captain Diamond's daughter; if it was she it certainly was her spirit. But was it not her spirit and something more?

The middle of September saw me again established among the theologic shades, but I made no haste to revisit the haunted house.

The last of the month approached—the term of another quarter with poor Captain Diamond—and found me indisposed to disturb his pilgrimage on this occasion; though I confess that I thought with a good deal of compassion of the feeble old man trudging away, lonely, in the autumn dusk, on his extraordinary errand. On the thirtieth of September, at noonday, I was drowsing over a heavy octavo, when I heard a feeble rap at my door. I replied with an invitation to enter, but as this produced no effect I repaired to the door and opened it. Before me stood an elderly Negress with her head bound in a scarlet turban and a white handkerchief folded across her bosom. She looked at me intently and in silence; she had that air of supreme gravity and decency which aged persons of her race so often wear. I stood interrogative, and at last, drawing her hand from her ample pocket, she held up a little book. It was the copy of Pascal's *Thoughts* that I had given to Captain Diamond.

"Please, sir," she said, very mildly, "do you know this book?"

"Perfectly," said I, "my name is on the flyleaf."

"It is your name—no other?"

"I will write my name if you like, and you can compare them," I answered.

She was silent a moment and then, with dignity—"It would be useless, sir," she said, "I can't read. If you will give me your word that is enough. I come," she went on, "from the gentleman to whom you gave the book. He told me to carry it as a token—a token—that is what he called it. He is right down sick, and he wants to see you."

"Captain Diamond—sick?" I cried. "Is his illness serious?"

"He is very bad—he is all gone."

I expressed my regret and sympathy, and offered to go to him immediately, if his messenger would show me the way. She assented deferentially, and in a few moments I was following her along the sunny streets. My conductress directed her steps toward the river and stopped at a decent little yellow house in one of the streets that descend to it. She quickly opened the door and led me in, and I very soon found myself in the presence of my old friend. He was in bed, in a darkened room, and evidently in a very feeble state. He lay back on his pillow staring before him, with his bristling hair more erect than ever, and his intensely dark and bright old eyes touched with the glitter of fever. His apartment was humble and scrupulously neat, and I could see that my guide was a faithful servant. Captain Diamond, lying there rigid and pale on his white sheets, resembled some ruggedly carven figure on the lid of a Gothic tomb. He looked at me silently, and my companion withdrew and left us alone.

"Yes, it's you," he said, at last, "it's you, that good young man. There is no mistake, is there?"

"I hope not; I believe I'm a good young man. But I am very sorry you are ill. What can I do for you?"

"I am very bad, very bad; my poor old bones ache so!" and, groaning portentously, he tried to turn toward me.

I questioned him about the nature of his malady and the length of time he had been in bed, but he barely heeded me; he seemed impatient to speak of something else. He grasped my sleeve, pulled me toward him, and whispered quickly:

"You know my time's up!"

"Oh, I trust not," I said, mistaking his meaning. "I shall certainly see you on your legs again."

"God knows!" he cried. "But I don't mean I'm dying; not yet a bit. What I mean is, I'm due at the house. This is rent day."

"Oh, exactly! But you can't go."

"I can't go. It's awful. I shall lose my money. If I am dying, I want it all the same. I want to pay the doctor. I want to be buried like a respectable man."

"It is this evening?" I asked.

"This evening at sunset, sharp."

He lay staring at me, and, as I looked at him in return, I suddenly understood his motive in sending for me. Morally, as it came into my thought, I winced. But, I suppose I looked unperturbed, for he continued in the same tone. "I can't lose my money. Someone else must go. I asked Belinda; but she won't hear of it."

"You believe the money will be paid to another person?"

"We can try, at least. I have never failed before and I don't know. But, if you say I'm as sick as a dog, that my old bones ache, that I'm dying, perhaps she'll trust you. She don't want me to starve!"

"You would like me to go in your place, then?"

"You have been there once; you know what it is. Are you afraid?"

I hesitated.

"Give me three minutes to reflect," I said, "and I will tell you." My glance wandered over the room and rested on the various objects that spoke of the threadbare, decent poverty of its occupant. There seemed to be a mute appeal to my pity and my resolution in their cracked and faded sparseness. Meanwhile Captain Diamond continued, feebly:

"I think she'd trust you, as I have trusted you; she'll like your face; she'll see there is no harm in you. It's a hundred and thirty-three dollars, exactly. Be sure you put them into a safe place."

"Yes," I said at last, "I will go, and, so far as it depends upon me, you shall have the money by nine o'clock tonight."

He seemed greatly relieved; he took my hand and faintly pressed it, and soon afterward I withdrew. I tried for the rest of the day not to think of my evening's work, but, of course, I thought of nothing else. I will not deny that I was nervous; I was, in fact, greatly excited, and I spent my time in alternately hoping that the mystery should prove less deep than it appeared, and yet fearing that it might prove too shallow. The hours passed very slowly, but, as the afternoon began to wane, I started on my mission. On the way, I stopped at Captain Diamond's modest dwelling, to ask how he was doing, and to receive such last instructions as he might desire to lay upon me. The old Negress, gravely and inscrutably placid, admitted me, and, in answer to my inquiries, said that the Captain was very low; he had sunk since the morning.

"You must be right smart," she said, "if you want to get back before he drops off."

A glance assured me that she knew of my projected expedition, though, in her own opaque black pupil, there was not a gleam of self-betrayal.

"But why should Captain Diamond drop off?" I asked. "He certainly seems very weak; but I cannot make out that he has any definite disease."

"His disease is old age," she said, sententiously.

"But he is not so old as that; sixty-seven or sixty-eight, at most."
She was silent a moment.

"He's worn out; he's used up; he can't stand it any longer."

"Can I see him a moment?" I asked; upon which she led me again to his room.

He was lying in the same way as when I had left him, except that his eyes were closed. But he seemed very "low," as she had said, and he had very little pulse. Nevertheless, I further learned the doctor had been there in the afternoon and professed himself satisfied. "He don't know what's been going on," said Belinda curtly.

The old man stirred a little, opened his eyes, and after some time recognized me.

"I'm going, you know," I said. "I'm going for your money. Have you anything more to say?" He raised himself slowly, and with a painful effort, against his pillows; but he seemed hardly to understand me. "The house, you know," I said. "Your daughter."

He rubbed his forehead, slowly, awhile, and at last, his comprehension awoke. "Ah, yes," he murmured, "I trust you. A hundred and thirty-three dollars. In old pieces—all in old pieces." Then he added more vigorously, and with a brightening eye: "Be very respectful—be very polite. If not—if not—" and his voice failed again.

"Oh, I certainly shall be," I said, with a rather forced smile. "But, if not?"

"If not, I shall know it!" he said, very gravely. And with this, his eyes closed and he sunk down again.

I took my departure and pursued my journey with a sufficiently resolute step. When I reached the house, I made a propitiatory bow in front of it, in emulation of Captain Diamond. I had timed my walk so as to be able to enter without delay; night had already fallen. I turned the key, opened the door and shut it behind me. Then I struck a light, and found the two candlesticks I had used before, standing on the tables in the entry. I applied a match to both of them, took them up and went into the parlor. It was empty, and though I waited awhile, it remained empty. I passed then into the other rooms on the same floor, and no dark image rose before me to check my steps. At last, I came out into the hall again, and stood weighing the question of going upstairs. The staircase had been the scene of my discomfiture before, and I approached it with profound mistrust. At the foot, I paused, looking up, with my hand on the balustrade. I was acutely expectant, and my expression was justified. Slowly, in the darkness above, the black figure that I had seen before took shape. It was not an illusion; it was a figure, and the same. I gave it time to define itself, and watched it stand and look down at me with its hidden face. Then, deliberately, I lifted up my voice and spoke.

"I have come in place of Captain Diamond, at his request," I said. "He is very ill; he is unable to leave his bed. He earnestly begs that you will pay the money to me; I will immediately carry it to him." The figure stood motionless, giving no sign. "Captain Diamond would have come if he were able to move," I added, in a moment, appealingly; "but, he is utterly unable."

At this the figure slowly unveiled its face and showed me a dim, white mask; then it began slowly to descend the stairs. Instinctively I fell back before it, retreating to the door of the front sitting room. With my eyes still fixed on it, I moved backward across the threshold; then I stopped in the middle of the room and set down my lights. The figure advanced; it seemed to be that of a tall woman, dressed in vaporous black crape. As it drew near, I saw that it had a perfectly human face, though it looked extremely pale and sad. We stood gazing at each other; my agitation had completely vanished; I was only deeply interested.

"Is my father dangerously ill?" said the apparition.

At the sound of its voice—gentle, tremulous, and perfectly human—I started forward; I felt a rebound of excitement. I drew a long breath, I gave a sort of cry, for what I saw before me was not a disembodied spirit, but a beautiful woman, an audacious actress. Instinctively, irresistibly, by the force of reaction against my credulity, I stretched out my hand and seized the long veil that muffled her head. I gave it a violent jerk, dragged it nearly off, and stood staring at a large fair person, of about five-and-thirty. I comprehended her at a glance; her long black dress, her pale, sorrow-worn face, painted to look paler, her very fine eyes—the color of her father's—and her sense of outrage at my movement.

"My father, I suppose," she cried, "did not send you here to insult me!" and she turned away rapidly, took up one of the candles and moved toward the door. Here she paused, looked at me again, hesitated, and then drew a purse from her pocket and flung it down on the floor. "There is your money!" she said, majestically.

I stood there, wavering between amazement and shame, and saw her pass out into the hall. Then I picked up the purse. The next moment, I heard a loud shriek and a crash of something dropping, and she came staggering back into the room without her light.

"My father—my father!" she cried; and with parted lips and dilated eyes, she rushed toward me.

"Your father—where?" I demanded.

"In the hall, at the foot of the stairs."

I stepped forward to go out but she seized my arm.

"He is in white," she cried, "in his shirt. It's not he!"

"Why, your father is in his house, in his bed, extremely ill," I answered.

She looked at me fixedly, with searching eyes.

"Dying?"

"I hope not," I stuttered.

She gave a long moan and covered her face with her hands.

"Oh, heavens, I have seen his ghost!" she cried.

She still held my arm; she seemed too terrified to release it. "His ghost!" I echoed, wondering.

"It's the punishment of my long folly!" she went on.

"Ah," said I, "it's the punishment of my indiscretion—of my violence!"

"Take me away, take me away!" she cried, still clinging to my arm. "Not there"—as I was turning toward the hall and the front door—"not there, for pity's sake! By this door—the back entrance." And snatching the other candles from the table, she led me through the neighboring room into the back part of the house. Here was a door opening from a sort of scullery into the orchard. I turned the rusty lock and we passed out and stood in the cool air, beneath the stars. Here my companion gathered her black drapery about her, and stood for a moment, hesitating. I had been infinitely flurried, but my curiosity touching her was uppermost. Agitated, pale, picturesque, she looked, in the early evening light, very beautiful.

"You have been playing all these years a most extraordinary game," I said.

She looked at me somberly, and seemed disinclined to reply. "I came in perfect good faith," I went on. "The last time—three months ago—you remember?—you greatly frightened me."

"Of course it was an extraordinary game," she answered at last. "But it was the only way."

"Had he not forgiven you?"

"So long as he thought me dead, yes. There have been things in my life he could not forgive."

I hesitated and then—"And where is your husband?" I asked.

"I have no husband—I have never had a husband."

She made a gesture which checked further questions, and moved rapidly away. I walked with her round the house to the road, and she kept murmuring—"It was he—it was he!" When we reached the road she stopped, and asked me which way I was going. I pointed to the road by which I had come, and she said—"I take the other. You are going to my father's?" she added.

"Directly," I said.

"Will you let me know tomorrow what you have found?"

"With pleasure. But how shall I communicate with you?"

She seemed at a loss, and looked about her. "Write a few words," she said, "and put them under that stone." And she pointed to one of the lava slabs that bordered the old well. I gave her my promise to comply, and she turned away. "I know my road," she said. "Everything is arranged. It's an old story."

She left me with a rapid step, and as she receded into the darkness, resumed, with the dark flowing lines of her drapery, the phantasmal appearance with which she had at first appeared to me. I watched her till she became invisible, and then I took my own leave of the place. I returned to town at a swinging pace, and marched straight to the little yellow house near the river. I took the liberty of entering without a knock, and, encountering no interruption, made my way to Captain Diamond's room. Outside the door, on a low bench, with folded arms, sat Belinda.

"How is he?" I asked.

"He's gone to glory."

"Dead?" I cried.

She rose with a sort of tragic chuckle.

"He's as big a ghost as any of them now!"

I passed into the room and found the old man lying there irredeemably rigid and still. I wrote that evening a few lines which I proposed on the morrow to place beneath the stone, near the well; but my promise was not destined to be executed. I slept that night very ill—it was natural—and in my restlessness left my bed to walk about the room. As I did so I caught sight, in passing my window, of a red glow in the northwestern sky. A house was on fire in the country, and evidently burning fast. It lay in the same direction as the scene of my evening's adventures, and as I stood

watching the crimson horizon I was startled by a sharp memory.
I had blown out the candle which lighted me, with my companion,
to the door through which we escaped, but I had not accounted
for the other light, which she had carried into the hall and dropped
—heaven knew where—in her consternation. The next day I walked
out with my folded letter and turned into the familiar crossroad.
The haunted house was a mass of charred beams and smoldering
ashes; the well cover had been pulled off, in quest of water, by the
few neighbors who had had the audacity to contest what they
must have regarded as a demon-kindled blaze, the loose stones
were completely displaced, and the earth had been trampled into
puddles.

At one point in this story, James compares Captain Diamond to "a
figure out of one of Hoffmann's tales." He refers, of course, to the
great German fantasist E. T. A. Hoffmann whose stories inspired such
stage works as *The Nutcracker, Coppelia,* and *Tales of Hoffmann.*
In the foreword to *Automata* (*Die Automate,* 1814) Hoffmann gives
the story of another girl who played ghost:

"Adelgunda was at one time the most blooming, vigorous, cheer-
ful creature to be seen. Her fourteenth birthday came, and a number
of her friends and companions had been invited to spend it with
her. They were all sitting in a circle in the shrubbery, laughing and
amusing themselves, taking little heed that the evening was getting
darker and darker, for the soft July breeze was blowing refreshingly,
and they were just beginning thoroughly to enjoy themselves. In
the magic twilight they set about all sorts of dances, pretending to
be elves and woodland sprites. Adelgunda cried, 'Listen, children!
I shall go and appear to you as the White Lady whom our gardener
used to tell us about so often while he was alive. But you must come
to the bottom of the garden, where the old ruins are.' She wrapped
her white shawl round her, and went lightly dancing down the leafy
path, the girls following her, in full tide of laughter and fun. But
Adelgunda had scarcely reached the old crumbling arches, when
she suddenly stopped, and stood as if paralyzed in every limb. The
castle clock struck nine.

" 'Look, look!' cried she, in a hollow voice of the deepest terror.
'Don't you see it? the figure—close before me—stretching her hand
out at me. Don't you see her?'

"The children saw nothing whatever; but terror came upon them, and they all ran away, except one, more courageous than the rest, who hastened up to Adelgunda, and was going to take her in her arms. But Adelgunda, turning pale as death, fell to the ground. At the screams of the other girl everybody came hastening from the castle, and Adelgunda was carried in. At last she recovered from her faint, and, trembling all over, told them that as soon as she reached the ruins she saw an airy form, as if shrouded in mist, stretching its hand out towards her."

After that, Adelgunda sees the phantom White Lady every evening when the clock strikes nine.

CHAPTER 11

The Face

by E. F. Benson

On January 10, 1895, Henry James had tea with the Archbishop of Canterbury, Edward White Benson. As they sat before the fire, the conversation turned to ghosts. James and the Archbishop agreed that all the good ghost stories had been told; then the prelate remembered an account he had heard of some children who were haunted by the ghosts of evil servants. James entered the Archbishop's tale in his notebook on January 12, 1895, and later developed it as *The Turn of the Screw*. While writing this he lived at Lamb House, an eighteenth-century mansion in Rye, Sussex, which boasted a haunted chamber. From 1934 to 1937, E. F. (Edward Frederic) Benson, the Archbishop's son, occupied the same haunted house.

———

Hester Ward, sitting by the open window on this hot afternoon in June, began seriously to argue with herself about the cloud of foreboding and depression which had encompassed her all day, and, very sensibly, she enumerated to herself the manifold causes for happiness in the fortunate circumstances of her life. She was young, she was extremely good-looking, she was well off, she enjoyed excellent health, and above all, she had an adorable husband and two small, adorable children. There was no break, indeed, anywhere in the circle of prosperity which surrounded her, and had the wishing cap been handed to her that moment by some beneficent fairy, she would have hesitated to put it on her head, for there was positively nothing that she could think of which would have been worthy of such solemnity. Moreover, she could not accuse herself of a want of appreciation of her blessings; she appreciated enormously, she enjoyed enormously, and she thoroughly wanted all those who so munificently contributed to her happiness to share in it.

She made a very deliberate review of these things, for she was really anxious, more anxious, indeed, than she admitted to herself, to find anything tangible which could possibly warrant this ominous feeling of approaching disaster. Then there was the weather to consider; for the last week London had been stiflingly hot, but if that was the cause, why had she not felt it before? Perhaps the effect of these broiling, airless days had been cumulative. That was an idea, but, frankly, it did not seem a very good one, for, as a matter of fact, she loved the heat; Dick, who hated it, said that it was odd he should have fallen in love with a salamander.

She shifted her position, sitting up straight in this low window seat, for she was intending to make a call on her courage. She had known from the moment she awoke this morning what it was that lay so heavy on her, and now, having done her best to shift the reason of her depression on to anything else, and having completely failed, she meant to look the thing in the face. She was ashamed of doing so, for the cause of this leaden mood of fear which held her in its grip, was so trivial, so fantastic, so excessively silly.

"Yes, there never was anything so silly," she said to herself. "I must look at it straight, and convince myself how silly it is." She paused a moment, clenching her hands.

"Now for it," she said.

She had had a dream the previous night, which, years ago, used to be familiar to her, for again and again when she was a child she had dreamed it. In itself the dream was nothing, but in those childish days, whenever she had this dream which had visited her last night, it was followed on the next night by another, which contained the source and the core of the horror, and she would awake screaming and struggling in the grip of overwhelming nightmare. For some ten years now she had not experienced it, and would have said that, though she remembered it, it had become dim and distant to her. But last night she had had that warning dream, which used to herald the visitation of the nightmare, and now that whole storehouse of memory crammed as it was with bright things and beautiful contained nothing so vivid.

The warning dream, the curtain that was drawn up on the succeeding night, and disclosed the vision she dreaded, was simple and harmless enough in itself. She seemed to be walking on a high sandy cliff covered with short down-grass; twenty yards to the left came the edge of this cliff, which sloped steeply down to the sea that lay at its foot. The path she followed led through fields bounded by low hedges, and mounted gradually upward. She went through some half dozen of these, climbing over the wooden stiles that gave communication; sheep grazed there, but she never saw another human being, and always it was dusk, as if evening was falling, and she had to hurry on, because someone (she knew not whom) was waiting for her, and had been waiting not a few minutes only, but for many years. Presently, as she mounted this slope, she saw in front of her a copse of stunted trees, growing crookedly under the continual pressure of the wind that blew from the sea, and when she saw those she knew her journey was nearly done, and that the nameless one, who had been waiting for her so long was somewhere close at hand. The path she followed was cut through this wood, and the slanting boughs of the trees on the seaward side almost roofed it in; it was like walking through a tunnel. Soon the trees in front began to grow thin, and she saw through them the gray tower of a lonely church. It stood in a graveyard, apparently long disused, and the body of the church, which lay between the tower and the edge of the cliff, was in ruins, roofless, and with gaping windows, round which ivy grew thickly.

At that point this prefatory dream always stopped. It was a troubled, uneasy dream for there was over it the sense of dusk and of the man who had been waiting for her so long, but it was not of the order of nightmare. Many times in childhood had she experienced it, and perhaps it was the subconscious knowledge of the night that so surely followed it, which gave it its disquiet. And now last night it had come again, identical in every particular but one. For last night it seemed to her that in the course of these ten years which had intervened since last it had visited her, the glimpse of the church and churchyard was changed. The edge of the cliff had come nearer to the tower, so that it now was within a yard or two of it, and the ruined body of the church, but for one broken arch that remained, had vanished. The sea had encroached, and for ten years had been busily eating at the cliff.

Hester knew well that it was this dream and this alone which had darkened the day for her, by reason of the nightmares that used to follow it, and, like a sensible woman, having looked it once in the face, she refused to admit into her mind any conscious calling up of the sequel. If she let herself contemplate that, as likely or not the very thinking about it would be sufficient to ensure its return, and of one thing she was very certain, namely, that she didn't at all want it to do so. It was not like the confused jumble and jangle of ordinary nightmare, it was very simple, and she felt it concerned the nameless one who waited for her. . . . But she must not think of it; her whole will and intention was set on not thinking of it, and to aid her resolution, there was the rattle of Dick's latchkey in the front door, and his voice calling her.

She went out into the little square front hall; there he was, strong and large, and wonderfully undreamlike.

"This heat's a scandal, it's an outrage, it's an abomination of desolation," he cried, vigorously mopping. "What have we done that Providence should place us in this frying pan? Let us thwart him, Hester! Let us drive out of this inferno and have our dinner at—I'll whisper it so that he shan't overhear—at Hampton Court!"

She laughed: this plan suited her excellently. They would return late, after the distraction of a fresh scene; and dining out at night was both delicious and stupefying.

"The very thing," she said, "and I'm sure Providence didn't hear. Let's start now!"

"Rather. Any letters for me?"

He walked to the table where there were a few rather uninteresting-looking envelopes with half penny stamps.

"Ah, receipted bill," he said. "Just a reminder of one's folly in paying it. Circular . . . unasked advice to invest in German marks. . . . Circular begging letter, beginning 'Dear Sir or Madam.' Such impertinence to ask one to subscribe to something without ascertaining one's sex. . . . Private view, portraits at the Walton Gallery. . . . Can't go: business meetings all day. You might like to have a look in, Hester. Some one told me there were some fine Vandycks. That's all. Let's be off."

Hester spent a thoroughly reassuring evening, and though she thought of telling Dick about the dream that had so deeply im-

printed itself on her consciousness all day, in order to hear the
great laugh he would have given her for being such a goose, she
refrained from doing so, since nothing that he could say would
be so tonic to these fantastic fears as his general robustness. Besides, she would have to account for its disturbing effect, tell him
that it was once familiar to her, and recount the sequel of the nightmares that followed. She would neither think of them, nor mention them: it was wiser by far just to soak herself in his extraordinary sanity, and wrap herself in his affection. . . . They dined
out of doors at a riverside restaurant and strolled about afterward,
and it was very nearly midnight when, soothed with coolness and
fresh air, and the vigor of his strong companionship, she let herself
into the house, while he took the car back to the garage. And now
she marveled at the mood which had beset her all day, so distant
and unreal had it become. She felt as if she had dreamed of ship-
wreck, and had awoke to find herself in some secure and sheltered
garden where no tempest raged nor waves beat. But was there,
ever so remotely, ever so dimly, the noise of far-off breakers
somewhere?

He slept in the dressing room which communicated with her
bedroom, the door of which was left open for the sake of air and
coolness, and she fell asleep almost as soon as her light was out,
and while his was still burning. And immediately she began to
dream.

She was standing on the seashore; the tide was out, for level
sands strewn with stranded jetsam glimmered in a dusk that was
deepening into night. Though she had never seen the place it was
awfully familiar to her. At the head of the beach there was a steep
cliff of sand, and perched on the edge of it was a gray church
tower. The sea must have encroached and undermined the body
of the church, for tumbled blocks of masonry lay close to her at
the bottom of the cliff, and there were gravestones there, while
others still in place were silhouetted whitely against the sky. To
the right of the church tower there was a wood of stunted trees,
combed sideways by the prevalent sea wind, and she knew that
along the top of the cliff a few yards inland there lay a path through
fields, with wooden stiles to climb, which led through a tunnel of
trees and so out into the churchyard. All this she saw in a glance,
and waited, looking at the sand cliff crowned by the church tower,

for the terror that was going to reveal itself. Already she knew
what it was, and, as so many times before, she tried to run away.
But the catalepsy of nightmare was already on her; frantically she
strove to move, but her utmost endeavor could not raise a foot
from the sand. Frantically she tried to look away from the sand
cliffs close in front of her, where in a moment now the horror
would be manifested. . . .

It came. There formed a pale oval light, the size of a man's face,
dimly luminous in front of her and a few inches above the level
of her eyes. It outlined itself, short reddish hair grew low on the
forehead, below were two gray eyes, set very close together, which
steadily and fixedly regarded her. On each side the ears stood no-
ticeably away from the head, and the lines of the jaw met in a short
pointed chin. The nose was straight and rather long, below it came
a hairless lip, and last of all the mouth took shape and color, and
there lay the crowning terror. One side of it, soft-curved and beautiful, trembled into a smile, the other side, thick and gathered
together as by some physical deformity, sneered and lusted.

The whole face, dim at first, gradually focused itself into clear
outline: it was pale and rather lean, the face of a young man. And
then the lower lip dropped a little, showing the glint of teeth, and
there was the sound of speech. "I shall soon come for you now,"
it said, and on the words it drew a little nearer to her, and the smile
broadened. At that the full hot blast of nightmare poured in upon
her. Again she tried to run, again she tried to scream, and now she
could feel the breath of that terrible mouth upon her. Then with
a crash and a rending like the tearing asunder of soul and body
she broke the spell, and heard her own voice yelling, and felt with
her fingers for the switch of her light. And then she saw that the
room was not dark, for Dick's door was open, and the next moment, not yet undressed, he was with her.

"My darling, what is it?" he said. "What's the matter?"

She clung desperately to him, still distraught with terror.

"Ah, he has been here again," she cried. "He says he will soon
come to me. Keep him away, Dick."

For one moment her fear infected him, and he found himself
glancing round the room.

"But what do you mean?" he said. "No one has been here."

She raised her head from his shoulder.

"No, it was just a dream," she said. "But it was the old dream, and I was terrified. Why, you've not undressed yet. What time is it?"

"You haven't been in bed ten minutes, dear," he said. "You had hardly put out your light when I heard you screaming."

She shuddered.

"Ah, it's awful," she said. "And he will come again. . . ."

He sat down by her.

"Now tell me all about it," he said.

She shook her head.

"No, it will never do to talk about it," she said, "it will only make it more real. I suppose the children are all right, are they?"

"Of course they are. I looked in on my way upstairs."

"That's good. But I'm better now, Dick. A dream hasn't anything real about it, has it? It doesn't mean anything?"

He was quite reassuring on this point, and soon she quieted down. Before he went to bed he looked in again on her, and she was asleep.

Hester had a stern interview with herself when Dick had gone down to his office next morning. She told herself that what she was afraid of was nothing more than her own fear. How many times had that ill-omened face come to her in dreams, and what significance had it ever proved to possess? Absolutely none at all, except to make her afraid. She was afraid where no fear was: she was guarded, sheltered, prosperous, and what if a nightmare of childhood returned? It had no more meaning now than it had then, and all those visitations of her childhood had passed away without trace. . . . And then, despite herself, she began thinking over that vision again. It was grimly identical with all its previous occurrences, except . . . And then, with a sudden shrinking of the heart, she remembered that in earlier years those terrible lips had said: "I shall come for you when you are older," and last night they had said: "I shall soon come for you now." She remembered, too, that in the warning dream the sea had encroached, and it had now demolished the body of the church. There was an awful consistency about these two changes in the otherwise identical visions. The years had brought their change to them, for in the one the encroaching sea had brought down the body of the church, in the other the time was now near. . . .

It was no use to scold or reprimand herself, for to bring her mind to the contemplation of the vision meant merely that the grip of terror closed on her again; it was far wiser to occupy herself, and starve her fear out by refusing to bring it the sustenance of thought. So she went about her household duties, she took the children out for their airing in the park, and then, determined to leave no moment unoccupied, set off with the card of invitation to see the pictures in the private view at the Walton Gallery. After that her day was full enough, she was lunching out, and going on to a matinee, and by the time she got home Dick would have returned, and they would drive down to his little house at Rye for the weekend. All Saturday and Sunday she would be playing golf, and she felt that fresh air and physical fatigue would exorcise the dread of these dreaming fantasies.

The gallery was crowded when she got there; there were friends among the sightseers, and the inspection of the pictures was diversified by cheerful conversation. There were two or three fine Raeburns, a couple of Sir Joshuas, but the gems, so she gathered, were three Vandycks that hung in a small room by themselves. Presently she strolled in there, looking at her catalogue. The first of them, she saw, was a portrait of Sir Roger Wyburn. Still chatting to her friend she raised her eye and saw it. . . .

Her heart hammered in her throat, and then seemed to stand still altogether. A qualm, as of some mental sickness of the soul overcame her, for there in front of her was he who would soon come for her. There was the reddish hair, the projecting ears, the greedy eyes set close together, and the mouth smiling on one side, and on the other gathered up into the sneering menace that she knew so well. It might have been her own nightmare rather than a living model which had sat to the painter for that face.

"Ah, what a portrait, and what a brute!" said her companion. "Look, Hester, isn't that marvelous?"

She recovered herself with an effort. To give way to this evermastering dread would have been to allow nightmare to invade her waking life, and there, for sure, madness lay. She forced herself to look at it again, but there were the steady and eager eyes regarding her; she could almost fancy the mouth began to move. All round her the crowd bustled and chattered, but to her own sense she was alone there with Roger Wyburn.

And yet, so she reasoned with herself, this picture of him—for it was he and no other—should have reassured her. Roger Wyburn, to have been painted by Vandyck, must have been dead near on two hundred years; how could he be a menace to her? Had she seen that portrait by some chance as a child; had it made some dreadful impression on her, since overscored by other memories, but still alive in the mysterious subconsciousness, which flows eternally, like some dark underground river, beneath the surface of human life? Psychologists taught that these early impressions fester or poison the mind like some hidden abscess. That might account for this dread of one, nameless no longer, who waited for her.

That night down at Rye there came again to her the prefatory dream, followed by the nightmare, and clinging to her husband as the terror began to subside, she told him what she had resolved to keep to herself. Just to tell it brought a measure of comfort, for it was so outrageously fantastic, and his robust common sense upheld her. But when on their return to London there was a recurrence of these visions, he made short work of her demur and took her straight to her doctor.

"Tell him all, darling," he said. "Unless you promise to do that, I will. I can't have you worried like this. It's all nonsense, you know, and doctors are wonderful people for curing nonsense."

She turned to him.

"Dick, you're frightened," she said quietly.

He laughed.

"I'm nothing of the kind," he said, "but I don't like being awakened by your screaming. Not my idea of a peaceful night. Here we are."

The medical report was decisive and peremptory. There was nothing whatever to be alarmed about; in brain and body she was perfectly healthy, but she was run down. These disturbing dreams were, as likely as not, an effect, a symptom of her condition, rather than the cause of it, and Dr. Baring unhesitatingly recommended a complete change to some bracing place. The wise thing would be to send her out of this stuffy furnace to some quiet place to where she had never been. Complete change; quite so. For the same reason her husband had better not go with her; he must pack her off to, let us say, the East Coast. Sea air and coolness and complete idleness. No long walks; no long bathings; a dip, and a deck chair on the sands. A lazy, soporific life. How about Rushton? He had no doubt that Rushton would set her up again. After a week or so, perhaps, her husband might go down and see her. Plenty of sleep —never mind the nightmares—plenty of fresh air.

Hester, rather to her husband's surprise, fell in with this suggestion at once, and the following evening saw her installed in solitude and tranquillity. The little hotel was still almost empty, for the rush of summer tourists had not yet begun, and all day she sat out on the beach with the sense of a struggle over. She need not fight the terror any more; dimly it seemed to her that its malignancy had been relaxed. Had she in some way yielded to it and done its secret bidding? At any rate no return of its nightly visitations had occurred, and she slept long and dreamlessly, and woke to another day of quiet. Every morning there was a line for her from Dick, with good news of himself and the children, but he and they alike seemed somehow remote, like memories of a very distant time. Something had driven in between her and them, and she saw them as if through glass. But equally did the memory of the face of Roger Wyburn, as seen on the master's canvas or hanging close in front of her against the crumbling sand cliff, become blurred and indistinct, and no return of her nightly terrors visited her. This truce from all emotion reacted not on her mind alone, lulling her with a sense of soothed security, but on her body also, and she began to weary of this daylong inactivity.

The village lay on the lip of a stretch of land reclaimed from the sea. To the north the level marsh, now beginning to glow with the pale bloom of the sea lavender, stretched away featureless till it lost itself in distance, but to the south a spur of hill came down to the shore ending in a wooded promontory. Gradually, as her physical health increased, she began to wonder what lay beyond this ridge which cut short the view, and one afternoon she walked across the intervening level and strolled up its wooded slopes. The day was close and windless, the invigorating sea breeze, which till now had spiced the heat with freshness, had died, and she looked forward to finding a current of air stirring when she had topped the hill. To the south a mass of dark cloud lay along the horizon, but there was no imminent threat of storm. The slope was easily surmounted, and presently she stood at the top and found herself on the edge of a tableland of wooded pasture, and following the path, which ran not far from the edge of the cliff, she came out into more open country. Empty fields, where a few sheep were grazing, mounted gradually upward. Wooden stiles made a communication in the hedges that bounded them. And there, not a mile in front of her, she saw a wood, with trees growing slantingly away from the push of the prevalent sea winds, crowning the upward slope, and over the top of it peered a gray church tower.

For the moment, as the awful and familiar scene identified itself, Hester's heart stood still: the next a wave of courage and resolution poured in upon her. Here, at last was the scene of that prefatory dream, and here was she presented with the opportunity of fathoming and dispelling it. Instantly her mind was made up, and under the strange twilight of the shrouded sky, she walked swiftly on through the fields she had so often traversed in sleep, and up to the wood, beyond which he was waiting for her. She closed her ears against the clanging bell of terror, which now she could silence forever, and unfalteringly entered that dark tunnel of wood. Soon in front of her the trees began to thin, and through them, now close at hand, she saw the church tower. In a few yards farther she came out of the belt of trees, and round her were the monuments of a graveyard long disused. The cliff was broken off close to the church tower: between it and the edge there was no more of the body of the church than a broken arch, thick hung with ivy. Round this she passed and saw below the ruin of fallen masonry, and the level sands strewn with headstones and disjected rubble, and at the edge of the cliff were graves already cracked and toppling. But there was no one here, none waited for her, and the churchyard where she had so often pictured him was as empty as the fields she had just traversed.

A huge elation filled her; her courage had been rewarded, and all the terrors of the past became to her meaningless phantoms. But there was no time to linger, for now the storm threatened, and on the horizon a blink of lightning was followed by a crackling peal. Just as she turned to go her eye fell on a tombstone that was balanced on the very edge of the cliff, and she read on it that here lay the body of Roger Wyburn.

Fear, the catalepsy of nightmare, rooted her for the moment to the spot; she stared in stricken amazement at the moss-grown letters; almost she expected to see that fell terror of a face rise and hover over his resting place. Then the fear which had frozen her lent her wings, and with hurrying feet she sped through the arched pathway in the wood and out into the fields. Not one backward glance did she give till she had come to the edge of the ridge above the village, and, turning, saw the pastures she had traversed empty of any living presence. None had followed; but the sheep, apprehensive of the coming storm, had ceased to feed, and were huddling under shelter of the stunted hedges.

Her first idea, in the panic of her mind, was to leave the place at once, but the last train for London had left an hour before, and besides, where was the use of flight if it was the spirit of a man long dead from which she fled? The distance from the place where his bones lay did not afford her safety; that must be sought for within. But she longed for Dick's sheltering and confident presence; he was arriving in any case tomorrow, but there were long dark hours before tomorrow, and who could say what the perils and dangers of the coming night might be? If he started this evening instead of tomorrow morning, he could motor down here in four hours, and would be with her by ten o'clock or eleven. She wrote an urgent telegram: "Come at once," she said. "Don't delay."

The storm which had flickered on the south now came quickly up, and soon after it burst in appalling violence. For preface there were but a few large drops that splashed and dried on the roadway as she came back from the post office, and just as she reached the hotel again the roar of the approaching rain sounded, and the sluices of heaven were opened. Through the deluge flared the fire of the lightning, the thunder crashed and echoed overhead, and presently the street of the village was a torrent of sandy turbulent water, and sitting there in the dark one picture leaped floating before her eyes, that of the tombstone of Roger Wyburn, already tottering to its fall at the edge of the cliff of the church tower. In such rains as these, acres of the cliffs were loosened; she seemed to hear the whisper of the sliding sand that would precipitate those perished sepulchres and what lay within to the beach below.

By eight o'clock the storm was subsiding, and as she dined she was handed a telegram from Dick, saying that he had already started and sent this off en route. By half-past ten, therefore, if all was well, he would be here, and somehow he would stand between her and her fear. Strange how a few days ago both it and the thought of him had become distant and dim to her; now the one was as vivid as the other, and she counted the minutes to his ar-

rival. Soon the rain ceased altogether, and looking out of the curtained window of her sitting room where she sat watching the slow
circle of the hands of the clock, she saw a tawny moon rising over
the sea. Before it had climbed to the zenith, before her clock had
twice told the hour again, Dick would be with her.

It had just struck ten when there came a knock at her door, and
the page boy entered with the message that a gentleman had come
for her. Her heart leaped at the news; she had not expected Dick
for half an hour yet, and now the lonely vigil was over. She ran
downstairs, and there was the figure standing on the step outside.
His face was turned away from her; no doubt he was giving some
order to his chauffeur. He was outlined against the white moonlight, and in contrast with that, the gas jet in the entrance just
above his head gave his hair a warm, reddish tinge.

She ran across the hall to him.

"Ah, my darling, you've come," she said. "It was good of you.
How quick you've been!" Just as she laid her hand on his shoulder
he turned. His arm was thrown out round her, and she looked into
a face with eyes close set, and a mouth smiling on one side, the
other, thick and gathered together as by some physical deformity,
sneered and lusted.

The nightmare was on her; she could neither run nor scream,
and supporting her dragging steps, he went forth with her into the
night.

Half an hour later Dick arrived. To his amazement he heard that
a man had called for his wife not long before, and that she had
gone out with him. He seemed to be a stranger here, for the boy
who had taken his message to her had never seen him before, and
presently surprise began to deepen into alarm; enquiries were made
outside the hotel, and it appeared that a witness or two had seen
the lady whom they knew to be staying there walking, hatless, along
the top of the beach with a man whose arm was linked in hers.
Neither of them knew him, but one had seen his face and could
describe it.

The direction of the search thus became narrowed down, and
though with a lantern to supplement the moonlight they came
upon footprints which might have been hers, there were no marks
of any who walked beside her. But they followed these until they
came to an end, a mile away, in a great landslide of sand, which

had fallen from the old churchyard on the cliff, and had brought down with it half the tower and a gravestone, with the body that had lain below.

The gravestone was that of Roger Wyburn, and his body lay by it, untouched by corruption or decay, though two hundred years had elapsed since it was interred there. For a week afterwards the work of searching the landslide went on, assisted by the high tides that gradually washed it away. But no further discovery was made.

E. F. Benson's ghosts, unlike those of Henry James, are definite and sometimes tangible. In "The Face," it seems Sir Roger Wyburn returns in body as well as spirit, like a vampire, but there is no suggestion that he wants the same sustenance a vampire would seek. Benson (1867–1940) did write two vampire stories: the title story of his collection *The Room in the Tower* and "Mrs. Amworth" in *Visible and Invisible*. Other ghostly tales are collected in *Spook Stories* and *More Spook Stories*.

CHAPTER 12

The Whistling Room

by William Hope Hodgson

Dracula, as Anthony Boucher points out in his introduction to the Heritage Press edition, is a horror novel "told in terms of the detective story." Dr. Abraham Van Helsing, the champion vampire fighter of that novel, is the very model of such psychic detectives as Algernon Blackwood's *John Silence,* Seabury Quinn's *Phantom-Fighter* Jules de Grandin, and William Hope Hodgson's *Carnacki, the Ghost-Finder.* Carnacki is the detective hero of "The Whistling Room." Unfortunately, the author tells us very little about Mr. Carnacki, except that he specializes in finding and chasing ghosts. But the main interest of this story is the intense and unusual haunting of the whistling room itself.

———

Carnacki shook a friendly fist at me as I entered, late. Then he opened the door into the dining room and ushered the four of us—Jessop, Arkright, Taylor, and myself—in to dinner.

We dined well, as usual, and equally as usual Carnacki was pretty silent during the meal. At the end we took our wine and cigars to our accustomed positions and Carnacki—having got himself comfortable in his big chair—began without any preliminary:—

"I have just got back from Ireland, again," he said. "And I thought you chaps would be interested to hear my news. Besides, I fancy I shall see the thing clearer after I have told it all out straight. I must tell you this, though, at the beginning—up to the present moment I have been utterly and completely 'stumped.' I have tumbled upon one of the most peculiar cases of 'haunting'— or devilment of some sort—that I have come against. Now listen.

"I have been spending the last few weeks at Iastrae Castle, about twenty miles northeast of Galway. I got a letter about a month ago from a Mr. Sid K. Tassoc, who it seemed had bought the place lately and moved in, only to find that he had got a very peculiar piece of property.

"When I reached there he met me at the station, driving a jaunting car and drove me up to the castle, which by the way, he called a 'house-shanty.' I found that he was 'pigging it' there with his boy brother and another American who seemed to be half servant and half companion. It appears that all the servants had left the place, in a body, as you might say, and now they were managing among themselves, assisted by some day help.

"The three of them got together a scratch feed and Tassoc told me all about the trouble while we were at table. It is most extraordinary and different from anything that I have had to do with, though that Buzzing case was very queer too.

"Tassoc began right in the middle of his story. 'We've got a room in this shanty,' he said, 'which has got a most infernal whistling in it, sort of haunting it. The thing starts any time, you never know when, and it goes on until it frightens you. It's not ordinary whistling and it isn't the wind. Wait till you hear it.'

" 'We're all carrying guns,' said the boy, and slapped his coat pocket.

" 'As bad as that?' I said, and the older brother nodded. 'I may be soft,' he replied, 'but wait till you've heard it. Sometimes I think it's some infernal thing and the next moment I'm just as sure that someone's playing a trick on us.'

" 'Why?' I asked. 'What is to be gained?'

" 'You mean,' he said, 'that people usually have some good reason for playing tricks as elaborate as this. Well, I'll tell you. There's a lady in this province by the name of Miss Donnehue who's going to be my wife, this day two months. She's more beautiful than they make them, and so far as I can see, I've just stuck my head into an Irish hornet's nest. There's about a score of hot young Irishmen been courting her these two years gone and now that I've come along and cut them out they feel raw against me. Do you begin to understand the possibilities?'

" 'Yes,' I said. 'Perhaps I do in a vague sort of way, but I don't see how all this affects the room?'

" 'Like this,' he said. 'When I'd fixed it up with Miss Donnehue I looked out for a place and bought this little house-shanty. Afterward I told her—one evening during dinner—that I'd decided to tie up here. And then she asked me whether I wasn't afraid of the whistling room. I told her it must have been thrown in gratis, as I'd heard nothing about it. There were some of her men friends present and I saw a smile go round. I found out after a bit of questioning that several people have bought this place during the last twenty odd years. And it was always on the market again, after a trial.

" 'Well, the chaps started to bait me a bit and offered to take bets after dinner that I'd not stay six months in this shanty. I looked once or twice at Miss Donnehue so as to be sure I was "getting the note" of the talkee-talkee, but I could see that she didn't take it as a joke at all. Partly, I think, because there was a bit of a sneer in the way the men were tackling me and partly because she really believes there is something in this yarn of the whistling room.

" 'However, after dinner I did what I could to even things up with the others. I nailed all their bets and screwed them down good and safe. I guess some of them are going to be hard hit, unless I lose; which I don't mean to. Well, there you have practically the whole yarn.'

" 'Not quite,' I told him. 'All that I know is that you have bought a castle with a room in it that is in some way "queer," and that you've been doing some betting. Also, I know that your servants have got frightened and run away. Tell me something about the whistling?'

" 'Oh, that!' said Tassoc. 'That started the second night we were in. I'd had a good look round the room in the daytime, as you can understand; for the talk up at Arlestrae—Miss Donnehue's place—had me wonder a bit. But it seems just as usual as some of the other rooms in the old wing only perhaps a bit more lonesome feeling. But that may be only because of the talk about it, you know.

" 'The whistling started about ten o'clock on the second night, as I said. Tom and I were in the library when we heard an awfully queer whistling coming along the East Corridor—the room is in the East Wing, you know.

" 'That's that blessed ghost!' I said to Tom and we collared the lamps off the table and went up to have a look. I tell you, even as we dug along the corridor it took me a bit in the throat, it was so beastly queer. It was a sort of tune in a way, but more as if a devil or some rotten thing were laughing at you and going to get round at your back. That's how it makes you feel.

" 'When we got to the door we didn't wait, but rushed it open, and then I tell you the sound of the thing fairly hit me in the face. Tom said he got it the same way—sort of felt stunned and bewildered. We looked all round and soon got so nervous, we just cleared out and I locked the door.

" 'We came down here and had a stiff peg each. Then we landed fit again and began to feel we'd been nicely had. So we took sticks and went out into the grounds, thinking after all it must be some of these confounded Irishmen working the ghost trick on us. But there was not a leg stirring.

" 'We went back into the house and walked over it and then paid another visit to the room. But we simply couldn't stand it. We fairly ran out and locked the door again. I don't know how to put it into words, but I had a feeling of being up against something that was rottenly dangerous. You know! We've carried our guns ever since.

" 'Of course we had a real turnout of the room next day and the whole house-place, and we even hunted round the grounds but there was nothing queer. And now I don't know what to think, except that the sensible part of me tells me that it's some plan of these wild Irishmen to try to take a rise out of me.'

" 'Done anything since?' I asked him.

" 'Yes,' he said. 'Watched outside of the door of the room at night and chased round the grounds and sounded the walls and floor of the room. We've done everything we could think of and it's beginning to get on our nerves, so we sent for you.'

"By this we had finished eating. As we rose from the table Tassoc suddenly called out:—'Ssh! Hark!'

"We were instantly silent, listening. Then I heard it, an extraordinary hooning whistle, monstrous and inhuman, coming from far away through corridors to my right.

" 'By God!' said Tassoc, 'and it's scarcely dark yet! Collar those candles, both of you, and come along.'

"In a few moments we were out of the door and racing up the stairs. Tassoc turned into a long corridor and we followed, shielding our candles as we ran. The sound seemed to fill all the passage as we drew near, until I had the feeling that the whole air throbbed under the power of some wanton immense force—a sense of an actual taint, as you might say, of monstrosity all about us.

"Tassoc unlocked the door then, giving it a push with his foot, jumped back and drew his revolver. As the door flew open the sound beat out at us with an effect impossible to explain to one who has not heard it—with a certain, horrible personal note in it, as if in there in the darkness you could picture the room rocking and creaking in a mad, vile glee to its own filthy piping and whistling and hooning, and yet all the time aware of you in particular. To stand there and listen was to be stunned by realization. It was as if someone showed you the mouth of a vast pit suddenly and said:— That's hell. And you *knew* that they had spoken the truth. Do you get it, even a little bit?

"I stepped a pace into the room and held the candle over my head and looked quickly round. Tassoc and his brother joined me and the man came up at the back and we all held our candles high. I was deafened with the shrill, piping hoon of the whistling and then, clear in my ear something seemed to be saying to me:— 'Get out of here—quick! Quick! Quick!'

"As you chaps know, I never neglect that sort of thing. Sometimes it may be nothing but nerves, but as you will remember, it was just such a warning that saved me in the 'Gray Dog' case and in the 'Yellow Finger' experiments, as well as other times. Well, I turned sharp round to the others: 'Out!' I said. 'For God's sake, *out* quick!' And in an instant I had them into the passage.

"There came an extraordinary yelling scream into the hideous whistling and then, like a clap of thunder, an utter silence. I slammed the door, and locked it. Then, taking the key, I looked round at the others. They were pretty white and I imagine I must have looked that way too. And there we stood a moment, silent.

" 'Come down out of this and have some whisky,' said Tassoc, at last, in a voice he tried to make ordinary; and he led the way. I was the back man and I knew we all kept looking over our shoulders. When we got downstairs Tassoc passed the bottle round. He took a drink himself and slapped his glass on to the table. Then sat down with a thud.

" 'That's a lovely thing to have in the house with you, isn't it!' he said. And directly afterward:—'What on earth made you hustle us all out like that, Carnacki?'

" 'Something seemed to be telling me to get out, *quick*,' I said. 'Sounds a bit silly—superstitious, I know, but when you are meddling with this sort of thing you've got to take notice of queer fancies and risk being laughed at.'

"I told him then about the 'Gray Dog' business and he nodded a lot to that. 'Of course,' I said, 'this may be nothing more than those would-be rivals of yours playing some funny game, but personally, though I'm going to keep an open mind, I feel that there is something beastly and dangerous about this thing.'

"We talked for a while longer and then Tassoc suggested billiards, which we played in a pretty half-hearted fashion, and all the time cocking an ear to the door as you might say, for sounds; but none came, and later after coffee he suggested early bed and a thorough overhaul of the room on the morrow.

"My bedroom was in the newer part of the castle and the door opened into the picture gallery. At the east end of the gallery was the entrance to the corridor of the East Wing; this was shut off from the gallery by two old and heavy oak doors which looked rather odd and quaint beside the more modern doors of the various rooms.

"When I reached my room I did not go to bed, but began to unpack my instrument trunk, of which I had retained the key. I intended to take one or two preliminary steps at once in my investigation of the extraordinary whistling.

"Presently, when the castle had settled into quietness, I slipped out of my room and across to the entrance of the great corridor. I opened one of the low, squat doors and threw the beam of my pocket searchlight down the passage. It was empty and I went through the doorway and pushed to the oak behind me. Then along the great passageway, throwing my light before and behind and keeping my revolver handy.

"I had hung a 'protection belt' of garlic round my neck and the smell of it seemed to fill the corridor and give me assurance; for as you all know, it is a wonderful 'protection' against the more usual Aeiirii forms of semi-materialization by which I supposed the whistling might be produced, though at that period of my investigation I was still quite prepared to find it due to some perfectly natural cause, for it is astonishing the enormous number of cases that prove to have nothing abnormal in them.

"In addition to wearing the necklet I had plugged my ears loosely with garlic and as I did not intend to stay more than a few minutes in the room, I hoped to be safe.

"When I reached the door and put my hand into my pocket for the key I had a sudden feeling of sickening funk. But I was not going to back out if I could help it. I unlocked the door and turned the handle. Then I gave the door a sharp push with my foot, as Tassoc had done, and drew my revolver, though I did not expect to have any use for it, really.

"I shone the searchlight all round the room and then stepped inside with a disgustingly horrible feeling of walking slap into a waiting danger. I stood a few seconds, expectant, and nothing happened, and the empty room showed bare from corner to corner. And then, you know, I realized that the room was full of an abominable silence—can you understand that? A sort of purposeful silence, just as sickening as any of the filthy noises the things have power to make. Do you remember what I told you about that 'Silent Garden' business? Well this room had just that same *malevolent* silence—the beastly quietness of a thing that is looking at you and not seeable itself, and thinks that it has got you. Oh, I recognized it instantly and I slipped the top off my lantern so as to have light over the *whole* room.

"Then I set to working like fury and keeping my glance all about me. I sealed the two windows with lengths of human hair, right across, and sealed them at every frame. As I worked a queer, scarcely perceptible tenseness stole into the air of the place and the silence seemed, if you can understand me, to grow more solid. I knew then that I had no business there without 'full protection,' for I was practically certain that this was no mere Aeiirii development, but one of the worse forms as the Saiitii, that 'Grunting Man' case—you know.

"I finished the window and hurried over to the great fireplace. This is a huge affair and has a queer gallows-iron, I think they are called, projecting from the back of the arch. I sealed the opening with seven human hairs—the seventh crossing the six others.

"Then just as I was making an end, a low, mocking whistle grew

in the room. A cold, nervous prickling went up my spine and round
my forehead from the back. The hideous sound filled all the room
with an extraordinary, grotesque parody of human whistling, too
gigantic to be human—as if something gargantuan and monstrous
made the sounds softly. As I stood there a last moment, pressing
down the final seal, I had little doubt but that I had come across
one of those rare and horrible cases of the *Inanimate* reproducing
the functions of the *Animate*. I made a grab for my lamp and went
quickly to the door, looking over my shoulder and listening for the
thing that I expected. It came just as I got my hand upon the
handle—a squeal of incredible, malevolent anger, piercing through
the low hooning of the whistling. I dashed out, slamming the door
and locking it.

"I leaned a little against the opposite wall of the corridor, feeling rather funny for it had been a hideously narrow squeak . . .
'thyr be noe sayfetie to be gained bye gayrds of holieness when
the monyster hath pow'r to speak throe woode and stoene.' So
runs the passage in the Sigsand MS. and I proved it in that 'Nodding Door' business. There is no protection against this particular
form of monster, except possibly for a fractional period of time;
for it can reproduce itself in or take to its purposes the very protective material which you may use and has power to 'forme
wythine the pentycle,' though not immediately. There is, of course,
the possibility of the Unknown Last Line of the Saaamaaa Ritual
being uttered but it is too uncertain to count upon and the danger
is too hideous and even then it has no power to protect for more
than 'maybe fyve beats of the harte' as the Sigsand has it.

"Inside of the room there was now a constant, meditative,
hooning whistling, but presently this ceased and the silence seemed
worse for there is such a sense of hidden mischief in a silence.

"After a little I sealed the door with crossed hairs and then
cleared off down the great passage and so to bed.

"For a long time I lay awake, but managed eventually to get
some sleep. Yet, about two o'clock I was waked by the hooning
whistling of the room coming to me, even through the closed
doors. The sound was tremendous and seemed to beat through the
whole house with a presiding sense of terror. As if (I remember
thinking) some monstrous giant had been holding mad carnival
with itself at the end of that great passage.

"I got up and sat on the edge of the bed, wondering whether to go along and have a look at the seal and suddenly there came a thump on my door and Tassoc walked in with his dressing gown over his pajamas.

" 'I thought it would have waked you so I came along to have a talk,' he said, *'I* can't sleep. Beautiful! Isn't it?'

" 'Extraordinary!' I said, and tossed him my case.

"He lit a cigarette and we sat and talked for about an hour, and all the time that noise went on down at the end of the big corridor.

"Suddenly Tassoc stood up:—

" 'Let's take our guns and go and examine the brute,' he said, and turned toward the door.

" 'No!' I said. 'By Jove—NO! I can't say anything definite yet but I believe that room is about as dangerous as it well can be.'

" 'Haunted—*really* haunted?' he asked, keenly and without any of his frequent banter.

"I told him, of course, that I could not say a definite *yes* or *no* to such a question, but that I hoped to be able to make a statement soon. Then I gave him a little lecture on the False Re-Materialization of the Animate Force through the Inanimate-Inert. He began then to understand the particular way in which the room might be dangerous, if it were really the subject of a manifestation.

"About an hour later the whistling ceased quite suddenly and Tassoc went off again to bed. I went back to mine also, and eventually got another spell of sleep.

"In the morning I walked along to the room. I found the seals on the door intact. Then I went in. The window seals and the hair were all right, but the seventh hair across the great fireplace was broken. This set me thinking. I knew that it might, very possibly have snapped, through my having tensioned it too highly; but then, again, it might have been broken by something else. Yet it was scarcely possible that a man, for instance, could have passed between the six unbroken hairs for no one would ever have noticed them, entering the room that way, you see; but just walked through them, ignorant of their very existence.

"I removed the other hairs and the seals. Then I looked up the chimney. It went up straight and I could see blue sky at the top. It was a big, open flue and free from any suggestion of hiding places or corners. Yet, of course, I did not trust to any such casual

examination and after breakfast I put on my overalls and climbed
to the very top, sounding all the way, but I found nothing.

"Then I came down and went over the whole of the room—
floor, ceiling and the walls, mapping them out in six-inch squares
and sounding with both hammer and probe. But there was nothing
unusual.

"Afterward I made a three-weeks' search of the whole castle
in the same thorough way, but found nothing. I went even farther
then for at night, when the whistling commenced, I made a microphone test. You see, if the whistling were mechanically produced
this test would have made evident to me the working of the
machinery if there were any such concealed within the walls. It
certainly was an up-to-date method of examination, as you must
allow.

"Of course I did not think that any of Tassoc's rivals had fixed
up any mechanical contrivance, but I thought it just possible that
there had been some such thing for producing the whistling made
away back in the years, perhaps with the intention of giving the
room a reputation that would insure its being free of inquisitive
folk. You see what I mean? Well of course it was just possible, if
this were the case, that someone knew the secret of the machinery
and was utilizing the knowledge to play this devil of a prank on
Tassoc. The microphone test of the walls would certainly have
made this known to me, as I have said, but there was nothing of
the sort in the castle so that I had practically no doubt at all
now but that it was a genuine case of what is popularly termed
'haunting.'

"All this time, every night, and sometimes most of each night
the hooning whistling of the room was intolerable. It was as if an
intelligence there knew that steps were being taken against it and
piped and hooned in a sort of mad, mocking contempt. I tell you, it
was as extraordinary as it was horrible. Time after time I went
along—tiptoeing noiselessly on stockinged feet—to the sealed floor
(for I always kept the room sealed). I went at all hours of the
night and often the whistling inside would seem to change to a
brutally jeering note, as though the half-animate monster saw me
plainly through the shut door. And all the time as I would stand,
watching, the hooning of the whistling would seem to fill the whole
corridor so that I used to feel a precious lonely chap messing about
there with one of hell's mysteries.

"And every morning I would enter the room and examine the different hairs and seals. You see, after the first week, I had stretched parallel hairs all along the walls of the room and along the ceiling, but over the floor, which was of polished stone, I had set out little colorless wafers, tacky side uppermost. Each wafer was numbered and they were arranged after a definite plan so that I should be able to trace the exact movements of any living thing that went across.

"You will see that no material being or creature could possibly have entered that room without leaving many signs to tell me about it. But nothing was ever disturbed and I began to think that I should have to risk an attempt to stay a night in the room in the electric pentacle. Mind you, I *knew* that it would be a crazy thing to do, but I was getting stumped and ready to try anything.

"Once, about midnight, I did break the seal on the door and have a quick look in, but I tell you, the whole room gave one mad yell and seemed to come toward me in a great belly of shadows as if the walls had bellied in toward me. Of course, that must have been fancy. Anyway, the yell was sufficient and I slammed the door and locked it, feeling a bit weak down my spine. I wonder whether you know the feeling.

"And then when I had got to that state of readiness for anything I made what, at first, I thought was something of a discovery:

"'Twas about one in the morning and I was walking slowly round the castle, keeping in the soft grass. I had come under the shadow of the East Front and far above me I could hear the vile, hooning whistling of the room up in the darkness of the unlit wing. Then suddenly, a little in front of me, I heard a man's voice speaking low, but evidently in glee:—

"'By George! You chaps, but I wouldn't care to bring a wife home to that!' it said, in the tone of the cultured Irish.

"Someone started to reply, but there came a sharp exclamation and then a rush and I heard footsteps running in all directions. Evidently the men had spotted me.

"For a few seconds I stood there feeling an awful ass. After all, *they* were at the bottom of the haunting! Do you see what a big fool it made me seem? I had no doubt but that they were some of Tassoc's rivals and here I had been feeling in every bone that I had hit a genuine case! And then, you know, there came the memory of hundreds of details that made me just as much in doubt

again. Anyway, whether it was natural or abnatural, there was a
great deal yet to be cleared up.

"I told Tassoc next morning what I had discovered and through
the whole of every night for five nights we kept a close watch round
the East Wing, but there was never a sign of anyone prowling
about and all this time, almost from evening to dawn, that grotesque
whistling would hoon incredibly, far above us in the darkness.

"On the morning after the fifth night I received a wire from
here which brought me home by the next boat. I explained to
Tassoc that I was simply bound to come away for a few days,
but told him to keep up the watch round the castle. One thing
I was very careful to do and that was to make him absolutely
promise never to go into the room between sunset and sunrise. I
made it clear to him that we knew nothing definite yet, one way or
the other, and if the room were what I had first thought it to be,
it might be a lot better for him to die first than enter it after dark.

"When I got here and had finished my business I thought you
chaps would be interested and also I wanted to get it all spread out
clear in my mind, so I rang you up. I am going over again tomorrow
and when I get back I ought to have something pretty extraordinary
to tell you. By the way, there is a curious thing I forgot to tell you.
I tried to get a phonographic record of the whistling, but it simply
produced no impression on the wax at all. That is one of the things
that has made me feel queer.

"Another extraordinary thing is that the microphone will not
magnify the sound—will not even transmit it, seems to take no
account of it and acts as if it were non-existent. I am absolutely and
utterly stumped up to the present. I am a wee bit curious to see
whether any of you dear clever heads can make daylight of it.
I cannot—not yet."

He rose to his feet.

"Good night, all," he said, and began to usher us out abruptly,
but without offence, into the night.

A fortnight later he dropped us each a card and you can imagine
that I was not late this time. When we arrived Carnacki took us
straight into dinner and when we had finished and all made ourselves comfortable he began again, where he had left off:—

"Now just listen quietly, for I have got something very queer to
tell you. I got back late at night and I had to walk up to the castle
as I had not warned them that I was coming. It was bright moon-

light, so that the walk was rather a pleasure than otherwise. When I got there the whole place was in darkness and I thought I would go round outside to see whether Tassoc or his brother was keeping watch. But I could not find them anywhere and concluded that they had got tired of it and gone off to bed.

"As I returned across the lawn that lies below the front of the East Wing I caught the hooning whistling of the room coming down strangely clear through the stillness of the night. It had a peculiar note in it I remember—low and constant, queerly meditative. I looked up at the window, bright in the moonlight, and got a sudden thought to bring a ladder from the stable-yard and try to get a look into the room from the outside.

"With this notion I hunted round at the back of the castle among the straggle of the office and presently found a long, fairly light ladder, though it was heavy enough for one, goodness knows! I thought at first that I should never get it reared. I managed at last and let the ends rest very quietly against the wall a little below the sill of the larger window. Then, going silently, I went up the ladder. Presently I had my face above the sill and was looking in, alone with the moonlight.

"Of course the queer whistling sounded louder up there, but it still conveyed that peculiar sense of something whistling quietly to itself—can you understand? Though for all the meditative lowness of the note, the horrible, gargantuan quality was distinct—a mighty parody of the human, as if I stood there and listened to the whistling from the lips of a monster with a man's soul.

"And then, you know, I saw something. The floor in the middle of the huge, empty room was puckered upward in the center into a strange, soft-looking mound parted at the top into an ever-changing hole that pulsated to that great, gentle hooning. At times, as I watched, I saw the heaving of the indented mound gap across with a queer, inward suction as with drawing of an enormous breath, then the thing would dilate and pout once more to the incredible melody. And suddenly as I stared, dumb, it came to me that the thing was living. I was looking at two enormous, blackened lips, blistered and brutal, there in the pale moonlight. . . .

"Abruptly they bulged out to a vast pouting mound of force and sound, stiffened and swollen and hugely massive and clean cut in the moonbeams. And a great sweat lay heavy on the vast upper lip. In the same moment of time the whistling had burst into a mad screaming note that seemed to stun me, even where I stood, outside of the window. And then the following moment I was staring blankly at the solid, undisturbed floor of the room—smooth, polished stone flooring from wall to wall. And there was an absolute silence.

"You can picture me staring into the quiet room and knowing what I knew. I felt like a sick, frightened child and I wanted to slide *quietly* down the ladder and run away. But in that very instant I heard Tassoc's voice calling to me from within the room for help, *help*. My God! but I got such an awful dazed feeling and I had a vague, bewildered notion that after all, it was the Irishmen who had got him in there and were taking it out of him. And then the call came again and I burst the window and jumped in to help him. I had a confused idea that the call had come from within the shadow of the great fireplace and I raced across to it, but there was no one there.

" 'Tassoc!' I shouted, and my voice went empty-sounding round the great apartment, and then in a flash I *knew that Tassoc had never called*. I whirled round, sick with fear, toward the window, and as I did so a frightful, exultant whistling scream burst through the room. On my left the end wall had bellied in toward me in a pair of gargantuan lips, black and utterly monstrous, to within a yard of my face. I fumbled for a mad instant at my revolver; not for It, but myself, for the danger was a thousand times worse than death. And then suddenly the Unknown Last Line of the Saaamaaa Ritual was whispered quite audibly in the room. Instantly the thing happened that I have known once before. There came a sense as of dust falling continually and monotonously and I knew that my life hung uncertain and suspended for a flash in a brief, reeling vertigo of unseeable things. Then *that* ended and I knew that I might live. My soul and body blended again and life and power came to me. I dashed furiously at the window and hurled myself out headforemost, for I can tell you that I had stopped being afraid of death. I crashed down on to the ladder and slithered, grabbing and grabbing and so came some way or other alive to the bottom. And there I sat in the soft, wet grass with the moonlight all about me, and far above through the broken window of the room, there was a low whistling.

"That is the chief of it. I was not hurt and I went round to the front and knocked Tassoc up. When they let me in we had a long yarn over some good whisky—for I was shaken to pieces—and I explained things as much as I could. I told Tassoc that the room would have to come down and every fragment of it be burned in a blast furnace erected within a pentacle. He nodded. There was nothing to say. Then I went to bed.

"We turned a small army on to the work and within ten days that lovely thing had gone up in smoke and what was left was calcined and clean.

"It was when the workmen were stripping the paneling that I got hold of a sound notion of the beginnings of that beastly development. Over the great fireplace, after the great oak panels had been torn down, I found that there was let into the masonry a scrollwork of stone with on it an old inscription in ancient Celtic, that here in this room was burned Dian Tiansay, jester of King Alzof, who made the 'Song of Foolishness' upon King Ernore of the Seventh Castle.

"When I got the translation clear I gave it to Tassoc. He was tremendously excited for he knew the old tale and took me down to the library to look at an old parchment that gave the story in detail. Afterward I found that the incident was well known about the countryside, but always regarded more as a legend, than as history. And no one seemed ever to have dreamt that the old East Wing of Iastrae Castle was the remains of the ancient Seventh Castle.

"From the old parchment I gathered that there had been a pretty dirty job done, away back in the years. It seems that King Alzof and King Ernore had been enemies by birthright, as you might say truly, but that nothing more than a little raiding had occurred on either side for years until Dian Tiansay made the 'Song of Foolishness' upon King Ernore and sang it before King Alzof, and so greatly was it appreciated that King Alzof gave the jester one of his ladies to wife.

"Presently all the people of the land had come to know the song and so it came at last to King Ernore who was so angered that he made war upon his old enemy and took and burned him and his castle; but Dian Tiansay, the jester, he brought with him to his own place and having torn his tongue out because of the song which he had made and sung, he imprisoned him in the room in the East Wing (which was evidently used for unpleasant purposes), and the jester's wife he kept for himself, having a fancy for her prettiness.

"But one night Dian Tiansay's wife was not to be found and in the morning they discovered her lying dead in her husband's arms and he sitting, whistling the 'Song of Foolishness', for he had no longer the power to sing it.

"Then they roasted Dian Tiansay in the great fireplace—probably from that self-same gallows-iron which I have already mentioned. And until he died Dian Tiansay 'ceased not to whistle' the 'Song of Foolishness' which he could no longer sing. But afterward 'in that room' there was often heard at night the sound of something whistling and there 'grew a power in that room' so that none dared to sleep in it. And presently, it would seem, the King went to another castle for the whistling troubled him.

"There you have it all. Of course, that is only a rough rendering of the translation from the parchment. It's a bit quaint! Don't you think so?"

"Yes," I said, answering for the lot. "But how did the thing grow to such a tremendous manifestation?"

"One of those cases of continuity of thought producing a positive action upon the immediate surrounding material," replied Carnacki. "The development must have been going forward through centuries, to have produced such a monstrosity. It was a true instance of Saiitii manifestation which I can best explain by likening it to a living spiritual fungus which involves the very structure of the ether fiber itself and, of course, in so doing acquires an essential control over the 'material substance' involved in it. It is impossible to make it plainer in a few words."

"What broke the seventh hair?" asked Taylor.

But Carnacki did not know. He thought it was probably nothing but being too severely tensioned. He also explained that they found out that the men who had run away had not been up to mischief, but had come over secretly merely to hear the whistling which, indeed, had suddenly become the talk of the whole countryside.

"One other thing," said Arkright, "have you any idea what governs the use of the Unknown Last Line of the Saaamaaa Ritual? I know, of course, that it was used by the Ab-human Priests in the Incantation of the Raaaee, but what used it on your behalf and what made it?"

"You had better read Harzam's Monograph and my addenda to it, on Astral and 'Astarral' Co-ordination and Interference," said Carnacki. "It is an extraordinary subject and I can only say here that the human vibration may not be insulated from the 'astarral' (as is always believed to be the case in interferences by the Ab-human), without immediate action being taken by those Forces that govern the spinning of the outer circle. In other words, it is being proved, time after time, that there is some inscrutable Protective Force constantly intervening between the human soul (not the body, mind you) and the Outer Monstrosities. Am I clear?"

"Yes, I think so," I replied. "And you believe that the room had become the material expression of the ancient jester—that his soul, rotted with hatred had bred into a monster—eh?" I asked.

"Yes," said Carnacki, nodding. "I think you've put my thought rather neatly. It is a queer coincidence that Miss Donnehue is supposed to be descended (so I heard since) from the same King Ernore. It makes one think some rather curious thoughts, doesn't it? The marriage coming on and the room waking to fresh life. If she had gone into that room, ever . . . eh? IT had waited a long time. Sins of the fathers. Yes, I've thought of that. They're to be married next week and I am to be best man, which is a thing I hate. And he won his bets, rather! Just think, *if* ever she had gone into that room. Pretty horrible, eh?"

He nodded his head, grimly, and we four nodded back. Then he rose and took us collectively to the door and presently thrust us forth in friendly fashion on to the embankment and into fresh night air.

"Good night," we all called back and went to our various homes. If she had, eh? If she had? That is what I kept thinking.

William Hope Hodgson (1875–1918) spent eight years at sea and distinguished himself for valor in World War I with the 171st Brigade of Royal Field Artillery. Besides *Carnacki, the Ghost-Finder,* from which "The Whistling Room" is taken, he is the author of *The Boats of the "Glen Carrig," The House on the Borderland, The Ghost Pirates, The Night Land Poems, Men of the Deep Waters, Cargunka, The Luck of the Strong, Captain Gault, Deep Waters,* and two posthumous collections of verse: *The Calling of the Sea* and *The Voice of the Ocean.* A collection of his unpublished tales is planned by Arkham House.

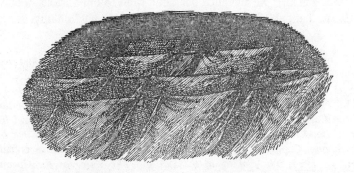

CHAPTER 13

The Grey Ones

by J. B. Priestley

J. B. (John Boynton) Priestley was born in 1894 and fought in World War I. After the war, he took honors in literature, history, and political science at Cambridge and went on to distinguish himself as an essayist, novelist, and dramatist. His 1927 novel *The Old Dark House* (in England, *Benighted*) became a first-rate, literate terror film in the capable hands of director James Whale. The cast was headed by Melvyn Douglas, Charles Laughton, Raymond Massey, Ernest Thesiger, Gloria Stuart, Lillian Bond, Eva Moore—and Boris Karloff as the ideal Charles Addams butler. There is nothing supernatural in *The Old Dark House,* but there are overtones. At one point in the film, the sudden appearance of a hand on a bannister has all the import of Horace Walpole's famous dream, ". . . a dream, of which all I could recover was, that I had thought myself in an ancient castle (a very natural dream for a head filled like mine with Gothic story), and that on the uppermost bannister of a great staircase I saw a gigantic hand in armour. In the evening I sat down, and began to write, without knowing in the least what I intended to say or relate." What he wrote was the first Gothic novel, *The Castle of Otranto,* which set the style for supernatural fiction since 1764.

"And your occupation, Mr. Patson?" Dr. Smith asked, holding his beautiful fountain pen a few inches from the paper.

"I'm an exporter," said Mr. Patson, smiling almost happily.

Really this wasn't too bad at all. First, he had drawn Dr. Smith instead of his partner Dr. Meyenstein. Not that he had anything against Dr. Meyenstein, for he had never set eyes on him, but he had felt that it was at least a small piece of luck that Dr. Smith had been free to see him and Dr. Meyenstein hadn't. If he had to explain himself to a psychiatrist, then he would much rather have one simply and comfortingly called Smith. And Dr. Smith, a broad-faced man about fifty with giant rimless spectacles, had nothing forbidding about him, and looked as if he might have been an accountant, a lawyer, or a dentist. His room, too, was reassuring, with nothing frightening in it; rather like a sitting room in a superior hotel. And that fountain pen really was a beauty. Mr. Patson had already made a mental note to ask Dr. Smith where he had bought that pen. And surely a man who could make such a mental note, right off, couldn't have much wrong with him?

"It's a family business," Mr. Patson continued, smiling away. "My grandfather started it. Originally for the Far East. Firms abroad, especially in rather remote places, send us orders for all manner of goods, which we buy here on commission for them. It's not the business it was fifty years ago, of course, but on the other hand we've been helped to some extent by all these trade restrictions and systems of export licences, which people a long way off simply can't cope with. So we cope for them. Irritating work often, but not uninteresting. On the whole I enjoy it."

"That is the impression you've given me," said Dr. Smith, making a note. "And you are reasonably prosperous, I gather? We all have our financial worries these days, of course. I know I have." He produced a mechanical sort of laugh, like an actor in a comedy that had been running too long, and Mr. Patson echoed him like another bored actor. Then Dr. Smith looked grave and pointed his pen at Mr. Patson as if he might shoot him with it. "So I think we can eliminate all that side, Mr. Patson—humph?"

"Oh yes—certainly—certainly," said Mr. Patson hurriedly, not smiling now.

"Well now," said Dr. Smith, poising his pen above the paper again, "tell me what's troubling you."

Mr. Patson hesitated. "Before I tell you the whole story, can I ask you a question?"

Dr. Smith frowned, as if his patient had made an improper suggestion. "If you think it might help——"

"Yes, I think it would," said Mr. Patson, "because I'd like to know roughly where you stand before I begin to explain." He waited a moment. "Dr. Smith, do you believe there's a kind of Evil Principle in the universe, a sort of super devil, that is working hard to ruin humanity, and has its agents, who must really be minor devils or demons, living among us as people? Do you believe that?"

"Certainly not," replied Dr. Smith without any hesitation at all. "That's merely a superstitious fancy, for which there is no scientific evidence whatever. It's easy to understand—though we needn't go into all that now—why anybody, even today, suffering from emotional stress, might be possessed by such an absurd belief, but of course it's mere fantasy, entirely subjective in origin. And the notion that this Evil Principle could have its agents among us might be very dangerous indeed. It could produce very serious antisocial effects. You realize that, Mr. Patson?"

"Oh—yes—I do. I mean, at certain times when—well, when I've been able to look at it as you're looking at it, doctor. But most times I can't. And that, I suppose," Mr. Patson added, with a wan smile, "is why I'm here."

"Quite so," Dr. Smith murmured, making some notes. "And I think you have been well advised to ask for some psychiatric treatment. These things are apt to be sharply progressive, although their actual progress might be described as regressive. But I won't worry you with technicalities, Mr. Patson. I'll merely say that you—or was it Mrs. Patson?—or shall I say both of you?—are to be congratulated on taking this very sensible step in good time. And now you know, as you said, where I stand, perhaps you had better tell me all about it. Please don't omit anything for fear of appearing ridiculous. I can only help you if you are perfectly frank with me, Mr. Patson. I may ask a few questions, but their purpose will be to make your account clearer to me. By the way, here we don't adopt the psychoanalytic methods—we don't sit behind our patients while they relax on a couch—but if you would find it easier not to address me as you have been doing—face to face——"

"No, that's all right," said Mr. Patson, who was relieved to discover he would not have to lie on the couch and murmur at the opposite wall. "I think I can talk to you just like this. Anyhow, I'll try."

"Good! And remember, Mr. Patson, try to tell me everything relevant. Smoke if it will help you to concentrate."

"Thanks, I might later on." Mr. Patson waited a moment, surveying his memories as if they were some huge glittering sea, and then waded in. "It began about a year ago. I have a cousin who's a publisher, and one night he took me to dine at his club—the Burlington. He thought I might like to dine there because it's a club used a great deal by writers and painters and musicians and theater people. Well, after dinner we played bridge for an hour or two, then we went down into the lounge for a final drink before leaving. My cousin was claimed by another publisher, so I was left alone for about a quarter of an hour. It was then that I overheard Firbright—you know, the famous painter—who was obviously full of drink, although you couldn't exactly call him drunk, and was holding forth to a little group at the other side of the fireplace. Apparently he'd just come back from Syria or somewhere around there, and he'd picked this idea up from somebody there though he said it only confirmed what he'd been thinking himself for some time."

Dr. Smith gave Mr. Patson a thin smile. "You mean the idea of an Evil Principle working to ruin humanity?"

"Yes," said Mr. Patson. "Firbright said that the old notion of a scarlet and black sulphuric Satan, busy tempting people, was of course all wrong, though it might have been right at one time, perhaps in the Middle Ages. Then the devils were all fire and energy. Firbright quoted the poet Blake—I've read him since—to show that these weren't real devils and their hell wasn't the real hell. Blake, in fact, according to Firbright, was the first man here to suggest we didn't understand the Evil Principle, but in his time it had hardly made a start. It's during the last few years, Firbright said, that the horrible thing has really got to work on us."

"Got to work on us?" Dr. Smith raised his eyebrows. "Doing what?"

"The main object, I gathered from what Firbright said," Mr. Patson replied earnestly, "is to make mankind go the way the social insects went, to turn us into automatic creatures, mass beings without individuality, soulless machines of flesh and blood."

The doctor seemed amused. "And why should the Evil Principle want to do that?"

"To destroy the soul of humanity," said Mr. Patson, without an answering smile. "To eliminate certain states of mind that belong essentially to the Good. To wipe from the face of this earth all wonder, joy, deep feeling, the desire to create, to praise life. Mind you, that is what Firbright said."

"But you believed him?"

"I couldn't help feeling, even then, that there was something in it. I'd never thought on those lines before—I'm just a plain business man and not given to fancy speculation—but I had been feeling for some time that things were going wrong and that somehow they seemed to be out of our control. In theory I suppose we're responsible for the sort of lives we lead, but in actual practice we find ourselves living more and more the kind of life we don't like. It's as if," Mr. Patson continued rather wildly, avoiding the doctor's eye, "we were all compelled to send our washing to one huge sinister laundry, which returned everything with more and more color bleached out of it until it was all a dismal grey."

"I take it," said Dr. Smith, "that you are now telling me what you thought and felt yourself, and not what you overheard this man Firbright say?"

"About the laundry—yes. And about things never going the right way. Yes, that's what I'd been feeling. As if the shape and color and smell of things were going. Do you understand what I mean, doctor?"

"Oh—yes—it's part of a familiar pattern. Your age may have something to do with it——"

"I don't think so," said Mr. Patson sturdily. "This is something quite different. I've made all allowance for that."

"So far as you can, no doubt," said Dr. Smith smoothly, without any sign of resentment. "You must also remember that the English middle class, to which you obviously belong, has suffered recently from the effects of what has been virtually an economic and social revolution. Therefore any member of that class—and I am one myself—can't help feeling that life does not offer the same satisfactions as it used to do, before the war."

"Dr. Smith," cried Mr. Patson, looking straight at him now, "I know all about that—my wife and her friends have enough to say about it, never stop grumbling. But this is something else. I may tell you, I've always been a Liberal and believed in social reform. And if this was a case of one class getting a bit less, and another class getting a bit more, my profits going down and my clerk's and

warehousemen's wages going up, I wouldn't lose an hour's sleep
over it. But what I'm talking about is something quite different.
Economics and politics and social changes may come into it, but
they're just being used."

"I don't follow you there, Mr. Patson."

"You will in a minute, doctor. I want to get back to what I
overheard Firbright saying, that night. I got away from it just to
make the point that I couldn't help feeling at once there was something in what he said. Just because for the first time somebody had
given me a reason why these things were happening." He regarded
the other man earnestly.

Smiling thinly, Dr. Smith shook his head. "The hypothesis of
a mysterious but energetic Evil Principle, Mr. Patson, doesn't offer
us much of a reason."

"It's a start," replied Mr. Patson, rather belligerently. "And of
course that wasn't all, by any means. Now we come to these
agents."

"Ah—yes—the agents." Dr. Smith looked very grave now. "It
was Firbright who gave you that idea, was it?"

"Yes, it would never have occurred to me, I'll admit. But if
this Evil Principle was trying to make something like insects out of
us, it could do it in two ways. One—by a sort of remote control,
perhaps by a sort of continuous radio program, never leaving our
minds alone, telling us not to attempt anything new, to play safe,
not to have any illusions, to keep to routine, nor to waste time
and energy wondering and brooding and being fanciful, and all
that."

"Did Firbright suggest something of that sort was happening?"

"Yes, but it wasn't his own idea. The man he'd been talking
about before I listened to him, somebody he'd met in the Near
East, had told him definitely all that non-stop propaganda was
going on. But the other way—direct control, you might call it—
was by the use of these agents—a sort of evil fifth column—with
more and more of 'em everywhere, hard at work."

"Devils?" enquired the doctor, smiling. "Demons? What?"

"That's what they amount to," said Mr. Patson, not returning
the smile but frowning a little. "Except that it gives one a wrong
idea of them—horns and tails and that sort of thing. These are quite
different, Firbright said. All you can definitely say is that they're
not human. They don't belong to us. They don't like us. They're

working against us. They have their orders. They know what they're doing. They work together in teams. They arrange to get jobs for one another, more and more influence and power. So what chance have we against them?" And Mr. Patson asked this question almost at the top of his voice.

"If such beings existed," Dr. Smith replied calmly, "we should soon be at their mercy, I agree. But then they don't exist—except of course as figures of fantasy, although in that capacity they can do a great deal of harm. I take it, Mr. Patson, that you have thought about—or shall we say *brooded over*—these demonic creatures rather a lot lately? Quite so. By the way, what do you call them? It might save time and possible confusion if we can give them a name."

"They're the Grey Ones," said Mr. Patson without any hesitation.

"Ah—the Grey Ones." Dr. Smith frowned again and pressed his thin lips together, perhaps to show his disapproval of such a prompt reply. "You seem very sure about this, Mr. Patson."

"Well, why shouldn't I be? You ask me what I call them, so I tell you. Of course, I don't know what they call themselves. And I didn't invent that name for them."

"Oh—this is Firbright again, is it?"

"Yes, that's what I heard him calling them, and it seemed to me a very good name for them. They're trying to give everything a grey look, aren't they? And there's something essentially grey about these creatures themselves—none of your gaudy, red and black, Mephistopheles stuff about *them*. Just quiet grey fellows busy greying everything—that's them."

"Is it indeed? Now I want to be quite clear about this, Mr. Patson. As I suggested earlier, this idea of the so-called Grey Ones is something I can't dismiss lightly, just because it might have very serious antisocial effects. It is one thing to entertain a highly fanciful belief in some mysterious Evil Principle working on us for its own evil ends. It is quite another thing to believe that actual fellow citizens, probably highly conscientious and useful members of the community, are not human beings at all but so many masquerading demons. You can see that, can't you?"

"Of course I can," said Mr. Patson, with a flick of impatience. "I'm not stupid, even though I may have given you the impression that I am. This idea of the Grey Ones—well, it brings the whole thing home to you, doesn't it? Here they are, busy as bees, round every corner, you might say."

The doctor smiled. "Yet you've never met one. Isn't that highly suggestive? Doesn't that make you ask yourself what truth there can be in this absurd notion? All these Grey Ones, seeking power over us, influencing our lives, and yet you've never actually come into contact with one. Now—now—Mr. Patson——" And he wagged a finger.

"Who says I've never met one?" Mr. Patson demanded indignantly. "Where did you get that idea from, doctor?"

"Do you mean to tell me——?"

"Certainly I mean to tell you. I know at least a dozen of 'em. My own brother-in-law is one."

Dr. Smith looked neither shocked nor surprised. He merely stared searchingly for a moment or two, then rapidly made some notes. And now he stopped sounding like a rather playful schoolmaster and became a doctor in charge of a difficult case. "So that's how it is, Mr. Patson. You know at least a dozen Grey Ones, and one of them is your brother-in-law. That's correct, isn't it? Good! Very well, let us begin with your brother-in-law. When and how did you make the discovery that he is a Grey One?"

"Well, I'd wondered about Harold for years," said Mr. Patson slowly. "I'd always disliked him but I never quite knew why. He'd always puzzled me too. He's one of those chaps who don't seem to have any center you can understand. They don't act from any ordinary human feeling. They haven't motives you can appreciate. It's as if there was nothing inside 'em. They seem to tick over like automatic machines. Do you know what I mean, doctor?"

"It would be better now if you left me out of it. Just tell me what you thought and felt—about Harold, for instance."

"Yes, Harold. Well, he was one of them. No center, no feeling, no motives. I'd try to get closer to him, just for my wife's sake, although they'd never been close. I'd talk to him at home, after dinner, and sometimes I'd take him out. You couldn't call him unfriendly—that at least would have been *something*. He'd listen, up to a point, while I talked. If I asked him a question, he'd make some sort of reply. He'd talk himself in a kind of fashion, rather like a leading article in one of the more cautious newspapers. Chilly stuff, grey stuff. Nothing exactly wrong with it, but nothing right about it either. And after a time, about half an hour or so, I'd find it hard to talk to him, even about my own affairs. I'd begin wondering what to say next. There'd be a sort of vacuum between us. He had a trick, which I've often met elsewhere, of deliberately not encouraging you to go on, of just staring, waiting for you to say something silly. Now I put this down to his being a public official. When I first knew him, he was one of the assistants to the clerk of our local borough council. Now he's the clerk, quite a good job, for ours is a big borough. Well, a man in that position has to be more careful than somebody like me has. He can't let himself go, has too many people to please—or rather, not to offend. And one thing was certain about Harold—and that ought to have made him more human, but somehow it didn't—and that was that he meant to get on. He had ambition, but there again it wasn't an ordinary human ambition, with a bit of fire and nonsense in it somewhere, but a sort of cold determination to keep on moving up. You see what I mean? Oh—I forgot—no questions. Well, that's how he was—and is. But then I noticed another thing about Harold. And even my wife had to agree about this. He was what we called a damper. If you took him out to enjoy something, he not only didn't enjoy it himself, but he contrived somehow to stop you from enjoying it. I'm very fond of a good show—and don't mind seeing a really good one several times—but if I took Harold along then it didn't matter what it was, I couldn't enjoy it. He wouldn't openly attack it or sneer at it, but somehow by just being there, sitting beside you, he'd cut it down and take all the color and fun out of it. You'd wonder why you'd wasted your evening and your money on such stuff. It was the same if you tried him with a football or cricket match, you'd have a boring afternoon. And if you asked him to a little party, it was fatal. He'd be polite, quite helpful, do whatever you asked him to do, but the party would never get going. It would be just as if he was invisibly spraying us with some devilish composition that made us all feel tired and bored and depressed. Once we were silly enough to take him on a holiday with us motoring through France and Italy. It was the worst holiday we ever had. He killed it stone dead. Everything he looked at seemed smaller and duller and greyer than it ought to have been. Chartres, the Loire country, Provence, the Italian Riviera, Florence, Siena—they were all cut down and greyed over, so that we wondered why we'd ever bothered to arrange such a trip and hadn't stuck to Torquay and Bournemouth. Then, before I'd

learnt more sense, I'd talk to him about various plans I had for
improving the business, but as soon as I'd described any scheme
to Harold I could feel my enthusiasm ebbing away. I felt—or he
made me feel—any possible development wasn't worth the risk.
Better stick to the old routine. I think I'd have been done for now
if I hadn't had sense enough to stop talking to Harold about the
business. If he asked me about any new plans, I'd tell him I hadn't
any. Now all this was long before I knew about the Grey Ones.
But I had Harold on my mind, particularly as he lived and worked
so close to us. When he became clerk to the council, I began to
take more interest in our municipal affairs, just to see what
influence Harold was having on them. I made almost a detective
job of it. For instance, we'd had a go-ahead, youngish chief education officer, but he left and in his place a dull timid fellow was
appointed. And I found out that Harold had worked that. Then
we had a lively chap as entertainments officer, who'd brightened
things up a bit, but Harold got rid of him too. Between them, he
and his friend, the treasurer, who was another of them, managed to put an end to everything that added a little color and
sparkle to life round our way. Of course they always had a good
excuse—economy and all that. But I noticed that Harold and the
treasurer only made economies in one direction, on what you might
call the anti-grey side, and never stirred themselves to save money
in other directions, in what was heavily official, pompous, interfer-
ing, irritating, depressing, calculated to make you lose heart. And
you must have noticed yourself that we never do save money in
those directions, either in municipal or national affairs, and that
what I complained of in our borough was going on all over the
country—yes, and as far as I can make out, in a lot of other countries too."

Dr. Smith waited a moment or two, and then said rather sharply:
"Please continue, Mr. Patson. If I wish to make a comment or ask
a question, I will do so."

"That's what I meant earlier," said Mr. Patson, "when I talked
about economies and politics and social changes just being used.
I've felt all the time there was something behind 'em. If we're
doing it for ourselves, it doesn't make sense. But the answer is of
course that we're not doing it for ourselves, we're just being
manipulated. Take communism. The Grey Ones must have almost
finished the job in some of those countries—they hardly need to

bother any more. All right, we don't like communism. We must make every possible effort to be ready to fight it. So what happens? More and more of the Grey Ones take over. This is their chance. So either way they win and we lose. We're farther along the road we never wanted to travel. Nearer the bees, ants, termites. Because we're being pushed. My God—doctor—can't you feel it yourself?"

"No, I can't, but never mind about me. And don't become too general, please. What about your brother-in-law, Harold? When did you decide he was a Grey One?"

"As soon as I began thinking over what Firbright said," replied Mr. Patson. "I'd never been able to explain Harold before—and God knows I'd tried often enough. Then I saw at once he was a Grey One. He wasn't born one, of course, for that couldn't possibly be how it works. My guess is that sometime while he was still young, the soul or essence of the real Harold Sothers was drawn out and a Grey One slipped in. That must be going on all the time now, there are so many of them about. Of course they recognize each other and help each other, which makes it easy for them to handle us humans. They know exactly what they're up to. They receive and give orders. It's like having a whole well-disciplined secret army working against us. And our only possible chance now is to bring 'em out into the open and declare war on 'em."

"How can we do that," asked Dr. Smith, smiling a little, "if they're secret?"

"I've thought a lot about that," said Mr. Patson earnestly, "and it's not so completely hopeless as you might think. After a time you begin to recognize a few. Harold, for instance. And our borough treasurer. I'm certain he's one. Then, as I told you at first, there are about a dozen more that I'd willingly stake a bet on. Yes, I know what you're wondering, doctor. If they're all officials, eh? Well no, they aren't, though seven or eight of 'em are—and you can see why—because that's where the power is now. Another two are up-and-coming politicians—and not in the same party neither. One's a banker I know in the city—and he's a Grey One all right. I wouldn't have been able to spot them if I hadn't spent so much time either with Harold or wondering about him. They all have the same cutting down and bleaching stare, the same dead touch. Wait till you see a whole lot of 'em together, holding a conference." Then Mr. Patson broke off abruptly, as if he felt he had said too much.

Dr. Smith raised his eyebrows so that they appeared above his spectacles, not unlike hairy caterpillars on the move. "Perhaps you would like a cigarette now, Mr. Patson. No, take one of these. I'm no smoker myself but I'm told they're excellent. Ah—you have a light. Good! Now take it easy for a minute or two because I think you're tiring a little. And it's very important you should be able to finish your account of these—er—Grey Ones, if possible without any hysterical overemphasis. No, no—Mr. Patson—I didn't mean to suggest there'd been any such overemphasis so far. You've done very well indeed up to now, bearing in mind the circumstances. And it's a heavy sort of day, isn't it? We seem to have too many days like this, don't we? Or is it simply that we're not getting any younger?" He produced his long-run actor's laugh. Then he brought his large white hands together, contrived to make his lips smile without taking the hard stare out of his eyes, and said finally: "Now then, Mr. Patson. At the point you broke off your story, shall we call it, you had suggested that you had seen a whole lot of Grey Ones together, holding a conference. I think you might very usefully enlarge that rather astonishing suggestion, don't you?"

Mr. Patson looked and sounded troubled. "I'd just as soon leave that, if you don't mind, doctor. You see, if it's all nonsense, then there's no point in my telling you about that business. If it isn't all nonsense——"

"Yes," said Dr. Smith, after a moment, prompting him, "if it isn't all nonsense——?"

"Then I might be saying too much." And Mr. Patson looked about for an ash tray as if to hide his embarrassment.

"There—at your elbow, Mr. Patson. Now please look at me. And remember what I said earlier. I am not interested in fanciful theories of the universe or wildly imaginative interpretations of present world conditions. All I'm concerned with here, in my professional capacity, is your state of mind, Mr. Patson. That being the case, it's clearly absurd to suggest that you might be saying too much. Unless you are perfectly frank with me, it will be very difficult for me to help you. Come now, we agreed about that. So far you've followed my instructions admirably. All I ask now is for a little more co-operation. Did you actually attend what you believed to be a conference of these Grey Ones?"

"Yes, I did," said Mr. Patson, not without some reluctance.

"But I'll admit I can't prove anything. The important part may be something I imagined. But if you insist, I'll tell you what happened. I overheard Harold and our borough treasurer arranging to travel together to Maundby Hall, which is about fifteen miles north of where I live. I'd never been there myself but I'd heard of it in connection with various summer schools and conferences and that sort of thing. Perhaps you know it, Dr. Smith?"

"As a matter of fact, I do. I had to give a paper there one Saturday night. It's a rambling early Victorian mansion, with a large ballroom that's used for the more important meetings."

"That's the place. Well, it seems they were going there to attend a conference of the New Era Community Planning Association. And when I overheard them saying that, first I told myself how lucky I was not to be going too. Then afterward, thinking it over, I saw that if you wanted to hold a meeting that no outsider in his senses would want to attend, you couldn't do better than hold it in a country house that's not too easy to get at, and call it a meeting or conference of the New Era Community Planning Association. I know if anybody said to me 'Come along with me and spend the day listening to the New Era Community Planning Association,' I'd make any excuse to keep away. Of course it's true that anybody like Harold couldn't be bored. The Grey Ones are never bored, which is one reason why they are able to collar and hold down so many jobs nowadays, the sort of jobs that reek of boredom. Well, this New Era Community Planning Association might be no more than one of the usual societies of busybodies, cranks, and windbags. But then again it might be something very different, and I kept thinking about it in connection with the Grey Ones. Saturday was the day of the conference. I went down to my office in the morning, just to go through the post and see if there was anything urgent, and then went home to lunch. In the middle of the afternoon I felt I had to know what was happening out at Maundby Hall, so off I went in my car. I parked it just outside the grounds, scouted round a bit, then found an entrance through a little wood at the back. There was nobody about, and I sneaked into the house by way of a servants' door near the pantries and larders. There were some catering people around there, but nobody bothered me. I went up some back stairs and after more scouting, which I enjoyed as much as anything I've done this year, I was guided by the sound of voices to a small door in a corridor upstairs. This door was locked on the inside, but a fellow had once shown me how to deal with a locked door when the key's still in the lock on the other side. You slide some paper under the door, poke the key out so that it falls on to the paper and then slide the paper back with the key on it. Well, this trick worked and I was able to open the door, which I did very cautiously. It led to a little balcony overlooking the floor of the ballroom. There was no window near this balcony so that it was rather dark up there and I was able to creep down to the front rail without being seen. There must have been between three and four hundred of them in that ballroom, sitting on little chairs. This balcony was high above the platform, so I had a pretty good view of them as they sat facing it. They looked like Grey Ones, but of course I couldn't be sure. And for the first hour or so, I couldn't be sure whether this really was a meeting of the New Era Community Planning Association or a secret conference of Grey Ones. The stuff they talked would have done for either. That's where the Grey Ones are so damnably clever. They've only to carry on doing what everybody expects them to do, in their capacity as sound conscientious citizens and men in authority, to keep going with their own hellish task. So there I was, getting cramp, no wiser. Another lot of earnest busybodies might be suggesting new ways of robbing us of our individuality. Or an organized covey of masquerading devils and demons might be making plans to bring us nearer to the insects, to rob us of our souls. Well, I was just about to creep back up to the corridor, giving it up as a bad job, when something happened." He stopped, and looked dubiously at his listener.

"Yes, Mr. Patson," said Dr. Smith encouragingly, "then something happened?"

"This is the part you can say I imagined, and I can't prove I didn't. But I certainly didn't dream it, because I was far too cramped and aching to fall asleep. Well, the first thing I noticed was a sudden change in the atmosphere of the meeting. It was as if somebody very important had arrived, although I didn't see anybody arriving. And I got the impression that the *real* meeting was about to begin. Another thing—I knew for certain now that this was no random collection of busybodies and windbags, that they were all Grey Ones. If you asked me to tell you in detail how I knew, I couldn't begin. But I noticed something else, after a minute or two. These Grey Ones massed together down there had now a positive quality of their own, which I'd never discovered before. It wasn't that they were just negative, not human, as they were at ordinary times; they had this positive quality, which I can't describe except as a sort of chilly hellishness. As if they'd stopped pretending to be human and were letting themselves go, recovering their demon natures. And here I'm warning you, doctor, that my account of what happened from then is bound to be sketchy and peculiar. For one thing, I wasn't really well placed up in that balcony; not daring to show myself and only getting hurried glimpses; and for another thing, I was frightened. Yes, doctor, absolutely terrified. I was crouching there just above three or four hundred creatures from some cold hell. That quality I mentioned, that chilly hellishness, seemed to come rolling over me in waves. I might have been kneeling on the edge of a pit of iniquity a million miles deep. I felt the force of this hellishness not on the outside but inside, as if the very essence of me was being challenged and attacked. One slip, a blackout, and then I might waken up to find myself running a concentration camp, choosing skins for lamp shades. Then somebody, something, arrived. Whoever or whatever they'd been waiting for was down there on the platform. I knew that definitely. But I couldn't see him or it. All I could make out was a sort of thickening and whirling of the air down there. Then out of that a voice spoke, the voice of the leader they had been expecting. But this voice didn't come from outside, through my ears. It spoke inside me, right in the center, so that it came out to my attention, if you see what I mean. Rather like a small, very clear voice on a good telephone line, but coming from inside. I'll tell you frankly I didn't want to stay there and listen, no matter what big secrets were coming out; all I wanted to do was to get away from there as soon as I could; but for a few minutes I was too frightened to make the necessary moves."

"Then you heard what this—er—voice was saying, Mr. Patson?" the doctor asked.

"Some of it—yes."

"Excellent! Now this is important." And Dr. Smith pointed his beautiful fountain pen at Mr. Patson's left eye. "Did you learn from it anything you hadn't known before? Please answer me carefully."

"I'll tell you one thing you won't believe," cried Mr. Patson. "Not about the voice—we'll come to that—but about those Grey

Ones. I risked a peep while the voice was talking, and what I saw nearly made me pass out. There they were—three or four hundred of 'em—not looking human at all, not making any attempt; they'd all gone back to their original shapes. They looked—this is the nearest I can get to it—like big semitransparent toads—and their eyes were like six hundred electric lamps burning under water, all greeny, unblinking, and shining out of hell."

"But what did you hear the voice say?" Dr. Smith was urgent now. "How much can you remember? That's what I want to know. Come along, man."

Mr. Patson passed a hand across his forehead and then looked at the edge of his hand with some astonishment, as if he had not known it would be so wet. "I heard it thank them in the name of Adaragraffa—Lord of the Creeping Hosts. Yes, I could have imagined it—only I never knew I had that sort of imagination. And what is imagination anyhow?"

"What else—what else—did you hear, man?"

"Ten thousand more were to be drafted into the Western Region. There would be promotions for some there who'd been on continuous duty longest. There was to be a swing over from the assault by way of social conditions, which could almost look after itself now, to the draining away of character, especially in the young of the doomed species. Yes, those were the very words," Mr. Patson shouted, jumping up and waving his arms. "Especially in the young of the doomed species. Us—d'you understand—us. And I tell you—we haven't a chance unless we start fighting back now—now—yes, and with everything we've got left. Grey Ones. And more and more of them coming, taking charge of us, giving us a push here, a shove there—down—down—down——"

Mr. Patson found his arms strongly seized and held by the doctor, who was clearly a man of some strength. The next moment he was being lowered into his chair. "Mr. Patson," said the doctor sternly, "you must not excite yourself in this fashion. I cannot allow it. Now I must ask you to keep still and quiet for a minute while I speak to my partner, Dr. Meyenstein. It's for your own good. Now give me your promise."

"All right, but don't be long," said Mr. Patson, who suddenly felt quite exhausted. As he watched the doctor go out, he wondered if he had not said either too much or not enough. Too much, he felt, if he was to be accepted as a sensible business man who happened to be troubled by some neurotic fancies. Not enough, perhaps, to justify, in view of the doctor's obvious skepticism, the terrible shaking excitement that had possessed him at the end of their interview. No doubt, round the corner, Drs. Smith and Meyenstein were having a good laugh over this rubbish about Grey Ones. Well, they could try and make him laugh too. He would be only too delighted to join them, if they could persuade him he had been deceiving himself. Probably that is what they would do now.

"Well, Mr. Patson," said Dr. Smith, at once brisk and grave, as he returned with two other men, one of them Dr. Meyenstein and the other a bulky fellow in white who might be a male nurse. All three moved forward slowly as Dr. Smith spoke to him. "You must realize that you are a very sick man—sick in mind if not yet sick in body. So you must put yourself in our hands."

Even as he nodded in vague agreement, Mr. Patson saw what he ought to have guessed before, that Dr. Smith was a Grey One and that now he had brought two more Grey Ones with him. There was a fraction of a moment, as the three of them bore down upon him to silence his warning forever, when he thought he caught another glimpse of the creature in the ballroom, three of them now like big semitransparent toads, six eyes like electric lamps burning under water, all greeny, unblinking, shining triumphantly out of hell. . . .

————————

Concise as it is, this story presents some puzzles that Hoffmann, Kafka, and Henry James might be proud of. Mr. Patson may be hallucinating but his fear cannot be dismissed as baseless. A clinical interpretation is possible but unlikely. The Caligaresque Dr. Smith—now there's an alias for you!—could have another name that sounds like "Adaragraffa, Lord of the Creeping Hosts." And what about the Grey Ones: are they cosmic invaders, demons of the pit, or both? The author has carefully erased everything that might give them a simple label. Likewise, he raises and dismisses politico-economic issues in favor of more subtle implications about the values and convictions of our time. The ultimate question seems to be: what are *we* becoming?

CHAPTER 14

The Stolen Body

by H. G. Wells

Though "The Grey Ones" may be extraterrestrial invaders, Priestley weaves the tale like an old account of diabolic possession, or a modern case of persecution complex. Conversely, "The Stolen Body" involves ghosts aplenty, but it is told in terms of speculative fiction. H. G. Wells is less concerned with ambiguous ghostly fears than with his own piquant ideas about the conditions of ghosthood. As always, his curiosity is catching, his narrative is swift and clear, and even the supernaturalism of this story seems quite natural.

Mr. Bessel was the senior partner in the firm of Bessel, Hart & Brown, of St. Paul's Churchyard, and for many years he was well known among those interested in psychical research as a liberal-minded and conscientious investigator. He was an unmarried man, and instead of living in the suburbs, after the fashion of his class, he occupied rooms in the Albany, near Piccadilly. He was particularly interested in the questions of thought transference and of apparitions of the living, and in November, 1896, he commenced a series of experiments in conjunction with Mr. Vincey, of Staple Inn, in order to test the alleged possibility of projecting an apparition of oneself by force of will through space.

Their experiments were conducted in the following manner: At a prearranged hour Mr. Bessel shut himself in one of his rooms in the Albany and Mr. Vincey in his sitting room in Staple Inn, and each then fixed his mind as resolutely as possible on the other. Mr. Bessel had acquired the art of self-hypnotism, and, so far as he could, he attempted first to hypnotize himself and then to project himself as a "phantom of the living" across the intervening space of nearly two miles into Mr. Vincey's apartment. On several evenings this was tried without any satisfactory result, but on the fifth or sixth occasion Mr. Vincey did actually see or imagine he saw an apparition of Mr. Bessel standing in his room. He states that the appearance, although brief, was very vivid and real. He noticed that Mr. Bessel's face was white and his expression anxious, and, moreover, that his hair was disordered. For a moment Mr. Vincey, in spite of his state of expectation, was too surprised to speak or move, and in that moment it seemed to him as though the figure glanced over its shoulder and incontinently vanished.

It had been arranged that an attempt should be made to photograph any phantasm seen, but Mr. Vincey had not the instant presence of mind to snap the camera that lay ready on the table beside him, and when he did so he was too late. Greatly elated, however, even by this partial success, he made a note of the exact time, and at once took a cab to the Albany to inform Mr. Bessel of this result.

He was surprised to find Mr. Bessel's outer door standing open to the night, and the inner apartments lit and in an extraordinary disorder. An empty champagne magnum lay smashed upon the floor; its neck had been broken off against the inkpot on the bureau and lay beside it. An octagonal occasional table, which carried a bronze statuette and a number of choice books, had been rudely overturned, and down the primrose paper of the wall inky fingers had been drawn, as it seemed for the mere pleasure of defilement. One of the delicate chintz curtains had been violently torn from its rings and thrust upon the fire, so that the smell of its smoldering filled the room. Indeed the whole place was disarranged in the strangest fashion. For a few minutes Mr. Vincey, who had entered sure of finding Mr. Bessel in his easy chair awaiting him, could scarcely believe his eyes, and stood staring helplessly at these unanticipated things.

Then, full of a vague sense of calamity, he sought the porter at the entrance lodge. "Where is Mr. Bessel?" he asked. "Do you know that all the furniture is broken in Mr. Bessel's room?" The porter said nothing, but, obeying his gestures, came at once to Mr. Bessel's apartment to see the state of affairs. "This settles it," he said, surveying the lunatic confusion. "I didn't know of this. Mr. Bessel's gone off. He's mad!"

He then proceeded to tell Mr. Vincey that about half an hour previously, that is to say, at about the time of Mr. Bessel's apparition in Mr. Vincey's rooms, the missing gentleman had rushed out of the gates of the Albany into Vigo Street, hatless and with disordered hair, and had vanished into the direction of Bond Street. "And as he went past me," said the porter, "he laughed—a sort of gasping laugh, with his mouth open and his eyes glaring—I tell you, sir, he fair scared me!—like this."

According to his imitation it was anything but a pleasant laugh. "He waved his hand, with all his fingers crooked and clawing—like that. And he said, in a sort of fierce whisper, *'Life.'* Just that one word, *'Life!'*"

"Dear me," said Mr. Vincey. "Tut, tut," and "Dear me!" He could think of nothing else to say. He was naturally very much surprised. He turned from the room to the porter and from the porter to the room in the gravest perplexity. Beyond his suggestion that probably Mr. Bessel would come back presently and explain what had happened, their conversation was unable to proceed. "It might be a sudden toothache," said the porter, "a very sudden and violent toothache, jumping on him suddenly-like and driving him wild. I've broken things myself before now in such a case . . ." He thought. "If it was, why should he say *'life'* to me as he went past?"

Mr. Vincey did not know. Mr. Bessel did not return, and at last Mr. Vincey, having done some more helpless staring, and having addressed a note of brief inquiry and left it in a conspicuous position on the bureau, returned in a very perplexed frame of mind to his own premises in Staple Inn. This affair had given him a shock. He was at a loss to account for Mr. Bessel's conduct on any sane hypothesis. He tried to read, but he could not do so; he went for a short walk, and was so preoccupied that he narrowly escaped a cab at the top of Chancery Lane; and at last—a full hour before his usual time—he went to bed. For a considerable time he could not sleep because of his memory of the silent confusion of Mr. Bessel's apartment, and when at length he did attain an uneasy slumber it was at once disturbed by a very vivid and distressing dream of Mr. Bessel.

He saw Mr. Bessel gesticulating wildly, and with his face white and contorted. And, inexplicably mingled with his appearance, suggested perhaps by his gestures, was an intense fear, an urgency to act. He even believes that he heard the voice of his fellow experimenter calling distressfully to him, though at the time he considered this to be an illusion. The vivid impression remained though Mr. Vincey awoke. For a space he lay awake and trembling in the darkness, possessed with that vague, unaccountable terror of unknown possibilities that comes out of dreams upon even the bravest men. But at last he roused himself, and turned over and went to sleep again, only for the dream to return with enhanced vividness.

He awoke with such a strong conviction that Mr. Bessel was in overwhelming distress and need of help that sleep was no longer possible. He was persuaded that his friend had rushed out to some dire calamity. For a time he lay reasoning vainly against this belief, but at last he gave way to it. He arose, against all reason, lit his gas and dressed, and set out through the deserted streets— deserted, save for a noiseless policeman or so and the early news carts—towards Vigo Street to inquire if Mr. Bessel had returned.

But he never got there. As he was going down Long Acre some unaccountable impulse turned him aside out of that street toward Covent Garden, which was just waking to its nocturnal activities. He saw the market in front of him—a queer effect of glowing yellow lights and busy black figures. He became aware of a shouting, and perceived a figure turn the corner by the hotel and run swiftly toward him. He knew at once that it was Mr. Bessel. But it was Mr. Bessel transfigured. He was hatless and disheveled, his collar was torn open, he grasped a bone-handled walking cane near the ferrule end, and his mouth was pulled awry. And he ran, with agile strides, very rapidly. Their encounter was the affair of an instant. "Bessel!" cried Vincey.

The running man gave no sign of recognition either of Mr. Vincey or of his own name. Instead, he cut at his friend savagely with the stick, hitting him in the face within an inch of the eye. Mr. Vincey, stunned and astonished, staggered back, lost his footing, and fell heavily on the pavement. It seemed to him that Mr. Bessel leapt over him as he fell. When he looked again Mr. Bessel had vanished, and a policeman and a number of garden porters and salesmen were rushing past toward Long Acre in hot pursuit.

With the assistance of several passers-by—for the whole street was speedily alive with running people—Mr. Vincey struggled to his feet. He at once became the center of a crowd greedy to see his injury. A multitude of voices competed to reassure him of his safety, and then to tell him of the behavior of the madman, as they regarded Mr. Bessel. He had suddenly appeared in the middle of the market screaming *"Life! Life!"* striking left and right with a blood-stained walking stick, and dancing and shouting with laughter at each successful blow. A lad and two women had broken heads, and he had smashed a man's wrist; a little child had been knocked insensible, and for a time he had driven everyone before him, so furious and resolute had his behavior been. Then he made a raid upon a coffee stall, hurled its paraffin flare through the window of the post office, and fled laughing, after stunning the foremost of the two policemen who had the pluck to charge him.

Mr. Vincey's first impulse was naturally to join in the pursuit of his friend, in order if possible to save him from the violence of the indignant people. But his action was slow, the blow had half stunned him, and while this was still no more than a resolution came the news, shouted through the crowd, that Mr. Bessel had eluded his pursuers. At first Mr. Vincey could scarcely credit this, but the universality of the report, and presently the dignified return of two futile policemen, convinced him. After some aimless inquiries he returned toward Staple Inn, padding a handkerchief to a now very painful nose.

He was angry and astonished and perplexed. It appeared to him indisputable that Mr. Bessel must have gone violently mad in the midst of his experiment in thought transference, but why that should make him appear with a sad white face in Mr. Vincey's dreams seemed a problem beyond solution. He racked his brains in vain to explain this. It seemed to him at last that not simply Mr. Bessel, but the order of things must be insane. But he could think of nothing to do. He shut himself carefully into his room, lit his fire—it was a gas fire with asbestos bricks—and, fearing fresh dreams if he went to bed, remained bathing his injured face, or holding up books in a vain attempt to read, until dawn. Throughout that vigil he had a curious persuasion that Mr. Bessel was endeavoring to speak to him, but he would not let himself attend to any such belief.

About dawn, his physical fatigue asserted itself, and he went to bed and slept at last in spite of dreaming. He rose late, unrested and anxious and in considerable facial pain. The morning papers had no news of Mr. Bessel's aberration—it had come too late for them. Mr. Vincey's perplexities, to which the fever of his bruise added fresh irritation, became at last intolerable, and, after a fruitless visit to the Albany, he went down to St. Paul's Churchyard to Mr. Hart, Mr. Bessel's partner, and so far as Mr. Vincey knew, his nearest friend.

He was surprised to learn that Mr. Hart, although he knew nothing of the outbreak, had also been disturbed by a vision, the very vision that Mr. Vincey had seen—Mr. Bessel, white and disheveled, pleading earnestly by his gestures for help. That was his impression of the import of his signs. "I was just going to look him up in the Albany when you arrived," said Mr. Hart. "I was so sure of something being wrong with him."

As the outcome of their consultation the two gentlemen decided to inquire at Scotland Yard for news of their missing friend. "He is bound to be laid by the heels," said Mr. Hart. "He can't go on at that pace for long." But the police authorities had not laid Mr. Bessel by the heels. They confirmed Mr. Vincey's overnight experiences and added fresh circumstances, some of an even graver character than those he knew—a list of smashed glass along the upper half of Tottenham Court Road, an attack upon a policeman in Hampstead Road, and an atrocious assault upon a woman. All these outrages were committed between half-past twelve and a quarter to two in the morning, and between those hours—and, indeed, from the very moment of Mr. Bessel's first rush from his rooms at half-past nine in the evening—they could trace the deepening violence of his fantastic career. For the last hour, at least from before one, that is, until a quarter to two, he had run amuck through London, eluding with amazing agility every effort to stop or capture him.

But after a quarter to two he had vanished. Up to that hour witnesses were multitudinous. Dozens of people had seen him, fled from him or pursued him, and then things suddenly came to an end. At a quarter of two he had been seen running down the Euston Road toward Baker Street, flourishing a can of burning colza oil and jerking splashes of flame therefrom at the windows of the houses he passed. But none of the policemen on Euston Road beyond the Waxwork Exhibition, nor any of those in the sidestreets down which he must have passed had he left the Euston Road, had seen anything of him. Abruptly he disappeared. Nothing of his subsequent doings came to light in spite of the keenest inquiry.

Here was a fresh astonishment for Mr. Vincey. He had found considerable comfort in Mr. Hart's conviction: "He is bound to be laid by the heels before long," and in that assurance he had been able to suspend his mental perplexities. But any fresh development seemed destined to add new impossibilities to a pile already heaped beyond the powers of his acceptance. He found himself doubting whether his memory might not have played him some grotesque trick, debating whether any of these things could possibly have happened; and in the afternoon he hunted up Mr. Hart again to share the intolerable weight on his mind. He found Mr. Hart engaged with a well-known private detective, but as that gentleman accomplished nothing in this case, we need not enlarge upon his proceedings.

All that day Mr. Bessel's whereabouts eluded an unceasingly active inquiry, and all that night. And all that day there was a persuasion in the back of Mr. Vincey's mind that Mr. Bessel sought his attention, and all through the night Mr. Bessel with a tear-stained face of anguish pursued him through his dreams. And whenever he saw Mr. Bessel in his dreams he also saw a number of other faces, vague but malignant, that seemed to be pursuing Mr. Bessel.

It was on the following day, Sunday, that Mr. Vincey recalled certain remarkable stories of Mrs. Bullock, the medium, who was then attracting attention for the first time in London. He determined to consult her. She was staying at the house of that well-known inquirer, Dr. Wilson Paget, and Mr. Vincey, although he had never met that gentleman before, repaired to him forthwith with the intention of invoking her help. But scarcely had he mentioned the name of Bessel when Dr. Paget interrupted him. "Last night—just at the end," he said, "we had a communication."

He left the room, and returned with a slate on which were certain words written in a handwriting, shaky indeed, but indisputably the handwriting of Mr. Bessel!

"How did you get this?" said Mr. Vincey. "Do you mean?——"

"We got it last night," said Dr. Paget. With numerous interruptions from Mr. Vincey, he proceeded to explain how the writing had been obtained. It appears that in her séances, Mrs. Bullock passes into a condition of trance, her eyes rolling up in a strange way under her eyelids, and her body becoming rigid. She then begins to talk very rapidly, usually in voices other than her own. At the same time one or both of her hands may become active, and if slates and pencils are provided they will then write messages simultaneously with and quite independently of the flow of words from her mouth. By many she is considered an even more remarkable medium than the celebrated Mrs. Piper. It was one of these messages, the one written by her left hand, that Mr. Vincey now had before him. It consisted of eight words written disconnectedly "George Bessel . . . trial excav^n . . . Baker Street . . . help . . . starvation." Curiously enough, neither Dr. Paget nor the two other inquirers who were present had heard of the disappearance of Mr. Bessel—the news of it appeared only in the evening papers of Saturday—and they had put the message aside with many others of a vague and enigmatical sort that Mrs. Bullock has from time to time delivered.

When Dr. Paget heard Mr. Vincey's story, he gave himself at once with great energy to the pursuit of this clue to the discovery of Mr. Bessel. It would serve no useful purpose here to describe the inquiries of Mr. Vincey and himself; suffice it that the clue was a genuine one, and that Mr. Bessel was actually discovered by its aid.

He was found at the bottom of a detached shaft which had been sunk and abandoned at the commencement of the work for the new electric railway near Baker Street Station. His arm and leg and two ribs were broken. The shaft is protected by a hoarding nearly twenty feet high, and over this, incredible as it seems, Mr. Bessel, a stout, middle-aged gentleman, must have scrambled in order to fall down the shaft. He was saturated in colza oil, and the smashed tin lay beside him, but luckily the flame had been extinguished by his fall. And his madness had passed from him altogether. But he was, of course, terribly enfeebled, and at the sight of his rescuers he gave way to hysterical weeping.

In view of the deplorable state of his flat, he was taken to the house of Dr. Hatton in Upper Baker Street. Here he was sub-

jected to a sedative treatment, and anything that might recall the
violent crisis through which he had passed was carefully avoided.
But on the second day he volunteered a statement.

Since that occasion Mr. Bessel has several times repeated this
statement—to myself among other people—varying the details as
the narrator of real experiences always does, but never by any
chance contradicting himself in any particular. And the statement
he makes is in substance as follows.

In order to understand it clearly it is necessary to go back to his
experiments with Mr. Vincey before his remarkable attack. Mr.
Bessel's first attempts at self-projection, in his experiments with
Mr. Vincey, were, as the reader will remember, unsuccessful. But
through all of them he was concentrating all his power and will
upon getting out of the body—"willing it with all my might," he
says. At last, almost against expectation, came success. And Mr.
Bessel asserts that he, being alive, did actually, by an effort of
will, leave his body and pass into some place or state outside
this world.

The release was, he asserts, instantaneous. "At one moment
I was seated in my chair, with my eyes tightly shut, my hands
gripping the arms of the chair, doing all I could to concentrate
my mind on Vincey, and then I perceived myself outside my
body—saw my body near me, but certainly not containing me, with
the hands relaxing and the head drooping forward on the breast."

Nothing shakes him in his assurance of that release. He
describes in a quiet, matter-of-fact way the new sensation he experienced. He felt he had become impalpable—so much he had
expected, but he had not expected to find himself enormously
large. So, however, it would seem he became. "I was a great
cloud—if I may express it that way—anchored to my body. It appeared to me, at first, as if I had discovered a greater self of which
the conscious being in my brain was only a little part. I saw the
Albany and Piccadilly and Regent Street and all the rooms and
places in the houses, very minute and very bright and distinct,
spread out below me like a little city seen from a balloon. Every
now and then vague shapes like drifting wreaths of smoke made
the vision a little indistinct, but at first I paid little heed to them.
The thing that astonished me most, and which astonishes me
still, is that I saw quite distinctly the insides of the houses as well
as the streets, saw little people dining and talking in the private

houses, men and women dining, playing billiards, and drinking in restaurants and hotels, and several places of entertainment crammed with people. It was like watching the affairs of a glass hive."

Such were Mr. Bessel's exact words as I took them down when he told me the story. Quite forgetful of Mr. Vincey, he remained for a space observing these things. Impelled by curiosity, he says, he stooped down, and with the shadowy arm he found himself possessed of attempted to touch a man walking along Vigo Street. But he could not do so, though his finger seemed to pass through the man. Something prevented his doing this, but what it was he finds it hard to describe. He compares the obstacle to a sheet of glass.

"I felt as a kitten may feel," he said, "when it goes for the first time to pat its reflection in a mirror." Again and again, on the occasion when I heard him tell this story, Mr. Bessel returned to that comparison of the sheet of glass. Yet it was not altogether a precise comparison, because, as the reader will speedily see, there were interruptions of this generally impermeable resistance, means of getting through the barrier to the material world again. But, naturally, there is a very great difficulty in expressing these unprecedented impressions in the language of everyday experience.

A thing that impressed him instantly, and which weighed upon him throughout all this experience, was the stillness of this place—he was in a world without sound.

At first Mr. Bessel's mental state was an unemotional wonder. His thought chiefly concerned itself with where he might be. He was out of the body—out of his material body, at any rate—but that was not all. He believes, and I for one believe also, that he was somewhere out of space, as we understand it, altogether. By a strenuous effort of will he had passed out of his body into a world beyond this world, a world undreamed of, yet lying so close to it and so strangely situated with regard to it that all things on this earth are clearly visible both from without and from within in this other world about us. For a long time, as it seemed to him, this realization occupied his mind to the exclusion of all other matters, and then he recalled the engagement with Mr. Vincey, to which this astonishing experience was, after all, but a prelude.

He turned his mind to locomotion in this new body in which he found himself. For a time he was unable to shift himself from his attachment to his earthy carcass. For a time this new strange cloud body of his simply swayed, contracted, expanded, coiled, and writhed with his efforts to free himself, and then quite suddenly the link that bound him snapped. For a moment everything was hidden by what appeared to be whirling spheres of dark vapor, and then through a momentary gap he saw his drooping body collapse limply, saw his lifeless head drop sideways, and found he was driving along like a huge cloud in a strange place of shadowy clouds that had the luminous intricacy of London spread like a model below.

But now he was aware that the fluctuating vapor about him was something more than vapor, and the temerarious excitement of his first essay was shot with fear. For he perceived, at first indistinctly, and then suddenly very clearly, that he was surrounded by *faces!* that each roll and coil of the seeming cloud stuff was a face. And such faces! Faces of thin shadow, faces of gaseous tenuity. Faces like those faces that glare with intolerable strangeness upon the sleeper in the evil hours of his dreams. Evil, greedy eyes that were full of a covetous curiosity, faces with knit brows and snarling, smiling lips; their vague hands clutched at Mr. Bessel as he passed, and the rest of their bodies was but an elusive streak of trailing darkness. Never a word they said, never a sound from the mouths that seemed to gibber. All about him they pressed in that dreamy silence, passing freely through the dim mistiness that was his body, gathering ever more numerously about him. And the shadowy Mr. Bessel, now suddenly fear-stricken, drove through the silent, active multitude of eyes and clutching hands.

So inhuman were these faces, so malignant their staring eyes, and shadowy, clawing gestures, that it did not occur to Mr. Bessel to attempt intercourse with these drifting creatures. Idiot phantoms, they seemed, children of vain desire, beings unborn and forbidden the boon of being, whose only expressions and gestures told of the envy and craving for life that was their one link with existence.

It says much for his resolution that, amid the swarming cloud of these noiseless spirits of evil, he could still think of Mr. Vincey. He made a violent effort of will and found himself, he knew not how, stooping toward Staple Inn, saw Vincey sitting attentive and alert in his armchair by the fire.

And clustering also about him, as they clustered ever about all that lives and breathes, was another multitude of these vain voiceless shadows, longing, desiring, seeking some loophole into life.

For a space Mr. Bessel sought ineffectually to attract his friend's attention. He tried to get in front of his eyes, to move the objects in his room, to touch him. But Mr. Vincey remained unaffected, ignorant of the being that was so close to his own. The strange something that Mr. Bessel has compared to a sheet of glass separated them impermeably.

And at last Mr. Bessel did a desperate thing. I have told how that in some strange way he could see not only the outside of a man as we see him, but within. He extended his shadowy hand and thrust his vague black fingers, as it seemed, through the heedless brain.

Then, suddenly, Mr. Vincey started like a man who recalls his attention from wandering thoughts, and it seemed to Mr. Bessel that a little dark red body situated in the middle of Mr. Vincey's brain swelled and glowed as he did so. Since that experience he has been shown anatomical figures of the brain, and he knows now that this is that useless structure, as doctors call it, the pineal eye. For, strange as it will seem to many, we have, deep in our brains—where it cannot possibly see any earthly light—an eye! At the time this, with the rest of the internal anatomy of the brain, was quite new to him. At the sight of its changed appearance, however, he thrust forth his finger, and, rather fearful still of the consequences, touched this little spot. And instantly Mr. Vincey started, and Mr. Bessel knew that he was seen.

And at that instant it came to Mr. Bessel that evil had happened to his body, and behold! a great wind blew through all that world of shadows and tore him away. So strong was this persuasion that he thought no more of Mr. Vincey, but turned about forthwith, and all the countless faces drove back with him like leaves before a gale. But he returned too late. In an instant he saw the body that he had left inert and collapsed—lying, indeed, like the body of a man just dead—had arisen, had arisen by virtue of some strength and will beyond his own. It stood with staring eyes, stretching its limbs in dubious fashion.

For a moment he watched it in wild dismay, and then he stooped toward it. But the pane of glass had closed against him again, and he was foiled. He beat himself passionately against this, and all about him the spirits of evil grinned and pointed and mocked. He gave way to furious anger. He compares himself to a bird that has fluttered heedlessly into a room and is beating at the windowpane that holds it back from freedom.

And behold! the little body that had once been his was now dancing with delight. He saw it shouting, though he could not hear its shouts; he saw the violence of its movements grow. He watched it fling his cherished furniture about in the mad delight of existence, rend his books apart, smash bottles, drink heedlessly from the jagged fragments, leap and smite in a passionate acceptance of living. He watched these actions in paralyzed astonishment. Then once more he hurled himself against the impassable barrier, and then, with all that crew of mocking ghosts about him, hurried back in dire confusion to Vincey to tell him of the outrage that had come upon him.

But the brain of Vincey was now closed against apparitions, and the disembodied Mr. Bessel pursued him in vain as he hurried out into Holborn to call a cab. Foiled and terror-stricken, Mr. Bessel swept back again, to find his desecrated body whooping in a glorious frenzy down the Burlington Arcade. . . .

And now the attentive reader begins to understand Mr. Bessel's interpretation of the first part of this strange story. The being whose frantic rush through London had inflicted so much injury and disaster had indeed Mr. Bessel's body, but it was not Mr. Bessel. It was an evil spirit out of that strange world beyond existence, into which Mr. Bessel had so rashly ventured. For twenty hours it held possession of him, and for all those twenty hours the dispossessed spirit body of Mr. Bessel was going to and fro in that unheard-of middle world of shadows seeking help in vain.

He spent many hours beating at the minds of Mr. Vincey and of his friend Mr. Hart. Each, as we know, he roused by his efforts. But the language that might convey his situation to these helpers across the gulf he did not know; his feeble fingers groped vainly and powerlessly in their brains. Once, indeed, as we have already told, he was able to turn Mr. Vincey aside from his path so that he encountered the stolen body in its career, but he could not make him understand the thing that had happened: he was unable to draw any help from that encounter. . . .

All through those hours the persuasion was overwhelming in Mr. Bessel's mind that presently his body would be killed by its furious tenant, and he would have to remain in this shadowland forevermore. So that those long hours were a growing agony of fear. And ever as he hurried to and fro in his ineffectual excitement innumerable spirits of that world about him mobbed him and confused his mind. And ever an envious applauding multitude poured after their successful fellow as he went upon his glorious career.

For that, it would seem, must be the life of these bodiless things of this world that is the shadow of our world. Ever they watch, coveting a way into a mortal body, in order that they may descend, as furies and frenzies, as violent lusts and mad, strange impulses, rejoicing in the body they have won. For Mr. Bessel was not the only human soul in that place. Witness the fact that he met first one, and afterward several shadows of men, men like himself, it seemed, who had lost their bodies even it may be as he had lost his, and wandered, despairingly, in that lost world that is neither life nor death. They could not speak because that world is silent, yet he knew them for men because of their dim human bodies, and because of the sadness of their faces.

But how they had come into that world he could not tell, nor where the bodies they had lost might be, whether they still raved about the earth, or whether they were closed forever in death against return. That they were the spirits of the dead neither he nor I believe. But Dr. Wilson Paget thinks they are the rational souls of men who are lost in madness on the earth.

At last Mr. Bessel chanced upon a place where a little crowd of such disembodied silent creatures was gathered, and thrusting through them he saw below a brightly lit room, and four or five quiet gentlemen and a woman, a stoutish woman dressed in black bombazine and sitting awkwardly in a chair with her head thrown back. He knew her from her portraits to be Mrs. Bullock, the medium. And he perceived that tracts and structures in her brain glowed and stirred as he had seen the pineal eye in the brain of Mr. Vincey glow. The light was very fitful; sometimes it was a broad illumination, and sometimes merely a faint twilight spot, and it shifted slowly about her brain. She kept on talking and writing with one hand. And Mr. Bessel saw that the crowding shadows of men about him, and a great multitude of the shadow spirits of that shadowland, were all striving and thrusting to touch the lighted regions of her brain. As one gained her brain or another was thrust away, her voice and the writing of her hand changed. So that what she said was disorderly and confused for the most part; now a fragment of one soul's message, and now a fragment of another's, and now she babbled the insane fancies of the spirits of vain desire. Then Mr. Bessel understood that she spoke for the spirit that had touch of her, and he began to struggle very furiously toward her. But he was on the outside of the crowd and at that time he could not reach her, and at last, growing anxious, he went away to find what had happened meanwhile to his body.

For a long time he went to and fro seeking it in vain and fearing that it must have been killed, and then he found it at the bottom of the shaft in Baker Street, writhing furiously and cursing with pain. Its leg and arm and two ribs had been broken by its fall. Moreover, the evil spirit was angry because his time had been so short and because of the pain—making violent movements and casting his body about.

And at that Mr. Bessel returned with redoubled earnestness to the room where the séance was going on, and so soon as he had thrust himself within sight of the place he saw one of the men who stood about the medium looking at his watch as if he meant that the séance should presently end. At that a great number of the shadows who had been striving turned away with gestures of despair. But the thought that the séance was almost over only made Mr. Bessel the more earnest, and he struggled so stoutly with his will against the others that presently he gained the woman's brain. It chanced that just at that moment it glowed very brightly, and in that instant she wrote the message that Dr. Wilson Paget preserved. And then the other shadows and the cloud of evil spirits about him had thrust Mr. Bessel away from her, and for all the rest of the séance he could regain her no more.

So he went back and watched through the long hours at the bottom of the shaft where the evil spirit lay in the stolen body it had maimed, writhing and cursing, and weeping and groaning, and learning the lesson of pain. And toward dawn the thing he had waited for happened, the brain glowed brightly and the evil spirit came out, and Mr. Bessel entered the body he had feared he should never enter again. As he did so, the silence—the brooding silence—ended; he heard the tumult of traffic and the voices of people overhead, and that strange world that is the shadow of our world—the dark and silent shadows of ineffectual desire and the shadows of lost men—vanished clean away.

He lay there for the space of about three hours before he was found. And in spite of the pain and suffering of his wounds, and of the dim damp place in which he lay; in spite of the tears—wrung from him by his physical distress—his heart was full of gladness to know that he was nevertheless back once more in the kindly world of men.

Science and society have already achieved a few of the things Herbert George Wells (1866–1946) envisioned, but his fiction wears well despite the inevitable obsolescence of predictions and inventions. Even Hollywood has not had the temerity to retitle *The Time Machine, The Invisible Man, The War of the Worlds, The First Men in the Moon, The Man Who Could Work Miracles* (one exception: *The Island of Dr. Moreau* was filmed as *The Island of Lost Souls,* and Wells disliked the movie). Reading such titles, who would not wish to read more? Wells brings out the child in every reader, aggressively inquisitive, eager to surmount any obstacle to see what lies ahead, and to project beyond that. This quality is essential in every generation, and it makes a gripping book.

CHAPTER 15

The Red Lodge

by H. Russell Wakefield

In the introduction to his last collection of supernatural tales, *Strayers from Sheol* (published by Arkham House in 1961), Herbert Russell Wakefield tells how he came to write his first ghost story:

Why was I persuaded into this arduous (ghost stories are very difficult to write) and unremunerative game? I am a skeptic by temperament, though not, I hope, a wooden one, and the skeptical temperament is essentially a fair, open-spirited one, ever avid to examine and, if necessary, to accept evidence adverse to its creed. And I received such evidence during two weekends spent in a superficially charming and harmonious Queen Anne house about a mile and a half from Richmond Bridge. I mustn't locate it more precisely because—and it is a significant fact—even the most rampant unbelievers often refuse to live in a reputedly haunted house.

And I can assure them they are very wise.

I visited this house in 1917, and during the previous thirty years it had known five suicides—the old gardener, strictly against orders, blurted out this ominous record in his cups, and it was verified. One had hanged herself in a powder closet. One shot himself in the tool shed. The others had drowned themselves in the river about a hundred yards away, always, it was said, at dawn. And now mark this! About a year after I went there, the valet of a famous nobleman also drowned himself in the river at first light. He was seen running down the path as though a fearful fiend were hard upon his heels

*and plunging in to his death. I think you'll agree that gives one some-
what somberly to think.*

*Someone who entered this house on a lovely summer day, know-
ing nothing of its record, remarked in astonishment, "How dark it
is in here!" And that was so. Always it seemed unnaturally dim, as
though seen through those "reducing" glasses artists use for ton-
ing down bright light.*

*The moment I passed its threshold, I knew a general feeling of
devitalization and psychic malaise, which remained with me till I
left. The household were affected in varying degrees. Remember,
some people simply cannot see or sense ghosts. The cook was one
of them; she couldn't begin to understand what the trouble was. But
one of the maids twice encountered a stranger, once in the room
with the powder closet, and once on the stairs. She couldn't "take it"
and left. The lady of the house had one of those rare temperaments
which are not frightened by ghosts, and yet she was always seeing and
hearing something; for, particularly after dark, that house was spark-
ing with venom, an obscure mode of energy, call it what you will.*

*My own particular bother consisted of a petrified insomnia. I
lay awake till dawn, oppressed by a fear without a name. Call it just
ghostly fear, if you like. I felt a craven and a worm, but I was utterly
unable to snap out of it. Only those who have experienced something
like it will sympathize. I had only one visual bother. I was sitting in
the garden one afternoon under the mulberry tree and happened to
glance up at the first floor windows. There was a blurred face at one
of them. It was a man's face, but there was no man in the house.
I wrote my first story about that house and called it "The Red
Lodge."*

I am writing this from an imperative sense of duty, for I consider
the Red Lodge is a foul deathtrap and utterly unfit to be a human
habitation—it has its own proper denizens—and because I know its
owner to be an unspeakable blackguard to allow it so to be used for
his financial advantage. He knows the perils of the place perfectly
well; I wrote him of our experiences, and he didn't even acknowl-
edge the letter, and two days ago I saw the ghastly pesthouse ad-
vertised in *Country Life*. So anyone who rents the Red Lodge in
future will receive a copy of this document as well as some uncomfortable words from Sir William, and that scoundrel Wilkes
can take what action he pleases.

I certainly didn't carry any prejudice against the place down to it with me: I had been too busy to look over it myself, but my wife reported extremely favorably—I take her word for most things—and I could tell by the photographs that it was a magnificent specimen of the medium-sized Queen Anne house, just the ideal thing for me. Mary said the garden was perfect, and there was the river for Tim at the bottom of it. I had been longing for a holiday, and was in the highest spirits as I traveled down. I was not in the highest spirits for long.

My first vague, faint uncertainty came to me so soon as I had crossed the threshold. I am a painter by profession, and therefore sharply responsive to color tone. Well, it was a brilliantly fine day, the hall of the Red Lodge was fully lighted, yet it seemed a shade off the key, as it were, as though I were regarding it through a pair of slightly darkened glasses. Only a painter would have noticed it, I fancy.

When Mary came out to greet me, she was not looking as well as I had hoped, or as well as a week in the country should have made her look.

"Everything all right?" I asked.

"Oh, yes," she replied, but I thought she found it difficult to say so, and then my eye detected a curious little spot of green on the maroon rug in front of the fireplace. I picked it up—it seemed like a patch of river slime.

"I suppose Tim brings those in," said Mary. "I've found several; of course, he promises he doesn't." And then for a moment we were silent, and a very unusual sense of constraint seemed to set a barrier between us. I went out into the garden to smoke a cigarette before lunch, and sat myself down under a very fine mulberry tree.

I wondered if, after all, I had been wise to have left it all to Mary. There was nothing wrong with the house, of course, but I am a bit psychic, and I always know the mood or character of a house. One welcomes you with the tail-writhing enthusiasm of a really nice dog, makes you at home, and at your ease at once. Others are sullen, watchful, hostile, with things to hide. They make you feel that you have obtruded yourself into some curious affairs which are none of your business. I had never encountered so hostile, aloof, and secretive a living place as the Red Lodge seemed when I first entered it. Well, it couldn't be helped, though it was disappointing; and there was Tim coming back from his walk, and the luncheon gong. My son seemed a little subdued and thoughtful, though he looked pretty well, and soon we were all chattering away with those quick changes of key which occur when the respective ages of the conversationalists are forty, thirty-three and six and one half, and after half a bottle of Meursault and a glass of port I began to think I had been a morbid ass. I was still so thinking when I began my holiday in the best possible way by going to sleep in an exquisitely comfortable chair under the mulberry tree. But I have slept better. I dozed off, but I had a silly impression of being watched, so that I kept waking up in case there might be someone with his eye on me. I was lying back, and could just see a window on the second floor framed by a gap in the leaves, and on one occasion, when I woke rather sharply from one of these dozes, I thought I saw for a moment a face peering down at me, and this face seemed curiously flattened against the pane—just a "carry-over" from a dream, I concluded. However, I didn't feel like sleeping any more, and began to explore the garden. It was completely walled in, I found, except at the far end, where there was a door leading through to a path which, running parallel to the right-hand wall, led to the river a few yards away. I noticed on this door several of those patches of green slime for which Tim was supposedly responsible. It was a dark little corner cut off from the rest of the garden by two rowan trees, a cool, silent little place I thought it. And then it was time for Tim's cricket lesson, which was interrupted by the arrival of some infernal callers. But they were pleasant people, as a matter of fact, the Local Knuts, I gathered, who owned the Manor House; Sir William Prowse and his lady and his daughter. I went for a walk with him after tea.

"Who had this house before us?" I asked.

"People called Hawker," he replied. "That was two years ago."

"I wonder the owner doesn't live in it," I said. "It isn't an expensive place to keep up."

Sir William paused as if considering his reply.

"I think he dislikes being so near the river. I'm not sorry, for I detest the fellow. By the way, how long have you taken it for?"

"Three months," I replied, "till the end of October."

"Well, if I can do anything for you I shall be delighted. If you are in any trouble, come straight to me." He slightly emphasized the last sentence.

I rather wondered what sort of trouble Sir William envisaged for me. Probably he shared the general opinion that artists were quite mad at times, and that when I had one of my lapses I should destroy the peace in some manner. However, I was duly grateful.

I was sorry to find Tim didn't seem to like the river; he appeared nervous of it, and I determined to help him to overcome this, for the fewer terrors one carries through life with one the better, and they can often be laid by delicate treatment in childhood. Curiously enough, the year before at Frinton he seemed to have no fear of the sea.

The rest of the day passed uneventfully—at least I think I can say so. After dinner I strolled down to the end of the garden, meaning to go through the door and have a look at the river. Just as I got my hand on the latch there came a very sharp, furtive whistle. I turned round quickly, but seeing no one, concluded it had come from someone in the lane outside. However, I didn't investigate further, but went back to the house.

I woke up the next morning feeling a shade depressed. My dressing room smelled stale and bitter, and I flung its windows open. As I did so I felt my right foot slip on something. It was one of those small, slimy, green patches. Now Tim would never come into my dressing room. An annoying little puzzle. How on earth had that patch—? Which question kept forcing its way into my mind as I dressed. How could a patch of green slime . . . ? How could a patch of green slime . . . ? Dropped from something? From what? I am very fond of my wife—she slaved for me when I was poor, and always has kept me happy, comfortable and faithful, and she gave me my small son Timothy. I must stand between her and patches of green slime! What in hell's name was I talking about? And it was a flamingly fine day. Yet all during breakfast my mind was trying to find some sufficient reason for these funny little patches of green slime, and not finding it.

After breakfast I told Tim I would take him out in a boat on the river.

"Must I, Daddy?" he asked, looking anxiously at me.

"No, of course not," I replied, a trifle irritably, "but I believe you'll enjoy it."

"Should I be a funk if I didn't come?"

"No, Tim, but I think you should try it once, anyway."

"All right," he said.

He's a plucky little chap, and did his very best to pretend to be enjoying himself, but I saw it was a failure from the start.

Perplexed and upset, I asked his nurse if she knew of any reason for this sudden fear of water.

"No, sir," she said. "The first day he ran down to the river just as he used to run down to the sea, but all of a sudden he started crying and ran back to the house. It seemed to me he'd seen something in the water that frightened him."

We spent the afternoon motoring round the neighborhood, and already I found a faint distaste at the idea of returning to the house, and again I had the impression that we were intruding, and that something had been going on during our absence which our return had interrupted.

Mary, pleading a headache, went to bed soon after dinner, and I went to the study to read.

Directly I had shut the door I had again that very unpleasant sensation of being watched. It made the reading of Sidgwick's *The Use of Words in Reasoning*—an old favorite of mine, which requires concentration—a difficult business. Time after time I found myself peeping into dark corners and shifting my position. And there were little sharp sounds; just the oak paneling cracking, I supposed. After a time I became more absorbed in the book, and less fidgety, and then I heard a very soft cough just behind me. I felt little icy rays pour down and through me, but I would *not* look round, and I *would* go on reading. I had just reached the following passage: "However many things may be said about Socrates, or about any fact observed, there remains still more that might be said if the need arose; the need is the determining factor. Hence the distinction between complete and incomplete description, though perfectly sharp and clear in the abstract, can only have a meaning—can only be applied to actual cases—if it be taken as equivalent to *sufficient* description, the sufficiency being relative to some purpose. Evidently the description of Socrates as a man, scanty though it is, may be fully sufficient for the purpose of the modest enquiry whether he is *mortal* or not"——when my eye was caught by a green patch that suddenly appeared on the floor beside me, and then another and another, following a straight line toward the door. I picked up the nearest one, and it was a bit of soaking slime. I called on all my will power, for I feared something worse to come, and it should *not* materialize—and then no more patches appeared. I got up and walked deliberately, slowly, to the door, turned on the light in the middle of the room, and then came back and turned out the reading lamp and went to my dressing room. I sat down and thought things over. There was something very wrong with this house. I had passed the stage of pretending otherwise, and my inclination was to take my family away from it the next day. But that meant sacrificing one hundred and sixty-eight pounds, and we had nowhere else to go. It was conceivable that these phenomena were perceptible only to me, being half a highlander. I might be able to stick it out if I were careful and kept my tail up, for apparitions of this sort are partially subjective—one brings something of oneself to their materialization. That is a hard saying, but I believe it to be true. If Mary and Tim and the servants were immune it was up to me to face and fight this nastiness. As I undressed, I came to the decision that I would decide nothing then and there, and that I would see what happened. I made this decision against my better judgment, I think.

In bed I tried to thrust all this away from me by a conscious effort to "change the subject," as it were. The easiest subject for me to switch over to is the myriad-sided, useless, consistently abused business of creating things, stories out of pens and ink and paper, representations of things and moods out of paint, brushes and canvas, and our own miseries, perhaps, out of wine, women, and song. With a considerable effort, therefore, and with the edges of my brain anxious to be busy with bits of green slime, I recalled an article I had read that day on a glorious word *Jugendbewegung,* the "Youth Movement," that pregnant or merely wind-swollen Teutonism! How ponderously it attempted to canonize with its polysyllabic sonority that inverted Boy Scoutishness of the said youths and maidens. "One bad, mad deed—sonnet—scribble of some kind—lousy daub—a day." Bunk without spunk, sauce without force, futurism without a past, merely a *transition* from one yelping pose to another. And then I suddenly found myself at the end of the garden, attempting desperately to hide myself behind a rowan tree, while my eyes were held relentlessly to face the door. And then it began slowly to open, and something which was horridly unlike anything I had seen before began passing through it, and *I* knew It knew I was there, and then my head seemed to burst and flamed asunder, splintered and destroyed, and I awoke trembling to feel that something in the darkness was poised an inch or two above me, and then drip, drip, drip, something began falling on my face. Mary was in the bed next to mine, and I *would not*

scream, but flung the clothes over my head, my eyes streaming
with the tears of terror. And so I remained cowering till I heard
the clock strike five, and dawn, the ally I longed for, came, and
the birds began to sing, and then I slept.

I awoke a wreck, and after breakfast, feeling the need to be
alone, I pretended I wanted to sketch, and went out into the garden.
Suddenly I recalled Sir William's remark about coming to see
him if there was any trouble. Not much difficulty in guessing
what he had meant. I'd go and see him about it at once. I wished I
knew whether Mary was troubled too. I hesitated to ask her, for, if
she were not, she was certain to become suspicious and uneasy if I
questioned her. And then I discovered that, while my brain had
been busy with its thoughts my hand had also not been idle, but
had been occupied in drawing a very singular design on the
sketching block. I watched it as it went automatically on. Was it a
design or a figure of some sort? When had I seen something like it
before? My God, in my dream last night! I tore it to pieces, and
got up in agitation and made my way to the Manor House along a
path through tall, bowing, stippled grasses hissing lightly in the
breeze. My inclination was to run to the station and take the next
train to anywhere; pure undiluted panic—an insufficiently analyzed
word—that which causes men to trample on women and children
when Death is making his choice. Of course, I had Mary and Tim
and the servants to keep me from it, but supposing they had no
claim on me, should I desert them? No, I should not. Why? Such
things aren't done by respectable inhabitants of Great Britain—a
people despised and respected by all other tribes. Despised as
Philistines, but it took the jawbone of an ass to subdue that hardy
race! Respected for what? Birkenhead stuff. No, not the noble
Lord, for there were no glittering prizes for those who went down
to the bottom of the sea in ships. My mind deliberately restricting
itself to such highly debatable jingoism, I reached the Manor
House, to be told that Sir William was up in London for the day,
but would return that evening. Would he ring me up on his return?
"Yes, sir." And then, with lagging steps, back to the Red Lodge.

I took Mary for a drive in the car after lunch. Anything to get
out of the beastly place. Tim didn't come, as he preferred to play
in the garden. In the light of what happened I suppose I shall be
criticized for leaving him alone with a nurse, but at that time I
held the theory that these appearances were in no way malignant,

THE RED LODGE 277

and that it was more than possible that even if Tim did see anything he wouldn't be frightened, not realizing it was out of the ordinary in any way. After all, nothing that I had seen or heard, at any rate during the daytime, would strike him as unusual.

Mary was very silent, and I was beginning to feel sure, from a certain depression and oppression in her manner and appearance, that my trouble was hers. It was on the tip of my tongue to say something, but I resolved to wait until I had heard what Sir William had to say. It was a dark, somber, and brooding afternoon, and my spirits fell as we turned for home. What a home!

We got back at six, and I had just stopped the engine and helped Mary out when I heard a scream from the garden. I rushed round, to see Tim, his hands to his eyes, staggering across the lawn, the nurse running behind him. And then he screamed again and fell. I carried him into the house and laid him down on a sofa in the drawing room, and Mary went to him. I took the nurse by the arm and out of the room; she was panting and crying down a face of chalk.

"What happened? What happened?" I asked.

"I don't know what it was, sir, but we had been walking in the lane, and had left the door open. Master Tim was a bit ahead of me, and went through the door first, and then he screamed like that."

"Did you see anything that could have frightened him?"

"No, sir, nothing."

I went back to them. It was no good questioning Tim, and there was nothing coherent to be learnt from his hysterical sobbing. He grew calmer presently, and was taken up to bed. Suddenly he turned to Mary, and looked at her with eyes of terror.

"The green monkey won't get me, will it, Mummy?"

"No, no, it's all right now," said Mary, and soon after he went to sleep, and then she and I went down to the drawing room. She was on the border of hysteria herself.

"Oh, Tom, what is the matter with this awful house? I'm *terrified*. Ever since I've been here I've been terrified. Do you see things?"

"Yes," I replied.

"Oh, I wish I'd known. I didn't want to worry you if you hadn't. Let me tell you what it's been like. On the day we arrived I saw a man pass ahead of me into my bedroom. Of course, I only *thought*

I had. And then I've heard beastly whisperings, and every time I pass that turn in the corridor I *know* there's someone just round the corner. And then the day before you arrived I woke suddenly, and something seemed to force me to go to the window, and I crawled there on hands and knees and peeped through the blind. It was just light enough to see. And suddenly I saw someone running down the lawn, his or her hands outstretched, and there was something ghastly just beside him, and they disappeared behind the trees at the end. I'm terrified every minute."

"What about the servants?"

"Nurse hasn't seen anything, but the others have, I'm certain. And then there are those slimy patches, I think they're the vilest of all. I don't think Tim has been troubled till now, but I'm sure he's been puzzled and uncertain several times."

"Well," I said, "it's pretty obvious we must clear out. I'm seeing Sir William about it tomorrow, I hope, and I'm certain enough of what he'll advise. Meanwhile we must think over where to go. It is a nasty jar, though; I don't mean merely the money, though that's bad enough, but the fuss—just when I hoped we were going to be so happy and settled. However, it's got to be done. We should be mad after a week of this filth-drenched hole."

Just then the telephone bell rang. It was a message to say Sir William would be pleased to see me at half past ten tomorrow.

With the dusk came that sense of being watched, waited for, followed about, plotted against, an atmosphere of quiet, hunting malignancy. A thick mist came up from the river, and as I was changing for dinner I noticed the lights from the windows seemed to project a series of swiftly changing pictures on its gray, crawling screen. The one opposite my window, for example, was unpleasantly suggestive of three figures staring in and seeming to grow nearer and larger. The effect must have been slightly hypnotic, for suddenly I started back, for it was as if they were about to close on me. I pulled down the blind and hurried downstairs. During dinner we decided that unless Sir William had something very reassuring to say we would go back to London two days later and stay at a hotel till we could find somewhere to spend the next six weeks. Just before going to bed we went up to the night nursery to see if Tim was all right. This room was at the top of a short flight of stairs. As these stairs were covered with green slime, and there was a pool of the muck just outside the door, we took him down to sleep with us.

The Permanent Occupants of the Red Lodge waited till the light was out, but then I felt them come thronging, slipping in one by one, their weapon, fear. It seemed to me they were massed for the attack. A yard away my wife was lying with my son in her arms, so I must fight. I lay back, gripped the sides of the bed and strove with all my might to hold my assailants back. As the hours went by I felt myself beginning to get the upper hand, and a sense of exultation came to me. But an hour before dawn they made their greatest effort. I knew that they were willing me to creep on my hands and knees to the window and peep through the blind, and that if I did so we were doomed. As I set my teeth and tightened my grip till I felt racked with agony, the sweat poured from me. I felt them come crowding round the bed and thrusting their faces into mine; and a voice in my head kept saying insistently, "You must crawl to the window and look through the blind." In my mind's eye I could see myself crawling stealthily across the floor and pulling the blind aside, but who would be staring back at me? Just when I felt my resistance breaking I heard a sweet, sleepy twitter from a tree outside, and saw the blind touched by a faint suggestion of light, and at once those with whom I had been struggling left me and went their way, and, utterly exhausted, I slept.

In the morning I found, somewhat ironically, that Mary had slept better than on any night since she came down.

Half-past ten found me entering the Manor House, a delightful nondescript old place, which started wagging its tail as soon as I entered it. Sir William was awaiting me in the library. "I expected this would happen," he said gravely, "and now tell me."

I gave him a short outline of our experiences.

"Yes," he said, "it's always much the same story. Every time that horrible place has been let I have felt a sense of personal responsibility, and yet I cannot give a proper warning, for the letting of haunted houses is not yet a criminal offense—though it ought to be—and I couldn't afford a libel action, and, as a matter of fact, one old couple had the house for fifteen years and were perfectly delighted with it, being troubled in no way. But now let me tell you what I know of the Red Lodge. I have studied it for forty years, and I regard it as my personal enemy.

"The local tradition is that the second owner, early in the eight-

eenth century, wished to get rid of his wife, and bribed his servants to frighten her to death—just the sort of ancestor I can imagine
that blackguard Wilkes being descended from.

"What devilries they perpetrated I don't know, but she is supposed to have rushed from the house just before dawn one day and
drowned herself. Whereupon her husband installed a small harem
in the house; but it was a failure, for each of these charmers one
by one rushed down to the river just before dawn, and finally the
husband himself did the same. Of the period between then and
forty years ago I have no record, but the local tradition has it that
it was the scene of tragedy after tragedy, and then was shut up for
a long time. When I first began to study it, it was occupied by two
bachelor brothers. One shot himself in the room which I imagine
you use as your bedroom, and the other drowned himself in the
usual way. I may tell you that the worst room in the house, the
one the unfortunate lady is supposed to have occupied, is locked
up, you know, the one on the second floor. I imagine Wilkes mentioned it to you."

"Yes, he did," I replied. "Said he kept important papers there."

"Yes; well, he was forced in self-defence to do so ten years ago,
and since then the death rate has been lower, but in those forty
years twenty people have taken their lives in the house or in the
river, and six children have been drowned accidentally. The last
case was Lord Passover's butler in 1924. He was seen to run down
to the river and leap in. He was pulled out, but had died of shock.

"The people who took the house two years ago left in a week,
and threatened to bring an action against Wilkes, but they were
warned they had no legal case. And I strongly advise you, more
than that, *implore* you, to follow their example, though I can
imagine the financial loss and great inconvenience, for that house
is a deathtrap."

"I will," I replied. "I forgot to mention one thing; when my
little boy was so badly frightened he said something about 'a green
monkey.'"

"He did!" said Sir William sharply. "Well then, it is absolutely
imperative that you should leave at once. You remember I mentioned the death of certain children. Well, in each case they have
been found drowned in the reeds just at the end of that lane, and
the people about here have a firm belief that 'The Green Thing,' or

'The Green Death'—it is sometimes referred to as the first and sometimes as the other—is connected with danger to children."

"Have you ever seen anything yourself?" I asked.

"I go to the infernal place as little as possible," replied Sir William, "but when I called on your predecessors I most distinctly saw someone leave the drawing room as we entered it, otherwise all I have noted is a certain dream that recurs with curious regularity. I find myself standing at the end of the lane and watching the river—always in a sort of brassy half light. And presently something comes floating down the stream. I can see it jerking up and down, and I always feel passionately anxious to see what it may be. At first I think that it is a log, but when it gets exactly opposite me it changes its course and comes toward me, and then I see that it is a dead body, very decomposed. And when it reaches the bank it begins to climb up toward me, and then I am thankful to say I always awake. Sometimes I have thought that one day I shall not wake just then, and that on this occasion something will happen to me, but that is probably merely the silly fancy of an old gentleman who has concerned himself with these singular events rather more than is good for his nerves."

"That is obviously the explanation," I said, "and I am extremely grateful to you. We will leave tomorrow. But don't you think we should attempt to devise some means by which other people may be spared this sort of thing, and this brute Wilkes be prevented from letting the house again?"

"I certainly do so, and we will discuss it further on some other occasion. And now go and pack!"

A very great and charming gentleman, Sir William, I reflected, as I walked back to the Red Lodge.

Tim seemed to have recovered excellently well, but I thought it wise to keep him out of the house as much as possible, so while Mary and the maids packed after lunch I went with him for a walk through the fields. We took our time, and it was only when the sky grew black and there was a distant rumble of thunder and a menacing little breeze came from the west that we turned to come back. We had to hurry, and as we reached the meadow next to the house there came a ripping flash and the storm broke. We started to run for the door into the garden when I tripped over my bootlace, which had come undone, and fell. Tim ran on. I had just tied the lace and was on my feet again when I saw something slip through the door. It was green, thin, tall. It seemed to glance back at me, and what should have been its face was a patch of soused slime. At that moment Tim saw it, screamed, and ran for the river. The figure turned and followed him, and before I could reach him hovered over him. Tim screamed again and flung himself in. A moment later I passed through a green and stenching film and dived after him. I found him writhing in the reeds and brought him to the bank. I ran with him in my arms to the house, and I shall not forget Mary's face as she saw us from the bedroom window.

By nine o'clock we were all in a hotel in London, and the Red Lodge was an evil, fading memory. I shut the front door when I had packed them all into the car. As I took hold of the knob I felt a quick and powerful pressure from the other side, and it shut with a crash. The Permanent Occupants of the Red Lodge were in sole possession once more.

———————

Herbert Russell Wakefield (1889–1964), the son of Bishop Wakefield of Birmingham, studied at Marlborough College and Oxford University. He wrote mysteries and television plays, but he is perhaps even better known for several collections of ghost stories: *They Return at Evening, Others Who Returned, Imagine a Man in a Box, Ghost Stories, A Ghostly Company, The Clock Strikes Twelve,* and *Strayers from Sheol.* A final collection of his ghostly tales will be published by Arkham House.

CHAPTER 16

The Visiting Star

by Robert Aickman

Robert Aickman is an English author and critic. He distinguishes the ghost story from horror stories and scientific extravaganzas as "an art form of altogether exceptional delicacy and subtlety" that "draws upon the unconscious mind in the manner of poetry." By that high standard, he estimates there are only thirty or forty first-class ghost stories in the whole of Western literature. But this reckoning is both conservative and modest; supernatural fiction is certainly enhanced by such stories as Robert Aickman's own "The Cicerones," "A Roman Question," and "The Visiting Star." The last story mentioned is not about ghosts. In fact, it can only be classified as unique.

The first time that Colvin, who had never been a frequent theater-goer, ever heard of the great actress Arabella Rokeby, was when he was walking past the Hippodrome one night and Malnik, the manager of the Tabard Players, invited him into his office.

Had Colvin not been awarded a grant, remarkably insufficient for present prices, upon which to compose, collate, and generally scratch together a book upon the once thriving British industries of lead and plumbago mining, he would probably never have set eyes upon this bleak town. Tea was over (today it had been pilchard salad and chips); and Colvin had set out from the Emancipation Hotel, where he boarded, upon his regular evening walk. In fifteen or twenty minutes he would be beyond the gaslights, the granite setts, the nimbus of the pits. (Lead and plumbago mining had long been replaced by coal, as the town's main industry.) There had been no one else for tea and Mrs. Royd had made it clear that the trouble he was causing had not passed unnoticed.

Outside it was blowing as well as raining, so that Palmerston Street was almost deserted. The Hippodrome (called, when built, the Grand Opera House) stood at the corner of Palmerston Street and Aberdeen Place. Vast, ornate, the product of an unfulfilled aspiration that the town would increase in size and devotion to the Muses, it had been for years unused and forgotten. About it like rags, when Colvin first beheld it, had hung scraps of posters: "Harem Nights. Gay! Bright! ! Alluring! ! !" But a few weeks ago the Hippodrome had reopened to admit the Tabard Players ("In Association with the Arts Council"), and, it was hoped, their audiences. The Tabard Players offered soberer joys: a new and respectable play each week, usually a light comedy or West End crook drama; but, on one occasion, *Everyman*. Malnik, their manager, a youngish bald man, was an authority on the British drama of the nineteenth century, upon which he had written an immense book, bursting with carefully verified detail. Colvin had met him one night in the saloon bar of the Emancipation Hotel; and, though neither knew anything of the other's subject, they had exchanged cultural life belts in the ocean of apathy and incomprehensible interests which surrounded them. Malnik was lodging with the sad-faced rector, who let rooms.

Tonight, having seen the curtain up on Act I, Malnik had come outside for a breath of the wind. There was something he wanted to impart and, as he regarded the drizzling and indifferent town, Colvin obligingly came into sight. In a moment, he was inside Malnik's roomy but crumbling office.

"Look," said Malnik.

He shuffled a heap of papers on his desk and handed Colvin a photograph. It was yellow, and torn at the edges. The subject was a wild-eyed young man with much dark curly hair and a blobby face. He was wearing a high stiff collar, and a bow like Chopin's.

"John Nethers," said Malnik. Then, when no light of rapture flashed from Colvin's face, he said, "Author of *Cornelia*."

"Sorry," said Colvin, shaking his head.

"John Nethers was the son of a chemist in this town. Some books say a miner, but that's wrong. A chemist. He killed himself at twenty-two. But before that I've traced that he'd written at least six plays. *Cornelia,* which is the best of them, is one of the great plays of the nineteenth century."

"Why did he kill himself?"

"It's in his eyes. You can see it. *Cornelia* was produced in London with Arabella Rokeby. But never here. Never in the author's own town. I've been into the whole thing closely. Now we're going to do *Cornelia* for Christmas."

"Won't you lose money?" asked Colvin.

"We're losing money all the time, old man. Of course we are. We may as well do something we shall be remembered by."

Colvin nodded. He was beginning to see that Malnik's life was a single-minded struggle for the British drama of the nineteenth century and all that went with it.

"Besides I'm going to do *As You Like It* also. As a fill-up." Malnik stooped and spoke close to Colvin's ear as he sat in a bursting leather armchair, the size of a judge's seat. "You see, Arabella Rokeby's *coming.*"

"But how long is it since—"

"Better not be too specific about that. They say it doesn't matter with Arabella Rokeby. She can get away with it. Probably in fact she can't. Not altogether. But all the same, think of it. Arabella Rokeby in *Cornelia*. In *my* theater."

Colvin thought of it.

"Have you ever seen her?"

"No, I haven't. Of course she doesn't play regularly nowadays. Only special engagements. But in this business one has to take a chance sometimes. And golly what a chance!"

"And she's willing to come? I mean at Christmas," Colvin added, not wishing to seem rude.

Malnik did seem slightly unsure. "I have a contract," he said. Then he added: "She'll love it when she gets here. After all: *Cornelia!* And she must know that the nineteenth-century theater is my subject." He had seemed to be reassuring himself, but now he was glowing.

"But *As You Like It?*" said Colvin, who had played Touchstone at his preparatory school. "Surely she can't manage Rosalind?"

"It was her great part. Happily you can play Rosalind at any

age. Wish I could get old Ludlow to play Jaques. But he won't."
Ludlow was the company's veteran.

"Why not?"

"He played with Rokeby in the old days. I believe he's afraid
she'll see he isn't the grand old man he should be. He's a good
chap, but proud. Of course he may have other reasons. You never
know with Ludlow."

The curtain was down on Act I.

Colvin took his leave and resumed his walk.

Shortly thereafter Colvin read about the "Nethers Gala" in the
local evening paper ("this forgotten poet," as the writer helpfully
phrased it), and found confirmation that Miss Rokeby was indeed
to grace it ("the former London star"). In the same issue of the
paper appeared an editorial to the effect that widespread disap-
pointment would be caused by the news that the Hippodrome
would not be offering a pantomime at Christmas in accordance
with the custom of the town and district.

"She can't 'ardly stop 'ere, Mr. Colvin," said Mrs. Royd, when
Colvin, thinking to provide forewarning, showed her the news, as
she lent a hand behind the saloon bar. "This isn't the Cumberland.
She'd get across the staff."

"I believe she's quite elderly," said Colvin soothingly.

"If she's elderly, she'll want special attention, and that's often
just as bad."

"After all, where she goes is mainly a problem for her, and perhaps Mr. Malnik."

"Well, there's nowhere else in town for her to stop, is there?"
retorted Mrs. Royd with fire. "Not nowadays. She'll just 'ave to
make do. We did for theatricals in the old days. Midgets once.
Whole troupe of 'em."

"I'm sure you'll make her very comfortable."

"Can't see what she wants to come at all for, really. Not at
Christmas."

"Miss Rokeby needs no *reason* for her actions. What she does
is sufficient in itself. You'll understand that, dear lady, when you
meet her." The speaker was a very small man, apparently of advanced years, white-haired, and with a brown sharp face, like a
Levantine. The bar was full, and Colvin had not previously noticed him, although he was conspicuous enough, as he wore an

overcoat with a fur collar and a scarf with a large black pin in the center. "I wonder if *I* could beg a room for a few nights," he went on. "I assure you I'm no trouble at all."

"There's only number Twelve A. It's not very comfortable," replied Mrs. Royd sharply.

"Of course you must leave room for Miss Rokeby."

"Nine's for her. Though I haven't had a word from her."

"I think she'll need two rooms. She has a companion."

"I can clear out Greta's old room upstairs. If she's a friend of yours, you might ask her to let me know when she's coming."

"Not a friend," said the old man, smiling. "But I follow her career."

Mrs. Royd brought a big red book from under the bar.

"What name, please?"

"Mr. Superbus," said the little old man. He had yellow, expressionless eyes.

"Will you register?"

Mr. Superbus produced a gold pen, long and fat. His writing was so curvilinear that it seemed purely decorative, like a design for ornamental ironwork. Colvin noticed that he paused slightly at the "Permanent Address" column, and then simply wrote (although it was difficult to be sure) what appeared to be "North Africa."

"Will you come this way?" said Mrs. Royd, staring suspiciously at the newcomer's scrollwork in the visitor's book. Then, even more suspiciously, she added: "What about luggage?"

Mr. Superbus nodded gravely. "I placed two bags outside."

"Let's hope they're still there. They're rough in this town, you know."

"I'm sure they're still there," said Mr. Superbus.

As he spoke the door opened suddenly and a customer almost fell into the bar. "Sorry, Mrs. Royd," he said with a mildness which in the circumstances belied Mrs. Royd's words. "There's something on the step."

"My fault, I'm afraid," said Mr. Superbus. "I wonder—have you a porter?"

"The porter works evenings at the Hippodrome nowadays. Sceneshifting and that."

"Perhaps I could help?" said Colvin.

On the step outside were what appeared to be two very large

suitcases. When he tried to lift one of them, he understood what Mr. Superbus had meant. It was remarkably heavy. He held back the bar door, letting in a cloud of cold air. "Give me a hand some-one," he said.

The customer who had almost fallen volunteered, and a short procession, led by Mrs. Royd, set off along the little dark passage to number Twelve A. Colvin was disconcerted when he realized that Twelve A was the room at the end of the passage, which had no number on its door and had never, he thought, been occupied since his arrival; the room, in fact, next to his.

"Better leave these on the floor," said Colvin, dismissing the rickety luggage stand.

"Thank you," said Mr. Superbus, transferring a coin to the man who had almost fallen. He did it like a conjuror unpalming something.

"I'll send Greta to make up the bed," said Mrs. Royd. "Tea's at six."

"At six?" said Mr. Superbus, gently raising an eyebrow. "Tea?" Then, when Mrs. Royd and the man had gone, he clutched Colvin very hard on the upper part of his left arm. "Tell me," enquired Mr. Superbus, "are you in love with Miss Rokeby? I overheard you defending her against the impertinence of our hostess."

Colvin considered for a moment.

"Why not admit it?" said Mr. Superbus, gently raising the other eyebrow. He was still clutching Colvin's arm much too hard.

"I've never set eyes on Miss Rokeby."

Mr. Superbus let go. "Young people nowadays have no imagination," he said with a whinny, like a wild goat.

Colvin was not surprised when Mr. Superbus did not appear for tea (pressed beef and chips that evening).

After tea Colvin, instead of going for a walk, wrote to his mother. But there was little to tell her, so that at the end of the letter he mentioned the arrival of Mr. Superbus. "There's a sort of sweet blossomy smell about him like a meadow," he ended. "I think he must use scent."

When the letter was finished, Colvin started trying to construct tables of output from the lead and plumbago mines a century ago. The partitions between the bedrooms were thin, and he began to wonder about Mr. Superbus's nocturnal habits.

He wondered from time to time until the time came for sleep; and wondered a bit also as he dressed the next morning and went to the bathroom to shave. For during the whole of this time no sound whatever had been heard from number Twelve A, despite the thinness of the plywood partition; a circumstance that Colvin already thought curious when, during breakfast, he overheard Greta talking to Mrs. Royd in the kitchen. "I'm ever so sorry, Mrs. Royd. I forgot about it with the crowd in the bar." To which Mrs. Royd simply replied: "I wonder what 'e done about it. 'E could 'ardly do without sheets or blankets, and this December. Why didn't 'e *ask?*" And when Greta said, "I suppose nothing ain't happened to him?" Colvin put down his porridge spoon and unobtrusively joined the party which went to find out.

Mrs. Royd knocked several times upon the door of number Twelve A, but there was no answer. When they opened the door, the bed was bare as Colvin had seen it the evening before, and there was no sign at all of Mr. Superbus except that his two big cases lay on the floor, one beside the other.

"What's he want to leave the window open like that for?" enquired Mrs. Royd. She shut it with a crash. "Someone will fall over those cases in the middle of the floor."

Colvin bent down to slide the heavy cases under the bed. But the pair of them now moved at a touch.

Colvin picked one case up and shook it slightly. It emitted a muffled flapping sound, like a bat in a box. Colvin nearly spoke, but stopped himself, and stowed the cases, end on, under the unmade bed in silence.

"Make up the room, Greta," said Mrs. Royd. "It's no use just standing about." Colvin gathered that it was not altogether unknown for visitors to the Emancipation Hotel to be missing from their rooms all night.

But there was a further little mystery. Later that day in the bar, Colvin was accosted by the man who had helped to carry Mr. Superbus's luggage.

"Look at that." He displayed, rather furtively, something which lay in his hand.

It was a sovereign.

"He gave it me last night."

"Can I see it?" It had been struck in Queen Victoria's reign, but gleamed like new.

"What d'you make of that?" asked the man.

"Not much," replied Colvin, returning the pretty piece. "But now I come to think of it, *you* can make about forty-five shillings."

When this incident took place, Colvin was on his way to spend three or four nights in another town where lead and plumbago mining had formerly been carried on, and where he needed to consult an invaluable collection of old records which had been presented to the public library at the time the principal mining company went bankrupt.

On his return, he walked up the hill from the station through a thick mist, laden with coal dust and sticky smoke, and apparently in no way diminished by a bitter little wind, which chilled while hardly troubling to blow. There had been snow, and little archipelagos of slush remained on the pavements, through which the immense boots of the miners crashed noisily. The male population wore heavy mufflers and were unusually silent. Many of the women wore shawls over their heads in the manner of their grandmothers.

Mrs. Royd was not in the bar, and Colvin hurried through it to his old room, where he put on a thick sweater before descending to tea. The only company consisted in two commercial travelers, sitting at the same table and eating through a heap of bread and margarine but saying nothing. Colvin wondered what had happened to Mr. Superbus.

Greta entered as usual with a pot of strong tea and a plate of bread and margarine.

"Good evening, Mr. Colvin. Enjoy your trip?"

"Yes, thank you, Greta. What's for tea?"

"Haddock and chips." She drew a deep breath. "Miss Rokeby's come . . . I don't think she'll care for haddock and chips, do you, Mr. Colvin?" Colvin looked up in surprise. He saw that Greta was trembling. Then he noticed that she was wearing a thin black dress, instead of her customary casual attire.

Colvin smiled up at her. "I think you'd better put on something warm. It's getting colder every minute."

But at that moment the door opened and Miss Rokeby entered.

Greta stood quite still, shivering all over, and simply staring at her. Everything about Greta made it clear that this was Miss Rokeby. Otherwise the situation was of a kind which brought to Colvin's mind the cliché about there being some mistake.

The woman who had come in was very small and slight. She had a triangular gazelle-like face, with very large dark eyes, and a mouth that went right across the lower tip of the triangle, making of her chin another, smaller triangle. She was dressed entirely in black, with a high-necked black silk sweater, and wore long black earrings. Her short dark hair was dressed like that of a faun; and her thin white hands hung straight by her side in a posture resembling some Indian statuettes which Colvin recalled but could not place.

Greta walked toward her and drew back a chair. She placed Miss Rokeby with her back to Colvin.

"Thank you. What can I eat?" Colvin was undecided whether Miss Rokeby's voice was high or low: it was like a bell beneath the ocean.

Greta was blushing. She stood, not looking at Miss Rokeby, but at the other side of the room, shivering and reddening. Then tears began to pour down her cheeks in a cataract. She dragged at a chair, made an unintelligible sound, and ran into the kitchen.

Miss Rokeby half turned in her seat, and stared after Greta. Colvin thought she looked quite as upset as Greta. Certainly she was very white. She might almost have been eighteen . . .

"Please don't mind. It's nerves, I think." Colvin realized that his own voice was far from steady, and that he was beginning to blush also, he hoped only slightly.

Miss Rokeby had risen to her feet and was holding on to the back of her chair.

"I didn't say anything that could frighten her."

It was necessary to come to the point, Colvin thought.

"Greta thinks the menu unworthy of the distinguished company."

"What?" She turned and looked at Colvin. Then she smiled. "Is that it?" She sat down again. "What is it? Fish and chips?"

"Haddock. Yes." Colvin smiled back, now full of confidence.

"Well. There it is." Miss Rokeby made the prospect of haddock sound charming and gay. One of the commercial travelers offered to pour the other a fourth cup of tea. The odd little crisis was over.

But when Greta returned, her face seemed set and a trifle hostile. She had put on an ugly custard-colored cardigan.

"It's haddock and chips."

Miss Rokeby merely inclined her head, still smiling charmingly.

Before Colvin had finished, Miss Rokeby, with whom further conversation had been made difficult by the fact that she had been
seated with her back to him, and by the torpid watchfulness of the
commercial travelers, rose, bade him good evening, and left.

Colvin had not meant to go out again that evening, but curiosity
continued to rise in him, and in the end he decided to clear his
thoughts by a short walk, taking in the Hippodrome. Outside it
had become even colder; the fog was thicker, the streets emptier.

Colvin found that the entrance to the Hippodrome had been
transformed. From frieze to floor, the walls were covered with
large photographs. The photographs were not framed, but merely
mounted on big sheets of pasteboard. They seemed to be all the
same size. Colvin saw at once that they were all portraits of Miss
Rokeby.

The entrance hall was filled with fog, but the lighting within
had been greatly reinforced since Colvin's last visit. Tonight the
effect was mistily dazzling. Colvin began to examine the photographs. They depicted Miss Rokeby in the widest variety of cos-
tumes and make-up, although in no case was the name given of
the play or character. In some Colvin could not see how he
recognized her at all. In all she was alone. The number of the
photographs, their uniformity of presentation, the bright swim-
ming lights, the emptiness of the place (for the box office had
shut) combined to make Colvin feel that he was dreaming. He
put his hands before his eyes, inflamed by the glare and the fog.
When he looked again, it was as if all the Miss Rokebys had
been so placed that the gaze converged upon the spot where he
stood. He closed his eyes tightly and began to feel his way to the
door and the dimness of the street outside. Then there was a flutter
of applause behind him; the evening's audience began to straggle
out, grumbling at the weather; and Malnik was saying "Hullo,
old man. Nice to see you."

Colvin gesticulated uncertainly. "Did she bring them all with
her?"

"Not a bit of it, old man. Millie found them when she opened
up."

"Where did she find them?"

"Just lying on the floor. In two whacking great parcels. Rokeby's
agent, I suppose, thought she appeared not to have one. Blest if I

know, really. I myself could hardly shift one of the parcels, let
alone two."

Colvin felt rather frightened for a moment; but he only said:
"How do you like her?"

"Tell you when she arrives."

"She's arrived."

Malnik stared.

"Come back with me and see for yourself."

Malnik seized Colvin's elbow. "What's she look like?"

"Might be any age."

All the time Malnik was bidding good night to patrons, trying
to appease their indignation at being brought out on such a night.

Suddenly the lights went, leaving only a pilot. It illumined a
photograph of Miss Rokeby holding a skull.

"Let's go," said Malnik. "Lock up, Frank, will you?"

"You'll need a coat," said Colvin.

"Lend me your coat, Frank."

On the short cold walk to the Emancipation Hotel, Malnik said
little. Colvin supposed that he was planning the encounter before
him. Colvin did ask him whether he had ever heard of a Mr.
Superbus, but he hadn't.

Mrs. Royd was, it seemed, in a thoroughly bad temper. To
Colvin it appeared that she had been drinking; and that she was
one whom drink soured rather than mellowed. "I've got no one to
send," she snapped. "You can go up yourself, if you like. Mr.
Colvin knows the way." There was a roaring fire in the bar, which
after the cold outside, seemed very overheated.

Outside number Nine, Colvin paused before knocking. Immediately he was glad he had done so, because inside were voices
speaking very softly. All the evening he had been remembering
Mr. Superbus's reference to a "companion."

In dumb show he tried to convey the situation to Malnik, who
peered at his efforts with a professional's dismissal of the amateur.
Then Malnik produced a pocketbook, wrote in it, and tore out the
page, which he thrust under Miss Rokeby's door. Having done
this, he prepared to return with Colvin to the bar, and await a
reply. Before they had taken three steps, however, the door was
open, and Miss Rokeby was inviting them in.

To Colvin she said, "We've met already," though without en-
quiring his name.

Colvin felt gratified; and at least equally pleased when he saw
that the fourth person in the room was a tall, frail-looking girl
with long fair hair drawn back into a tight bun. It was not the sort
of companion he had surmised.

"This is Myrrha. We're never apart."

Myrrha smiled slightly, said nothing, and sat down again. Colvin
thought she looked positively wasted. Doubtless by reason of the
cold, she wore heavy tweeds, which went oddly with her air of
fragility.

"How well do you know the play?" asked Malnik at the earliest
possible moment.

"Well enough not to play in it." Colvin saw Malnik turn gray.
"Since you've got me here, I'll play Rosalind. The rest was lies.
Do you know," she went on, addressing ·Colvin, "that this man
tried to trick me? You're not in the theater, are you?"

Colvin, feeling embarrassed, smiled and shook his head.

"*Cornelia* is a masterpiece," said Malnik furiously. "Nethers
was a genius."

Miss Rokeby simply said "Was" very softly, and seated herself
on the arm of Myrrha's armchair, the only one in the room. It was
set before the old-fashioned gas fire.

"It's announced. Everyone's waiting for it. People are coming
from London. They're even coming from Cambridge." Myrrha
turned away her head from Malnik's wrath.

"I was told—another English classic. Not an outpouring by little
Jack Nethers. I won't do it."

"*As You Like It* is only a fill-up. What more is it ever? *Cornelia* is the whole point of the Gala. Nethers was *born* in this town.
Don't you understand?"

Malnik was so much in earnest that Colvin felt sorry for him.
But even Colvin doubted whether Malnik's was the best way to
deal with Miss Rokeby.

"Please play for me. Please."

"Rosalind only." Miss Rokeby was swinging her legs. They
were young and lovely. There was more than one thing about this
interview which Colvin did not care for.

"We'll take it over in my office tomorrow." Colvin identified
this as a customary admission of defeat.

"This is a horrid place, isn't it?" said Miss Rokeby conversationally to Colvin.

"I'm used to it," said Colvin, smiling. "Mrs. Royd has her softer side."

"She's put poor Myrrha in a cupboard."

Colvin remembered about Greta's old room upstairs.

"Perhaps she'd like to change rooms with me? I've been away and haven't even unpacked. It would be easy."

"How kind you are! To that silly little girl! To me! And now to Myrrha! May I see?"

"Of course."

Colvin took her into the passage. It seemed obvious that Myrrha would come also, but she did not. Apparently she left it to Miss Rokeby to dispose of her. Malnik sulked behind also.

Colvin opened the door of his room and switched on the light. Lying on his bed and looking very foolish was his copy of Bull's *Graphite and Its Uses*. He glanced round for Miss Rokeby. Then for the second time that evening, he felt frightened.

Miss Rokeby was standing in the ill-lit passage, just outside his doorway. It was unpleasantly apparent that she was terrified. Formerly pale, she was now quite white. Her hands were clenched, and she was breathing unnaturally deeply. Her big eyes were half shut, and to Colvin it seemed that it was something she smelled that was frightening her. This impression was so strong that he sniffed the chilly air himself once or twice, unavailingly. Then he stepped forward, and his arms were around Miss Rokeby, who was palpably about to faint. Immediately Miss Rokeby was in his arms, such emotion swept through him as he had never before known. For what seemed a long moment, he was lost in the wonder of it. Then he was recalled by something that frightened him more than anything else, though for less reason. There was a sharp sound from number Twelve A. Mr. Superbus must have returned.

Colvin supported Miss Rokeby back to number Nine. Upon catching sight of her, Myrrha gave a small but jarring cry, and helped her on to the bed.

"It's my heart," said Miss Rokeby. "My absurd heart."

Malnik now looked more black than gray. "Shall we send for a doctor?" he enquired, hardly troubling to mask the sarcasm.

Miss Rokeby shook her head once. It was the sibling gesture to her nod.

"Please don't trouble about moving," she said to Colvin.

Colvin, full of confusion, looked at Myrrha, who was being resourceful with smelling salts.

"Good night," said Miss Rokeby, softly but firmly. And as Colvin followed Malnik out of the room, she touched his hand.

Colvin passed the night almost without sleep, which was another new experience for him. A conflict of feelings about Miss Rokeby, all of them strong, was one reason for insomnia: another was the sequence of sounds from number Twelve A. Mr. Superbus seemed to spend the night in moving things about and talking to himself. At first it sounded as if he were rearranging all the furniture in his room. Then there was a period, which seemed to Colvin timeless, during which the only noise was of low and unintelligible muttering, by no means continuous, but broken by periods of silence and then resumed as before, just as Colvin was beginning to hope that all was over. Colvin wondered whether Mr. Superbus was saying his prayers. Ultimately the banging about recommenced. Presumably Mr. Superbus was still dissatisfied with the arrangement of the furniture; or perhaps was returning it to its original dispositions. Then Colvin heard the sash window thrown sharply open. He remembered the sound from the occasion when Mrs. Royd had sharply shut it. After that silence continued. In the end Colvin turned on the light and looked at his watch. It had stopped.

At breakfast, Colvin asked when Mr. Superbus was expected down. "He doesn't come down," replied Greta. "They say he has all his meals out."

Colvin understood that rehearsals began that day, but Malnik had always demurred at outsiders being present. Now, moreover, he felt that Colvin had seen him at an unfavourable moment, so that his cordiality was much abated. The next two weeks, in fact, were to Colvin heavy with anticlimax. He saw Miss Rokeby only at the evening meal, which, however, she was undeniably in process of converting from tea to dinner, by expending charm, will power, and cash. Colvin participated in this improvement, as did even such few of the endless commercial travelers as wished to do so; and from time to time Miss Rokeby exchanged a few pleasant generalities with him, though she did not ask him to sit at her table, nor did he, being a shy man, dare to invite her. Myrrha never appeared at all; and when on one occasion Colvin referred to her interrogatively, Miss Rokeby simply said, "She pines, poor lamb," and plainly wished to say nothing more. Colvin remembered Myrrha's wasted appearance, and concluded that she must be an invalid. He wondered if he should again offer to change rooms. After that single disturbed night, he had heard no more of Mr. Superbus. But from Mrs. Royd he had gathered that Mr. Superbus had settled for several weeks in advance. Indeed, for the first time in years the Emancipation Hotel was doing good business.

It continued as cold as ever during all the time Miss Rokeby remained in the town, with repeated little snow storms every time the streets began to clear. The miners would stamp as they entered the bar until they seemed likely to go through to the cellar beneath; and all the commercial travelers caught colds. The two local papers, morning and evening, continued their efforts to set people against Malnik's now diminished Gala. When *Cornelia* was no longer offered, the two editors pointed out (erroneously, Colvin felt) that even now it was not too late for a pantomime: but Malnik seemed to have succeeded in persuading Miss Rokeby to reinforce *As You Like It* with a piece entitled *A Scrap of Paper*, which Colvin had never heard of, but which an elderly local citizen whom the papers always consulted upon matters theatrical described as "very old-fashioned." Malnik caused further comment by proposing to open on Christmas Eve, when the unfailing tradition had been Boxing Night.

The final week of rehearsal was marred by an exceedingly distressing incident. It happened on the Tuesday. Coming in that morning from a cold visit to the Technical Institute Library, Colvin found in the stuffy little saloon bar a number of the Tabard Players. The Players usually patronized an establishment nearer to the Hippodrome; and the fact that the present occasion was out of the ordinary was emphasized by the demeanor of the group, who were clustered together and talking in low, serious voices. Colvin knew none of the players at all well, but the group looked so distraught that, partly from curiosity and partly from compassion, he ventured to enquire of one of them, a middle-aged actor named Shillitoe to whom Malnik had introduced him, what was the matter. After a short silence, the group seemed collectively to decide upon accepting Colvin among them, and all began to enlighten him in short strained bursts of overeloquence. Some of

the references were not wholly clear to Colvin, but the substance
of the story was simple.

Colvin gathered that when the Tabard Players took possession
of the Hippodrome, Malnik had been warned that the "grid"
above the stage was undependable, and that scenery should not be
"flown" from it. This restriction had caused grumbling, but had
been complied with until, during a rehearsal of *A Scrap of Paper,*
the producer had rebelled and asked Malnik for authority to use
the grid. Malnik had agreed; and two stagehands began gingerly
to pull on some of the dusty lines which disappeared into the almost complete darkness far above. Before long one of them had
cried out that there was "something up there already." At these
words, Colvin was told, everyone in the theater fell silent. The
stagehand went on paying out line, but the stage was so ample and
the grid so high that an appreciable time passed before the object
came slowly into view.

The narrators stopped, and there was a silence which Colvin
felt must have been like the silence in the theater. Then Shillitoe
resumed: "It was poor old Ludlow's body. He'd hanged himself
right up under the grid. Eighty feet above the floor of the stage.
Some time ago, too. He wasn't in the Christmas plays, you know.
Or in this week's play. We all thought he'd gone home."

Colvin learned that the producer had fainted right away; and,
upon tactful enquiry, that Miss Rokeby had fortunately not been
called for that particular rehearsal.

On the first two Sundays after her arrival, Miss Rokeby had been
no more in evidence than on any other day; but on the morning of
the third Sunday Colvin was taking one of his resolute lonely
walks across the windy fells which surrounded the town when
he saw her walking ahead of him through the snow. The snow lay
only an inch or two deep upon the hillside ledge along which the
path ran; and Colvin had been wondering for some time about the
small footsteps which preceded him. It was the first time he had
seen Miss Rokeby outside the Emancipation Hotel, but he had no
doubt that it was she he saw, and his heart turned over at the sight.
He hesitated; then walked faster, and soon had overtaken her. As
he drew near, she stopped, turned, and faced him. Then, when
she saw who it was, she seemed unsurprised. She wore a fur coat

with a collar which reached almost to the tip of her nose; a fur hat; and elegant boots which laced to the knee.

"I'm glad to have a companion," she said gravely, sending Colvin's thoughts to her other odd companion. "I suppose you know all these paths well?"

"I come up here often to look for lead workings. I'm writing a dull book on lead and plumbago mining."

"I don't see any mines up here." She looked around with an air of grave bewilderment.

"Lead mines aren't like coal mines. They're simply passages in hillsides."

"What do you do when you find them?"

"I mark them on a large-scale map. Sometimes I go down them."

"Don't the miners object?"

"There are no miners."

A shadow crossed her face.

"I mean, not any longer. We don't mine lead any more."

"Don't we? Why not?"

"That's a complicated story."

She nodded. "Will you take me down a mine?"

"I don't think you'd like it. The passages are usually both narrow and low. One of the reasons why the industry's come to an end is that people would no longer work in them. Besides, now the mines are disused, they're often dangerous."

She laughed. It was the first time he had ever heard her do so. "Come on." She took hold of his arm. "Or aren't there any mines on this particular hillside?" She looked as concerned as a child.

"There's one about a hundred feet above our heads. But there's nothing to see. Only darkness."

"Only *darkness*," cried Miss Rokeby. She implied that no reasonable person could want more. "But you don't go down all these passages only to see darkness?"

"I take a flashlight."

"Have you got it now?"

"Yes." Colvin never went to the fells without it.

"Then that will look after *you*. Where's the mine? Conduct me."

They began to scramble together up the steep snow-covered

slope. Colvin knew all the workings round here; and soon they were in the entry.

"You see," said Colvin. "There's not even room to stand, and a fat person couldn't get in at all. You'll ruin your coat."

"I'm not a fat person." There was a small excited patch in each of her cheeks. "But you'd better go first."

Colvin knew that this particular working consisted simply in a long passage, following the vein of lead. He had been to the end of it more than once. He turned on his flashlight. "I assure you, there's nothing to see," he said. And in he went.

Colvin perceived that Miss Rokeby seemed indeed to pass along the adit without even stooping or damaging her fur hat. She insisted on going as far as possible, although near the end Colvin made a quite strenuous effort to persuade her to let them return.

"What's that?" enquired Miss Rokeby when they had nonetheless reached the extremity of the passage.

"It's a big fault in the limestone. A sort of cave. The miners chucked their debris down it."

"Is it deep?"

"Some of these faults are supposed to be bottomless."

She took the light from his hand, and, squatting down on the brink of the hole, flashed it round the depths below.

"Careful," cried Colvin. "You're on loose shale. It could easily slip." He tried to drag her back. The only result was that she dropped the flashlight, which went tumbling down the great hole like a meteor, until after many seconds they heard a faint crash. They were in complete darkness.

"I'm sorry," said Miss Rokeby's voice. "But you did push me."

Trying not to fall down the hole, Colvin began to grope his way back. Suddenly he had thought of Malnik, and the irresponsibility of the proceedings upon which he was engaged appalled him. He begged Miss Rokeby to go slowly, test every step, and mind her head; but her unconcern seemed complete. Colvin tripped and toiled along for an endless period of time, with Miss Rokeby always close behind him, calm, sure of foot, and unflagging. As far into the earth as this, it was both warm and stuffy. Colvin began to fear that bad air might overcome them, forced as they were to creep so laboriously and interminably. He broke out in heavy perspiration.

Suddenly he knew that he would have to stop. He could not

even pretend that it was out of consideration for Miss Rokeby. He subsided upon the floor of the passage and she seated herself near him, oblivious of her costly clothes. The blackness was still complete.

"Don't feel unworthy," said Miss Rokeby softly. "And don't feel frightened. There's no need. We shall get out."

Curiously enough, the more she said, the worse Colvin felt. The strange antecedents to this misadventure were with him; and, even more so, Miss Rokeby's whole fantastic background. He had to force his spine against the stone wall of the passage if he were not to give way to panic utterly and leap up screaming. Normal speech was impossible.

"Is it me you are frightened of?" asked Miss Rokeby, with dreadful percipience.

Colvin was less than ever able to speak.

"Would you like to know more about me?"

Colvin was shaking his head in the dark.

"If you'll promise not to tell anyone else."

But, in fact, she was like a child, unable to contain her secret.

"I'm sure you won't tell anyone else . . . It's my helper. He's the queer one. Not me."

Now that the truth was spoken Colvin felt a little better. "Yes," he said in a low, shaken voice, "I know."

"Oh, you know . . . *I* don't see him or—" she paused—"or encounter him, often for years at a time. Years."

"But you encountered him the other night?"

He could feel her shudder. "Yes . . . You've seen him?"

"Very briefly . . . How did you . . . encounter him first?"

"It was years ago. Have you any idea how many years?"

"I think so."

Then she said something that Colvin never really understood; not even later, in his dreams of her. "You know I'm not here at all, really. Myrrha's me. That's why she's called Myrrha. That's how I act."

"How?" said Colvin. There was little else to say.

"My helper took my own personality out of me. Like taking a nerve out of a tooth. Myrrha's my personality."

"Do you mean your soul?" asked Colvin.

"Artists don't have souls," said Miss Rokeby. "Personality's the word . . . I'm anybody's personality. Or everybody's. And

when I lost my personality, I stopped growing older. Of course I
have to look after Myrrha, because if anything happened to
Myrrha—well, you do see," she continued.

"But Myrrha looks as young as you do."

"That's what she *looks*."

Colvin remembered Myrrha's wasted face.

"But how can you live without a personality? Besides," added
Colvin, "you seem to me to have a very strong personality."

"I have a mask for every occasion."

It was only the utter blackness, Colvin felt, which made this
impossible conversation possible.

"What do you do in exchange? I suppose you must repay your
helper in some way?"

"I suppose I must . . . I've never found out what way it is."

"What else does your helper do for you?"

"He smooths my path. Rids me of people who want to hurt me.
He rid me of little Jack Nethers. Jack was mad, you know. You
can see it even in his photograph."

"Did he rid you of this wretched man Ludlow?"

"I don't know. You see, I can remember Ludlow. I think he
often rids me of people that I don't know want to hurt me."

Colvin considered.

"Can you be rid of him?"

"I've never really tried."

"Don't you *want* to be rid of him?"

"I don't know. He frightens me terribly whenever I come near
him, but otherwise . . . I don't know . . . But for him I should
never have been down a lead mine."

"How many people know all this?" asked Colvin after a pause.

"Not many. I only told you because I wanted you to stop being
frightened."

As she spoke the passage was filled with a strange sound. Then
they were illumined with icy December sunshine. Colvin perceived
that they were almost at the entry to the working, and supposed
that the portal must have been temporarily blocked by a miniature
avalanche of melting snow. Even now there was, in fact, only a
comparatively small hole, through which they would have to
scramble.

"I told you we'd get out," said Miss Rokeby. "Other people
haven't believed a word I said. But now *you*'ll believe me."

Not the least strange thing was the matter-of-fact manner in which, all the way back, Miss Rokeby questioned Colvin about his researches into lead and plumbago mining, with occasionally, on the perimeter of their talk, flattering enquiries about himself; although equally strange, Colvin considered, was the matter-of-fact manner in which he answered her. Before they were back in the town he was wondering how much of what she had said in the darkness of the mine had been meant only figuratively; and after that he wondered whether Miss Rokeby had not used the circumstances to initiate an imaginative and ingenious boutade. After all, he reflected, she was an actress. Colvin's hypothesis was, if anything, confirmed when at their parting she held his hand for a moment and said: "Remember! *No one.*"

But he resolved to question Mrs. Royd in a business-like way about Mr. Superbus. An opportunity arose when he encountered her after luncheon (at which Miss Rokeby had not made an appearance), reading *The People* before the fire in the saloon bar. The bar had just closed, and it was, Mrs. Royd explained, the only warm spot in the house. In fact it was, as usual, hot as a kiln.

"Couldn't say, I'm sure," replied Mrs. Royd to Colvin's firm enquiry, and implying that it was neither her business nor his. "Anyway, 'e's gone. Went last Tuesday. Didn't you notice, with 'im sleeping next to you?"

After the death of poor Ludlow (the almost inevitable verdict was suicide while of unsound mind), it was as if the papers felt embarrassed about continuing to carp at Malnik's plans; and by the opening night the editors seemed ready to extend the Christmas spirit even to Shakespeare. Colvin had planned to spend Christmas with his mother; but when he learned that Malnik's first night was to be on Christmas Eve, had been unable to resist deferring his departure until after it, despite the perils of a long and intricate railway journey on Christmas Day. With Miss Rokeby, however, he now felt entirely unsure of himself.

On Christmas Eve the town seemed full of merriment. Colvin was surprised at the frankness of the general rejoicing. The shops, as is usual in industrial districts, had long been offsetting the general drabness with drifts of Christmas cards and whirlpools of tinsel. Now every home seemed to be decorated and all the shops to be proclaiming bonus distributions and bumper share-outs.

Even the queues, which were a prominent feature of these celebrations, looked more sanguine, Colvin noticed, when he stood in one of them for about half an hour in order to send Miss Rokeby some flowers, as he felt the occasion demanded. By the time he set out for the Hippodrome, the more domestically-minded citizens were everywhere quietly toiling at preparations for the morrow's revels; but a wilder minority, rebellious or homeless, were inaugurating such a carouse at the Emancipation Hotel as really to startle the comparatively retiring Colvin. He suspected that some of the bibbers must be Irish.

Sleet was slowly descending as Colvin stepped out of the sweltering bar in order to walk to the Hippodrome. A spot of it sailed gently into the back of his neck, chilling him in a moment. But, notwithstanding the weather, notwithstanding the claims of the season and the former attitude of the press, there was a crowd outside the Hippodrome such as Colvin had never previously seen there. To his great surprise, some of the audience were in evening dress; many of them had expensive cars, and one party, it appeared, had come in a closed carriage with two flashing black horses. There was such a concourse at the doors that Colvin had to stand a long time in the slowly falling sleet before he was able to join the throng which forced its way, like icing onto a cake, between the countless glittering photographs of beautiful Miss Rokeby. The average age of the audience, Colvin observed, seemed very advanced, and especially of that section of it which was in evening dress. Elderly white-haired men with large noses and carnations in their buttonholes spoke in elegant Edwardian voices to the witchlike ladies on their arms, most of whom wore hot-house gardenias.

Inside, however, the huge and golden Hippodrome looked as it was intended to look when it was still named the Grand Opera House. From his gangway seat in the stalls Colvin looked backward and upward at the gilded satyrs and bacchantes who wantoned on the dress-circle balustrade; and at the venerable and orchidaceous figures who peered above them. The small orchestra was frenziedly playing selections from *L'Etoile du Nord*. In the gallery distant figures, unable to find seats, were standing watchfully. Even the many boxes, little used and dusty, were filling up. Colvin could only speculate how this gratifying assembly had been collected. But then he was on his feet for the "National Anthem," and the faded crimson and gold curtain, made deceivingly splendid by the footlights, was about to rise.

The play began, and then: "Dear Celia, I show more mirth than I am mistress of, and would you yet I were merrier? Unless you could teach me to forget a banished father, you must not learn me how to remember any extraordinary pleasure."

Colvin realized that in his heart he had expected Miss Rokeby to be good, to be moving, to be lovely; but the revelation he now had was something he could never have expected because he could never have imagined it; and before the conclusion of Rosalind's first scene in boy's attire in the forest, he was wholly and terribly bewitched.

No one coughed, no one rustled, no one moved. To Colvin, it seemed as if Miss Rokeby's magic had strangely enchanted the normally journeyman Tabard Players into miracles of judgment. Plainly her spell was on the audience also; so that when the lights came up for the interval, Colvin found that his eyes were streaming, and felt not chagrin, but pride.

The interval was an uproar. Even the bells of fire engines pounding through the wintry night outside could hardly be heard above the din. People spoke freely to unknown neighbors, groping to express forgotten emotions. "What a prelude to Christmas!" everyone said. Malnik was proved right in one thing.

During the second half, Colvin, failing of interest in Sir Oliver Martext's scene, let his eyes wander round the auditorium. He noticed that the nearest dress-circle box, previously unoccupied, appeared to be unoccupied no longer. A hand, which, being only just above him, he could see was gnarled and hirsute, was tightly gripping the box's red velvet curtain. Later in the scene between Silvius and Phebe (Miss Rokeby having come and gone meanwhile), the hand was still there, and still gripping tightly; as it was (after Rosalind's big scene with Orlando) during the Forester's song. At the beginning of Act V, there was a rush of feet down the gangway, and someone was crouching by Colvin's seat. It was Greta. "Mr. Colvin! There's been a fire. Miss Rokeby's friend jumped out of the window. She's terribly hurt. Will you tell Miss Rokeby?"

"The play's nearly over," said Colvin. "Wait for me at the back." Greta withdrew, whimpering.

After Rosalind's Epilogue the tumult was millennial. Miss

Rokeby, in Rosalind's white dress, stood for many seconds not bowing but quite still and unsmiling, with her hands by her sides as Colvin had first seen her. Then as the curtain rose and revealed the rest of the company, she began slowly to walk backward up-stage. Doorkeepers and even stagehands, spruced up for the pur-pose, began to bring armfuls upon armfuls of flowers, until there was a heap, a mountain of them in the center of the stage, so high that it concealed Miss Rokeby's small figure from the audience. Suddenly a bouquet flew through the air from the dress-circle box. It landed at the very front of the heap. It was a hideous dusty laurel wreath, adorned with an immense and somewhat tasteless purple bow. The audience were yelling for Miss Rokeby like Dionysians; and the company, flagging from unaccustomed emotional expendi-ture, and plainly much scared, were looking for her; but in the end the stage manager had to lower the safety curtain and give orders that the house be cleared.

Back at the Emancipation Hotel, Colvin, although he had little title, asked to see the body.

"You wouldn't ever recognize her," said Mrs. Royd. Colvin did not pursue the matter.

The snow, falling ever more thickly, had now hearsed the town in silence.

"She didn't 'ave to do it," wailed on Mrs. Royd. "The brigade had the flames under control. And tomorrow Christmas Day!"

Robert Aickman, who was born in 1914, is the grandson of Richard Marsh, author of *The Beetle*. So far, Mr. Aickman's ghostly output includes *Dark Entries, Powers of Darkness,* and, with Elizabeth Jane Howard, *We Are for the Dark.* He has compiled two anthologies, *The Fontana Book of Great Ghost Stories* and *A Second Fontana Book of Great Ghost Stories.* His admirable story "The Cicerones" is included in August Derleth's *Travellers By Night* (1967), and this, I believe, constitutes Mr. Aickman's first appearance in America. He has also written a novel, *The Late Breakfasters,* and two books about the rivers and canals of England.

CHAPTER 17

Midnight Express

by Alfred Noyes

Reading this story is like seeing your own ghost, for it embodies the subtle terror of the *Doppelgänger* or phantom double of a living person. The German poet Goethe believed he saw his own Doppelgänger several times. E. T. A. Hoffmann elaborated the idea as an expression of the individual's many-faceted personality. But in "Midnight Express," the English Poet Alfred Noyes conforms to the ancient folk belief that the Doppelgänger is an omen of death.

It was a battered old book, bound in red buckram. He found it, when he was twelve years old, on an upper shelf in his father's library; and, against all the rules, he took it to his bedroom to read by candlelight, when the rest of the rambling old Elizabethan house was flooded with darkness. That was how young Mortimer always thought of it. His own room was a little isolated cell, in which, with stolen candle ends, he could keep the surrounding darkness at bay, while everyone else had surrendered to sleep and allowed the outer night to come flooding in. By contrast with those unconscious ones, his elders, it made him feel intensely alive in every nerve and fiber of his young brain. The ticking of the grandfather clock in the hall below; the beating of his own heart; the long-drawn rhythmical "ah" of the sea on the distant coast, all filled him with a sense of overwhelming mystery; and, as he read, the soft thud of a blinded moth, striking the wall above the candle, would make him start and listen like a creature of the woods at the sound of a cracking twig.

The battered old book had the strangest fascination for him, though he never quite grasped the thread of the story. It was called *The Midnight Express,* and there was one illustration, on the fiftieth page, at which he could never bear to look. It frightened him.

Young Mortimer never understood the effect of that picture on him. He was an imaginative, but not a neurotic youngster; and he avoided that fiftieth page as he might have hurried past a dark corner on the stairs when he was six years old, or as the grown man on the lonely road, in the *Ancient Mariner,* who, having once looked round, walks on, and turns no more his head. There was nothing in the picture—apparently—to account for this haunting dread. Darkness, indeed, was almost its chief characteristic. It showed an empty railway platform—at night—lit by a single dreary lamp; an empty railway platform that suggested a deserted and lonely junction in some remote part of the country. There was only one figure on the platform: the dark figure of a man, standing almost directly under the lamp, with his face turned away toward the black mouth of a tunnel, which—for some strange reason—plunged the imagination of the child into a pit of horror. The man seemed to be listening. His attitude was tense, expectant, as though he were awaiting some fearful tragedy. There was nothing in the text, so far as the child read, and could understand, to account for this waking nightmare. He could neither resist the fascination of the book, nor face that picture in the stillness and loneliness of the night. He pinned it down to the page facing it, with two long pins, so that he should not come upon it by accident. Then he determined to read the whole story through. But, always, before he came to page fifty, he fell asleep; and the outlines of what he had read were blurred; and the next night he had to begin again; and again, before he came to the fiftieth page, he fell asleep.

He grew up, and forgot all about the book and the picture. But half way through his life, at that strange and critical time when Dante entered the dark wood, leaving the direct path behind him, he found himself, a little before midnight, waiting for a train at a lonely junction; and, as the station clock began to strike twelve, he remembered; remembered like a man awaking from a long dream—

There, under the single dreary lamp, on the long glimmering platform, was the dark and solitary figure that he knew. Its face was turned away from him toward the black mouth of the tunnel. It seemed to be listening, tense, expectant, just as it had been thirty-eight years ago.

But he was not frightened now, as he had been in childhood. He would go up to that solitary figure, confront it, and see the face that had so long been hidden, so long averted from him. He would walk up quietly, and make some excuse for speaking to it: he would ask it, for instance, if the train was going to be late. It should be easy for a grown man to do this; but his hands were clenched, when he took the first step, as if he, too, were tense and expectant. Quietly, but with the old vague instincts awaking, he went toward the dark figure under the lamp, passed it, swung round abruptly to speak to it; and saw—without speaking, without being able to speak—

It was himself—staring back at himself—as in some mocking mirror, his own eyes alive in his own white face, looking into his own eyes, alive—

The nerves of his heart tingled as though their own electric currents would paralyze it. A wave of panic went through him. He turned, gasped, stumbled, broke into a blind run, out through the deserted and echoing ticket office, on to the long moonlit road behind the station. The whole countryside seemed to be utterly deserted. The moonbeams flooded it with the loneliness of their own deserted satellite.

He paused for a moment, and heard, like the echo of his own footsteps, the stumbling run of something that followed over the wooden floor within the ticket office. Then he abandoned himself shamelessly to his fear; and ran, sweating like a terrified beast, down the long white road between the two endless lines of ghostly poplars each answering another, into what seemed an infinite distance. On one side of the road there was a long straight canal, in which one of the lines of poplars was again endlessly reflected. He heard the footsteps echoing behind him. They seemed to be slowly, but steadily, gaining upon him. A quarter of a mile away, he saw a small white cottage by the roadside, a white cottage with two dark windows and a door that somehow suggested a human face. He thought to himself that, if he could reach it in time, he might find shelter and security—escape.

The thin implacable footsteps, echoing his own, were still some way off when he lurched, gasping, into the little porch; rattled the latch, thrust at the door, and found it locked against him. There was no bell or knocker. He pounded on the wood with his fists until his knuckles bled. The response was horribly slow. At last, he heard heavier footsteps within the cottage. Slowly they descended the creaking stair. Slowly the door was unlocked. A tall shadowy figure stood before him, holding a lighted candle, in such a way that he could see little either of the holder's face or form; but to his dumb horror there seemed to be a cerecloth wrapped round the face.

No words passed between them. The figure beckoned him in; and, as he obeyed, it locked the door behind him. Then, beckoning him again, without a word, the figure went before him up the crooked stair, with the ghostly candle casting huge and grotesque shadows on the whitewashed walls and ceiling.

They entered an upper room, in which there was a bright fire burning, with an armchair on either side of it, and a small oak table, on which there lay a battered old book, bound in dark red buckram. It seemed as though the guest had been long expected and all things were prepared.

The figure pointed to one of the armchairs, placed the candlestick on the table by the book (for there was no other light but that of the fire) and withdrew without a word, locking the door behind him.

Mortimer looked at the candlestick. It seemed familiar. The smell of the guttering wax brought back the little room in the old Elizabethan house. He picked up the book with trembling fingers. He recognized it at once, though he had long forgotten everything about the story. He remembered the inkstain on the title page; and then, with a shock of recollection, he came on the fiftieth page, which he had pinned down in childhood. The pins were still there. He touched them again—the very pins which his trembling childish fingers had used so long ago.

He turned back to the beginning. He was determined to read it to the end now, and discover what it all was about. He felt that it must all be set down there, in print; and, though in childhood he could not understand it, he would be able to fathom it now.

It was called *The Midnight Express;* and, as he read the first paragraph, it began to dawn upon him slowly, fearfully, inevitably—

It was the story of a man who, in childhood, long ago, had chanced upon a book, in which there was a picture that frightened him. He had grown up and forgotten it, and one night, upon a lonely railway platform, he had found himself in the remembered scene of the picture; he had confronted the solitary figure under the lamp; recognized it, and fled in panic. He had taken shelter in a wayside cottage; had been led to an upper room, found the book awaiting him and had begun to read it right through, to the very end, at last.—And this book, too, was called The Midnight Express. *And it was the story of a man who, in childhood—It would go on thus, forever and forever, and forever. There was no escape.*

But when the story came to the wayside cottage, for the third time, a deeper suspicion began to dawn upon him, slowly, fearfully, inevitably—Although there was no escape, he could at least try to grasp more clearly the details of the strange circle, the fearful wheel, in which he was moving.

There was nothing new about the details. They had been there all the time; but he had not grasped their significance. That was all. *The strange and dreadful being that had led him up the crooked stair—who and what was That?*

The story mentioned something that had escaped him. The strange host, who had given him shelter, was about his own height. Could it be that he also—And was this why the face was hidden?

At the very moment when he asked himself that question, he heard the click of the key in the locked door.

The strange host was entering—moving toward him from behind —casting a grotesque shadow, larger than human, on the white walls in the guttering candlelight.

It was there, seated on the other side of the fire, facing him. With a horrible nonchalance, as a woman might prepare to remove a veil, it raised its hands to unwind the cerecloth from its face. He knew to whom it would belong. But would it be dead or living?

There was no way out but one. As Mortimer plunged forward and seized the tormentor by the throat, his own throat was gripped with the same brutal force. The echoes of their strangled cry were indistinguishable; and when the last confused sounds died out together, the stillness of the room was so deep that you might have heard—the ticking of the old grandfather clock, and the long-drawn rhythmical "ah" of the sea, on a distant coast, thirty-eight years ago.

But Mortimer had escaped at last. Perhaps, after all, he had caught the midnight express.

It was a battered old book, bound in red buckram . . .

Alfred Noyes was born at Wolverhampton, Staffordshire, in 1880 and studied at Exeter College, Oxford. His poems attained wide popularity with the *Loom of Years; Drake: An English Epic; The Golden Hynde and Other Poems; Tales of the Mermaid Tavern; Dick Turpin's Ride.* In the novel *No Other Man* and several short stories Mr. Noyes delved into the weird and fantastic.

About the Editor and Illustrator

HENRY MAZZEO was born in Yonkers, New York and attended parochial schools there, becoming interested in writing and art, as he recalls, somewhere about the fourth grade. While in high school he took summer classes in drawing and painting at Columbia University, where he returned to earn his B.A. and M.A. degrees (in sixteenth-century English literature). He also found time to play both Count Dracula and the Frankenstein Monster in Fordham University radio dramatizations. Mr. Mazzeo won a scholarship in art to Cooper Union and a teaching fellowship in English literature to Ohio State University but did not accept them. Instead, he went to work as a copywriter, first for several advertising agencies, then for Scholastic Magazines and Book Services, and currently for *Esquire Magazine* and *Gentleman's Quarterly*. His other interests include folklore, photography, and cinema. Presently he is at work on a translation of "Vourdalak," a vampire story by Aleksei Konstantinovich Tolstoy.

EDWARD GOREY, apart from illustrating books, also writes them, the most recent being *The Other Statue* and *The Blue Aspic*.